I0589214

The Wrong Road Home
A story of treachery and deceit inspired by true events

Ian A. O'Connor

Pegasus Publishing & Entertainment Group

The Wrong Road Home - A Story of Treachery and Deceit Inspired by True Events.

Pegasus Publishing & Entertainment Group
March 2016© Ian A. O'Connor. All rights reserved
First Printing, March 2016

Cover art by: SelfPubBookCovers.com/DianasGraphics

Visit the author at: www.ianaoconnor.com
Contact the author at: ianaoconnor@ianaoconnor.com

This is a work of fiction.

ISBN: 978-0-692-56965-8

Manufactured in the United States of America

Dedication

This book is dedicated to my wife, Candice Myers O'Connor, my forever very best friend.

Acknowledgment

I owe an extra special thanks to Margaret Datsmann O'Connor who undertook the unenviable task of editing my manuscript.

<u>Fiction Titles by Ian A. O'Connor</u>
The Twilight of the Day
The Seventh Seal
The Barbarossa Covenant
The Wrong Road Home

<u>Nonfiction Titles by Ian A. O'Connor</u>
With Howard C. "Scrappy" Johnson
SCRAPPY: Memoir of a U. S. Fighter Pilot in Korea and Vietnam

<u>Short Story Title by Ian A. O'Connor</u>
"The Last Grandmaster"

FOREWORD

"The road to hell is paved with good intentions."

There is a smell unique to poverty, an odor known only to the truly poor. It's the stench of hopelessness and despair. It's that awful knowing of having lost life's fight without ever having been given the opportunity to sally forth, raise the standard, and compete. It's called reality for eighty-five percent of the people on earth.

"Blessed are the poor in spirit, for theirs is the kingdom of heaven."

My countrymen have long believed that their reward was not to be a temporal one, that one day their suffering would end. And just as Christ had made a promise from the cross to the good thief, so, too, He would whisper similar words as their time drew near: *"Today you shall be with me in paradise."*

Our faith with its promise of eternal life, has sustained us. It is the bedrock of Irish Christianity. Simply put: we believe. But we also believe in the timeless adage: *"God helps those who help themselves."* Maybe it's not an Irish proverb, but it should be. It's why my forebears left that cold, bleak, sea-swept isle and set forth to America and the promise of her shores.

The smell of poverty can fade with time yet it never truly leaves a soul. How can it? Poverty remains a haunting memory embedded in the spirit, and leaves one to live in mortal fear of its rebirth. No matter what riches or accolades are showered upon the anointed, that fear is as constant as the North Star. *This, too, can pass.* Fortunes made, fortunes lost. Ask Job.

And should the rainbow fade into the ether before the day is done, what is left, pray tell?

Poverty.

This pervasive fear of its return can cloud all judgment. I should know. It did mine.

PROLOGUE

I arrived at the law offices of Middleton and Ives, P.A., in Coral Gables, Florida, at nine o'clock on a clear November morning in 1992. Eighteen months earlier, I had been seriously injured in an auto accident and still wore a cumbersome neck and back brace. Pain was my constant companion.

The task this day was to prepare me for a pre-trial deposition scheduled for midweek. My attorneys had realized soon after filing a claim in court that things could turn dicey simply because I was a longtime friend of the car's driver, Kathy Murray. Indeed, her insurance carrier had remained steadfast in refusing to entertain any thoughts of a settlement and had drawn a new line in the sand by hiring a top Miami attorney named Carl Weston.

"Relax, Desmond," my friend Mike Middleton said. "Your case is a slam dunk. Just answer all questions truthfully, and don't volunteer any information."

"You know this insurance company lawyer?"

Mike chuckled. "Yeah, I know Carl. He's no Perry Mason, but he can turn into one tough little bulldog if he smells blood. But Carl has nothing to go after here because the facts are the facts." Mike led me into the conference room and then headed for the gargantuan leather chair at the head of the table while motioning me to take the seat on his right. As he reached for a yellow legal pad, his partner entered.

"Sorry I'm late," Drew Ives said, and with a nod, signaled for Mike to begin.

They went over the facts of the accident at least a dozen times, all the while lobbing every imaginable question at me. They then helped polish my responses and three hours later, pronounced me ready. "Just tell the truth," was Mike's last piece of advice.

Michael Middleton and Drew Ives oozed confidence from every pore.

*   *   *

We were ushered into the floor-to-ceiling book-lined conference room of the law firm of Weston, Hailey and Strunk, P.A., at three o'clock on the afternoon of November 20, 1992. After the requisite introductions and going over a few technical legal housekeeping matters, the lawyers started the deposition at 3:20 P.M., and it lasted ninety minutes. A court stenographer videotaped the proceeding.

Carl Weston began by guiding me through the preliminaries, those mundane, innocuous items, such as having me state my full name, age, place of birth, city of residence, and marital status.

I began to relax. I had answered the last question by saying I was a widower these past eighteen years, as my wife, Margaret had died in childbirth with our child.

Carl Weston wore a suitably sad face as he listened to my recounting.

Then he moved on to wanting to know about my education, beginning in Chicago. I said I had attended college at Loyola University, followed by medical school in Cork, Ireland.

"When did you start these Irish medical studies, and when did you finish?"

"Nineteen sixty-nine until nineteen seventy-six."

"It was a seven-year course?" Carl Weston couldn't keep the surprise out of his voice as he peered at me over the rim of his half-frames.

"Well, it's normally five, but I did some other things while I was there." I then went on to explain away my particular circumstances. Mike remained silent. And why not? The facts were facts, and he had heard me parrot them *ad nauseam*.

"So, from nineteen sixty-nine to nineteen seventy-six you were a student at the medical school in Ireland?"

"Yes."

"That's seven years?" Carl Weston was now repeating himself.

"It is."

"Did you finally get your degree?"

"Of course."

"And what degree did you get?"

"Similar to an American M.D. degree."

"Which is…?"

"An MB., Bch., BAO."

"That's quite the mouthful of alphabet soup. Just what do all those letter mean?"

"MB and Bch., stand for Medical Bachelor, and Bachelor of Surgery. BAO, Bachelor of Obstetrics and Gynecology."

"So in other words, you got these MB, Bch., BAO degrees in Ireland*?*"

"I did." I was beginning to think this hotshot lawyer was somewhat slow in the understanding department. And still Mike said nothing.

Weston then wanted to know what hospital I had attended for my clinical training while in Cork, and I told him there were several the students rotated through. That answer seemed to satisfy him. He next queried the date and the facts leading up to my marriage, then delicately probed for more details about Margaret's demise and that of our child.

Next, he led me through a recitation of events from the time I left Ireland, until my being hired by St. Anslem's Hospital in Coral Gables, a dozen years earlier.

"And at St. Anslem's you wear a white doctor's coat?"

"Of course."

"And it has Desmond Donahue, M.D. embroidered over the left breast?"

"It does."

Weston scribbled a quick notation, rifled through some pages, selected one, and began asking about my life and duties at St. Anslem's. He wanted to know how much was I paid. How long was my workday? What *exactly* did I do at the hospital? He then followed with in depth questions regarding the general state of my health before the accident and my several life insurance policies and their beneficiaries. Ditto for my disability coverage. Then, he wanted to know about my relationship with the defendant, Kathy Murray. I explained she was the widow of a long-time friend who had died of lymphoma three years earlier.

Finally, after many repeated questions, the discussion turned to the accident. Carl Weston led me through the mishap, minute-by-minute, blow-by-blow, my many injuries being duly noted. He then asked for the names of all the physicians who had, and still were, treating me.

The session ended with a probing of my limited surgical work schedule since the accident, with me explaining how my injuries had curtailed most of the activities I had enjoyed prior to that fateful day.

At last, it was over. I sank into my chair, exhausted.

Twenty minutes later, I was riding back to Coral Gables with Mike. "Went well," he said as we crawled along in bumper-to-bumper traffic on South Dixie Highway. "I told you Carl's a bulldog! Get him fixated on a line of questioning and he will beat it to frigging death. Hell, there were times in there I had no idea where the man was going." Mike let loose a whoop of delight. "Poor old Carl went on a fishing expedition only to find there were no fish in the pond. You handled him great, Desmond."

*   *   *

I got a call from Mike two days before the end of the year. "I need you in my office as soon as possible."

"Well, I'm kind of tied up for the next..."

"You're not listening, Desmond" he interrupted. "As soon as possible means just that." No ranting, no raving, just a command.

I immediately went on red alert. Something big was up. "Then I'll be there this afternoon. Care to tell me what it's about?"

"This afternoon will be fine. I'll see you then."

I made my appearance shortly after two o'clock when a poker-faced Mike Middleton walked me into the conference room and shut the door. He strode over to the table and scooped up an overstuffed manila envelope, which he began waving in front of my nose. "This was delivered by courier from Carl Weston's office at nine o'clock this morning. Care to guess what's inside?"

I immediately knew the answer. Carl Weston had dug deep into my past and had struck the mother lode of all mother lodes. Mike Middleton's tenacious little bulldog had done what no one else had been able to do in twenty years—he had discovered that my life was a lie and that I was a fraud.

I hung my head in silent disgrace inside my brace and collar, too mortified to look Mike in the eye.

"Sit down, Desmond," Mike finally said, and then heeding his own advice, sank wearily into his oversized chair and began a vigorous rubbing of his face, a ritual I had witnessed many times.

"It's time for you to come clean, *Doctor* Donahue," he finally said in a voice as dry as dust, deliberately emphasizing the word doctor. "I want the truth, but first, answer me this: Is your real name even Desmond Donahue? Because if it isn't, I sure as hell need to know that particular fact right up front."

I shook my head and sighed. "Desmond Donahue is my real name."

"Well, that's a start, I suppose. Forget that we've been friends for ten years, I want to hear only the truth from here on out. No bullshitting, no spinning, no you deciding what to tell and what to withhold. I need to know everything about you from the day you were born because very soon, you're going to be facing one really pissed-off judge who could send you away for a very long time. Do you understand what I'm saying?"

I nodded, took a deep breath, held it for what seemed like an eternity, then exhaled in one long swoosh and began to talk.

CHAPTER ONE

The first time I saw the ocean was the week before I was to start school. Now, more than a half century later, I had no idea why my mother took me there because the journey was some fifteen miles from home, and the trip by donkey cart took the better part of a day. But there we were, standing on the rugged cliffs of Clew Bay, huddled close for protection from the bitter wind and driving rain. A hundred feet below, the surf crashed against lichen-covered rocks, creating a gossamer curtain of salty mist that rose to mingle with the unceasing rain. I remember how the seagulls screeched in angry protest each time a wave flung great beds of brown kelp their way and forcing them to abandon their slippery perches in the crags, while interrupting their never-ending search for food.

And there we stood, the only two people in the world. I clutched her hand as tightly as only a five-year old can anchor to his mother, mesmerized by the awesome power of the sea.

"Is it cold, Mamma?" I yelled up at the woman who stood as transfixed as I.

"That it is, Desmond, and dangerous, too," she yelled back. "The sea has never taken kindly to men, yet that has never stopped them from tempting her." She then fell silent, lost in her own thoughts, dreaming of that which might have been, dreaming of that which could never be. And I just stood there, glad with all my heart to be nestled in the safe harbor of her arms.

At some point, the rain stopped and the smallest patch of blue appeared, allowing the sun to shine through if only for a moment.

"Look, Desmond," she said, suddenly excited, "a rainbow!" And indeed there was. Originating somewhere in the mist behind us and having painted its pre-ordained arc, the beautiful image disappeared from view far out over the gray, undulating sea. "I give it to you as a gift, my son. Isn't it lovely?"

My response was to grab her hand all the tighter.

"That rainbow's a magic staircase," she continued. "One day it will return, and when it does, you cannot tarry. You must be ready to climb those magical stairs, Desmond, because once you've reached the top, then you can slide down the other side."

"Where will it take me, Mamma?" I was both thrilled and scared at the thought of such a journey. "To heaven?"

She shook her head as she brushed my sopping hair with her fingers, and then stared sadly out at sea and my now-disappearing rainbow, its beauty fading right before our eyes. "America," she answered, "the next best place to heaven."

"Are you coming, too, Mamma?" I asked tremulously, trying to picture this journey to a place I'd never heard of. I suddenly found myself not liking the prospect one bit.

Her sigh was audible. "Desmond, this is your rainbow," and with her next sentence confirmed the worst. "There'll be room enough for only one, I'm afraid." She looked down at me and smiled, feeling my anguish through her fingertips. "But that won't be for a long, long time, lad."

After a few more minutes of standing on that cruelest of coasts, she announced it was time to leave. We made our way cautiously along the narrow granite pathway on the face of the cliffs back to the village of Westport. It would be many years before I would again be alone like that with my mother. Oh, what ransom I would have gladly paid to be able to savor just one fleeting moment with her again!

*   *   *

I've often wondered what went through my mother's mind when she saw Ballymorris for the first time. She had been born and raised in Lancashire, England, of hard-working, middle class Irish parents, had graduated from secondary school, and was on her way to becoming an accomplished violinist. But love changed all that. She met Arthur Donahue, an Irish laborer who had come to England out of sheer desperation. This was the mid nineteen-thirties, and although the entire world was mired in the worst depression in history, the situation was so appallingly bad in Ireland that Arthur Donahue was forced to leave to seek employment elsewhere. He found occasional day labor jobs and soon earned a reputation for being solid and dependable. But there were times when days, then weeks, would pass before some meager job would become available. It was a hand-to-mouth existence in every sense of the word. From what little money he earned, he somehow managed to send a pittance back to Ireland to his destitute, extended family. It was not just a godsend: it was a true lifeline. And despite the times, he managed to court young Angela Cunningham. Her parents were aghast. In spite of their vociferous objections, Angela accepted Arthur Donahue's proposal of marriage.

And so in the spring of 1936, Arthur Donahue returned to Ireland with his twenty-three-year-old bride and took her to the village of Ballymorris in County Mayo on the rugged and primitive West Coast. This became her home for the remaining fifty years of her life, and never once in all that time did either any of my twelve surviving siblings or I ever hear a word of despair part from her lips. Her unshakable faith sustained her through unspeakable deprivation until the day she died.

It must have seemed like a journey back in time for the young woman from England. Conditions defied description. What must she have thought as she made her way from the village in a donkey cart, her husband beside her and all her worldly possessions literally resting on her lap? When pressed by me for an answer so many years later, she only smiled, patted my hand as though I were her little boy once more, and simply replied, "Desmond, I was going home."

Home to a three-room structure. A "council house," erected by the government to shelter the indigent. It was a refuge from the elements, but nothing more. Built entirely of concrete, it had four windows and a fireplace. And it was whitewashed inside and out. That was it. No electricity, no kitchen, no water, no toilet, no well. No amenity of any description. Yet, this was a far better abode than that of most of her neighbors, and they were truly envious of her good fortune. Their homes were all at least two hundred-years-old built from field rock and mortar, maybe two rooms and one window, a fireplace, a thatched roof, and a dirt floor. Mean structures all, and passed from one generation to the next. It was pitiful. Our house sat on twenty acres, which we grandly referred to as a "farm."

But three other families also had houses on the land, and all four somehow expected to eke out an existence from this woefully inadequate setting. One half was peat bog, thus impossible to cultivate; the remainder was used to plant potatoes, cabbages and beets. There were two cows, two horses, and one donkey, several sheep, a smattering of chickens, some ducks, and a few geese. The farm. And four families depended on this cornucopia for their survival.

It was here that I came screaming and kicking into the world in the dead of night, on October 5, 1938, following my sister Sheila by almost seventeen months. As with Sheila, my mother was aided by a midwife from the village, delivering her second child by candlelight and without the benefit of sedatives or painkillers. The fee for my delivery was one shilling, duly paid. My father had long before left the house to walk the five miles into Ballymorris to celebrate my arrival with his friends. He would follow this ritual a total of fourteen times. Drink was the bane of his existence, as sadly, too, it is for untold numbers of my countrymen. It was only many years later that I could come to terms with this affliction and truly understand that drink released him, however briefly, from the cruelties of everyday life. I do not condone, but I do understand. It is a true curse and must in large measure be held responsible for some of the backwardness of the country I hold so dear. What greatness could have sprung from this land were it not for drink? God only knows.

*   *   *

The first five years of my life were uneventful, mainly because my entire universe was either the house or its surrounding fields. During these years the family grew by two, so by the time I started school, there were six mouths to feed. Other than that one trip to the ocean, nothing of importance registers in my mind except the anticipation I felt at starting school. Sheila had been attending for a year now, and she would come home full of tales of wonder, recounting to my mother and father all she had learned. My father was a strong believer in education and although he had only been able to attend school for three years before his parents were forced to have him labor in the fields in order to bring home pennies a day for twelve hours work—and this at eight years of age.

I remember that morning as though it were yesterday. I know I didn't sleep a wink that night, and I was up and dressed before dawn, champing at the bit to start the four-mile trek to the one-room schoolhouse at Glenanemon. Sheila was an old hand. She had just turned seven, and if maybe she did not quite know everything, she certainly took pains to constantly remind me that I knew absolutely nothing!

After gobbling down breakfast of bread and fat drippings along with a little warm tea, I set out accompanied by my sister and father, who would introduce me this first day to my teacher. We walked through the rain, the two of us children racing ahead of daddy while calling out to other children already on the road, all heading in the same direction. *Hurry, hurry, hurry!* The miles flew by, and suddenly, there it was: Glenanemon School. One room, three teachers, fifty to sixty students, my window to the world from age five until my graduation nine years later at age fourteen.

The year was 1943. The terrible depression of the thirties was history, replaced now by a tragedy of far greater proportions. The world was at war. Ireland was a non-combatant nation, but untold thousands of her sons were in the British and American armies, so even the very youngest of us were aware of the struggle taking place beyond our shores. We knew that Germany was the foe, and the fighting raging in North Africa and on the continent was described in letters sent home from the front. The news was passed from family to family.

Much has been said and written of that time, the implication being that Ireland favored a German victory in this war because it was the enemy of our age-old enemy, Great Britain. This simply was not the case. True, there existed more than just a few souls who felt this way, Irish patriots who had fought in the Dublin uprising in 1916, members of the Sinn Fein Movement, men who had struggled alongside Kevin Barry that awful bloody Easter Sunday many years before, men who had cheered for Sir Roger Casement after he was captured by the Crown for gun-running. But to ascribe this feeling of enmity toward Britain as indicative of the feelings of the entire country is just not true. But what did a five year old rushing to his first day of school know of such worldly matters?

I was introduced to my teacher, Mrs. Noonan, and assigned my very own desk. She would be my teacher for the next three years, followed by Mrs. O'Boyle, then finally by Mr. Connolly, who also happened to be Mrs. Noonan's brother.

At the end of that first day I could hardly wait to get home and tell my mother what I had learned. "I can read!" I exclaimed for all the world to hear as I exploded into her presence.

"And what can you read, Desmond?" She was as excited as I.

"I can read *A*."

"*A*?"

"Aye, *A*."

She burst out laughing and tried to give me a hug, but I danced out of her reach and whirled around the room. "Oh, Desmond, I'm so proud. Wait until we tell your father. Now, you have only twenty-five more letters to learn. Soon there will be nothing more to teach you. And to think you learned all this in just one day!"

We both shared my joy to full measure.

* * *

That year flew by, and although I certainly lost some of my initial enthusiasm, I truly enjoyed school. I wish I could report that I was a brilliant student, but, alas, I can't. Of those subjects I enjoyed, the learning came with very little effort, and those subjects I did not care for—such as arithmetic—suffice to say, I remained marginally proficient.

The government of Ireland took education very seriously, and compulsory learning was the law of the land for all up to the age of fourteen. Sadly, many parents could not afford to keep their children in school: the wages they could earn were so desperately needed at home, and the idea of added income, no matter how meager was too great a temptation. There were times when my father wanted to have me leave school and go to work, but my mother would never hear of it. "We'll do without, Arthur," she would say quietly but firmly, and in this matter, her word was law. It was the only subject on which she had the last word, and her decision always stood. In his heart of hearts, he knew she was right. But in all other things, my father was king, a monarch with absolute powers. And as any dutiful and fearful subject knows, one goes to great lengths to never, ever, upset the king.

*   *   *

Arthur Donahue had been born on this land in 1908, the last of sixteen children with only eleven surviving to adulthood. Times were so desperate in the early years of the century that as each male child reached the age of eight or nine, he followed the father into the fields to work for the few very wealthy landholders on vast holdings of the finest farmland in Ireland. These estates dated back hundreds of years, many to the days of Oliver Cromwell. The occupants were landed gentry in every sense of what that quaint phrase denotes. Ireland had no middle class in those days, so the gulf between the truly poor and the truly rich was so vast that neither could comprehend how the other lived. The homes of the wealthy were—and still are—magnificent edifices, monuments all to the grandeur of class and privilege. Over time, many of these families had become more British than the inhabitants of that Sceptered Isle even to the extent of abandoning their Irish Catholic faith to become Anglicans. Many were duly elected members of the House of Commons, and their ranks were also well represented in the House of Lords.

My father toiled on several of these huge holdings alongside his father, siblings, uncles, and their offspring. Most of the neighbors were similarly employed, and all lived on the ragged edge. As the century matured and things began to deteriorate even further, Arthur's remaining brothers and sisters who were still living at home at the time approached the father to announce their intention to immigrate to America. They wanted permission to take the fourteen-year old with them. The year was 1922. The father was furious.

"Leave, if ye will," he thundered. "Go to America with all o' the rats who've abandoned this land before you. Go and find the soft life which ye think is yourn for the taking. But you'll not carry the bairn, too. He'll inherit the birthright! Be gone!"

Arthur and his mother wept as the brothers and sisters departed, none ever to return, nor to be seen again. A few letters were written back and forth, the time between each becoming longer and longer, until one day they ceased altogether.

Arthur Donahue worked the land with his father, and over the years became something of an expert on soil and its potential for sustaining crops. His was a gift, pure and simple. He could take a fistful of dirt, hold it up to his nose, smell it, put it to his mouth and taste it, rub it slowly between his fingers, and then pronounce with uncanny accuracy what crop would thrive that growing season. In later life the central government hired him sporadically to test the soil in various parts of the country, and utilizing this most unscientific of methods, had him report his findings to the agricultural ministry. Alas, our land never underwent any miraculous change as a result of my father's unique ability. Our land was just tired and remained such.

It was Arthur's lot to remain in his father's house until the mid-thirties when circumstances drove him to England, where he met Angela Cunningham, married her, and returned to his birthright.

*   *   *

Daily life was a hardscrabble existence, and what was already difficult became only more so as the family grew. By the time I was ten, there were three more children in the Donahue household, bringing the clan to nine souls. We all rose with the weak light of dawn in the summer months and in an inky darkness during the long, hard winters. There were chores to be attended to before setting off to school, and we all dashed about on our appointed rounds. Sheila and I had the task of fetching water, both for the household and for the animals. This meant taking galvanized buckets to a brook that meandered through the farm about a hundred yards away from our front door. It was cold, wretched work, made all the more so because more often than not the job was accomplished in the rain. The buckets were heavy, and as we struggled back to the house, they would invariably bang against our shins, spilling ice-cold water down our bare legs and into our perennially damp, rubber Wellington boots.

After the needs of the household had been satisfied, it was back outside to repeat the process for the animals. The two horses and the donkey would be sating themselves on their morning ration of oats, and as I approached their stall, all would make leery eye contact, then with a toss of their heads seem to command, "Just leave it in the trough, sonny, we'll get to it soon enough." They would chew contentedly, and for many years I actually thought they were laughing at me as I struggled with their morning libations.

These animals had a hard life. They worked six days a week in the interminable cold and rain, pulling plows and carts laden to overflowing with turf to be used as fuel for the fire, and tools and equipment to be traded back and forth among neighbors, and God only knows what else. I can count on one hand the number of times I ever saw these creatures run for the sheer joy of running. When outdoors and idle—with idleness a very rare condition—they would stand dejectedly in the rain with hindquarters to the wind, their heads lowered to almost touching the ground, and they would stare at their hooves for hours. However, they were treated with a fair modicum of human kindness in that they were always fed and watered on time. Not necessarily out of feelings of tenderness and love, but because they were desperately needed for work. They earned their keep a thousandfold.

After all the animals and the various species of birds had been taken care of, it was time for us to eat. Oatmeal, bread, and potatoes in every form imaginable were the mainstay of our morning meal. Milk was a luxury we could not afford. Only the very youngest were given small amounts, the rest sold, but only after the cream had been skimmed off to later be churned into butter. Butter for selling, not for consumption at home. In those days, tuberculosis was rampant in Ireland, the result of the bacillus being passed from cow to human via contaminated milk. There was no pasteurization enforcement, so people were highly susceptible to this germ. Because the entire population was generally unhealthy and most were easy targets for the disease. It was many years later that the Government initiated a rigorous program to eradicate this killer, and by the time I was in my late teens, pasteurization was strictly enforced. All dairy stock were inoculated, and no animal could be sold or even used in dairy production, unless it had papers attesting to its good health.

People would not be treated so well until much later!

Those of us old enough to be going to school were out of the house by eight o'clock, running through the fields, taking shortcuts across neighbors' lands, covering the four miles in a little over twenty-five minutes. Arriving at the schoolhouse, we would find a fire burning in the huge hearth, the smoke from the turf spreading a haze throughout the entire room, so much so that soon fifty students and three teachers would spend the rest of the day coughing and sneezing, choking and gagging in the noxious air. The clothes we all wore were eternally wet—not just damp, but wet—and as these garments begrudgingly released their moisture into the atmosphere, it made an already bad situation worse. And we all toiled oblivious to our unhealthy condition. It was nothing more than an extension of the way things were inside our own homes and every other family. It's a miracle we were not all dead of pneumonia by the time we reached ten.

At noontime, classes came to a halt for forty-five minutes, ostensibly for lunch. More often than not, lunch consisted of a boiled potato, a piece of bread, and at times an apple liberated from a neighbor's tree, snatched on the run. There was no such thing as a school lunch program in those days, so after our meager rations were wolfed down, the room emptied as the younger children ran outside to play, while the older boys disappeared to share a Woodbine cigarette, one smoke for maybe a dozen youths. Then, it was back to class until the bell sounded four, and we were dismissed. That was Ireland in the days of my youth. However, I must admit that during that time, I was really not aware of just how precarious our situation truly was. My parents loved us all equally, and although life was harsh, I did find time to enjoy some of the days of my childhood. But they were few and far between.

CHAPTER TWO

Is **D..d.e.s.m.o.n.d r..r..ready..?"** Michael O'Shane stuttered as he craned his thin neck way back in order to look my father in the eye. At eight and older than me by four months, Michael was the size of a five-year old.

"Inside with you," the giant replied, ignoring the question. "You're letting all the heat out." And in a louder voice over his shoulder commanded, "Desmond, get a move on!"

So began my Saturday afternoon ritual. All the children in the village who'd made their first communion—as I'd done earlier that year—were expected to go to weekly confession, a must prior to receiving the Holy Sacrament the following morning at mass.

A moment later I stood beside my friend.

"Off with the both of you."

My mother called from somewhere within, obscured by the perpetual haze from the turf fire. "Be back by five. Remember, it's bath night."

We dashed out the door and set a course for Ballymorris and St. Agnes' Church where we would humbly kneel in the dark confessional and recite our sins in a timeworn litany to God's intermediary on earth, Father Seamus Jennings.

As I now hearken back to those days, I feel genuinely sorry for the man. He had to suffer in that cold, damp, dark little cubicle for untold hours every Saturday afternoon, listening to children mumble their terrible misdeeds of the week just past. And mumble it was, hoping against hope that Father didn't really hear you, but would grant absolution nonetheless. My heart would race all the faster as the line got shorter, until it was my turn to disappear behind that penitent's door to humble myself before God and man.

Sometimes Father Jennings would be in a foul mood and yell at the supplicant huddled in that tiny box trying not to be identified through the screen separating saint from sinner.

"What in the name of all that's holy would a young girl do something like that for, Colleen McGrath?" he would boom for all to hear. And those in line would become paralyzed with fear, yet still have the capacity to wonder what Colleen McGrath had done? Our eight-year-old brains could not begin to imagine what terrible doings had taken place in Colleen's life to warrant such a tirade. We would trade wide-eyed stares up and down the queue while holding our collective breaths. Soon there would follow some indecipherable whispering on the part of the cleric, followed by a very audible, "For your penance say ten Our Fathers and ten Hail Marys."

Ten? Oh my God!

"Now, make a good act of contrition." And Colleen's soul would instantly be made chaste. But at what price? The mortified child would slink out of the confessional to face her friends. With eyes clouded by tears and her head hung in shame, she would walk to the front of the church and reaching the brass altar rail, would drop to her knees and begin to recite her penance. And the next sinner would reluctantly enter that cubicle to lay bare his or her soul.

Oh, the terrors of those Saturday afternoon confessions, but, ah, the ecstasy of the absolution that followed!

Go forth and sin no more, commanded God's vicar on earth.

I promise I won't sin ever again! Never! In fact, dear Jesus, strike me dead this instant so that my soul might join You in heaven for all eternity!

Alas, He did not see it in His infinite wisdom to do my bidding. Maybe next week. But let the record show that on any given Saturday, any one of us could—and would—get the same treatment that befell our hapless friend Colleen McGrath. None was exempt. To our complete mortification, at one time or another, we were all Colleens.

Once outside the church, Michael O'Shane and I joined forces with John Mannion and John O'Connell, and the four of us headed down the one main street of the village, no destination in mind, simply content just being together. We stopped in front of the Central Cinema and studied the posters pinned inside the crude glass case affixed to the wall. The price of admission was two pence, a king's ransom. We sighed as we looked at the pictures of cowboys in mortal combat, six-guns blazing, Indians falling willy-nilly right and left, but not before splitting open some hapless soul's head with a bloodied tomahawk. I think Gary Cooper was enshrined that Saturday behind the glass, but I can't be sure.

On down the street we strolled, looking in all the store windows, content to shove and jostle one another every few paces, and laugh like deranged hooligans at our own puerile antics. We passed a couple of the pubs, and out of habit I stole a glance into the darkened doorways to see any evidence of my father, until I remembered he had still been at home when I left. As we came abreast Curran's Sweet Shoppe, Michael O'Shane surprised us all by producing a penny. *A penny!* Not a farthing, not a ha'penny, a whole penny!

Into Curran's we marched and spent the next five minutes deciding what would constitute our feast to follow. We settled on jellybeans. Out the door and down the street we went, savoring the delights of that small paper bag. And all too soon it was four o'clock, and time to start home.

"Bye, I'll be at the eight o'clock mass," I announced.

"Me, too," they chorused, and with that we all went our own way home.

*   *   *

Saturday night, bath night. I will never forget that particular Saturday and the events which followed. Bath night meant that all the Donahues in turn—starting with my parents—climbed into a huge, galvanized tub, the water for this cleansing having been placed in several large kettles and pans, and then heated at the hearth for hours. This was no mean production. The children were shooed from the main room until my parents were finished then it was our turn. One by one, the youngsters were washed, hot water being added after some colder water was drawn off so that the tub remained relatively hot for the next in line—and relatively clean as well. When my mother called out my turn, there were two of the younger siblings still in the tub. Sheila had finished and was in the process of drying her hair. I started to peel off my clothes, and as I removed my trousers, a half-crown spilled noisily onto the concrete. All stopped in mid-stride whatever they were doing and followed the spinning coin as it danced its way to the corner. It became a freeze-frame moment captured in my memory for all time.

I must digress momentarily to explain how I was the possessor of such a coin. Every year on my birthday, my godfather, Ned Donahue, a relative—but just how close a relative I don't know to this day—would come and visit from his home some fifteen miles away to wish me a happy birthday and present me with a half-crown.

And as soon as he left, my mother would confiscate the coin and put it to good use. Well, on my eighth birthday, some two weeks past, my half-crown was duly given, and my half-crown duly liberated.

This was neither just, nor fair. It was mine! So three days later I went into my mother's purse and transferred it to my pants pocket, where it resided until that fateful Saturday night. Even Sammy, the dog we had gotten barely a month before, followed the progress of that shiny coin as it skittered across the floor and out of sight. Then all hell broke loose. The two infants in the tub leaped out, spraying water everywhere. Sheila dropped her towel, and in an instant was on all fours in hot pursuit, followed by myself, my mother, my father, and the dog, all in that order. Pandemonium reigned. But there was never a doubt who would rule triumphant. The King. Tossing wife, and children, and dog aside with the strength of a Samson, he emerged from the fray victorious. He glowered at me for a long moment, then without a word, left the house and headed for Ballymorris.

My mother stood looking at me for an eternity. Finally, she spoke. "So that's what happened to the money. You know what you've done, don't you, Desmond? That was money to feed the children." There was no trace of bitterness in her voice, only total resignation. Her words spoke volumes.

Yes, I knew. Now, my father would be gone all night, drinking with his friends, no thought of kith and kin as he sunk into an alcoholic stupor. I wanted to die.

"Finish your bath," she said, as she began to clean the mess we had all created. "I'll think up some story to tell your father." She shook her head sadly at the thought of having to utter a lie. "I'll tell him that Uncle Ned had just given you the money a couple of days ago and that you simply forgot to give it to me." She let loose a sigh. "When everyone's clean, we'll say the rosary." She left the room, her arms laden with dirty clothes, and her heart burdened with the weight of the world.

*   *   *

Sundays without rain were usually pleasant days for my neighbors and me. After mass, the children would stay in town, bringing breakfast and oftentimes lunch with them. Breakfast, because we had to fast from midnight in order to receive communion. I was always ravenous by the time mass was over. But as I look back on those years, I now realize I was *always* hungry. There was simply never enough food, and the pangs in my stomach were very real and very sore. That hunger, coupled with the interminable cold, took its toll, and there was many a day when I would weep from the agony of being chilled to the bone, knowing there was no respite. It was a situation which bred despair, and many a day I prayed to die. There is nothing worse than to be so cold. Nothing. And this was an integral part of life in Ireland for most of the population. My brothers and sisters likewise wept from the pain of the same affliction, as I'm sure did my mother, but never in sight of her children. But on those few clear Sundays, I would meet up with my mates and we would play football for most of the afternoon. We became quite good, and as we got older, formed a team and played teams from surrounding villages. I can modestly report that we always gave a solid accounting of ourselves.

*   *   *

The days at the beginning of each month were brighter and happier than those which crowded the back-end of the calendar. Was it because God chose to bless and favor us according to some heavenly edict, or maybe because of the astrological placement of the planets? Nothing so cosmic, I'm afraid. Simply put, my parents could look forward to another welfare check. I never remember a time that we did not receive monetary assistance from Dublin, but this was never a cause for embarrassment because the condition was universal, at least it was with everyone I knew. There would be more and better food available as the calendar unfurled—sometimes even a piece of fruit—but mostly just more. If we were to taste meat, it would be during that first week; then as the days wore on, the largess would taper down in direct proportion to the number of days from the date our check was cashed. Come the twentieth day, the diet would again be porridge, bread, potatoes, cabbage and beets. And us all anticipating the start of a new month. That rhythm of life was as fixed as the tides, dependable, and unwavering in its cycle.

Finding clothing for the family was a constant headache for my mother. Everyone wore hand-me-downs with warmth, not fashion dictating our wardrobe. From head to toe, we boys were like miniature soldiers, all dressed in dark, short pants and dark sweaters. The same with my sisters, only they wore skirts instead of pants. And we all had Wellington boots. Socks were unheard of, so newspaper was stuffed into the bottoms of these always cold, always damp rubber boots. They chafed our feet and legs raw, and our toes were constantly covered with agonizing chilblains. Colors were always dark. Dark clothes hid the dirt. They could be worn to the point of disintegration and often were.

The seasons turned. Spring slipped into summer, autumn became winter, the latter truly dreaded for the additional hardships it brought: days of constant rain and sleet, plunging temperatures, and bone-chilling winds, which swept down from the Arctic. Daylight was from eight until three, so my journey to and from school was always made in the dark.

It was during a winter such as this that my sister Bernadette was born. I was ten at the time, so I reason Bernadette had to be the eighth child. She was a hard delivery, and finally struggled into this world in the early morning hours during a dreadful storm. She was woefully underweight and exhausted from the sheer effort of birth. Poor Bernadette. Within days she developed whooping cough, and that was her death warrant.

It's a terrible disease caused by the bacillus *Bordetella pertussis,* characterized by a thick mucus discharge from the nose and by bouts of coughing which end in a forced intake of breath creating a whooping sound. Thus the name. This valiant infant struggled for three weeks, cradled day-and-night in my mother's arms, held upright so that she could draw in tiny breaths of air between the horrific rounds of coughing which wracked her entire little body. Neighborhood women were constantly in the house to offer some modicum of relief for my mother, and they would force her to relinquish the child while she dropped into a sleep brought on from sheer exhaustion.

How terrible were the sounds from my little sister as the life ebbed out of her. All night long that frightening, tortured whoop. Such agony for my mother to endure. To be so helpless. We prayed and prayed for Bernadette, rosary after rosary, tears streaming down all our faces, but God chose not to hear our prayers, and finally it was over. There were no vaccines available in Ireland in those days, so the outcome was inevitable. Three weeks to the day, she shuddered one last time and died in my mother's arms. The woman was inconsolable.

Two of her friends from the village were with her when Bernadette died, and they did their best to ease the pain.

"Angela, your little Bernadette's with God, in heaven for all eternity. Angela, love, remember, you now have a saint in paradise. She's with the angels."

They were not just words of comfort; those ladies truly believed. Such is the faith. It gave meaning to my mother. And the strength to carry on.

"Desmond, go and collect your father," Mrs. Tiernan told me in a quiet voice. "He's over at the Donnelly place. Take the donkey cart, son, it'll be faster."

I remember that six-mile trip in the pouring rain as though it were yesterday. I wept the entire journey, tears for Bernadette, tears for Desmond. With all my heart and soul, I cried out to God take me so that I might join my little sister. I was tired of the hunger, the cold, the misery of life, a life with no respite from the deprivation which was our lot. The future held no promise. I would grow old trapped in these circumstances. I would never get the chance to truly live. I wanted peace.

We buried our little saint two days later during a snowstorm. The entire village attended the funeral mass and accompanied the family to the cemetery. This was the first time I saw my father cry. And the sight of him reduced to tears made mine flow all the faster.

Somehow life carried on.

* * *

I mentioned that I enjoyed school, and in subjects I liked, I excelled. English literature, grammar, and dictionary were my favorites. I loved to read, and my tastes in the written word were catholic. If a piece of paper held writing, I would read it. My mother often joked that if toilet paper had print, I would study each sheet and probably not use it for the purpose intended.

Ballymorris did boast of having one small, well-used library. Reading was an escape for grown-ups and children alike, and books could be found in every home. The written word is very important to the Irish, and we are extremely proud of the contributions made to literature by our sons and daughters. I spent untold hours in that library with my brothers and sisters, and when our homework was done, we would spend hours at home huddled around the table reading, each jockeying for a position closest to the candles. Reading helped keep my sanity in check.

It was during my middle years at school that Mrs. O'Boyle began holding competitions for the best composition. We were graded on content, spelling, grammar, use of words, and neatness. This was my milieu, and I excelled. A prize went to the best student, so the competition was fierce. It was a "winner take all" situation, and to place second was to be "an also ran". The prize was always two biscuits and two sweets. Every once in a while, I would fall short, but not often. At times my friend Michael O'Shane would displace me as top dog by a mere fraction of a point, and I would be furious with myself for days. He would savor those delicacies in front of me on our way home from school, while never offering me the slightest morsel.

"Wait until next time, Michael O'Shane, you just wait!" And sure enough, next time I would be back in my rightful place and would enjoy the fruits of my labor in front of him. Sometimes I would share my good fortune with Tess O'Boyle—not because she was the teacher's daughter—but because I had a crush on her! Throughout those years of competition, I was always the odds-on-favorite to win, but more importantly, it gave me a solid foundation in the correct usage of language and all its beautiful nuances.

Of course school was not all composition. Education was important to the Irish, and the central government is strict in laying out a curriculum to be followed without deviation. Arithmetic, algebra, and geometry, depending on the grade. Social studies, Irish history, world history, and geography. English, Irish Gaelic, Latin, and French. Zoology, chemistry, biology, and botany. For the girls, home economics, and for all, a course in hygiene in our senior year. By the time one matriculated, it was fair to say that individual had a reasonable understanding of the world and, hopefully, the means in which to prosper. At least that was the intention. Sadly, most were too poor to go on to higher education. They became adults at fourteen. Childhood was over.

Rare was the student who played hooky. Not only would he have to answer to Mr. Connolly, the senior teacher, but to Mr. Connolly, the disciplinarian. He was stone-deaf when it came to excuses. Sickness, along with a note from a parent, passed muster, all other excuses were just that: excuses. The malefactor would be brought to the front of the room to explain. He would plead his case in whispers, while the other students pretended to be engrossed in their work. We all knew what was coming, we just didn't know when. The anticipation was more than one could endure! Mr. Connolly would be talking quietly when suddenly, and without warning, he would lash out and whack the criminal a blow to the side of the head, or maybe let loose with a well-placed kick to the rear. The result was invariably the same. The student would be flattened and reduced to tears, then forced to crawl that hundred-mile journey back to his desk. More often than not, he would be given a note to take to his parents, which meant he could reasonably expect more of the same once he got home. There was no such thing as double jeopardy in our school system. If for some insane reason such behavior was repeated, then the police would be informed and that meant big trouble for student and parents alike. This situation only rose twice during my tenure at Glenanemon School. The consequences were simply not worth it!

Upon arrival back home from school in the waning daylight hours, and before dinner and homework, there were chores to be done. As in the morning, we each went about our appointed tasks. Animals had to be fed, stalls cleaned, water brought to the house, and whatever other jobs my mother needed doing. This occupied us until it was time for dinner. Sammy, our dog, would lie in the front yard with his head on his paws waiting with the patience of Job for his master to appear.

I must take a moment to tell you about Sammy. Sammy came to us as a pup from one of the neighboring farms, a medium-sized dog with a beautiful white and gray coat, an eager smile, and a devotion to my father that bordered on adoration. Sammy was the smartest of dogs and self-taught in most things. When my father would whistle and point to the cows and sheep grazing in the field and command *"fetch,"* that dog would streak out into the pasture to round up those not-too-smart beasts, nipping at their heels all the while as he drove them into the barn. Sammy was a sight to behold. And as I said, loved my father without reservation. My undemonstrative father loved that dog to full measure. The family could always gauge my father's mood even before he reached the house. If Sammy began barking and jumping up and down the moment he spotted my father, then we knew that all was right in the kingdom. But if Sammy just slunk alongside the master with his ears drawn back and his feathery tail held low, then we would all magically shrink to about six inches in height and stay well out of sight of the monarch. Sometimes it worked, sometimes it didn't. But we all kept our eye on Sammy, the forecaster of moods. Throughout the many years we had Sammy, he remained an absolute joy, and my father took steps to see that he would live forever. Whenever a dog at one of the surrounding farms came into heat, Sammy would be called on for services, and my father would get the pick of the litter. Sammy always performed magnificently, and after the litter was born, my father would inspect the progeny. Most often he would pass, and none would join Sammy, but sometimes he would call for his right. At times there were as many as three dogs in our lives. Sammy died at eighteen, mourned by all, but especially by my father.

Years later, a dog bearing the same name as the one who started the lineage was in residence, and like the original, adored my father and spent his entire day by his side. By now dad was well into his sixties and retired. He became ill shortly after his sixty-eighth birthday, grew worse, and died within days. My mother was heartbroken, and although Arthur Donahue had not been the easiest of souls to live with, he had loved my mother and his children with all his heart, and we knew it.

Shortly after the funeral, Sammy disappeared, and it wasn't until several days later that a neighbor came to the house to tell my mother he had spotted Sammy lying on Arthur's grave. Sammy would not budge. My mother and youngest sister brought food and water twice a day to that most faithful friend, until one morning two weeks later they arrived to find Sammy dead. Sweet, gentle Sammy had died of a broken heart. Had it been permitted, my mother would have buried that loving animal beside her Arthur Donahue.

Looking back from the vantage point of a man over seventy, my mind now tells me that those years rushed by, but I can honestly say that was not the way it seemed at the time. But that milestone day finally arrived. The day I graduated from Glenanemon. Just before the ceremony got underway, Mrs. O'Boyle took me aside. She had tears in her eyes.

"Desmond, what will become of you?" she asked tenderly. "You've been a good boy, and you do so take to education. I wish with all my heart that you could go on and get more schooling. You're one who would appreciate it." She brushed aside the tears and smiled. "I know you must work and help your parents, but, Desmond, if the opportunity ever presents itself that you can go back to school, promise me you will?"

Until that moment I had no idea she had such faith in me. I was shocked. But more, I was proud. "I promise, Mrs. O'Boyle."

And so, at noon, on a dreary day at the end of June 1952, I graduated from Glenanemon School. Now a man, I was expected to earn my keep. My education was over, and with it, my youth.

CHAPTER THREE

*M*y **summer vacation** lasted three days. On the morning of the fourth, my father woke me at six o'clock. "Up with you, Desmond. Time to be going to work."

What was he talking about? "I don't have a job, yet," I said through a fog.

"Yes, you do, boy. I spoke to Mr. Simpson from the Public Roads Department about you yesterday. He needs a lad to fetch water and do other odd jobs for the road crews as they make their way around the county. I told him you were just the ticket and that you could use the donkey and cart. He wants to meet you at seven in front of the theater."

I certainly had no desire to work on the roads, but I was too scared to say so to my father. I crawled out of my warm bed, grabbed a quick bite, hitched up the donkey and headed into town, grumbling every inch of the way.

"My lord, yer half the size of nothing," Mr. Simpson said, peering over his glasses at me sitting in the cart. "Arthur Donahue led me to believe you were a strapping lad. You sure you're not the wrong boy?"

"I'm Desmond Donahue, sir. I'm the one my father spoke to you about."

Simpson shook his head, skepticism painted on his weathered face. "You'll not last till noon," he observed. "This job requires you to fetch and lift all manner of things, the least of which is water in five-gallon containers. The days are long and hard, and the pay is two pounds a week. You think yer man enough to do all that?"

"Yes, Mr. Simpson, I can do it." Deep in my heart, I was hoping he would call me a liar and fire me on the spot.

"Well, you're here, so let's see if you can do a man's job."

So started my employment. I worked the roads of the county for fourteen long, miserable, cold, terrible months, hating every moment of every interminable day. I dragged water, asphalt, paint, shovels, spades, tar, brushes, and God knows what else, to the crews as they repaired and beautified the roads of the republic. My days started before dawn and ended well after dark. Most of the time my only companion was Neddy, our very patient mule who seldom raised his voice in protest. I made sure he was always well-fed and watered. That little donkey must have walked ten thousand miles in that year-and-a-half, and he must have grown sick of my voice as I spoke and sang to him hour after lonely hour, more often than not in the incessant rain.

Shortly after my sixteenth birthday, I was in Ballymorris on a Saturday afternoon when I spotted Mike McAdam coming out of the theater. Mike was almost a year older than I, and although we weren't close, we played on the same soccer team.

"Will you be playing tomorrow, McAdam?" I called out.

He turned to see who was talking to him. "That I will, Donahue. The question is, will you be able to do a better job defending our goal than last week?"

"I bloody well hope so!" I was still smarting from the five to nothing drubbing we had suffered the week before. Losses were a rarity for us, and as goalkeeper, I had taken more than my fair share of criticism for the debacle.

We fell into step, talking about this and that, when out of the blue Mike asked, "What do you see yourself doing ten years from now, Desmond?"

I hadn't really given the future a lot of thought. And ten years from now? Well, that was a lifetime. "I shan't be working on the bloody roads, that's for sure," I spat out, self-pity making the words stick in my throat.

"Have you ever thought of leaving?"

"My parents would never let me."

"I'm not talking about getting permission from your parents or anybody else. I'm talking about up and leaving." He snapped his fingers. "Just like that." *Snap.* "Think about what I said, Donahue. We'll talk some more after the game."

Is there ever a good time to run away from home? Is one time of the year better than another? One day better than the next? Or do you seize the moment, take advantage of opportunity, and act?

That's exactly what we did. Mike had an older brother in London who promised he could find us work and a place to stay. We planned on leaving the second weekend in December, and it was all I could do to maintain a semblance of normalcy as I continued my daily drudgery. I furtively began to gather my meager belongings, and on the appointed day, crept out of the house before dawn and met up with Mike by the post office. I shoved an envelope into the letterbox. It was addressed to my mother, and I knew she would receive it on Monday. In my letter I tried to explain my actions, beseeched her not to worry, and promised I would write from England.

We took the ferry across from Dublin to Wales, then a train into London. I carried fifteen pounds, that princely sum being my entire life's savings.

We were met at London's Victoria station by Matt McAdam, Mike's brother.

"Can't go back home now, boys," he said to the two scared, dejected figures before him. And boy, we were scared! But, too, we were filled with anticipation and a heady sense of adventure.

London was dressed in her Christmas finery, her streets packed with thousands of happy citizens, all window-shopping this dreary Saturday afternoon.

"I've got you staying at St. Ann's Hostel," Matt explained, as we walked rapidly in the fading light toward the East End. "Father Timothy runs the place, and his rules are few but fair. However, break any of them even once, mind you, and you're out on your ear. No second chance with Father Timothy. Remember that."

St. Ann's was a renovated reform school, taken over by the Oblate Fathers and turned into a safe haven for male, Irish immigrants. It was not a home for the indigent, nor the ne'er do well. Far from it. Everyone was expected to work, pay rent, prosper, and then move on, thus allowing room for others to follow in their footsteps. Father Timothy met us in the foyer, smiling kindly at his newest guests.

"Welcome to St. Ann's, lads. I know you must be tired, so I suggest a little something to eat, and then off to bed with you. But only if you feel so inclined. Time enough to go over the rules of the house in the morning after mass." Just like that. No fanfare, no threatening, no talk about toeing the mark. We were being treated like adults. I took an instant liking to the man.

I had been assigned a small room to myself; and for the first time in my life, I climbed into a bed not occupied by two or three other bodies. This was heaven! And the next morning, I had my first shower. No more galvanized tubs in a cold, dank kitchen. Real hot water and lots of it. What more could one possibly ask for? I shook my lathered head. There was nothing left in life to top this. Nothing!

On Monday morning Father Timothy sent McAdam and me over to see a Mr. John Piper, project engineer for a construction firm called Higgs and Hills, Contractors, LTD.

Higgs and Hills was one of the largest builders in England, and at the moment, was erecting a huge office complex not far from St. Ann's. Mike and I didn't hold out much hope of being hired mere days before Christmas.

"I can use both of you," Mr. Piper announced after interviewing us for less than five minutes. First, he gave McAdam his marching orders. "Go and find Ken Witherspoon somewhere on the first floor and tell him I said to put you to work. Tell him you're to be a navvy."

"A what, sir?"

Piper laughed. "A navvy," he repeated. "Just tell Witherspoon. He'll know what to do with you."

Mike shrugged his shoulders and went in search of the man who would transform him. By the end of the day, his aching body would know full well what it meant to be a navvy.

"And now for you, Desmond. I want you for a tea boy. It'll be your job to make sure the men are fed in the morning, at least those who want it, and then to make sure they have hot tea available throughout the day."

A tea boy? I ran away from home to become a tea boy? Absolutely not!

"Mr. Piper, I want to be a carpenter, a mason, or even a plumber. I want to learn a craft."

"That so? Well, let me tell you the facts of life, Master Desmond Donahue. I have all of those I need at the moment. And all with over ten years' experience. How much experience do you have to draw on, pray tell?"

"None, sir," I replied, my voice barely above a whisper. Instantly I was reduced to feeling like a whining, ten-year-old brat. And Mr. Piper never raised his voice. He didn't need to. He could speak volumes with just a look, and at the moment, he was throwing an entire set of encyclopedia in my direction.

"Let this be your first lesson. Never, ever, argue with the boss. Understood?"

I just nodded.

"There are one hundred forty-four men on this project," Piper said, "correction, one hundred forty-six, counting you and your friend, and I'm responsible for the lot. Now, the one thing I desperately need this very moment is a tea boy. That's what I'm hiring you for. There will be ample opportunity down the road to move onward and upward, but this is where you start. Do we see eye to eye on things, Desmond?"

We did.

*   *   *

Thus, I became a tea boy. The job was more demanding than I could have ever imagined. But it turned out to be a most profitable venture, and I learned many skills in the course of the next several months. Let me explain.

Higgs and Hills operated a canteen on the site, and I arrived in the dark every morning at six o'clock sharp. I was always the first person there and would spend the next hour readying breakfast for the men. Through trial and error, I learned how many workers could be expected to eat on any given day. I learned to prepare what they wanted to eat, and more importantly, learned how much to prepare simply because it was a part of my job to first purchase the food out of my own money, cook it, and then sell it at a profit. So, if I purchased food that no one would eat, then I suffered the loss. And believe me, in the early days, I learned the bitter lesson of having food ignored because I purchased what I thought they'd want. After twice crawling to Mr. Piper for an advance, he took me aside for some friendly advice.

"Desmond, ask the blokes what they want to eat. Make the rounds and ask 'em. They'll tell you. Then buy accordingly. Keep this up, you'll soon be stone-broke. But worse, I'll have an unhappy crew. And if that day comes, then I'll be a very unhappy boss. Do you get my drift, son?"

"Yes, sir."

Things changed overnight. I was on my way to becoming a successful entrepreneur, being paid nine pounds a week by Mr. Donovan. But soon my culinary skills had matured to a point that the "business" was generating another fifteen to twenty pounds a week. All profit, but before taxes. I was sure to become a millionaire, and I was still only sixteen years old.

You laugh? Allow me to digress so that I may put my status in perspective. The average forty-year-old carpenter—or any other skilled craftsman for the purpose of this lecture—made about thirty pounds per week. Before taxes. Now, more than likely, the man was married with a couple of kids. Thus, four people depended on his weekly paycheck. I was making almost the same amount with only myself to take care of. As I said, I was well on my way to becoming a millionaire.

All transactions were credit transactions, and the men would keep a running tally of what they owed me. Every week, as soon as they were paid, they settled up their accounts. And none ever welshed. Not one soul in the several months I had the job. I wonder if the same could be said today?

*   *   *

One of Father Timothy's rules was that all residents of St. Ann's were required to write home once a week and were also encouraged to send money. Send what you think you can afford was his only advice. These letters would be left in a brass tray in the front hallway, and he would place a stamp on each, then hand-carry the lot to the post office. This was a Saturday morning ritual, and all letters had to be written by ten o'clock. No exceptions, no excuses.

Every week I would write of my adventures in London, and faithfully enclose a fiver. I enjoyed writing—a holdover from my school days—and some weeks my letters would run four to five pages. And in the process, I learned another invaluable lesson.

'As you sow, so shall you reap.'

You see, all my family soon began writing in return. At first, it was just my mother, but in no time I was getting letters from my brothers and sisters as well. And at times even my father would add a line or two to one of the letters! By now I felt good about having made the decision to leave, and my parents had long ago forgiven me for 'scaring the daylights out of us when you just disappeared, son,' as my mother put it in her first communication. Without fail, her opening sentence in every letter carried words of thanks for the money I was sending. And I would glow with pride. I knew it was a godsend, easing her crushing burden, if only slightly.

On Friday and Saturday nights, a group of us would go to the pictures, and then afterwards stop in at any of several dances being sponsored by the various trade guilds or churches in the neighborhood. I would dress in my one good suit, purchased as carefully as if it had been acquired on Saville Row instead of a secondhand store in Piccadilly Circus. My mirror would convincingly lie, affirming its reflected presence of a dashing young man within. But by the time I stepped into the dance hall, my ersatz bravado invariably withered and died at the first sight of the girls grouped together in animated little knots. Soon the music would start, and a handful of daring souls would single out a prospective partner. With heads held high, they would cross that no-man's land to ask the chosen for the pleasure of this dance. Oh, how I envied those stalwart individuals! But, alas, sometimes the object of the quest would refuse the invitation for whatever reason, thus forcing that intrepid warrior to undertake a perilous journey back to friendly lines while the searchlight-like beams from a hundred pairs of eyes illuminated every step. Never once did I muster up the nerve to make that journey, utter coward that I was. "Next week," I always vowed silently as I walked home to St. Ann's with my friends. "Next week will be different. That's when I'll take the plunge." But next week came and went, and so too, the week after, *ad infinitum*. I never once crossed into enemy territory. Not once. I could only dream and adore those beautiful creatures from afar.

*   *   *

"Desmond, I've got a proposition for you to consider. You don't have to say yes, and it's certainly not an order." It was late June, and I had been working for Mr. Piper exactly six months.

"Yes, sir?"

"We're going to be starting a new project in Wales, probably before the end of July. We're all but finished here, and some of the lads will be going north to work on the warehouses we're putting up in Bristol. Now, if you want, you're welcome to go to Bristol, but I would like you to consider coming with me to Wales. The job there involves building an addition to a pretty fair-sized glass factory, and I want you to come as my assistant. It's time for you to learn more about this business. You've got a good head on your shoulders, son. You could learn to be a good craftsman, but I think you have the capability to do much more." He paused, a frown crossing his brow. "I could be wrong, mind you, but I don't think so."

"What would I do as your assistant, Mr. Piper?"

"You'd become my third and fourth hands, Desmond. You'd do things which would free me up for other tasks. I need someone I can trust to follow instructions, someone I can count on to make my busy life a little easier."

"I'd like to give it a go, sir." If Piper had faith in me, wasn't it time for me to have a little of that same faith in myself?

I spent the next two years in Wales working for Mr. Piper. He proved a demanding boss, but I learned so much. My time was spent mostly in the town of Pontypool, the site of the glass factory, but there were times I had to return and work in our London offices from a few days, to a stretch lasting upward of two weeks. Of course, I had moved out of St. Ann's once I had left the London jobsite, but I still visited whenever I was back in town. It was a psychological anchor, a refuge whenever events seemed to overwhelm.

In Wales, I lived in a boarding house, which provided breakfast and dinner six days a week. Sundays, everyone fended for himself. The cost was three pounds a week, not unreasonable for the times.

Mr. Piper by now had raised my salary to twenty pounds a week, but I was still far short of the almost thirty I had been earning as a tea boy.

Piper knew this. "We should all make sacrifices today for the prospect of a better tomorrow." Easy for him to say, I thought at the time. How true, I would finally agree, but only many years later.

Yet, it was hard. I was still sending five pounds a week home, but by the time taxes were paid, there wasn't much left for me to spend. Or save. Thank God there was not much of a social life in Pontypool, so at Piper's urging, I signed up for classes in the construction arts at the local college. Here, I was exposed to the reading of blueprints and wiring diagrams. I was also taught how to set footings and how to erect scaffolding so that the whole structure didn't come tumbling down like so many pick-up-sticks. I was learning the trade from professionals. But the best teacher was Piper himself.

Two years later the job was finished. Mr. Piper took me to dinner in London, the first and last time he did so.

"Desmond," he began, "my work in England is over. I've been asked by the directors to become the project manager on a building program we've contracted for in South Africa. I should be gone for at least four years. After that, I'll retire, hopefully to Dorset. That's been my dream for as long as I can remember." He seemed inexplicably sad to be telling me all this. "You've been a fine assistant, Desmond, and you've a good future ahead of you. I've taken the liberty to contact a friend of mine with our competitors over at Halloway Brothers. His name is Ian Potter, and he's offered you a job, sight unseen based on my recommendation to be his personal assistant. You'd be staying on in Wales, doing for him what you've done for me." He played with his teaspoon as he spoke. "They're starting a big project, building a paper goods factory for a bunch of Yanks. The job should last from three to four years. I told Potter you were earning thirty-five pounds a week and worth every penny. He didn't blink an eye. It's yours for the taking, lad. Just be in Cardiff a week from Monday."

What could I say? Mr. Piper had been the best boss and mentor a lad as green as Ireland's sod could have ever hoped for. I would sorely miss him. I thanked him for everything, and we solemnly shook hands. Mr. Piper handed me a letter of recommendation to be tucked away for future use. We said our good-byes rather stiffly, hoping to mask our mutual sadness. We parted company, and I never saw him again. I only hope that he was able to retire to Dorset and fulfill his dream.

He proved generous to a fault right to the end. In his letter he had placed a parting bonus of fifty pounds.

So, with a week off and nothing to do, I decided to go home and visit my family. It was long overdue.

*   *   *

This was only my second visit home in three years. A new addition to the clan had been born three months prior, bringing the number of siblings to thirteen. My older sister, Sheila, was now a nurse living in Northern England, and the two brothers next to me in line were champing at the bit. They had been pestering my parents for months to allow them to join me in England. At least they were going about the process the right way: they had no intention of following precisely in my footsteps by simply up and running away.

"They're ready," I told my parents when the subject was finally broached. "When I get back, let me get in touch with Father Timothy and see when would be a good time for them to go to St. Ann's. I know they'll have no difficulty finding jobs, but let's do it in an orderly fashion." This last I directed toward my brothers. Such grown-up advice.

They agreed, but pestered me to get on with it as quickly as possible. I promised I would.

On the last day of my visit, my mother informed me that my old school chum and sometime composition nemesis, Michael O'Shane, had dropped dead of a cerebral hemorrhage barely two months before. *Michael O'Shane dead?* It was beyond comprehension. He was always so full of life! And not yet twenty! It was a heavy blow.

"I'll write a letter to his mom as soon as I get back to Wales," I promised.

"She'll appreciate it, Desmond. He was the light of her life, and I know too well the heartbreak she's feeling. She always asks about you, by the way." She smiled and touched my head, a faraway look clouding her eyes. "Remember him in your prayers, son." She quickly blessed herself as she spoke. "We've all being saying novenas for the repose of his immortal soul."

*   *   *

True to his word, Mr. Ian Potter hired me as his assistant. "Glad to have you hook up with us, Desmond. I guarantee you're going to enjoy working for Holloway Brothers. This is one of the biggest projects we've ever attempted, so you're going to have the devil's own time keeping me out of trouble. Think you're up to the task?"

I had to laugh. And he laughed right along with me. "I'll do my level best, sir."

He was a small man, much younger than Mr. Piper, and a veritable dynamo. I had somehow pictured him as a character out of a Dickens novel, taciturn in nature, devoid of mirth, a regular bloody slave to the Protestant work ethic espoused and so much admired in the literature of his countrymen. Not even close!

To begin with, I never saw the man without a cigarette. Often he would have two or even three going at the same time, and any room he entered soon became enshrouded in a heavy, blue haze. He was oblivious to the discomfort this might cause others, but in all other things, he was a most considerate man. He did not rule by intimidation, as Piper had been able to do by merely staring a man down. No, Potter was the boss everyone went out of his way to please. He was long on praise for a job well done and quick to forgive when something went wrong.

And, oh, how he loved this assignment! We were to build an entire factory to house the largest paper-box manufacturing facility in Europe. As this was for an American corporation, money was no object. We were looking three to four years down the road to fully complete our task, but part of the factory had to be up and running in twelve months.

"It's going to be a grand challenge, lad," Potter observed that first week as we pored over a mountain of blueprints. "I figure to have my crews hired within a month, and I plan to excavate the first foundation thirty days after that." He stood back and vigorously rubbed his hands with glee. "This is an opportunity any engineer would kill for, Desmond. It's the dream job of a lifetime, and it's mine! By Jove, I can't wait to get started!"

It took months for the untrained eye to see the slightest hint of progress. There were about seventy men on site when we started, but by late November, their ranks had swelled to over two hundred. I had never been associated with so mammoth an undertaking, and the dynamo named Potter was in motion fourteen hours a day.

A week before Christmas, we were advised to expect a visit from a group out of the clients' headquarters in New York. This would be my first exposure to Americans.

Potter was everywhere, making sure that we were prepared for our guests. The entire area was cleared of all unnecessary equipment, and mounds of rubbish were carted away. To mention this in no way implies that Potter ran a dirty site. He didn't. It's that he wanted everything to be just so. He had readied a presentation for these men from on high, a briefing that included many impressive charts, depicting what he called "cost flow, and work-in-progress analyses."

"Yanks love pictures, Desmond," he said. "They're not too keen on a lot of words. Bullshit, they call it. But they gobble up graphs and charts. They call that eyewash." He stood back to admire his handiwork. "That's not to say they're stupid," he continued. "Far from it. And, I repeat, they hate to be razzle-dazzled with bullshit. But believe me, if there's a problem, they'll spot it in an instant. Some of our countrymen think all Americans are gum-chewing fools, but I'm here to tell you otherwise. These people now rule the world, Desmond, and they sure as hell didn't get to be king of the mountain because they're a nation of bloody nitwits."

I was in awe of these masters of the universe. I had heard so much about them growing up, and now I was finally going to meet some members of this race of supermen.

Potter stubbed out his cigarette and blew an atomic bomb-sized cloud smack into my face. "Remember, Desmond, don't call them Yanks. It's certainly not a derogatory term, but just say American, when referring to the country and its people."

"I understand, Mr. Potter."

There were four of them, and my first thought was, *they're not much older than I am!* They showed up in old work clothes, and after introductions all-around, they insisted on being addressed by their first names, an unheard of practice in the very proper, very stuffy, British Isles.

"Ian, if you or any of your men calls me Mr. Carter one more time, well, I'm folding my tent, taking my gang, and hightailing it back to New York. My dad's called Mr. Carter; I'm just plain old Bob."

Potter laughed. "Yes, sir. Plain old Bob it is."

And that's how it went for three days. They were the greatest group of men I had ever met. And they were everything I wanted to be. One day, I vowed, I'm going to be just like them. I'm going to be an American. They were my heroes.

"Ian, you guys are doing a bang-up job here," Bob congratulated us as they were leaving. "Now, remember, if there's anything you need, get on the horn, and call me in New York. And if I'm needed back here, just say the word and I'll be on the next plane." He turned to me. "Desmond, if you ever get tired of working for this tyrant, you just holler, okay? I'll snap you up in an instant."

And cheeky Desmond replied, "Yes, sir, plain old Bob."

Potter pretended to cuff me, and our visitors departed amidst gales of laughter.

The months flew by. By the end of that year, my two brothers had moved to London, were living at St. Ann's, and employed in the city. As for me, my life was all I could have hoped for. Except I now dreamed constantly of America. I knew that I had a future in the construction business and couldn't envision a better way of life. I was saving money, and my dream was to buy a house. Maybe someday. Maybe in America!

And fate stepped smartly into the picture, changing my life by turning a boy's dream into reality.

It was the summer of 1959, and the factory in Cardiff was about finished. Mr. Potter was being reassigned to London to undertake the job of project manager for building a bank in Whitehall. He had assumed I would be coming with him, and, of course, I let him know that I would.

The fate I mentioned took place on a train from Cardiff to London. I was traveling for the express purpose of finding a place to live.

At dinnertime, I went into the dining car and was seated at a table already occupied by one other person.

"Hi'ya, pal. I'm Pete Frank, Centralia, Illinois." He shot his hand out for me to shake.

An American! "Desmond Donahue," I replied.

"Pleased to meetcha, Desmond."

"Likewise, I'm sure."

Pete Frank, from Centralia, Illinois, explained that he was a high school teacher touring the British Isles for two months. He entertained me for the next hour with stories of life in the Midwest. I was spellbound.

"Didja ever think about visitin' the States?" he concluded, nursing a warm beer.

"I think what I would really like would be to live there," I replied, wistfully. I then spoke of the Americans I had met, and how impressed I had been with everything they stood for.

"That's the great thing about America, Desmond. You can do anything you want. Just set your sights, then, bam, go for it."

"All I know is that to immigrate to America you've got to be sponsored by someone, and I don't know a living soul who would do that for me."

"Ah, hell, I'd do it for ya, Desmond. No sweat."

The train was slowing down on its approach into London. We would be in the station in five minutes.

"Would you really, Mr. Frank?" I wasn't embarrassed to flaunt my excitement and enthusiasm.

"Tell you what, pal. Here's my address and phone number back in the U.S. of A. I'll be there one month from today. You start the ball rolling on this end, then contact me. Remember, Desmond, Rome wasn't built in a day."

"I don't know what you mean."

He handed me a sheet of paper on which I wrote my address in Ireland, explaining that by the time I contacted him a month from now, I would have a London address and telephone number.

"What I mean is the process will take at least a year, pal," he said. "So if this is what you want, then get started at once. And keep in touch."

We parted on the platform with me promising to write a month from now, detailing just what I had done to start the ball rolling, to borrow his phrase.

I couldn't believe my good fortune. Or my nerve. Oh my God, I'm going to America! The song "California, Here I Come!" popped into my head, so that's what I attempted to whistle as I made my way to the line of taxis crowding the curb before me.

CHAPTER FOUR

The **hour of** reckoning was at hand. I had just spent the past five days at my parents' home enjoying a well-deserved vacation, and now, on this last morning, everyone was expecting to accompany me to the train station for the start of my journey back to England. It had been wonderful seeing my family once more, the children sprouting like weeds, and, oh, so proud of their big brother. Sheila was still in England, and the two boys next in line to me were gainfully employed in London. It was money well spent on my part, having sponsored them to come to England. And the money I had been able to save and send home over the years had helped my parents beyond words. I basked in the adoration of my siblings. But, as I said, the hour of truth was at hand. We were seated around the table, our breakfast dishes piled high, all of us happy and content to have this last time together.

I was nervous. I had a terrible fear that somehow they would all feel that I was abandoning them, and this phobia had gnawed at my innards for weeks. Now was my moment. No longer could I keep my silence.

"Mama, Dad," I began, "I'm not going back to England. I'm going to America. To Chicago, actually," I added lamely, the words so woefully inadequate to convey the excitement and conflicting emotions within. My ears were ringing from the rush of blood coursing through my body, brought on by a natural infusion of adrenaline. I could barely hear my own voice. The world stood still. The announcement caught my father mid-stride as he was bringing a now-cold cup of tea up to his mouth, and my mother froze with her hand reaching out for my youngest sister's head.

"What did you say, Desmond?" my father asked. His expression was as if I had just told them that I had signed on for the first trip to the moon. He was thunderstruck. His lips continued to move, but no further sound came forth.

I smiled weakly and nodded. "America. Chicago. I leave from Heathrow Airport first thing in the morning." The silence was deafening.

Finally, my father regained limited use of his voice, but only just. His words came out in a ragged whisper. "In the name of God, Desmond, why? Lad, you have a wonderful job in London, a fine future ahead of you. Why in the name of all that is holy would you chuck that aside to go to America?" He was in shock. It was 1922 all over again, and in his mind, it was the scene being replayed of his brothers and sisters telling grandfather that they were off to the New World. And he had to stay behind. They were never seen again, so it would be with me. It was too much. For the second time in my life, my father burst into tears, tears that turned into huge wracking sobs. His reaction frightened me. In that moment he had been reduced to a wizened old man, a shell of himself, worn to the bone by the hardships of the past, terrified by the uncertainty of the future. The reaction of my family was far worse than I could have possibly imagined. The children took their cue from dad, and they, too, were soon reduced to tears of anguish. I was fast approaching that same condition myself. The situation was spinning out of control. I did not know what to do. In desperation I turned to my mother, who for some unknown reason had remained the Rock of Gibraltar.

"You understand don't you, Mama? You understand?" I repeated, my eyes pleading. My worst fears had been realized. The news was more than they could handle. Their pain was my pain, and it struck like a thousand knives to the very core of my being. She sat there a long minute before moving her head, moving it ever so slightly, but a small up and down motion nonetheless. And finally, "I do, son. I understand." The words said one thing, her eyes another.

"Well, I don't!" My father got up from the table and still sobbing, shuffled miserably from the room. He pulled open the front door, Sammy fast at his heels, but he failed to retrieve his coat from its peg, so we knew he was not going far. He just needed to be alone in his moment of grief.

My mother reached over and patted my hand. "Don't worry about your father, he'll be fine. It's a shock for him, Desmond," she explained, then gave a short, mirthless laugh and added, "It's a shock to all of us!" She stood and brushed her skirt, the sudden activity a catharsis and, looking around the room, her eyes came to rest on the clock. Seemingly mesmerized by the exposed pendulum, that mechanical harbinger of my imminent departure, she spoke to my brothers and sisters who were all still in tears. "I want you children to clear the table and do the dishes. Desmond and I are going for a short walk." She pulled me towards the door where we donned our coats, and then set out, mother and son together for one last time. She took my hand in hers and just walked, saying nothing for at least five minutes.

"Years ago, Desmond," she finally said, "we were at the seaside, oh, I think you were about five at the time, and we saw a rainbow." She smiled at the memory. "I'm sure you don't remember, son, you were such a wee boy at the time, but I told you that the rainbow was special."

"You gave it to me, Mama. I've never forgotten. You told me to be ready because one day it would come back, and because it was a magic staircase, it would take me to America."

"You remembered!" she exclaimed, with genuine amazement. "All those years ago, and you remembered. I can't believe it!"

We both laughed, and that broke the tension. We walked on, hand in hand, as we did those many years ago, just the two of us alone in the entire world.

"Go to America, my child, and go with my blessing. All those who've gone before you weren't wrong, Desmond. America is the New World," she said, "and that's where you belong. Europe is tired. That last war ruined us. Things will never be the same here. No, you're doing the right thing," she repeated. "To think, my son; going to Chicago! I hear it's a grand city."

"That's what I hear, too, Mama. 'The Windy City,' they call it."

"Indeed?" She chuckled, "then you'll be right at home." In addition, we both laughed at her wit as we walked slowly, going nowhere. No sign of my father, but neither of us was worried. The day was warm and clear, unusual for September. My mother let out a sigh, then stopped in the middle of the road. "You know, Desmond,

Arthur's been a good husband and father, but God forgive him, the drink has cursed him all the days of his life. It has made life impossible for all of us around him. Desmond, it's the ruination of a person. You've seen it. Once the drink has a hold of you there's no letting go. You're up on the back of a runaway tiger. What I'm saying, child, is don't start. The drink will kill you and destroy those who love you. Don't start," she repeated. "Promise me that one thing, and I will die a happy woman."

I looked down at that lovely face, now framed with snow-white hair. My mother was probably in her early forties at that time, and over the years I had witnessed her hair turn from a luxuriant black, to streaked with gray, to all-gray, and finally to this. Surprisingly, she did not look old. She wore it like a halo. A halo fully earned, paid for in pain and hardship, paid without a whisper of complaint. If there was a saint in our family beside my long-departed infant sister, it was this woman, my mother.

"It's a promise I make gladly, Mama. That's all I can say."

"And that's enough. Now, let's go and find your father. You've got to pack, son. You're leaving on a rainbow, and you can't be late!"

*   *   *

On September 30, 1960, at nine fifteen in the morning, I sat in the sixth row of a Trans-Canada Airlines DC-8, petrified at the thought of flying across the Atlantic. Months ago I had ruled out the idea of making the passage by ship. I got seasick every time I set foot in a boat, so I knew I would die if I attempted a five-day crossing. Better I endure seven hours of stark terror. At least that was my rationale those many months ago. Now, I was not so sure as I sat in that giant jet awaiting departure. With all the professionalism of a master spy, I had kept secret my plans to emigrate. There were the many trips to the American Embassy in London for documentation; approval for this, approval for that. Sorry, you need to re-accomplish this form. Oops! So sorry, old chap, we seem to have misplaced your photograph. Yes, you are indeed scheduled for your physical examination next Tuesday. No, not this Tuesday. And on, and on, and on. Until one day, I was handed a document which in essence told me I was being granted entry into the United States. "Good luck, young man," said a very sincere consular officer as he gave me final instructions. "Do your parents proud."

I was jolted from my reverie by the spooling-up of the four huge turbines. The racket was mind-numbing. The metal behemoth groaned and shook, until finally the captain released the brakes and we started—imperceptibly at first—to move down the runway. Faster and faster we went, the scenery starting to blur as I peeked out the small sphere of Perspex; and when we reached a speed closing in on one million miles an hour, the plane pointed its nose straight up toward heaven, and the aluminum-skinned monster lifted gracefully into the sky, carrying me and one hundred fifty other souls to the New World. Later, I learned this was the inaugural westward flight of Trans-Canada's jet service. I was partaking in history, but I was too terrified to appreciate what that meant!

In no time we were far above the clouds, and the aircraft settled down to a smoothness which rivaled that of a flying carpet. My heart ceased its rib-bruising pounding, and my breathing stabilized. I was on my way. For the hundredth time I re-read the last letter I had received from Pete Frank in Illinois. It was full of instructions. Upon arrival in Chicago, I would be met by his best friend, Don Parisi, who had offered not only to help me get settled, but had further promised to assist me in finding employment. I was in awe of the fact that a total stranger was willing to give so generously of his time to help an inconsequential Irish immigrant. Had he been family, or even someone I had met in London, it would have made sense. But a total stranger? Such absolute goodness. Now, more than fifty years later, Don has remained a dear friend. His youngest son is my godchild. His family my family. I cannot sing highly enough of his praises.

I set foot on the North American continent at the airport in Montreal. Because I was a through passenger, I was not processed by Canadian customs here, or our other stop, Toronto. Toward late afternoon, we swooped low over Lake Michigan and landed at Chicago's O'Hare Field. At last! The United States of America! I felt ten feet tall as I swaggered into the main terminal, but was soon overwhelmed by the enormity of it all and the thousands of people hurrying in and out of the building.

"Desmond Donahue, Please contact the Trans-Canada Information Desk for a message." I came to an abrupt halt. Someone was calling my name over the loudspeaker system, the message being boomed all over the building. What was I supposed to do? How would I answer? I had no idea!

"Lost, buddy?" A Chicago policeman was standing in front of me. I explained my dilemma, and with a crook of his finger, he motioned me to follow. He led me to a bank of telephones and explained that I should pick-up the white one and that a person on the other end would take over and guide me as to what to do next. With a kindly salute, he left in search of other strays.

Following directions, I came to the Trans-Canada Information Desk, but before I could open my mouth, a giant appeared beside me. I mean a real giant. He stood six foot six and looked like Charles Atlas.

"Desmond? Desmond Donahue?"

"Yes, sir."

"Hi, I'm Don Parisi. Welcome to Chicago." He extended the biggest hand I ever saw. While we were shaking hands, he tucked my one suitcase under his left arm and, talking all the while, led me out of the building and into the parking area. He could see that I was all but paralyzed with fear, so to help me relax he kept up a steady stream of chatter, interspersed with simple questions which required monosyllabic replies. He told me a little about himself during the drive downtown, his gentle and caring manner having a soothing effect on this newest arrival to the Windy City. He explained that he was a dentist, having graduated from the University of Chicago that past spring, and had just commenced a four-year residency program at Cook County Hospital. He lived with a fellow dentist, Brook Masterson, who was also enrolled in the same course. He went on to say that they lived in a rather rundown section of the city, but that the rent was right, and of equal importance, the location was close to the hospital.

"You'll stay with Brook and me," he explained, as if I were his long lost cousin. "No arguments. Okay, kid?"

I would have had to have a death wish to argue, so I just nodded, delighted at my good fortune. My wallet contained slightly over one hundred English pounds. That was it. Here, I'd been in America less than an hour, and because of this man's kindness, did not have to worry about having to find shelter. I recited a silent prayer of gratitude.

Ten minutes later we pulled up in front of his apartment. The neighborhood was everything he had described. The building housed a small Italian restaurant and bar on the first floor and somehow had managed to squeeze two Lilliputian apartments onto the second. The one on the right belonged to him and Kenneth. 1721 Adams Street. I'll never forget that address. I was home. "We'll dump your bag upstairs, then scoot over to Cook County Hospital and pick-up Brook. I'll need to spend a few minutes with some patients, and then we'll all grab a bite to eat. Sound good?"

All I could do was nod.

* * *

The hour which followed forever changed the direction my life would take. With my inaugural visit to that huge medical complex, I suddenly and inexplicably knew what it was I wanted to do with my life, and the knowing seared my brain. I walked through those mammoth portals straight into bedlam. It was as powerful a force as that which had struck Saul of Tarsus on the road to Damascus. Saul, who would become known to Christendom as St. Paul, realized in that instant what God wanted of him. So, too, with me, Desmond of Ireland. It was as though God had spoken. I was to become a doctor. Dr. Desmond Donahue.

* * *

Cook County General Hospital defies description. To simply say that it is huge is a gross understatement; descriptive adjectives cannot convey any sense of size. It goes on forever. It's a facility with over two thousand beds, a house staff numbering well into the thousands who daily cope with every illness known to man. It has a patient population which converses in every language. Nothing in medicine can compare with Cook County. Its reputation at the time was world-renowned. A physician had only to acknowledge that he had first, interned then followed-on with a residency at Cook, and his peers knew instantly he was a doctor of the highest caliber. It was the Harvard of hospitals, the ultimate teaching facility. I honestly don't know if the same can be said of it today.

The scene upon entering could only be described as organized chaos. I say organized because somehow there was a semblance of order, but it was certainly not evident to the uninitiated.

"Keep close to me, Desmond," Don Parisi commanded, as he strode purposefully down those linoleum-covered hallways. People were crowded everywhere. They were sitting in chairs, sitting on floors, leaning against walls, sleeping against walls, chewing gum unobtrusively and individually in corners, or partaking in family picnics right in the middle of the main lobby. Never in my life had I seen anything to compare with this spectacle. Don led me through this bobbing sea of humanity without a faltering step. Through scores of swinging doors we marched, up halting elevators we rode, down endless corridors we strode, until finally, we entered a small, dimly-lit room in the middle of this maze. In a corner a lone man sat, hunched over a microscope.

"Brook, guess who's here?" Don slapped the back of the scrunched-up figure.

Brook Masterson turned, peered myopically through non-existent glasses, gave me a thorough once-over, then burst into tribute. "Oh my God! As I live and breathe, I can't believe my eyes. Albert Einstein. Wait till I tell ma!" He began a mad charade of fanning himself.

We both laughed at his antics.

"Sorry, pal. I can understand the mistake, given the wretched lighting in this hovel, and indeed the similarity is striking. But, alas, no, not Albert, but Desmond. Desmond Donahue, our young adventurer from Ireland."

Brook jumped off his stool and shook my hand with all the vigor of a man priming a pump. His enthusiasm was genuine and intoxicating. I liked him instantly.

"Desmond, how are you? Welcome to America. Welcome to Chicago. And saving the best for last, welcome to Cook County's very own madhouse," he said, with an all-encompassing sweep of his free hand.

"I'm fine, thank you," I replied, grinning from ear to ear. I felt as though I had known him all my life. It was wonderful.

Don interrupted. "Brook, do me a favor and take our young friend on a tour of the wards." He glanced at his watch. "I've got to look in on tomorrow's pre-ops. Give me about forty to forty-five minutes, and I'll meet up with you both at the front doors. Let's say six o'clock, bang on, okay?"

"Six o'clock it shall be, sport," Brook replied. Turning to me he said, "Give me a sec to put this equipment away; then I'm going to take you on the tour of your life."

And what a tour it was.

Suffice to say I was a changed individual when we met up with Don Parisi right on schedule at the front doors of the hospital. I will not recount at this time all I saw that day as I intend to later describe and discuss in great detail my affection for this hospital and its dedicated staff of workers. I spent many wonderful hours among their ranks, but that all came later. However, that hour with Kenneth changed my life. To this day I have difficulty putting into words the transformation which came over me, but it was most assuredly a watershed. My life was forever changed as a result.

The three of us walked a couple of blocks to a Greek restaurant for my first-ever sampling of that delicious ethnic cuisine. I learned later it was a hangout for the staff physicians and nurses at Cook, a place where they could unwind after a day of dealing with the harsh realities of life. It was a place they could discuss their cases, admit their failures, revel in triumphs, share joy and share sorrow, all with knowing that they would not be judged by their fellows. The sanctity of this sanctuary would never be breached.

Don and Brook knew everybody. They were well-liked, but as dentists, took a fair amount of good-natured ribbing from their medical colleagues. But they gave as good as they got, and no-one ever bettered those two in the art of hurling quick-witted barbs at imagined foes.

I was introduced to the chiefs of various departments, men with international reputations, men whose work was studied and read throughout the world. All went out of their way to make this poor, uneducated immigrant feel welcome. I would become a regular customer in the months and years to follow, and always the recipient of encouragement and affection.

I finally tumbled into bed sometime after midnight, utterly exhausted, but joyous in the knowledge that I knew what direction my life was going to take.

*   *   *

First, I needed a job. Don told me the best place to start the search was with the Sunday edition of the *Chicago Tribune*, so that's what I did. Employment opportunities abounded in Chicago in the fall of 1960, and I narrowed my focus to those positions which would allow me time to study. Study what? you might ask. Study for my high school equivalency diploma. Remember, my formal education had come to an end at fourteen, so I had to rectify this deficiency before embarking on my quest. I was full of the resolve of youth, and with encouragement from my newfound friends, I knew I wouldn't fail.

Six days later I was hired by the Union League Club as a busboy. No raucous Irish pub, this. The Union League was one of America's premier private men's clubs. Its members and guests were the captains and kings of industry, men who came daily to mingle and to dine with their peers. The judiciary was also well-represented, as were politicians of every stripe and persuasion. Decisions affecting all aspects of life in America were made in the main dining room of this venerable institution, decisions which I would like to think were always made to advance the common good. Such was my good fortune to find employment here.

My schedule called for me to work lunch, which meant that I arrived shortly before ten o'clock to help set up the stations and perform any other tasks demanded of me by the dining room captain. Lunch was a major undertaking. We often served fifteen hundred meals in a four-hour period and accomplished all this with apparent ease and grace. We were feeding guests who were often on a tight schedule. Meals were always delivered hot, and complaints were rare. Good service was the order of the day, and those employees who would not, or could not, live up to those highest of standards were soon seeking employment elsewhere.

By four o'clock my work would be finished, and I was free to leave, which meant I was free to study. Don Parisi had called the Chicago School Board and had found out what I needed to sit for a GED, the General Equivalency Diploma. The authorities told him what areas would be covered in the examination and suggested a list of books for me to use in preparation. Thus armed, I went to the public library every day and studied for four hours, driven not only by my own desire, but, too, by the mortal fear of disappointing my friends.

I sat the examination on a cold, blustery day in mid-February, along with some five hundred other hopefuls, all desperately seeking that coveted piece of paper. The waiting for my results was one of the longest periods of my life.

Back at work, I had been promoted to waiter, which meant my income had risen dramatically due to the fact that I was now the recipient of generous tips. I loved my work, and the Club could not have treated me better.

Three weeks later I received notice from the Chicago Board of Education that I had earned a grade of eighty-nine and was now the equal of a regular high school graduate. A very official diploma attesting this fact was enclosed. The first hurdle had been successfully cleared. I was now on my way. America was living up to every promise I had ever imagined. I daily gave thanks for my good fortune and again at mass every Sunday. How far I had come in so short a time. The phrase *With faith, men can move mountains* took up a permanent residency inside my brain, and I've managed a smile over the years when those words pop into my consciousness, seemingly always at the oddest hours of the day or night.

CHAPTER FIVE

Sitting in the back seat of a taxi inching its way toward Chicago's O'Hare Airport, I was a nervous wreck. I must have patted my jacket pocket twenty times in as many minutes, each pat a much-needed reassurance that all my documents were secure.

Nine busy years had passed, and I was now thirty-two. It was finally happening. I was on my way to Ireland to start medical school. The last few days had been a non-stop blur since receiving the letter of acceptance from no less a person than Dr. Beckler, the President of University College, Cork.

What a week it had been. I had had to secure an American passport along with a visa for entry into Ireland, a feat accomplished in a record-breaking three days. My employer had to be informed, ditto my landlady, clothes purchased and packed, airplane tickets bought, plus a million other must-do tasks seen to their conclusion. The deadline was October 5. Today. My birthday.

After all those years of working in various hospitals, my time had finally come. I had taken several courses in the sciences and liberal arts at local colleges over the years, but nothing really which could be construed as being truly preparatory to the task at hand. Nevertheless, the focus of my efforts had never wavered. One day I would become a doctor.

I had worked in two different pathology departments, assisting some of the city's most respected names in this, the quietest field of medicine. I had spent untold hours as part of a team doing post-mortems, assisting in cases as diverse and far-ranging as the examining of a day-old child dead from known or unknown causes to the octogenarian who had simply expired from old age. The former were heartwrenching, the latter merely interesting in that the patient had lived well beyond the biblically allotted threescore and ten. It was during these years I was introduced to the wonders of surgery and the challenges unique to the practice of invasive medicine. Thank God for those years. They allowed me to stay focused on my dream so that one day I would become as good a surgeon as those with whom I had worked during those years in Chicago. By the time I left for Ireland, I had a solid grasp of anatomy, a fair understanding of physiology, and I certainly knew hematology! It was my background in hematology that had been the deciding factor for my receiving the letter from Dr. Beckler, directing me to medical school in Ireland. So, yes, those long, intervening years were most assuredly ones well spent.

I had worked in several hematology labs where I had learned about the hidden wonders of the blood. This river of life coursing through all living things is truly a miracle fluid, one that only grudgingly gives up its secrets. To the botanist, it's called xylem and phloem, the blood-like liquid of the plant kingdom; to the hematologist it's simply blood.

I worked on innumerable blood studies during those years, and even today I feel that my knowledge in this field is without a doubt superior to that of the average physician. This is no idle boast. Anyway, they were all years well spent, and I don't regret a one.

That last night in America I had a farewell dinner with Don and Brook. They were as happy for me as if I had been family.

"Good things comes to those who wait," Don toasted, holding his glass aloft for the three of us to clink rims. "And God knows you've certainly had to wait, Desmond. Cheers!"

"Do us proud, Albert Einstein," Brook admonished, taking me back to the first time we met.

"Thank you. What more can I say?" I could feel a lump the size of a house welling in my throat. This day had been nine years in the making, and, secretly, I think they had given up all hope. But here it was. "Without your support we wouldn't be here tonight, so I toast you both with all the love and gratitude a poor country boy can muster."

"Hear, hear!"

We drank to my future success.

"Desmond, remember, if you find you've forgotten to pack something in all the rushing around, call us right away, and we'll ship it to you. Don't wait for the mail, especially if it's important. Anyway, we're both delighted for you, kiddo; you deserve this break." Don then reached over and pretended to punch me on the shoulder. It was the best send-off dinner anyone could have hoped for. For a parting gift they presented me with a 14K gold Cross pen and pencil set with *Desmond Donahue, M.D.* embossed in delicate script.

"You'll grow into them," Brook said. "Study hard so that we don't have to go to Ireland to take them back. Also, no prescription writing until those M.D. initials become legit." We all had a good laugh at that.

"Never fear!" I replied.

*   *   *

By noon, the Pan-Am 707 Clipper reached the East Coast, and then lazily banked left, taking up a northerly track as it began its Atlantic crossing via the great circle route. The captain assured us that we would arrive at Shannon on schedule, which would put me back on Irish soil just before ten P.M. The weather was to be favorable all the way across, and he promised a smooth flight. Sleep was out of the question, so for me it was a journey without end. I couldn't read, I couldn't eat, and I couldn't even look out the window as there was nothing to see at this altitude. I was a prisoner trapped inside my own head, a prisoner too joyous to complain. I still couldn't believe it was happening. But a small voice sounding oh, so like Don's, repeated over and over, *Believe it, kid. This is for real!*

We landed on time, but it was almost two o'clock in the morning before I left Shannon in my rental car and headed out toward Cork.

I crossed the River Shannon at Limerick, the streets of the city all but deserted at this hour. Within minutes, the lights of civilization were far behind me, and I made my way cautiously on the narrow, dark, winding roadway, its faint, rain-washed white centerline stripe beckoning me southward. It felt strange to be driving on the wrong side of the road, and with a fog already forming, I knew I had better stay alert. Accidents in these parts invariably tended to be bad, and it oftentimes took hours for help to arrive.

You don't want to enter Cork in a pine box, Desmond, I lectured myself. Take it slow; enjoy the scenery. I smiled as I stole a quick glance off to my right. The world seemed coated in lampblack save for the twin beams of light reaching out from the grillwork of my rented Vauxhall. To stay awake, I rolled down my window and began to recite in loud voice—and from memory—the letter from Dr. Beckler summoning me to Cork.

16 September 1969

Dear Mr. Donahue:

I take this opportunity to say that you have been selected as a candidate to enter the beginning medical year class commencing on 12 October 1969.

Your admittance to University College, School of Medicine, was granted based on a consideration of extraordinary circumstances. This acceptance was bestowed not as a consequence of your limited academic record, but more so on extenuating factors, including, but not limited to, work experience and mature years.

Much will be demanded of you, but we at University College, Cork, feel you are equal to the task. Very few are afforded such an opportunity, and it was only after most careful consideration that your request for admittance to the College of Medicine was granted. Do not disappoint those of us who have placed so much faith in your abilities.

You must register in person on 6 October 1969, there being no exception to this requirement. This is necessary to ensure that any potential conflicts regarding class schedules are resolved before the opening date of the college year.

Should you experience any difficulties during registration, or subsequently, please feel free to contact my office at any time.

I extend my congratulations, and on behalf of the entire faculty and staff at University College, I welcome you as a student to our university.

The academic year will begin with a celebration of solemn High Mass at the Cathedral of Cork for all faculty members and students, the celebrant being His Excellency, Sean D. Lucey, Bishop of Cork. Holy mass will commence at 8 o'clock in the morning on 12 October 1969.

Sincerely,

Anthony Beckler, A.B., M.Sc., Ph.D.
President,
University College, Cork, Ireland

I knew every word, every comma, every fullstop—or period, as is the American word—of that letter. Its contents were burned into my brain for all time. And to think that I had left this wearied land to seek a better life in America, and in the strangest of ironies, my salvation was to spring from the confines of my native Ireland.

To further speed me on my way, I sang every song I could remember, sometimes banging out the tempo on the horn. I was in rare form. The miles slipped by, one village after another falling behind me in the fog-shrouded night: Croom, Killmallock, Mallow, Blarney; then just before sunrise, the ancient city of Cork appeared before me like an apparition. A beautiful stone heraldic sign by the side of the road welcomed me to its gates.

Although I had lived in Ireland until I was sixteen, I had never traveled outside County Mayo, so this was my first encounter with this ancient seaport city. And what a rich heritage this garden spot of Ireland could boast. Founded in the seventh century by the monk St. Finbar, religion had long wielded a strong influence on life in the region—ever since the written word had been introduced to Ireland by clerics from the continent.

By the tenth century, Cork was an established and bustling trading hub, and it grew to become a center of political intrigue. The city was subdued in the mid-sixteen hundreds by Oliver Cromwell, who secured it as another jewel in the Crown for England. Forty years earlier it had been captured after a bitter siege by John Churchill, who had declared the city a prize for William of Orange. What a rich history this city could proudly boast.

Today, with the deep-water harbor at scenic Bantry Bay, Cork was a thriving, modern trading and manufacturing center with goods flowing in and out on the tides to every corner of the globe. Her citizens were rightfully proud of their beautiful city, and I, too, was proud at the thought of becoming a part of this cultural oasis for the next several years.

After a hurried breakfast, I drove up to the college, but found myself rudely stopped at the entrance by a uniformed guard.

"You canno' park yer car on the grounds, sur, na withoot a sticker. It'll be too'd away in a flash."

Here I was in Cork being verbally thrashed by a man whose Scottish brogue I could cut with a knife. I smiled, then replied with a perplexed look.

"Then we have a problem. You see, I just flew in from America for a meeting with President Beckler, and after flying all night to get here, I suspect he'll be rather upset when I tell him I was late because the guard wouldn't let me park on campus.

"Why did'na ya say so, sur? O' course y' can park any place y' see fit." He handed me a card. "Just leave it on the dash, an' no'un'll tamper wi' yoor car. We just have the devil's own time tryin' ta keep the students oot."

I nodded, smiled, and then proceeded up the spacious graveled drive towards the magnificent, ivy-covered administration building. So, I hadn't been exactly honest with the man, but I absolved myself by suggesting that I didn't know all the rules and regulations yet.

Even though it was just past eight o'clock, the place hummed like a hive, people everywhere. There were signs posted directing the academically unwashed to various parts of this building and others, depending upon for which school one was registering. I spotted my sign.

School of Medicine, Science Building, Registrar's Office, Room 110.

It took me ten minutes to find the right building and the right room. Things were indeed hopping here too, but the situation had not yet deteriorated into chaos.

"Good morning, I'm Desmond Donahue, here to register," I explained to one of several comely young women standing on the other side of a long mahogany counter.

"Right." She picked up a list containing several pages of names typed single-spaced, and flipped toward the front of the alphabet. After a minute of going back and forth among the pages she asked without looking up, "That's Donahue, with a '*D*?'"

"Correct."

"School of Medicine?" Still not looking up.

"Correct again."

"Hmm." By now her brow was creased. She finally looked up at me. "Can't seem to find your name anywhere, Mr. Donahue."

"Maybe this will help." I offered her my letter from the president. She took a moment to read it, then giving me a quick nod, walked into an adjoining room. She reappeared a full five minutes later, trailing an older, no-nonsense looking woman who was now clutching my letter in no-nonsense pudgy hands.

"You need to go to Doctor Beckler's office, young man," she said in a no-nonsense voice. "I'm sure he'll explain." She handed me my letter, and in a no-nonsense manner began walking smugly back to her office in her no-nonsense orthopedic lace-up shoes.

This was the last straw. Here I was, one day past my thirty-second birthday, being treated like a child. "Stop, right there," I commanded, tone harsh, voice loud. All activity in the room ceased. She slowly turned in mid-stride, a look of utter astonishment spreading across her face.

"Are you talking to me, young man?" she asked, as if addressing a maggot.

"Bloody right I'm talking to you!" I was in no mood for her supercilious manner. "I've been traveling non-stop from the United States for the past twenty-four hours, and I am not about to be rudely bossed about like an errant school-boy. If you are having a problem understanding the contents of that letter from Doctor Beckler, then I suggest you show me to the Dean's office." I was now waving the page before me, and at least ten pairs of eyes followed its every flutter.

"Very well, come to this side of the counter and follow me."

Three minutes later, I was ushered in to Dean Standiford's office. He looked distinctly uncomfortable as he shook hands and motioned me to sit. He rustled some papers on his desk, giving me the impression this was simply a delaying tactic.

"Mr. Donahue," he began after a long sigh, "I'm afraid I have some rather disturbing news. Contrary to the contents of the letter from Doctor Beckler, I must inform you that you have not been accepted as a first year student at the college of medicine."

My ears refused to believe what this man was telling me. I found myself unable to breathe, somehow trapped inside a nightmare. *It couldn't be!* Obviously, he would say with his next breath that yes, of course, I had been accepted. Ha, ha! A little humor, don't you know? Really had you going there for a moment, what? But no such words came forth.

"This was a decision reached by a consensus of the admissions faculty," his disembodied voice was saying, "and I'm afraid the decision is final. You see, your academic achievements to date do not warrant that an exception be granted. However, it was agreed by all that you could enroll in the undergraduate program, and upon satisfactory completion, then you would be considered for admission to the medical school at that time. Anything else is out of the question, I'm afraid. I'm sorry."

I was feeling that the only thing he was sorry about was the embarrassment the entire affair was causing him at this very minute. But for me, his words were a death sentence. Nine years of hope and hard work dashed to smithereens in a moment in time. It was beyond comprehension.

Although speechless, my brain was nonetheless overloading with frenetic electrical activity. This can't be happening! *It just goddamn well can't be happening!* My breath spilled out in ragged gasps. After an eternity of staring frog-eyed at the man, I finally spoke, surprising myself at how rational I sounded. My mental state had now turned to one of righteous anger. I pulled out all the stops. "How in the hell can a letter from the president of the university be in error?" I asked, up on my feet. "I left my employment, my home, my entire life back in America based on the strength of this correspondence, and you sit there and tell me that it was sent in error?"

He was uncomfortable to the extreme and played for time by squirming around in his big leather chair, seeking sanctuary, but with nowhere to hide. Wisely, he must have seen that this was not the time to call me up short for my unseemly language. He chewed on the inside of his cheek, then finally said, "I'm really very sorry, but the president had no right to send that letter, and I must say, it was done without the final approval of me or the rest of the committee. I'm in charge of the medical college, and in matters of acceptance of any student, it is I who has the final say. My word is law."

"So, I just turn around and go back to America, is that it?" I was furious. At this point I had nothing to lose, and he was certainly no god to fear. What the hell, I thought, go for broke, Desmond. All or nothing, as the Americans are so fond of saying.

"Why not let me enroll? Give me one semester to prove myself? See it as a chance to gracefully rectify a wrong. I'm here, and I'm ready to work day and night to show you what I am capable of doing."

As if spring-loaded, he shot out of his chair and faced me on an equal footing. "Absolutely out of the question! Impossible! Can't consider it for a moment!" He was shaking his massive head. "No, my suggestion stands. Go and see Doctor Beckler and have him enroll you in the pre-medical program. That's the best I can offer. Now, I really must be about other business. I'm sorry, Mr. Donahue, but that's the best I can do. Good day, sir."

I was dismissed.

And the no-nonsense woman smiled daggers of evil satisfaction as I walked that mile-long walk down the hallowed hall to the main door of the Science Building. I felt them penetrate my back every miserable step of the way.

Forty-five minutes later, I concluded an equally embarrassing meeting with the president of the college. Walking me to his office door, he placed a hand on my shoulder and said, "Give yourself a day to think about it. Get some sleep, and when you're in a better frame of mind, I'm sure you'll agree to stay with us and enter the undergraduate program."

"What about registration day?" I asked, all bitterness and bile. "Your letter said the sixth, no exceptions."

"On this I can make an exception, and I can assure you, no one has the authority to override me. No, come back tomorrow, and I'll see to it." He shook my hand. "I'm dreadfully sorry for the way this has turned out, Desmond, truly, I am. But, let's make the best of it, shall we? Let's show them your stuff!"

"I'll sleep on it," I replied, without a trace of enthusiasm. "I'll give you my answer tomorrow."

I walked back to my car, the full weight of the world an all but impossible burden. I found myself becoming light-headed, the fresh air having no effect on reversing the condition. Nobody could have been further down than I that morning, unless he was already six feet under, and idly waiting for something to happen. That's where I wanted to be. Dead. All hope had been dashed from my soul. As I reached my car, I suddenly doubled over, and amidst the most horrible retching sounds, sprayed my breakfast in huge unsightly globs all over the parking lot.

With my now-empty stomach cramped in breath-robbing knots, I struggled weakly into the driver's seat and stole away.

*   *   *

The wooden sign with its white lettering on a kelly-green field jumped out at me from amidst the shadows. Waving its painted arms, it seemed to scream: *Stop, you've arrived!* The Shamrock Inn. I had been driving aimlessly for the past two hours, my mind in a trance and my body paralyzed with malaise. I had no idea what my future might hold, but I was desperately tired, and this small manor house of a hotel nestled on the banks of the River Lee looked like the perfect place to stop.

Despite my troubles, I was fast asleep the minute my head hit the pillow.

At seven-thirty that evening, I walked into the small pub on the first floor, neither hungry nor thirsty, but after a hot bath and a shave, found myself too antsy to stay in my room. I ordered a gin and tonic, specifying that I would like it with ice. The red-faced man standing next to me looked over and smiled. He had come to the bar at the same time I had, leaving a party of two men at one of the few small tables in the room.

"American?" he asked, pointing a stubby finger toward my glass. "It's the ice, you know, dead giveaway you're a Yank."

"County Mayo actually, but Chicago for the past few years," I replied as politely as I could, not relishing the idea of engaging in small talk.

"Roger Connolly," he continued, choosing to ignore the tone of my voice. He offered his hand. By now his drink had arrived. He acknowledged the lady serving. "Ta, mum."

"Desmond Donahue," I replied mechanically.

"What brings you to Cork? Visiting professor, perhaps?"

I had to laugh in spite of myself at that one. "No, came to enroll in the medical school, actually." That wasn't a lie, but neither did it convey my immediate status either.

"Well, well! Small bloody world! I'm in my last year there," replied Roger, as he hoisted his glass and downed a long swallow. "Taken me nine years to get to this point, but the gods are now looking down upon my countenance with favor, and I do believe I will manage to get my M.B. B.Ch., blah, blah, blah, sometime this year." He was, in a roundabout way, referring to a bachelor's of medicine and surgery, the equivalent to a M.D. from an American college.

Coddling his glass with swollen fingers, he beckoned me to follow. "Come, Desmond Donahue, let me introduce you to a couple of my friends."

In the seconds it took us to reach the table, I wondered just who in the hell this man really was. No one took nine years to complete a five-year course of study; and from my reception at the university this morning, I knew that Dean Standiford would brook no such nonsense. I was soon to learn otherwise!

Roger Connolly was about my age, a man of medium height and florid complexion, a man who carried more than a few extra pounds on his frame. He was expensively dressed, although casually so, and had the air of one used to the finer things in life. The world had obviously been kind to Roger, and his remark about the gods looking favorably upon his person was definitely not far off the mark.

The two men he introduced were Joe Brennan, a local dentist, and Seamus Williams, a stockbroker. All three had apparently been friends since their grammar school days, and they took me into their small group that night without a moment's hesitation. We ordered another round, and Roger explained how indeed he had been a student in off-and-on good standing for nine years. It seemed that he came from a wealthy family, and, over the course of the past decade, his father had made sizable contributions to the college's endowment fund. Certain shortcomings on Roger's part were discreetly overlooked, and he was given the benefit of the doubt at every turn. He exhibited no embarrassment recounting these facts, and as he did, all three enjoyed a good laugh. I sat and listened, thinking that I wished to God some of his bloody good luck would rub off on me!

At about nine o'clock, Roger drained his glass and stood. "Let's go pop over to Kerrigan's. I hear Margaret's in town for a couple of days."

Joe Brennan immediately agreed. "Righto. She might have some sweet looking lassies with her."

"Ma, we're leaving," Roger called out to the woman behind the bar. The place was now packed, the air blue from a million cigarettes and pipes. Knots of people were engaged in animated conversation as the beer and whiskey flowed. It was a scene being played in concert in ten thousand other pubs throughout the Republic.

"Does everybody call the lady, Ma? I asked Roger, as the four of us made our way out to the parking lot. I was really just making conversation.

"I should bloody well hope not," he hooted in reply. "I've two older sisters who call her Ma, but that's all that I'm aware of. No, she's my mum, all right. We own the hotel, and Ma likes to work. The woman loves people, so it's fun for her to be in the pub. Besides, that way she can keep her eye on me."

"Oh."

We rode over to Kerrigan's in Roger's car and dashed for cover just as the heavens opened up. Irish eyes were smiling, and I was starting to feel a whole lot better than I had a few short hours ago. I vowed I was going to enjoy the balance of the evening with my newfound acquaintances and told myself to let the cards fall where they may tomorrow.

Kerrigan's was not crowded. Roger explained that the place did not come into its own until ten o'clock on weekdays. It was that kind of a pub. A stern-faced man and an equally intense woman were engaged in a death struggle at the lone dartboard a few paces from a rock fireplace big enough to belong in a castle, while a smattering of people chatted at heavy oak tables in the large, comfortable room. It was a scene from every brochure featuring Ireland after dark.

"Hello, Mrs. 'K!'" Roger called out to the woman behind the bar as the four of us made our way towards her.

"And a g'day to you, too, Dr. Connolly," she replied, smiling as she busied herself wiping the highly polished counter top. She appeared to be in her late forties, very attractive, and exuding that natural confidence of someone at ease in any setting. She was an independent woman, and it showed. "What's your pleasure, gentlemen?"

We placed our orders, and while she was preparing the drinks, she turned her head sideways and called out towards a back room.

"Margaret, come see what the cat's dragged in."

"In a tick, mum," a disembodied voice replied. "As soon as I've cleaned the pigs' trotters. I'm doing the last one now."

We all laughed at the image of a pig getting a bath, but of course, we knew she was referring to pigs' feet which would never again see the dirt of a barnyard, but more immediately the innards of an oven.

A minute later out she came, and I caught my first glimpse of Margaret Kerrigan.

CHAPTER SIX

She was without a doubt the most beautiful woman I had ever laid eyes on. This radiant vision stood five-foot-seven, resplendent with long, luxuriant, anthracite hair, an alabaster face carved from the finest Irish china, and blessed by the Almighty with features of exquisite beauty. Classic cheekbones, eyes black as night, a nose so tailored and true as to defy description, and a mouth mere mortal men would sell their souls to kiss just once. Margaret Kerrigan, God's ultimate handiwork.

Time stood still.

She greeted everybody with a smile and a laugh.

"Margaret, when are you going to run away with me?" Seamus asked.

"Maybe soon, maybe never, you'll just have to wait and see."

"She's waiting for me," chimed in Roger, winking at the mother as he spoke.

A throaty laugh was her only reply. She then looked in my direction, arched an eyebrow, and asked, "And who might your silent friend be, Roger?"

"Ah, you must mean Desmond. Margaret, this is Desmond Donahue. Desmond, meet Margaret, the most ravishing beauty in all of Ireland. Next to her mother, of course," Roger added hastily, ever the diplomat, scoring a million points with his charm.

"How do you do?" We spoke the greeting in unison, and put forth our hands simultaneously. I was faint and driven to the verge of catatonia merely by her touch.

"Desmond joins us from Chicago. In America." This from Joe Brennan, who was as captured by her beauty as the rest of us.

"Ah, Joe, thank you for the geography lesson. I've always wondered where Chicago was, and no one seemed to know. Bless you."

We all hooted at Joe's expense, but he didn't mind a whit. Such was the power of Margaret Kerrigan. She then turned to me. "Desmond, I have work to do back in the kitchen. That is if anyone plans to eat later. Come and keep me company," she commanded, flashing a smile that could melt diamonds. "You can tell me all about Chicago, which I have only recently learned is in America," she said, sticking her tongue out at Joe. She took my hand in hers and led me, the most willing of lambs, to the slaughter.

She chatted while she worked, and I just sat in idle adoration, the contents of my cup cascading.

"Desmond, have you heard a single word I've said?" she admonished at one point with mock severity. "Would you rather be somewhere else? You're a million miles away."

My whole body gave an involuntary shudder. "No, I haven't heard a word you said. I mean…yes…of course I'm listening." I was strangling on my tongue.

"Why don't you tell me all about Chicago while I work on these vegetables," she said as she began to dice and chop. "Some say it's called the Windy City. Is that true?"

I spoke for the next twenty minutes with her asking questions and me answering with wit and charm. My words flowed like honey that night. I was such a man of the world. Reality was that I was convinced she saw right through me and had sized me up for the country clod that I was. Yet, she seemed genuinely interested in what I had to say. This was a moment I wanted to last forever. I was in ecstasy.

"Margaret, what in God's name are you two doing in here?" Mrs. Kerrigan asked, entering the kitchen, a twinge of exasperation in her voice. "People are getting hungry! Please, Margaret, get the lead out." She turned and went back to her station behind the bar. Margaret mimed a comic response toward her mother's departing back, then wheeled, and grinned at me. "You heard the woman. Let's get the lead out, Desmond. *Move, move!*"

Ten minutes later, we had the repast of pigs' feet and steamed vegetables lined up on the bartop and stood back in satisfaction as the assembled patrons dashed forward to enjoy a late supper. We retreated to the sanctuary of the kitchen.

We sat and ate, with me trying my damnedest not to just sit and stare. The food tasted like sawdust I suspect because my brain needed all the power it could muster to channel huge amounts of energy to my eyes, all at the expense of my other senses. I could not have cared less.

Finally, Margaret leaned back in her chair and let out a long, contented sigh. "So, Desmond, now that I know all about Chicago, tell me, what brings you to Cork?"

"Medical school."

"What did you say?"

"Medical school," I repeated.

Her entire body stiffened upon hearing my words, and that too-beautiful face transmogrified like melted wax into something truly grotesque. The transmutation was complete within a moment, and the hellish apparition before me was no longer Margaret, but a figure from the lowest circle of the damned. Then, it spat venom. I was shocked speechless by the diatribe that poured forth from that once-lovely mouth. The hairs on my neck and arms stood erect, my body now fully reacting to true fright. Atavistic reflex and instinct took over, preparing me for the classic flight or fight defense. Either seemed a very real possibility. *What in the name of God was happening?* And utter evil continued to pour forth. Unabated. A torrent of filth from a truly tortured soul. Until she was completely out of breath. In an instant I had been exiled from Nirvana by a capricious and malicious god and thrown unmercifully into the Inferno. Then just as suddenly, there came silence.

Now totally spent and gasping for air, her whole body was given to heaving and shuddering, with hands one second flailing uncontrollably and the next vigorously swatting at unseen demons crawling upon her skin. She was a dervish of uncoordinated activity. *What in the name of God was happening?* She then jumped out of her chair and fled the room. I couldn't move. Events had so completely overtaken me that I began to shake.

And this is how Margaret found me when she returned ten minutes later. She was totally composed, and although very pale, her face had become a serene mask devoid of all expression, but no longer of the netherworld. She poured herself a glass of water and downed the entire contents without a pause, all the while looking at me over the rim, her eyes speaking volumes, pleading for forgiveness. Margaret Kerrigan was back.

I waited for her to speak.

The words finally came in a whisper. "I'm sorry, Desmond. I don't expect forgiveness, but you are entitled to an explanation. That moment had been building up inside me for several months now, and regrettably, you were in the wrong place at the wrong time. When you mentioned that you had come to Cork to attend medical school, everything snapped. I lost all control, and you saw a Margaret Kerrigan no one else has ever seen before. You see, I was engaged to be married to a doctor. In fact, the wedding was to have taken place this very week but it didn't happen." She was speaking above a whisper now, but bitterness bathed every word. "One day in the merry month of May, he up and ran off to Australia with another woman and without so much as a by your leave. No goodbye, no explanation. Here one day, *poof,* gone the next. Well, a girl just doesn't like to be treated that way, Desmond." Then a moment later, she added in a voice as hard as diamonds, "Especially not this girl!"

What could I say? She looked so vulnerable, misery announcing its unwanted presence in every fiber of her being. Who could guess what torture she had endured? And I was thinking: what man in his right mind would give up such a perfect woman, abandon her for someone who would have to pale by comparison?

"I understand." How pathetically inadequate, but that was the sum of my response. Such a man of the world. So schooled in the art of offering comfort and solace to those in need. The word *callow* aptly described me that night. But my heart wept for Margaret Kerrigan, knowing such rejection would have been every woman's worst nightmare.

She reached over and gathered my hands in hers. "Thank you, Desmond. Thank you for being so kind." She stood up, a tentative, brave smile forming around the small, quivering of her lips. "Tell you what. Let me take you to dinner tomorrow night to make it up to you. Please say yes, Desmond. It's my last night here, and I would love to spend it with you." Expectancy was written all over her face. How could I refuse?

"I'll pick you up at seven-thirty?"

"Perfect, I'll be ready." She took my hand and guided me to the public room. "Let's go find Robin Hood and his band of merry men so you can get on home. I'm really looking forward to tomorrow." She placed a kiss on her hand, and as gently as the flutter of a butterfly's wings, mimed blowing it in my direction. Ecstasy once more became my middle name.

* * *

What a difference a day makes! I was up, dressed, had breakfast, and was waiting to see Dr. Beckler, just shy of eight o'clock. His secretary informed me he would be in at nine and promised he would spare me a moment before his first appointment. With a bounce in my step and a smile on my face, I decided to explore the grounds that would be my home for the next several years. And the reason for this sudden change in attitude? Why, Margaret Kerrigan, of course!

I set a course into a brisk wind, gathering my bearings, identifying the various buildings, and as the hour of my non-existent appointment approached, I was a full-fledged expert as to where everything was located. Such a quick learner, this intrepid navigator from the New World.

My meeting with the president was anti-climactic. He seemed pleased with my decision to register in the pre-med program, and he hastily scratched out a note for the registrar, using the biggest gold-filled fountain pen I had ever seen to make his flowing words the law of the land.

Tearing the sheet from the pad, he dried it with a strip of blotting paper—a ritual I had not seen performed since the days of my youth—and handed it to me with a flourish. This document did not need the triviality of sealing wax. It was my passport into the world of academia, signed by the lord himself, and no lowly serf would have the temerity to inform me that I was a day late and a dollar short!

"I'm glad you've chosen to start out on this path, Desmond. And to quote from an Arab infidel of long ago; 'Each journey starts with the first step'."

For some insane reason, I couldn't resist the temptation to correct him, and the words were out of my mouth before I could stifle them.

"'The journey of a thousand miles begins with a first step,'" I said. "It's from Mao Tse-Tung's book *The Long March*, and he was quoting the Chinese philosopher Lao-tse."

Beckler stared at me as though I had just dropped down from Mars. He finally cleared his throat in the same manner I'd seen acted out in a dozen movies when the brilliant mind gets pulled up short. "Yes…well…I do believe you're right. Very good."

It was *not* very good. It was bloody stupid, and my only saving grace was that the words had obviously sprung forth involuntarily. I had fostered no conscious intention to correct the president of one of the world's great learning centers, but it happened. Thank God, he did not seem to take offense. Surprised, yes, and puzzled, too, that I would know of such things. But he was not offended.

"The registrar will fix you up," he said, and in a replay of the day before, escorted me to his door with a hand to my shoulder. We shook hands.

Fifty minutes later, I found myself outside a downtown post office, not quite knowing what to do next. I had been prepared to pay my tuition in American dollars, but alas, I was informed such a transaction was not allowed. A money order would be fine, and the best place to get one was at the post office. But the resident postal bureaucrats politely let me know that they, too, had no use for dollars either, and finished by snootily reminding me that today was a bank holiday.

"Can I help you, lad?"

I turned to face an elderly man who had just preceded me from inside and was now leaning against a new Mercedes.

"I'm afraid no one can, thank you just the same." I then explained my dilemma.

"How many dollars did you say you needed changed?"

"Six hundred Irish pounds' worth," I replied, oblivious to the fact that my statement sounded rather stupid in that I was after all in Ireland, and the pound was the official currency of the land. "Seventeen hundred and ten dollars," I added.

Without another word, he reached into his pocket and extracted the biggest rabbit I had ever seen. Except this long-eared rodent was masterfully disguised as a wad of banknotes large enough to choke that special horse. He licked the thumb of his left hand, almost swallowing it in the process, and began to count aloud. Right there on the pavement. At least half a dozen people passed around us during the transaction, and not one gave us a second look.

"Right you are. Six hundred pounds. That should fix you up." He handed me the worn bills, and I in turn gave him a fistful of new American notes. With that, the curbside bank closed for the day, its lone transaction completed.

"What's your name, lad?"

"Desmond Donahue."

He openly scrutinized me, embarrassingly so, for more than a long moment, and then floored me with his next statement. "From Chicago. You're here for medical school."

I nodded, dumbfounded.

He laughed. "No big secret, lad. I'm Daniel Connolly, Roger's father, and he told me all about you this morning. Spoke quite highly of you, he did, and I can see why. You're not a youngster looking for a good time away from home pretending to be seeking an education. I like that. Where will you be staying for the year?"

"I really don't know."

"I own The Shamrock Inn, so if that suits you, you can keep your room for the year. I'll give you a good rate."

"Thank you." What more could I possibly say?

"Stop in the pub later tonight for a drink. I want to talk to you, Desmond. I think you could be a good influence on my son, and that is what I'll ask from you in return. I know you've got to hop on back up to the college and pay them, so I won't keep you." He started into his car, then stopped and faced me again. "I recommend the Bank of Cork. See Barry Driscoll and Harry Moore over there. Tell them I sent you. They'll treat you right as rain." And with a wave which looked suspiciously like a salute, he started the Mercedes and drove slowly away.

By two o'clock, I was back in my room having registered for the coming school year and was now making plans for the following day to visit the bank, turn in my rental car, and purchase a vehicle. After that, I would go to Ballycommon and visit my parents whom I hadn't seen in nine years. But, first, I had a dinner date with Margaret Kerrigan.

* * *

Cary Grant flashed that special smile at me from inside the mirror. You know the smile. The one that makes every woman swoon and transforms maidens into the most pliable putty in his hands. I turned away, the lingering image of magnificence still visible to my mind's eye. *Desmond Donahue, you look smashing!* I was dressed in all new finery. My suit was cut in the latest style, the lapels considerably widened from the narrow Beatles-look which had dominated men's fashion for most of the sixties. French cuffs, silk tie, new Bostonian black leather shoes shined to a mirror-finish, and to top it all off, a handkerchief the color of alpine snow resided casually in my breast pocket. I was a vision and I knew it. This Irish-American Emperor really did have some splendid new clothes!

The hour was at hand. I rang the bell at Margaret's front door, the Kerrigan home being a part of—but separate from—the pub. It was a beautiful two-story stone structure built at the turn of the century as the retirement home for a ship's captain. The door opened on the last note of the chimes, and she stood before me, breathtakingly beautiful.

"My, my, don't you look dashing," Margaret said, taking my hand to guide me inside.

I had had the presence of mind to stop to get her a small bouquet of flowers, which I presented with a flourish and a grin. "For you, *mademoiselle,* and may I say you, too, look marvelous."

"Oh, Desmond, you shouldn't have bothered! But, I'm glad you did. They're beautiful, thank you." She took the bouquet, and in one fluid motion, leaned forward and kissed me lightly on the cheek. "Let me get my coat and give these to mother to put in water for me. I'll just be a sec." She ran from my presence like a schoolgirl, and, true to her word, reappeared buttoning her coat as she walked.

"I think you'll like the restaurant I've picked, Desmond. It's very posh, but not snobbish, if you know what I mean." She entwined her arm with mine as we walked to the car, me hoping that the entire world would stop and stare at this perfect couple.

Our reservations were for eight o'clock, and we entered The Pembroke Lodge with several minutes to spare. The place was packed. Stepping up to the maitre d's desk, Margaret whispered her name, bestowing upon the man a smile that lit up the entire county. He was an instant goner, but to all appearances, a man delighting in his fate. "Give me two minutes, Miss Kerrigan, that's all I need." He disappeared into the main dining room.

"Well, hello, Margaret," a voice called out from behind us.

We turned to face two middle-aged men, all smiles, but with eyes only for Margaret.

"Why, hello, Dr. O'Connor, Dr. Moraghan, how are you both?"

Both were in heaven. She chatted for a second or two more, exchanging pleasantries, then introduced me.

We shook hands, but I could read their racing minds. How in the hell do you rate being with this ravishing creature? Return from whence you came, you unwelcome interloper. I just nodded politely and replied with equal silence, *Drop dead, you jealous old buzzards.* "How do you do, gentlemen?"

We were beckoned to our table.

"They're both at the University," Margaret explained, as we were seated. "I'm sure you'll be seeing a lot of them from now on. But, no more about that for tonight. This evening is for us alone." She reached over and gave my hand a squeeze, lingering with her touch before letting go, leaving me floating high above all the mortal inhabitants of the planet. "You're my guest for this evening, Desmond, so I would like to do the honors." She turned to the sommelier, hovering nearby. "We've decided on a bottle of Dom Perignon, a sixty-seven, perhaps, hmm?"

"Excellent choice," he groveled and backed away with mincing steps, almost, but not quite, bowing deferentially in the presence of royalty.

What a feast we had that night. I could not help but marvel that people actually lived this way, and from their numbers, more than I had ever imagined. Here was I, in my rightful place, *tête-à-tête* with the most beautiful woman in the world. And the most interesting, as well.

Margaret told me about herself. She was an only child, her father dying of a heart attack the day she was born. Apparently, he had been consumed for months with the thought that the child would be a son, and when God chose instead to bless him with a daughter, the man went into cardiac arrest and expired within minutes of her birth! Such is the grist of Victorian novels, but here was living proof that life was indeed stranger than fiction. However, in this story, the mother raised her only child alone, turning away an untold number of suitors over the ensuing years.

Margaret was an accomplished student and had graduated from the university with honors. She had accepted a position with Thomas Cook, the travel giant, to represent their interests in Paris. She had been residing in the City of Light for the better part of two years, fully devoted to a very demanding job yet somehow finding time to pursue graduate work at the Sorbonne. She was fluent in Gaelic, English, French, Spanish, and passably familiar with both German and Italian. She went on to explain that her duties took her back to Ireland quite often to evaluate and then grant her imprimatur upon different holiday resorts, hotels, and restaurants throughout the Republic, all of which were anxious to accommodate French tourists. Because of her recognized influence, she stayed at the finest hotels and ate in the best restaurants, all in the name of promoting Ireland as a land for tourists to visit on a Thomas Cook Tour. To think that Margaret—and people like her—were actually paid for doing this?

Never once did she mention her departed fiancé.

Course after sumptuous course came and went, the two of us sharing bites, then whetting our palates with the finest champagne France had to offer. Before I knew it, my watch told me it was ten o'clock. I did not want this night to end. Margaret had mentioned earlier that she was departing Cork the following afternoon, needing to stop briefly in Dublin for a meeting before catching an evening flight back to the continent.

She refused my protests that I should pay, reminding me that this was her treat, that I was her guest, and that she did not want any argument.

"Desmond, you can buy me a nightcap at The Shamrock Inn, agreed?" This to mollify my manly pride.

"Whatever m' lady's pleasure."

Twenty minutes later we entered the small, cozy pub and were greeted warmly by the woman I now knew to be Mrs. Connolly. "Well, hello, you two! Daniel had mentioned that you'd be stopping by."

It had completely slipped my mind! My face became diffused with blood rushing to fill all the capillaries in my face. In other words I was blushing a dark shade of red, a condition brought about by acute embarrassment. How could I have done this to Mr. Connolly after he had been so kind? I wanted to roll up into a microscopic ball and vanish.

Mrs. Connolly, bless her heart, immediately sized up my dilemma and sallied forth to my rescue. "Daniel could'na make it, Desmond. He's sorry, but hopes you can do it tomorrow night."

"Please let him know tomorrow would be perfect, Mrs. Connolly. Thank you."

"Here, let me make you both a nice Irish coffee." She kissed Margaret on the cheek. "It's so good to see you again, dear. Please say hello to your mother and let her know I'll be calling in the next couple of days."

"I will."

Placing the piping hot glasses before us, her face lit up at a sudden thought. She beckoned us to pick up our drinks and follow her from the pub. "Here, come tarry in this parlor. No need to stay in that noisy room. This is comfy, and you can talk undisturbed." The room in question was a small living room, every bit as comfy as she had described, made perfect by a low fire still burning in the grate. She winked at us. "In fact, lock the door behind me when I leave, so no one will barge in on you."

The moment Mrs. Connolly was out the door, Margaret made fast the lock, removed the big metal key from its berth, and tossed it nonchalantly onto a chair with an amused, exaggerated flip of her wrist. She mischievously turned to face me with a dimpled grin. "You are now my prisoner, Desmond Donahue. There is no escape." She switched off the one small lamp in the room, leaving the orange glow of the embers to cast long shadows everywhere. My heart was pounding itself into oblivion. Looking at me coyly, she took a swallow from her coffee, then patted the space beside her on the settee. I obliged, the most willing and grateful prisoner in history, yet I trembled as I obeyed. Margaret gently placed her glass on the small table behind her, and then with her face a scant inch from mine, whispered, "Kiss me, Desmond."

Oh, the delights of the flesh which unfolded with that first kiss. In no time at all, passion ran rampant, and clothing was soon discarded with abandon. We somehow moved from the sofa to the rug in front of the fireplace, an octopus-like tangle of arms and legs. We were both breathing in shallow gasps, snatching small breaths of life-giving air before plunging back into the fray, resuming long, passionate probes with our tongues.

"I have no protection; we'll have to stop." That was the last thing I wanted, but somehow managed to whisper nonetheless.

"It's all right: I'm on the pill," Margaret replied in a hurried, throaty murmuring.

We were at the point of no return, and we joined in the fiercest of embraces, both moaning with abandon from the sheer pleasure of the moment. Margaret clutched at me all the tighter if that were possible, and as one, we were both transported to another world, a world whose only active sense was one of total bliss. Our bodies shuddered involuntarily and in unison; then we collapsed, totally spent. I could not talk. I had fully experienced heaven right here on earth. There was nothing more in life I could hope for after this.

"I know I was clumsy," I apologized softly a few moments later. "I couldn't control myself. I'm sorry, Margaret."

"Shush." She placed her finger gently on my lips. "Shush," she repeated. "We'll have many other moments to perfect our pleasure,

Desmond. Speaking for myself, I can't wait," she added, ending her little speech with a giggle. Then, she propped herself up on one elbow and laughed conspiratorially. "I hope to God that they didn't hear us in the rest of the house! I would just die!" She then collapsed into gales of stifled laughter.

"Margaret, I think I've fallen in love."

"Desmond, that's the sweetest thing I've ever heard," she whispered back. "We are going to spend a lot of time together; I just know it. I will be back as often as I can, but meanwhile, you must keep busy studying. Then I'll know that you won't have time to be chasing other women and forget about me."

"Believe me, Margaret, I will never forget you. *Never!"*

"Desmond, those are the words every woman would die for just to hear. Thank you, my sweet."

Reluctantly, we dressed, and after carefully scrutinizing each other to see that our clothes were in perfect array, we returned to the pub to say our goodnights. We left arm-in-arm a few minutes later to take Margaret home. I was beside myself, truly the happiest man on earth because this most beautiful of creatures had chosen me. I was indescribably in love, and it tore my heart just to think that I would be separated from her within a few minutes.

She must have read my thoughts. "I don't want you to feel down when I'm gone, Desmond. It'll only be for a short while. We can write and phone each other, so it's really not so bad. Now give me a big hug and a long goodnight kiss. We'll be together again before you know it."

This moth had been fully drawn into the flame.

CHAPTER SEVEN

My plan was to finish my chores in Cork by the following afternoon, and then drive to Ballycommon to spend a couple of days with my parents.   But like all best-laid plans, this proved an unrealistic timetable, and it was not until a full day later that I was able to set out in my brand new, fire-engine red, Ford Escort. It took the better part of two days to complete the deal, and I had thought I could do it in a single morning!

I followed Mr. Connolly's advice and opened an account at the Bank of Cork. Just the mention of his name had the management jumping through hoops. I was quickly learning that Daniel Connolly was a force to be reckoned with in Cork. Now, with all my tasks completed, it was time to go home.

What a glorious homecoming it was. Gone nine years. A lifetime. My eyes welled as I embraced my parents in the front yard, my mother laughingly telling me later how they had been up and waiting since seven o'clock, dressed in their Sunday clothes and wanting everything just right for my return.

The years had taken their toll. Not so much on my mother. Discernible? Yes, of course, yet she was as serene as I'd remembered. But my father was now an old man. Chronologically, he had just passed his sixty-first birthday, yet looked every day an octogenarian. Shriveled and stooped, a sparse whispering of white hair arrayed in a thin fringe above a face both gaunt and tight, ears and nose protruding, creating a cruel caricature of the man he had once been. He walked hesitantly, supported by a sturdy cane, his once-proud step now palsied by the inexorable passage of time. But his eyes remained full of fire, sparkling with a special radiance through tears of joy at my return.   And his latest Sammy dashed madly to and fro, fully caught up in the excitement of the moment. Three of my brothers and one sister were there to join in the celebration, all sniveling unabashedly, hugging and kissing me, over and over. The Donahues were never a demonstrative family, but this day we outdid any

Mediterranean clan with our manifestations of love and affection. How indescribable my joy to be among them once more.

I must confess, my heart sang with pride upon seeing firsthand the changes I had been able to provide over the years, changes which had brought some small measure of comfort to my parents' simple house. Two were most evident. The first, and most dramatic, was electricity. In 1964 I was drafted, and while stationed with the U.S. Army in Germany, I paid the Irish government one thousand pounds to erect and string a mile of utility poles to bring power to the farm. Hard as is it to imagine now, this was a cost the tax base would not support; and if a family wanted electricity, then it had to pay for the transmission lines and subsequent hook-up. And this only five years before Neil Armstrong walked on the moon! Such was the backwardness of Ireland at the time.

The second change was the bathroom built onto the side of the house. A real bathroom with a real flush toilet. True, they still had to walk outside in the elements to use it, but nonetheless, it was a godsend. Such small pleasures we who have them take for granted. But not my parents. Daily they marveled and gave thanks to the Almighty for their blessings.

Those were three of the happiest days of my life. My parents were bursting with pride for their son who was soon to become a doctor. That first night home, my mother produced a copy of the weekly newspaper serving the myriad small communities of Galway and Mayo. I was front-page headline news! *LOCAL MAN RETURNS FROM AMERICA TO BECOME A DOCTOR.* Armed with details provided by my mother, Neil Gallagher, the reporter, had devoted four columns to my story and had even reproduced a photo of me in my army uniform to accompany the article.

"Neil made me promise that you would give him a follow-up interview sometime soon. You won't let your old mother down now, will you?" she asked, an embarrassed little smile crossing her face.

I smiled back, and gave her a hug. "I won't make a liar out of you, Mamma. I promise, Neil will get the rest of his story."

To celebrate my visit, almost two dozen of the neighbors crowded into our small house the following evening for a party.

Along with other treasures, I had brought home several bottles of whiskey and gin; and although my mother was not too keen on knowing what joy this elixir would bring to her Arthur, nonetheless, the contents of those bottles warmed the cockles of many a heart that night. Everyone fawned over me and called me 'Doctor Donahue."

In Ireland, as soon as a person is accepted into medical school, that individual immediately becomes known—and addressed by all—as doctor. And instantly, as if on cue, everyone tells you of his or her aches and pains. I reveled in the non-stop attention showered on me that night.

Even though I was the proudest man in all of Ireland, I still suffered a slight twinge of shame. I had not informed my family of my slight reversal of fortune necessitating me to first complete the medical undergraduate program. They knew nothing of this, and I had made a conscious decision not to enlighten. It was a mere technicality, I told myself, a trifle of a detail. Looking back, that moment was a watershed, for it marked my first tentative step down the path of self-destruction. In retrospect, I know there were many such similar instances where each in its own right was barely consequential, but taken cumulatively, who knows? I don't. But I did not dwell on such thoughts that festive night.

Too soon my visit was over, and I had to return to Cork. I departed vowing I would come home as often as I could. I'm proud to say I kept that vow.

* * *

I settled into the academic scene with a seamless grace, and even though I was a dozen years older than my peers—and a Yank to boot—my lot was their lot. The course load was staggering. Organic and inorganic chemistry, anatomy, physics, zoology, with several evening labs in each. My days started before dawn and finished well into the witching hour. The library became my second home, and I knew early on I had to develop good study habits if I were to survive.

Every morning I would arrive at the student union for breakfast. Most days, that was seven o'clock. I would sit down to tea and toast, my head buried in the local paper, catching up on the comings and goings of my fellow man. America was mired in a losing battle half a world away in a hellhole called Vietnam. Day after senseless day, the same monotonous story of death and destruction was recounted. Johnson's War had now become Nixon's War, and his oft-touted secret plan to end the conflict must have been so secret that his cronies—having hidden the plan blueprint from prying eyes—evidently had forgotten where they had misplaced the document. Meanwhile, people on both sides were dying, and the light at the end of General Westmoreland's tunnel was visible to but a precious few. Daily, I thanked God that I had served my tour in the army before this awful conflict had become a household word.

Things were not much better in Ireland. Bombings, burnings, and killings were the norm in Ulster, the six counties controlled by Great Britain. The Irish Republican Army was stirring from its period of self-imposed hibernation, and its actions were cause for concern in Dublin. The whole world was a mess, keeping alive the poet Santayana's observation that the human species seemed doomed to repeat its mistakes. The wrong crowd was reading the history books.

My first class started at eight, and I would dash nonstop from one to the other until one o'clock. Then, I had a two-hour break, after which it was back in the saddle until five. Night labs then followed from seven until nine. It was all mind-numbing.

Don't think for a moment that I had gotten over the fiasco surrounding my false start in medical school. I hadn't. It galled no end. But I suppressed my anger by staying busy and praying for the years to unfold at the speed of light.

My all-consuming source of joy was Margaret. True to our pact, we spoke to each other twice a week and wrote long letters in-between.

Toward the end of October, she phoned to say that she would be in Ireland for several days starting in the middle of the following month and asked me to join her for a weekend in Donegal. *Yes!*

It was all I could do to concentrate on my studies as I counted down the days.

I fell into the routine of visiting Mr. Connolly right after my morning classes. We would eat lunch at his home, he seeming to survive on tea and biscuits, but insisting I partake of a more substantial fare. I got to know him quite well over the ensuing months, and he turned out to be a fascinating character. Connolly was self-made, rising over a thirty-year span to assume the presidency of one of the largest printing companies in Ireland. Five years ago, ill-health had forced him into retirement. He had just turned seventy when I met him and was suffering from a host of ailments, but emphysema was the one that was killing him. And still he attempted to smoke! He would sink into horrible coughing jags while gasping and whooping for air, his empurpled face teetering on the brink of exploding, fully reflecting the tortures of the body. I couldn't help but think of my long-lost sister, Bernadette, as I stood helplessly by, waiting for those endless moments to pass. He always had a portable oxygen system nearby, but had once explained, "I'm scared as all get-out to use it. The damn things blow up, lad. Can't smoke around 'em, either!"

Sometimes Roger would join us, sometimes Mrs. Connolly, sometimes both. And much to the father's annoyance, Roger would often put in his appearance more drunk than sober. Junior would then rant and rave about everything and nothing, have another drink and depart, sometimes to school, sometimes to a pub. The monarch was not happy with his student prince and did not shy away from voicing his displeasure.

"I'm hoping you'll come to have a steadying influence on Roger," he had told me. "If he doesn't wrap up his studies this year, then, that's it, I'm afraid. Last chance. And I get that warning from no less a source than Dean Standiford. The man refuses to put up with any more of Roger's shenanigans." He grabbed the arms of his chair in anger, shook his head wildly, and shouted. *"I'm at my wits end with the boy!"*

The boy? The boy being discussed was a thirty-year-old man. However, to be fair, I should point out that the use of the word *boy* in the south of Ireland is as common as rain. Even men such as Roger are called boy. Boy is simply a substitution for a male's given name, a colloquialism.

Roger was his youngest, and as the only son, had been spoiled rotten. And the family, now having sowed haphazardly in that season for growing, found itself bitter with the harvest about to be reaped.

"I'll try, Mr. Connolly."

"I know you will, boy. I don't expect a miracle: the time for that is long past. I just want to see him graduate before I die." This sentiment triggered another attack, a fit brought on by exasperation and not tobacco.

Daniel Connolly loved Irish politics in general and IRA politics in particular. He could stay on the subject for hours. In those early days of our friendship, he would feel me out, trying to learn my persuasion, as he diplomatically put it. I felt this was dangerous ground for me to be treading upon, so one afternoon I spoke up.

"My persuasion, as you put it, Mr. Connolly, is that I'm an American citizen and as such must steer clear of Irish politics. I'm now a guest in the land of my birth, here to study medicine, so I must be cautious about expressing any opinion on political matters. I could be deported, don't you know? Then, where would I be?"

"Oh, go on with you, Desmond! I'm not suggesting you join the movement. I just hoped that your sentiments were still with your Irish brothers and sisters. We have more than enough men to serve the cause. I'd just like to know where you stand."

As I said, this was dangerous ground indeed, a minefield, and I wanted nothing to do with the movement. It took all of my limited diplomatic skills not to upset this aged warrior, who was so kind to me. With a slight shrug of his bony shoulder, he dropped the subject and never mentioned it again.

Horses were his second love. He could talk about them for hours and often did. Every morning he would read the racing forms, and then place bets both in Ireland and on the continent. He told me many times—and always with a wry smile on his face, "I'm lucky with horses, lad. I have a feel for the nags." But, to repeat, he avoided any further discussion of the IRA in my presence, and I, in turn, was grateful for that respect and kindness.

I wish I could say the same for Roger. Many a night he would be fully into his cups and would rail against the British, whom he referred to as the "Bloody Black and Tans," a slur in remembrance of the occupying force dispatched from London after the uprising of 1916. Roger had nothing good to say about the English. He hated them with a passion. Yet, this staunch defender of liberty, this feared Celtic thorn in side of the Crown, saw fit to marry an Englishwoman before the following year was out! And this while doing an internship in an English hospital! The Americans refer to such conduct as *chutzpah*. It's the perfect word. The father cursed the son until his dying day that he had lived long enough to witness such treachery. He had seen one daughter marry an Englishman, but this, *this was just too much*! Such is the misguided sentiment of a handful of my fellow Irishmen.

However, I enjoyed my visits with Mr. Connolly, and I know he looked forward to me keeping him company. And as for me being a good influence on Roger? You decide. But only after I give you much more information with which to form your opinion.

*   *   *

Margaret and I rendezvoused in Donegal, a county on the northwest coast. I had set out after my last class that Friday afternoon and drove in the most miserable weather I had encountered since my return. All indications were that winter was planning to visit the Emerald Isle with a vengeance that year.

Margaret was evaluating an expensive resort that catered mainly to wealthy Americans, who came to fish for salmon and to play on some of the most challenging golf courses in the Western World. The Cove House, nestled between the villages of Bundoran and Ballyshannon, overlooked the treacherous coastline of Donegal Bay. The recently remodeled hotel had the retained the appearance of a stately manor house of indeterminate age. Constructed of fieldstone, it rose an imposing four stories to stand guard over the ever-moving kelp beds swirling at the base of the cliffs. As my American friends would say, this was a first-class operation.

Margaret was waiting for me under the portico. She smiled and waved, and I do believe gave a little jump for joy on spotting my new red car. She rushed forward and flung open my door, leaving the startled doorman marooned in her wake. I was greeted with an exuberant kiss, targeted for my lips but ending on my chin because I was half-in, half-out of the car at the moment of impact.

"Mmmmmm." She gave me a quick hug, then a second, longer, more passionate kiss once I was clear of the door. "I'm *sooo* glad you could come, Desmond." She broke free, then whispered. "By the way, you're my husband, Dr. Kerrigan. It's for appearance's sake. Remember, love, this is still Ireland. We aren't yet quite as understanding as the French, or the Americans, when it comes to affairs of the heart. Or should I say the flesh?"

I returned her kiss, mine unabashedly lustier than hers. "Whatever you say, Mrs. Kerrigan. How about we retire right now for the night?" I breathed heavily in her ear.

She giggled as she drew away. "You randy rascal! First, we've got to meet the owners. Then after you clean up, we're to have dinner with them at eight-thirty. Be a dear, Desmond. Remember, this is my job. I'll make it worth your while later, I promise."

The owners were seeking to expand their market to include not only Americans, but anyone from the continent with money to spend. They pulled out all the stops that weekend to impress Margaret, and by extension, me. Nothing was too good for this royal couple. It was a lifestyle I had only seen in Mr. Cecil B. DeMille's movies, but here I was living such a fantasy. They apologized for the inclement weather, but little did they know that the unstable atmospherics suited my randy leanings to a tee. We spent long stretches behind closed doors, venturing forth only twice on Saturday, to see, and be seen. We wanted to leave the impression with our gracious hosts that we were serious about the job Margaret was here to accomplish. On Sunday evening, she spent two hours in their company, touring the facility, asking questions and offering suggestions, and ended by complimenting them on their beautiful resort. She told them that with the right promotion, their property would prosper from the new client base they were seeking to nurture. All parties were pleased with what had been a very successful weekend, weather notwithstanding.

In Margaret's line of work, one was comped by the hotels and restaurants she visited. Comped means she paid nothing. Tourism was, and still is big business in Ireland, so the merchants and hoteliers bend over backward to treat well those in positions to steer business their way. If Margaret was enthusiastic about a hotel, resort, restaurant, or golf course, then her good offices could mean much in favorable economic benefits to those businesses. This was not graft: it wass her job. I saw her wined and dined by people desperate to curry favor, some even going so far as to offer money in hopes for a well-placed word. She was always polite but firm in her refusal, but once we were alone, she would explode in righteous anger.

"That disgusting little man will get no help from me! His bloody dump will most assuredly not be on my list of places to visit," she would fume. "The gall of that cretin to think I could be bought for thirty pieces of silver!" Or words to that effect.

However, such conduct was rare. Those types invariably went out of business simply because they were incapable of delivering service and value. Margaret loved her job, and she always exuded an air of warmth and genuine friendliness. She was a natural. The business people loved her and oftentimes said she was the best representative Thomas Cook had ever hired. Of course, being a beautiful young woman didn't hurt either. And when I was with her on such occasions, I, too, was treated with respect and kindness. Reflected glory. But to me the best part was simply being with Margaret. She was passionate, and being in her presence made every day a perfect day. *I was madly in love!*

That trip to Donegal was typical of the many we would take over the years, and as I look back to those days, one thing strikes me as strange now although for some reason it didn't at the time. Maybe because I never dwelt on it. You see, never once did Margaret ask me how my studies were going. She would query me about the doings of various people we both knew, but there was never any discussion of my academic pursuits. The topic was simply never broached. Strange you ask? Strange indeed.

*   *   *

On the first day of December, I awoke to find the city blanketed under fifteen inches of snow and more coming down. The wind was howling, scattering the powder in a million different directions. As I stepped outside, my eyes were assaulted to the point of blindness.

The gale drove me backward, immobilizing me alongside the door which had slammed shut behind me. It took every ounce of strength I could muster to force it back open. Chicago had never seen anything to match this. *Windy City, indeed!* There were definitely not going to be classes today. In fact, there wasn't going to be much of anything today. Back in my room, I turned on the radio. The U.S. Armed Forces Radio Network, transmitting from Luxembourg, intoned that the entire continent was being pounded by the worst weather in fifty years. Two freighters had gone down in the North Atlantic during the night with no hope for survivors. Conditions were expected to get worse, and the experts on such matters were predicting another forty-eight hours of misery. My thoughts turned to my parents. Thank God they had electricity. As long as it didn't fail, then at least they'd be safe and warm. I pitied those countrymen not so fortunate.

The storm lasted three days. I studied in my room until I thought I would go mad, then went downstairs and pitched in, helping out in the bar and dining room. No member of the hotel staff was able to make it to work those first two days, so the guests willingly took up the slack and created a self-help operation. The bar did a brisk business. I know because I became the bartender and a popular one, too, I should add. Mrs. Donavon suggested later when she took inventory that my popularity probably had something to do with my heavy hand! But I did not turn into a socialist during my stint of duty. I charged market price for all ablutions, collecting money either at the point of sale or having the total added to the guests' room charge. Anyway, we all survived, and by Wednesday, the storm blew itself out. But over two hundred people had perished in Europe, and untold numbers of cattle and sheep were found frozen in the fields. Officially, winter was still three weeks away.

On Thursday, I stopped by the post office for a package the postmaster had been holding for almost a week. It was a Christmas present from Don and Brook. One of them had written on the wrapper in bold letters: *OPEN IMMEDIATELY. PERISHABLE.* Back in my room, I followed the instructions but could not find a reason for the recommendation. The two beautiful sweaters wrapped in Christmas paper did not appear to be under imminent attack from moths or other vermin. I was puzzled. Then spying an envelope, I tore it open and read the short note written by Don but signed by both. In essence, they wished me happy holidays and told me to look for another envelope wrapped inside one of the sweaters. I found it and noticed that the sender was another friend, Walt Seddon. He and I shared the same dream. We both wanted to become doctors.

I had met Walt at Loyola University. He was an ex-marine, having served four years as an officer. He had struggled with the decision whether to stay in the corps and make it a career, or resign his commission and try for medical school. He had followed his heart only to run into obstacles at every turn, such as "Sorry, but at twenty-five you're just too old for medical school. Or: You know, you really need more sciences." Or a thousand other reasons all saying the same thing. *No!*

But Walt Seddon was no quitter. He enrolled in the graduate program at Loyola working towards a master's in chemistry and would graduate in the spring. Meanwhile, he had flooded the academic landscape with applications to every medical school in the United States and Canada. *Semper fidelis.* Always faithful. The Marine Corps motto could have been penned for Walt. It described the man perfectly. He was faithful to himself and to his dream. Walt was an inspiration to me.

Why do I tell this? Because it was Walt, who had originally told me of the program at Cork, open only to a select number of American citizens who had been born in Ireland. It was Walt who had shown how I could turn my dream into a reality.

I read his letter twice. Then, I sat on the bed and read it again. My hands were shaking as I carefully studied it for a third time. If what he was telling me was true, then my dashed hopes were about to be resurrected. Because he described a pilot program, offered by a handful of medical schools in the United States, whereby American citizens studying in foreign medical schools could, upon the successful completion of their second year, transfer back to a school in America and graduate from that college two years hence with an M.D. degree. By now I felt as if I might faint. I actually lay down on the bed, my mind racing. My possibilities suddenly seemed endless.

As far as Walt knew, I was enrolled in my first year of medical school at University College, so he saw this news as a godsend to me if I should want to graduate from an American school.

I picked up the letter and re-read his last paragraph.

If this is of interest to you, Desmond, let me know, and I'll send you all the information I can get my hands on. It certainly looks like a program you should, at the very least, consider carefully, weighing the pros and cons before coming to a decision. I'll be happy to forward application forms, etc., etc., etc. Let me know, and I'll get right on it.

Meanwhile, have a great Christmas. Keep your nose to the grindstone and your powder dry.

Semper fi. Walt.

I whooped and hollered, but only inwardly. Outwardly, I thrashed about on my bed, beside myself with glee. *Oh, God, Yes!* Holy Mother of Jesus, I've got to get in touch with Walt right away, and have him send me everything.

Still shaking, I sat at my small desk and drafted a reply. It took me almost an hour to get the wording just right. I looked at my watch. Three-oh-six. I could get it into today's mail if I hustled. I grabbed my coat and flew out of the hotel. At two minutes to four, my letter was on its way to America.

Now came the hard part. Waiting for a response. I wasn't going to be worth a tinker's damn until then.

Why this sudden euphoria?

Hidden in the recesses of my mind, an idea was germinating, taking on life.

CHAPTER EIGHT

The thought of spending Christmas with my family flooded my mind with conflicting emotions. A harkening back to the holidays of my youth did not fill my soul with nostalgia for those days long dead. Truth be known, they were best left dead. There certainly hadn't been money for gifts and definitely none for a Christmas feast. I realize now this must have been the most dreaded time of year for my parents, especially when they looked at the anticipatory faces of the youngest children who could not understand that Santa Claus would not be visiting our home—again.

"Why not, Ma?" I remembered hearing. "We have a fine chimney for him to slide down. All we have to do is make sure the fire is out, so he doesn't burn his beard. We can do it, Ma, I just know we can!"

Well, not this anniversary year of our Savior's birth. I was determined Santa would visit our home this Christmas, and that jolly old man was jolly-well going to make up for his shortcomings of Christmases Past. I spent my free time that next week shopping for all of them, and although I put a sizable dent in my budget, I didn't begrudge a single penny spent. My plan was to arrive home two days before the holiday and get everybody into the proper mood. Sad as it sounds, I knew they would have to be coached, but I was equal to the task. The last thing on my list was a turkey, a treat the children had never tasted, and I suspected, neither had my parents.

Margaret called to invite me to Paris for New Year's. Her schedule was such that she was not going to get home to be with her mother, but she told me not to worry: she had a dozen invitations from friends who had begged for the pleasure of her company on Christmas Day. However, New Year's was to be a special gala. She had been invited to a private party being hosted by the Irish Embassy but held in one of the grand hotels of Paris. Margaret had accepted, informing the hosts that she and Dr. Donahue, her escort, were looking forward to the festivities.

"Don't worry, love, it's not black tie, so don't get your knickers in a knot," she admonished, her voice betraying the laughter she was trying to contain. She was a step ahead of me. "Your dark suit is just the ticket, Desmond. I've arranged for you to come over on Aer Lingus. Your flight leaves Shannon on the twenty-ninth at four P.M. and gets into Paris about an hour later. I'll meet you at the terminal and we can go right to dinner from there. It should be a smashing good time, love."

"I wish it were tomorrow."

"Me, too, Desmond, but the time will fly. Anyway, enjoy Christmas and bring me something nice. Besides you, of course," she added, blowing me a kiss through the receiver. "Got to run, love. See you soon. Bye.

As the days of December unfolded, Cork's social calendar blossomed. Roger and his parents knew everybody who was anybody in society and were invited to scores of parties and fancy dinners in honor of the season. Mr. and Mrs. Connolly declined most and insisted I attend in their stead. "I need you to keep an eye on Roger," explained the father. "I'm too old to be running all over town, but someone's got to make sure the boy doesn't make a complete ass of himself. Besides, his mother's scared to death he'll have far too much to drink and kill himself on the roads, the stupid sod!"

So, acting as Roger's keeper during that season of comfort and joy, I made the rounds of some of the most fashionable homes and hotels of that fair city and was introduced to the movers and shakers of Cork. The clergy was always well represented at most of these functions, as were many senior staff members of the university. I spoke politely to Doctor Beckler and Doctor Standiford on more than one occasion, the former always pleasant and friendly and the latter always haughty and cold, seemingly eyeing me as though I were a party-crasher. Standiford was a snob.

On the night before I left for home, the Connollys hosted a party in the main dining room of the Imperial Hotel. The invited numbered just shy of one hundred, the two guests of honor being the Lord Mayor and the Bishop of Cork. Much to his father's annoyance,

Roger showed up in white tie and tails even though the invitations had specified business attire.

"Are you deliberately trying to upset me, boy?"

"Hell, no, Father. This was the first suit I could find in my closet. Anyway, I felt like putting on the Ritz tonight," Roger said, already well into his cups.

"Watch yer tongue, boy." Daniel Connolly then shot me a look meant to kill. *Thought you were to see that something like this wouldn't happen*, his eyes said.

"Ho, ho, ho! Meeeeerry Christmas," a voice boomed from behind Mr. Connolly. He wheeled to face the source of this joviality, anger still written all over his face. It was the Bishop of Cork.

"Hello, Sean," Mr. Connolly said as his features softened. The two were friends from the time they were toddlers.

"My, my, don't you look spiffy, Roger," the bishop remarked, giving him a lingering once-over.

"My court jester's got his holidays all mixed up," interjected the father. "I suspect he thinks it's Halloween."

The bishop laughed. Grabbing Daniel by the arm, he steered his friend away from Roger and me, but not before winking at the two of us. "Come, buy me a drink, Danny Boy, and tell me how much of your winnings from the horses you're planning on dropping in the plate at Christmas Eve mass."

"Roger, please don't piss-off your old man any more tonight, okay?" I really didn't need Mr. Connolly turning on me.

Roger rubbed his swollen hands together, all the while scanning the assemblage. "Righto, Desmond, me boy," he replied absently, his gaze finally coming to rest on a comely young woman having a word with Mrs. Kerrigan. At that moment, Margaret's mother spotted me and waved.

"That's Meg Dougherty," Roger said, with a slight jerk of his head in the direction of the two women. "All peaches and cream," he observed with a derisive snort. "Biggest bloody round heels in all of Cork, she is," his eyes never leaving the angelic face of Meg Dougherty. She certainly looked most prim and proper. "Regular little mink, that one," he continued, suddenly talking like a gangster with the words spilling from the side of his mouth. Roger was on a roll. "If she ever plans on getting married, she'd better move to someplace like Alaska because she's slept with every living, breathing man between here and there. Our Peaches and Cream is a regular little queen of tarts!"

"Not every man," I blurted out.

Roger laughed. "I can soon remedy that." He then draped his arm clumsily around my neck and propelled us both in Meg's direction.

"Roger, I'll be quite happy to be the one man in Ireland who has not sampled her charms, thank you, very much!" I hissed.

Mrs. Kerrigan greeted us both with a kiss and a hug. I really liked this woman. She introduced me to Meg, who primly shook my hand and wished me a happy holiday season. *Peaches and Cream.* Roger instantly linked arms with a very willing Meg and escorted her away.

Mrs. Kerrigan smiled at me. "A little bird tells me you will be visiting my Margaret over New Year's. I wish she was coming here, but I'm glad you'll be going there, Desmond. Give her a big hug from her old mum. Tell her I miss her." She squeezed my hand as she spoke.

"I will."

A gong sounded, calling us to the banquet. This crowd was fully into the festivities of the season, and it took several minutes for everyone to find their assigned places. Glasses clinked, everyone toasting everyone else, laughter and gaiety the order of the day. Roger had changed Meg's place card with that of some powdered dowager, so she was now seated to his right. Peaches and Cream was in heaven.

A hundred people dined that night like royalty, feasting on roast goose and pheasant. Spectacular. That one word described the night perfectly.

It was almost midnight by the time the last of the guests had departed and I found myself alone in the empty room save for Mrs. Connolly.

"Thank you, Mrs. Connolly, for everything. Your dinner tonight was the finest I've ever eaten, and I know everyone else thought so, too."

"It did go rather well, didn't it?" A smile lit up her tired face. She was rightfully pleased with the evening's success. Then she added while a frown creased her forehead, "I wonder where Roger disappeared to?"

"I think he took Meg Dougherty home."

"Humph! To his or to hers?"

I turned red and shrugged my shoulders. Silence, at times such as this, is indeed golden. It appeared that everybody knew about Peaches and Cream.

"Oh, well." She mimicked my gesture. "Good night, Desmond. Happy Holidays."

*   *   *

Christmas that year made up for all the bleak Christmases Past. The dinner I prepared was a smashing success. We all attended midnight mass, me willingly making two trips in my little red Escort to ferry everyone to and from the church. We then stayed up until dawn opening presents and having a grand time. Of course, several of my brothers and sisters were absent, many being with their own families this day. Where, oh, where, had the years gone?

"Desmond, do you remember the Christmas Eve your father came home full of celebration and tried to find an open window to climb in, all the while yelling his fool-head off that he was Santa Claus?" My mother was on a stroll down memory lane, and she laughed at the thought of that long-ago night. "I could have strangled him for waking up the young'uns with his carrying on!"

How could I ever forget? He had come home in the wee hours and had started banging on the windows as he made his way around the house. He would sing a few lines of one Christmas carol, then segue off-key into another. Then, he would stop mid-sentence and yell out: "Ho, ho, ho! Merry Christmas everybody! Come out and see what Santa's brought you."

The younger children, now fully awake, were in stitches. Mother was not. "Get away from those windows, Arthur Donahue, and come in the house this instant."

We heard a shuffling, followed moments later by a muffled 'aagghh,' followed by a loud thump. It was obvious he had fallen.

"Bloody hell!" he bellowed. "All me bloody oranges are all over the bloody yard!"

Oranges?

The three of us older children were out the front door in a streak, eyes to the ground in search of the scattered treasure. We recovered just two, squished by father as he fell on them, the remainder gone, having rolled off to God knows where. We would have to wait until morning to find them.

At first light we were back outside, but found only three more. Our pigs had ferreted out the rest. The salvaged fruit was washed and sliced, with everyone getting at least one slice—except father.

Arthur Donahue had had the good sense not to argue with his wife that Christmas morning.

Now, my father grinned sheepishly, vaguely remembering. Funny now, heartbreaking then.

The next day I made arrangements to give Neil Gallagher a follow-on interview for the newspaper. We met for lunch at the one nice inn in Ballycommon. I had known Neil since childhood, and this day he was more interested in hearing about life in America than learning more about me.

"Desmond, I'm thirty-three years old and going nowhere," he began. "My salary's an embarrassment, and I'll die writing for a paper nobody reads." He was on the verge of tears. "No, I take that back. Everybody in the two counties reads every damn page, only because they have nothing else to do. No one of significance sees what I write. I have a degree in journalism, but I'm wasting my education here. How in the hell do I get out, Desmond? Help me."

Happy-go-lucky Neil Gallagher, *hail fellow well met*, daily dying a thousand deaths bred of despair. His life over at thirty-three—the same age Christ had accomplished His life's work and had left His mark on humanity as had no other in recorded history.

"Desmond, could I make a go of it in America?"

That was an easy one. "Neil, everybody can make a go of it in America." I smiled as I drained my beer and signaled for two more. "The bible says that Israel is the Promised Land," I continued. "Well, as the Yanks say, bullshit! I'm here to tell you that America is. It is God's chosen Eden, and the people His chosen people. End of sermon, case closed." I sat back, wearing a smug look on my face.

Gallagher slammed his draught down on the table with such force that the contents slopped over the rim and puddled beneath his pewter mug. He pounded the bare tabletop with his fists causing other patrons to turn and stare at the two wild men in their midst.

"By God, I'll do it!" His face took on a determined look. "The timing's perfect!" A new year, a new decade, a new beginning. I'm going to get in touch with the American Embassy right after the holidays and start the ball rolling. Thanks for your advice, Desmond. As for your story, I'll do a great follow-up piece. Guarantee I'll do you proud."

True to his word, a very flattering article appeared three weeks later. My mother sent me a copy shortly after it hit the streets, and I must confess to feeling more than just a tad of embarrassment reading Neil's words of praise. He hinted that the whole country was rooting for me and, at the very least, I would one day occupy a place in the pantheon of medical greats, actually naming Albert Schweitzer and William Harvey as two who would have to squeeze together on that august pedestal in order to make room for one Desmond Donahue.

On the twenty-ninth, I left for Shannon for my rendezvous with Margaret. The snows of two days ago had disappeared, replaced by a miserable cold drizzle of sleet that made driving a chore. I had not told my family about this wonderful woman, although it took all my willpower to keep quiet on the subject. However, I knew my mother would not condone my going off to stay in her home unchaperoned. Angela Donahue could have cared less that I was thirty-plus years old. Sin was sin. Period. This sounds so old fashioned and prissy now as I recount those days from forty-plus years ago, but believe me, my mother would have gone into cardiac arrest at the very thought of such a tryst. Once enlightened as to my falling, she would be obligated to pray endless novenas for the saving of my immortal soul, prayers that would rival those of St. Monica, who had prayed for her own wayward lad, St. Augustine.

*   *   *

My flight to Paris was uneventful, and I arrived at the same moment Margaret came running into the terminal at Le Bourget Field, waving wildly at me from behind the glass partition. The universally dour customs officials ushered me through without an order to open my suitcase and declare all the contraband I was bringing into the City of Light. The cold wind rivaled that of Dublin, and Margaret informed me after we had clambered into a taxi that it had been bloody godawful for days. She gave me a breath-snatching hug once we were nestled in the warm interior and had given directions in flawless French to our sullen driver. "We won't let the weather slow us down, Desmond." She peered at me through the darkness. "Have you been here before?"

"Once," I replied. "Back in the early sixties when I was stationed with the army in Germany." I recounted that time to her as we drove. Not pleasant.

"Well, that gives me the perfect opportunity to show you my Paris, and I assure you, it's a far cry from the city you've just described. You'll fall in love with her by the time you leave."

We ate dinner at a bistro not far from her apartment, she telling me nonstop of all the places we would visit.

"Margaret, I'm here for three days, not three months," I interrupted with a laugh. "Save something for next time, OK?"

She smiled and waved a breadstick under my nose. "You're right, of course. It's just that I love this city, and I want you to feel the way I do. It's a passion I have, *mon cher*." She reached over and stroked my cheek. "Let's go home, shall we?"

Oui! Her command was music to my ears. In a taxi, she informed me that we had the place to ourselves, her two roommates being out of town for the holidays.

And the band in my head played on!

Home was on a well-lit residential street of townhouses, not unlike those found in fashionable sections of London or Dublin.

Because of the cold, we beat a hasty retreat up to Margaret's second floor apartment. I don't know what I had expected, but I admit, I was roundly impressed. Not only was it spacious, but the rooms were meticulously furnished, and the twelve-foot-high ceilings with their ornate inlaid plasterwork made the residence somehow feel palatial. Compared to what I was used to, it was palatial!

Margaret busied herself in the kitchen preparing *café au lait*, and called out saying I would find brandy in the sideboard and ordered me to pour us each a generous helping. Seizing the largest snifters I could find, I did her bidding, sipping mine as I went into the kitchen to watch her work. We then took our treasures into the bedroom, and within moments were under the covers, propped up amidst multiple goose down pillows. A king and his queen surveying their softly lit kingdom.

"Nice digs?"

"Very nice digs," I replied, alternating sips from my brandy and coffee.

"It takes three of us to be able to afford to live like this," she explained. "Thomas Cook gives me an additional housing allowance, but even so, some months it gets pretty tight. However, it's important to have a fashionable address, so I see it as money well spent." She then turned to face me. "Finish your drink, love, then flip off the light."

"Then what?" I asked, full of feigned innocence.

"Then we rut, that's what. *Now hurry!*"

The next day, Margaret had us up and on the street by eight-thirty. The day was as clear as a Cartier diamond and, although cold, there were many people about, all bundled up to their chins.

"We're going to walk for a while," she explained, as we hoofed it smartly down the street toward the Place de la Concorde.

"Where to?" I puffed.

"The Louvre. It's time I introduced you to some culture, young man," she admonished, a laugh in her voice.

"Taxis from here on out, nature girl," I said fifteen minutes later in my no-argument-permitted voice as we entered the museum. I was frozen.

It was not long before my discomfort was forgotten, and I spent the next two hours marveling at the many wonders before me, some dating back to antiquity. Too soon, our time was up. Margaret suggested a quick lunch, and then a tour of Notre Dame.

I was a fearless knight as I rode with m'lady to the cathedral in a heated bus. Margaret snuggled, her cheeks more rosy than pink, a reflection of the wine we had consumed at lunch. A discreet little burp escaped her lips, a most fitting testament to her sense well-being.

The next day we did the obligatory ascent of M. Eiffel's tower, followed by a cultural happening, as Margaret put it, with an afternoon tour of the Paris Opera House.

As dusk descended over the city, she announced, "Time to go home, take a bath, and get ready for our party tonight. I think you've done rather well in the culture department, my love. I'm proud of you."

At ten minutes to ten, we entered the banquet room of the Hotel St.-Germain and found ourselves back in Dublin. The entire expat community was there, and it seemed everyone knew Margaret. She was kissed by a thousand worshippers, each wishing her a Happy New Year while her escort, *moi,* was treated like a celebrity and not some unwelcome appendage. Within minutes I was conversing with long-lost friends just met. What a night! At the stroke of midnight, hundreds of party favors were blown, all screeching a raucous heralding in of the New Year; and after another round of kissing and hugging, the revelers broke out in a chorus of "Auld Lang Syne." We finally staggered out of the hotel at dawn. It had truly been a night to remember. I was beat.

January 1, 1970, was a lost day, and I was still woozy and weak when Margaret took me to the airport for my flight home twenty-four hours later.

"Getting too old for this, are we?" she taunted, full of the vitality of youth.

"Sad to say, but we are." I smiled back weakly. "I just need to sleep for a month; then I'll be as good as new."

"Of course you will, love. Now give me a kiss to last a while."

I complied, the most willing of servants. "Thanks, Margaret. That was the best New Year's ever. I hope it's not our last."

"Of course it isn't, silly! Now, off with you."

Four and a half hours later, I was back in my own bed, sleeping the sleep of the dead.

*   *   *

1970. It was hard writing that unfamiliar number on the top of my checks as I paid bills the next morning. A new decade. A time for greatness. And I was ready for whatever lay ahead.

After I dropped my mail off at the post office, I collected an armload in return; and tucked away in the middle of the heap was a large envelope from Walt Seddon. I sat in my car and tore into my treasure. True to his word, Walt had sent everything I would need to start the ball rolling. I sat back and contemplated my next move. There was only one stumbling block to overcome, and it was a hurdle of monumental proportions.

All the paperwork Walt had sent me was obviously geared toward the second year medical student. I was no kind of medical student, but as I had mentioned before, a plan was germinating in my mind. This was a plan so audacious, so preposterous, that if I embarked upon it, there would be no turning back. It was a very scary thought. So where would I turn for counsel? Who could I trust to help me accomplish what I had in mind? Or tell me if what I had planned was even possible?

Only one name kept popping up. Roger Connolly. The time had come for me to expose my soul to another human being and allow a hint of the corruption spawning within. Desmond was turning into Faust.

Having made up my mind, I let loose a long breath, then went in search of my friend.

CHAPTER NINE

Roger was nowhere to be found. I tried every place I could think of, but he had disappeared. Maybe he was with Peaches and Cream. I had left messages for him all over Cork, and by dawn of the third day, I was fuming.

On my way to my first class that Friday morning, whom should I spy strolling across the quadrangle, heading towards the science building with nary a care in the world?

"Roger, hold on!" I yelled, much louder than I had intended. He had just fallen into step with John O'Banion, a fifth year med student, and now the two of them paused, waiting for me to catch up. "Where the hell have you been?" I asked, still shouting, venting my wrath at the prodigal son.

"Good morning to you, too, Desmond," Roger said nonchalantly, an unlit cigarette dangling from the corner of his mouth. "Forgive me, boy, but I didn't realize I had to report my bloody comings and goings to you."

"Roger, I need to talk to you."

"Well, talk."

"I mean alone. In private. I need your advice." There. I had said it.

John O'Banion took not the slightest offense. "Hello, Desmond, goodbye, Desmond." He waved and set off at a fast clip towards the science building.

"That was bloody rude of you, Desmond."

"Roger, I'm sorry, but I need to get together with you later."

"Okay. I'll meet you in your room at seven this evening. You can tell me what's on your mind, and then we'll go downstairs and have a Guinness." Without a goodbye, he turned and followed O'Banion, striking out with a purposeful stride, eager student that he was! A man on the move, a man actually going places. *Goddamn him!*

At seven sharp he knocked and entered my room at The Shamrock Inn and immediately spotted the papers from Walt Seddon strewn all over the bed. "OK, out with it, boy." He smiled to show he harbored no hard feelings from this morning.

"Roger, I think I've found a way to become a doctor, to even graduate from an American school, and do all this in a little over three years from right now." I was wound tighter than a watch's mainspring, my words all running together.

"Now that would be quite the feat, Desmond. I think you'd better start at the beginning. But slowly, boy, slowly." He drew up the lone chair and plunked himself down, gesturing for me to sit on the bed facing him.

I spoke for the next twenty minutes, bringing Roger up-to-date on all that I had learned from Walt. He sat and listened, paying close attention, or so it seemed. Sometimes, you can't be sure with Roger. At least he wasn't drunk, so maybe he was assimilating what I was imparting. I could only hope.

He shifted his weight and rocked the chair back on its hind legs. "So, let me see if I've got this right. Your American friend has told you about a program whereby Yankee citizens studying in foreign medical schools can, under certain conditions, transfer into an American medical college to complete their last two years?"

"Right."

"But in order to be accepted, you must sit an exam called 'The Part One of the National Board of Medical Examiners.' You called it the N.B.M.E., for short?"

"Exactly."

"Quite a mouthful," he observed, then continued. "Also, you can supposedly take the test at the end of your first year as a non-candidate, a kind of trial-run sort of thing; then at the end of your second year, you get to go back and sit the exam as a full-blown candidate? Meanwhile, you must apply to one or several schools participating in this core transfer program?"

"It's called the Cortrans, but, yes, that's it."

"But to be able to do all this, you've got to show you're an American citizen, give them passport numbers, copies of naturalization papers and what have you in order to prove you're legitimate?"

"Right again." I was impressed. Roger was on top of this.

"But in order to be admitted to sit this test, you must have a signed and sealed affidavit from the dean of your medical school attesting to your good standing and the fact that you will be a second year student at the appropriate time. Then, the entire package must be sent directly from the university to this place in Texas?"

I let out a deep breath and nodded. He definitely understood.

"Remember, I can get the papers signed and sealed now while still in my first year attesting that I am a student in good standing and that I will have completed two years by the time I take the test for real at the end of my second year. It sounds kind of complicated, but it really isn't. But yes, that's it in a nutshell." Then, I added an afterthought. "They strongly recommend that the student gets as much clinical experience as possible. They say it will be a big help for taking the test." I shook my head, wondering how I would tackle that one.

Roger's chair came back down on all fours with a loud thump. He clicked his tongue several times, lost in thought. Finally, "Don't worry about clinics. I can take care of that when the time comes. However, first things first. Do you really think Standiford would sign that paper saying you're a first year student in good standing and that a year from this May attest that you will have completed two years?"

"Not bloody likely!"

"So, are you planning on forging his signature?"

"Can't," I replied. "Wouldn't do any good. The document's got to be sealed, and it's got to be sent through the university mail system directly to Texas." I shook my head. "I sure wish it was as easy as forging a signature; I could have that done in a flash. I'm stuck, Roger. That's why I need your advice. You've got to find the answer."

Roger rose from his chair and lit a cigarette. He drew deeply, holding the smoke in his lungs for about two years, then tilted his head towards the ceiling and blew out a cloud to rival that ancient plume from Mount Vesuvius. I can barely tolerate the smell of cigarettes under the best of circumstances and was repulsed at the thought of this noxious air befouling my room, but I said not a word in protest that night. Roger was hard at work on my behalf. *Puff all you want, my friend*, I thought. *Two at a time, if it'll help you think. I'm not a total ingrate.*

Squinting from the smoke creeping into his eyes, he motioned to me with one hand, while flicking ashes on the floor with the other. This was really pushing it!

"Show me that instruction sheet you were talking about. The one where it tells you how to have the dean sign, stamp, seal, and then kiss the bloody thing."

I handed him the page. He read it a couple of times, then handed it back. "Good. I don't see a problem."

"Good? You don't see a problem? Have you heard a word I've said?"

"Of course I have, boy. The problem is you didn't read the instructions carefully."

"I what?" In one fluid motion, I snatched the paper from his hands and read it again. And again. Then a third time. By now I was thoroughly exasperated. "What in the goddamn hell are you talking about, Roger?" I was now yelling, just like this morning, my exasperation transformed into anger.

"It says, boy, the bloody thing can be signed and sealed by the dean *or the registrar*. That's the key, boy. *The registrar.* Dr. Andrew Bloody Quinn. He's your ticket back to America."

"Roger, what difference can it make?"

"All the difference in the world," Roger said, lighting up another cigarette. "Quinn is a befuddled, blind, buffoon." A giant cloud of smoke blossomed in front of his face. *"Blind as a bloody bat!"* I didn't know Roger had the power of alliteration in him. "Dear Doctor Quinn will sign anything put in front of his face. I'm telling you, boy, your prayers have been answered."

Holy Mother of God, could it be that simple? I broke out in goose bumps.

"I'll introduce you to the old coot. You get all the paperwork filled out up to the point where he has to attest to your good standing and the fact that you meet all the requirements. Quinn will sign, have no fear. I guarantee it. He'll be glad to appear useful, to show he's still on top of things. Believe me, you're home free, Desmond."

I handed him the same empty cup he had used to extinguish his first cigarette. He tossed in the dying butt and absently handed the cup back, both remnants floating in a puddle of tea like battered twins. Disgusting!

Roger stretched and yawned. "Enough work for tonight, my Machiavellian friend. Let's skedaddle downstairs and exercise our drinking arms by hoisting a jar or two. All this jabbering has built-up a terrible thirst in me, boy." He wore a look that suggested he had certainly earned his keep this day. And he was right. As walked down the hallway, he leered, "Tell me all about *Gay Paree.* Tell me about your dalliance with our fair Margaret, and don't leave out a single, dirty detail, *mon ami.*"

"Only after you tell me every dirty detail about your time with Peaches and Cream."

"Fat bloody chance!" Roger replied, then burst into laughter.

*   *   *

I spent the entire weekend either at the library or in my room, filling out ten thousand forms, applications, personal history statements, and God knows what else. Remember, this was in the days before photocopiers so there was no practice run before completing the official forms. I was painstakingly correct with each word I committed to paper, my dictionary always at the ready. Double check, triple check, and check again.

Roger and a group of friends had gone to Dublin for a rugby match between a strong Irish team and a band of iron warriors from Scotland. Of course, I had been invited to join them, and of course, I had declined. I was not unhappy. Far from it. I was doing something constructive to enhance my career. Anyway, the weather had turned bitterly cold. The wind howled for hours that weekend, and the constant squalls made any outdoor activity the strict preserve of stouthearted men. Or fools. By Sunday evening, I had completed the package.

I wanted everything on its way to America as soon as possible. True, I was preparing almost sixteen months in advance, but my rationale was that I had to strike now. Once everything was in the hands of the American officials, then I would be on record as a bona fide candidate for a transfer at the appropriate time. The instructions had strongly suggested that one get the paperwork started immediately, and that's what I was doing. Following instructions!

However, I was truly fearful that if old Dr. Quinn was as feeble-minded a soul as had been painted by Roger, then maybe a suddenly observant administrator would soon replace him. That would definitely not be in my best interests.

And it all came down to a little four-inch by six-inch green card I was now holding in my hand. Again, I looked at the few blocks needing Quinn's attention.

IS THE ABOVE NAMED INDIVIDUAL A STUDENT IN
GOOD STANDING?
YES___ NO___

PRINT THE INCLUSIVE DATES THE STUDENT HAS
ATTENDED YOUR MEDICAL SCHOOL. FROM:
MONTH____ YEAR____TO: MONTH____ YEAR____

WILL YOU ATTEST TO THE HIGH MORAL CHARACTER
OF THE APPLICANT?
YES___ NO___

SIGNATURE OF OFFICIAL_____
ACADEMIC POSITION_____
NAME OF UNIVERSITY_____

UNIVERSITY SEAL: (NOTE: SEAL STAMP MUST
OVERLAY AFFIXED PHOTOGRAPH OF STUDENT)

That was it! Please, Dr. Quinn, you just do your stuff, and I will worship you to your dying day. And mine.

A changed collective mindset now enveloped the campus, an affliction run rampant. The cause? Mid-year exams. Every student wore a serious face, and the library had become the most popular building on campus.

Even Roger was struck with the fever, and long days and longer nights was the remedy the doctor now ordered. This malady had a life span of about ten days, and it struck twice a year, once in January and again in June. It was as predictable as the tides or the phases of the moon.

During this time I learned Dr. Quinn had been hospitalized with a viral pneumonia. This was deadly serious. A bacterial pneumonia can be treated with antibiotics such as penicillin or one of a host of broad-spectrum derivatives. Not so a viral *pneumonitis*. This was no frivolous matter in a man of his advanced years. It's an illness which takes a terrible, yet mercifully swift toll on the aged. Fully aware of this possible outcome, I sincerely prayed for his recovery. I think everybody else in the medical college did too, though their motivations were pure. Although no longer the possessor of the sharpest of minds, Dr. Quinn was universally loved. He was an institution, and institutions are something we all respect. Even cynics like Roger. Anyway, prayers were answered, and after two weeks Dr. Quinn was sent home to recuperate under the watchful eye of his wife.

Sometime during the first week of February, O'Banion, Roger and I were walking from the science building to the student union, not really hurrying even though there was a slight drizzle. We all felt good about our performances on the mid-year exams. Ninety days from now, those two could expect to graduate as full-fledged physicians.

"Well, bless my soul!" O'Banion exclaimed, studying the figure heading towards the building we had just left. "Roger, could that be Lazarus I'm spying with my little eye?"

Roger squinted. "Indeed it is, my boy."

"Who? Who is it?" I had no idea who was approaching. All I could see was a stooped, wizened gnome, a man dressed in an outlandish overcoat with his head covered by a tam o'shanter. *No one wore those things anymore!* Except for this elf making his way across the quadrangle.

"Good morning, Dr. Quinn. How are you feeling?"

"Not bad, not bad." The little man stopped and peered at the figures before him. "Who asks?"

"Roger Connolly, John O'Banion, and an American student by the name of Desmond Donahue," Connolly said, answering for us all.

Quinn squinted at us through the thickest glasses I had ever seen, making his eyes appear as giant orbs. The effect was beyond comical. Yet none of us laughed.

"Ah, Roger, my boy, how are you?" Quinn stood right under Roger's chin and gazed up at his face. "Will you finally be leaving us, Roger? Is this the year we have all been waiting for since the days of our youth?" He chuckled at his own humor.

And Roger chuckled back. "I sure hope so, Doctor Quinn. So does everybody in Ireland for that matter. I feel as though I have worn out my welcome amongst these hallowed halls of learning. It's time for me to be about my uncle's business." He sighed, the weight of the world a terrible burden for him to carry. "I shall miss all this," he said with a giant sweep of his hands. "I truly shall."

"Yes, Roger, I'm sure you will. How is your Uncle Edmund, by the way?" Dr. Quinn was speaking of Roger's uncle, a well-known surgeon in the city. "Give him my regards, next time you see him. Tell him I'm ready for our card games again."

"I will. Oh, by the way, Doctor, Desmond Donahue here needs to drop by your office to have some forms signed. Desmond will be transferring back to America to finish medical school, but he needs a moment of your time for a signature."

The gaze shifted myopically to me. "American, eh?"

"Yes, sir."

"Great country. Great people. Good food, too, and plenty of it. And it's all so bloody big, isn't it?"

"Indeed it is."

"Bring the boy by, Roger. Any time. Good-bye, lads, always good to see you." And off he went, the woolen ball in the middle of his headpiece bobbing jauntily as he faded into the mist.

"The deed is as good as done, lad," Roger pontificated from his throne.

I was weak-kneed. "Thank you, Roger. I owe you at least a million dollars. I'll start to pay you back right away. How does a dollar a week sound?" I was now laughing from sheer joy. "I'll be your servant forever. Or at least until I pay you the million."

"Right you are, boy, and don't you forget it. You're a witness, John. You heard the Yankee braggart."

"I've no idea what I'm a witness to, but me feels me doesn't want to know, either." We were now entering the student union, joining at least two hundred of our fellows in this noisy, cavernous room. "Anyway, whatever it is, good luck with Quinn." He winked at us both and left.

"Seriously, thank you, Roger. Do you think we can see him this week before he forgets?"

"Aye, that we will, Desmond. I don't trust the old rascal myself to remember much anymore. We'll do it Friday."

"Thank you!" I groveled willingly at the feet of the mightiest dealmaker in all of Christendom.

And Roger looked down at me with mock scorn. "Out of my sight now, knave, I must be about the important business of managing my affairs of state."

"Not the affairs of Peaches and Cream?" I laughed heartily, nimbly dodging away from a feigned swing of his right arm.

"You ungrateful little bastard!" he called out to my departing back, and then he, too, broke out in laughter.

What a great day to be alive!

* * *

I don't think I got three hours of uninterrupted sleep that Thursday night, but I was full of vigor on Friday morning. I had repeatedly gone over in my mind how I was going to approach Dr. Quinn, and my instincts kept telling me: keep it simple, stupid. My game plan called for me to present the old gent with Dr. Beckler's letter showing my acceptance into the school of medicine, then explain in the briefest of terms the program allowing me to transfer back to an American school to finish my last two years. Next, I would hand him the green card to sign, date, and stamp with the official seal of the college, and mail off to Texas using the university mail system to validate the contents as being authentic. I think I had the scenario down pat. Keep it simple. Get in, get out.

I met up with Roger outside Dr. Quinn's office that afternoon. Roger punched me lightly on the shoulder for good luck, then rapped loudly on the old man's door.

"I'm half-blind, not half-deaf!" Quinn called out. "Come forth, and be recognized."

I sure hoped he was being humorous.

Roger led the way, announcing us as we entered. "Hello, Doctor Quinn. It's me, Roger Connolly, along with the American student, Desmond Donahue. We spoke to you on the quadrangle earlier this week."

"I remember. Pick a chair, boys, and sit."

You would expect me to describe an office in total chaos. Books and papers scattered helter-skelter, dust an inch thick and blanketing every horizontal surface, a world in turmoil. Not so. The room was immaculate. The order and neatness would have warmed any drill sergeant's stone-cold heart.

"Dr. Quinn, I've got to dash off to a clinic, so I'll leave Desmond in your capable hands. Goodbye, sir." Such a polite, diplomatic young man, our Roger! I waved my thanks in his direction, and he gave me a thumbs up as he left, closing the door quietly behind him.

There was nothing on the chair to clear off, so I maneuvered it a couple of paces towards Dr. Quinn's desk and sat.

He was dressed in an overcoat, and in place of his tam o' shanter, had a scarf pulled up over his head, a hideous tartan affair from some obscure clan domiciled in the Outer Hebrides within spitting distance of the North Pole.

"All right, my young American friend, what can I do for you?"

Holding fast to my canned presentation, I explained what it was I needed. He just sat staring at me, eyes like marbles behind those horrific lenses, but occasionally nodding his head to let me know he understood what I was saying.

He reached out and took possession of my passport to Nirvana. He held the card up to a point almost touching his nose and read the bold print, following along the lines with a misshapen, arthritic index finger. A kind of mumbling sound accompanied this procedure. I kept silent.

"Well, as much as we hate to lose a good student, I understand and appreciate your desire to graduate from an American college. It makes life so much easier for following-on in your internship and residency program." He now studied me closely. "You have all the other forms prepared?"

Silently, I handed over the rest of the package. Quinn took his time studying every page. No evidence of a bumbling buffoon here! Blind, yes, but not those other attributes described by Roger a couple of weeks ago. My heart started to pound. If he commenced to ask me questions about how my first year was going, he could quite possibly trip me up, and I would be finished. The upshot would be that in all likelihood I would be banished from the pre-med program with no hope of later being admitted to the medical college. *Dear God, let's get this over with.*

"Everything looks to be in order," he observed. "Neat, too, I might add. Neatness is so important. Unfortunately, not enough young people realize that nowadays. Everything's hurry, hurry, hurry."

I nodded my concurrence with an exaggerated movement of my head, hoping he could see by my action he had a staunch ally in me.

He picked up the green card, placed it on the desk, and then fumbled inside about twenty layers of clothing until finally producing a big, multicolored, marbleized, fountain pen. Laboriously, he unscrewed the cap and started to write.

I sat on the edge of my seat and craned my neck as much as I could, trying to see what he was doing. He was signing his name in red ink. *Red ink! Nobody signs official documents in bloody red ink!* Apparently, Dr. Quinn never had never gotten the word. His finished signature was a magnificent copperplate, rivaling that of John Hancock.

He rubbed his nose as he paused to admire his handiwork. Satisfied, he next filled in the dates of my attendance, and then blew on the card. Next, he painstakingly put a red check mark in the appropriate boxes, responding favorably to the questions pertaining to my good character and pristine academic standing.   Opening the middle drawer of his highly polished desk, he reverently extracted the Great Seal of University College, School of Medicine, Cork, and with a surprisingly steady hand, affixed the seal's image to the card, making sure that part of the raised lettering covered the photograph I had pasted in its proper place only a couple of hours earlier.

Mission accomplished. I could have kissed him.

After placing the seal back in its resting place, he held the card up close to his nose for one final look.   "Excellent, lad," he proclaimed. "I will place all of this in a college envelope and mail it today."

"Excuse me, Doctor, but I think they would like you to use the envelope they have provided. All you need is to make sure it's mailed through the university system so that the proper postmark appears."

"Very well, boy. We'd better show the Americans we can follow instructions, right?"

"Right!" I rose and stuck my hand out. "Thank you for your time, Dr. Quinn. I very much appreciate your assistance."

"Always glad to be of help to our students. That's what I'm here for. To help." He surprised me with the vitality of his grip, and he pumped my hand several times before relaxing his hold. "If there's anything else I can do, just let me know. Don't be shy, lad."

"Thank you, Doctor."

It was only after I was clear of the campus and driving towards the Connollys home, where I had promised to meet up with Roger that I began to whoop and holler at the top of my lungs. I had done it! Jesus, Mary and Joseph, I was on my way back to America, to complete the last two years of medical school and without the inconvenience of having had to attend the first two. What a bloody great coup! Desmond, you're nothing short of a blooming genius, I crowed to the appreciative audience residing inside my head.

CHAPTER TEN

I **confess that** the weekend following the foray into Dr. Quinn's *sanctum sanctorum* found Roger and me reduced to rubble. Maybe my cause for celebration was a tad premature, but I didn't think so. It was a weekend of pub crawling, a weekend where days and nights became a blur. Roger was in rare form. He had done reasonably well on his mid-year exams, the only hurdle he now faced before receiving the coveted M.B. B.Ch. B.A.O. was his orals, scheduled for the third week in June.

Late Saturday night, we were joined by two of Roger's pals, Argus Kennedy and James Cocharan, men who were already practicing physicians in Cork. We happened to be at Kerrigan's Pub when Roger dropped a bombshell.

"I've accepted an internship at the Royal Infirmary, Huddersfield, in Northern England. I leave the day after graduation."

"Tell me you jest, boy." Kennedy looked truly dumbfounded.

"May God strike me dead this instant if I'm not telling the truth," Roger replied.

"He bloody well may," Cocharan chimed in.

And me? I kept drinking. It did not take a genius to know that Roger was in for an unmerciful time. And well-deserved, I hasten to add. To think that this news was coming from our Roger, the same Roger who took the greatest of pleasure in castigating everything English. This stalwart Irish patriot who refused to even stand next to an Englishman at the pub! *The bloody nerve of the boy!*

"Have you told Daddy Connolly?" Kennedy asked, ready to milk this for all it was worth.

"Hell, no! Do you think I'm daft? I probably won't even have him know until I'm gone. Mother can tell him. She's good at stuff like that."

Cocharan shook his head, a look of exaggerated sadness etched onto his face. "You miserable, cowardly weasel, fool that you are! You would have been better served if you had stayed in the seminary those many years ago. Daddy's going to have you shot by the I.R. bloody A!"

Hearing all this, Kennedy fell forward, spraying his drink as he burst out laughing, and the three of us jumped back lest we fall under the shower. Choking, he turned to me and stammered between fits of coughing, "You ever been told of Roger's boyhood dreams of becoming a saint?"

I shook my head and glanced at Roger, now blushing in embarrassment.

"Two years in the seminary, or maybe it was a monastery," Kennedy said, "I forget which. Two years without wine, women and song." He then made a harrumphing sound of implied disgust. "*That* disgusting beggar," he said, pointing a finger at the accused, "was the most pious, mealy-mouthed, bloody little monk you ever laid eyes on." He turned to Roger. "Isn't that so, boy?"

Roger took his time finishing his beer, then let out a long, resonant belch. "That's what I think of my foolish days amongst the eunuchs. You must admit, though, to my everlasting credit, I did see the error of my ways and got the hell out."

"And broke your poor mum's heart," chimed in a man who had just come up to our table.

We all laughed. The newcomer was introduced to me as John Templeton, another doctor. Kennedy and Cocharan lost no time informing Templeton of Roger's postgraduate plans. When they were finished, John made an exaggerated display of blessing himself, followed by pretending to move his chair away from the self-infected leper in our midst.

"You'll probably come home after a year, dragging along a wife and a squalling little English bugger to boot. Serve you right, you bloody stupid twit!" If only any of us could have known just how prophetic Templeton's words would prove that night of unchecked revelry.

We tormented the topic for all it was worth, and, at the end, Roger reminded me to say nothing of his plans during any of my lunch visits with his father. I swore myself to secrecy, and we moved on to other foolishness. It was a weekend to remember. Or forget. To his everlasting credit, Roger was a good sport throughout.

On the last day of February, I received a letter from Texas. My paperwork had been found to be in order, and I was given an identification number to use with all future correspondence. I was informed I could sit the Part One, as a non-candidate, this coming June. They gave me a list of cities to choose from and instructed me to let them know as soon as I had finalized my plans. They also suggested that I make time after the exam to visit the three schools in the program. These would not be courtesy calls but interviews with the faculty. *Hot damn!* I couldn't wait to tell Roger my good news.

During the first week of March, Margaret came home to attend meetings scheduled for both Dublin and Shannon. Apparently, this was to be the year that the charms of Ireland and her people were to be made known far and wide, a year to convince those of Irish descent to return to their roots. True, the majority of the ad money would target North America, but Europe was also to be a part of this unprecedented media blitz. Good for Margaret. *Very* good for Desmond! For the next three weekends, I was able to be with her. I made no mention of my plans for returning to America for two years simply because that event was still a year from this coming June, and I didn't want her to wonder if this would lead to a condition known as out-of-sight, out-of-mind. On my part. Certainly not hers.

In mid-March, I visited my parents and noticed something for the first time. True, it was not something I was unaware of: it was simply something I had given no thought to until now. Their home had bare concrete floors. Sure, there were small area rugs scattered about, but they did nothing to hide the obvious.

I stayed over the following Monday, cutting classes, and took my mother and father to Connemara to pick out tiles for the home. My mother kept insisting it wasn't necessary, but I could tell she was overjoyed at the prospect. After looking at a thousand samples, she settled on one, and we placed the order.

"We'll have it delivered in three weeks, Dr. Donahue," the salesman promised. "It's stocked in our warehouse in Belfast. Three weeks. Guaranteed."

True to his word, the tile arrived at my parents' home two days short of the deadline, and I went back that following weekend. With the help of one brother and two neighbors, we tiled that house in two days. And what a difference it made. My mother loved that tile. She referred to it as her pride and joy until the day she died. I thank God I was able to bring a little added brightness to my parents' lives. I only wish I had done it sooner!

*   *   *

March roared in like a lion and went out like a bigger, nastier, one. Come to think about it, every month in Ireland seems to follow this same monotonous pattern. Blustery is the best description of the weather that spring, but I didn't care. I had made a monumental decision. I no longer attended classes. For what? To what end? Officialdom in America now recognized me as a medical school student, so who was I to disappoint them?

However, the real reason was that I simply did not have the time. My days were now spent dashing from one hospital—or clinic—to another and eating my meals on the fly. Rare was the day now I could pop in and have lunch with Mr. Connolly, a ritual I had grown to like.

Let me explain how I was able to attend the clinics.

Remember, it was Roger who had told me not to worry about the clinics when we were thrashing out how I was going to get my paperwork signed, sealed, and delivered. I didn't worry then, but I did now. Again, it was Roger to the rescue.

"Not to worry, boy, we'll get you started today."

After lunch, we went to the administration offices of the medical college.

"In order to attend clinics, you've got to have a little red booklet," he explained, holding up his current book for me to see. "It's how the college keeps track of your attendance. After every session, the physician will sign, or just scrawl, his initials on the appropriate page. Each book is good for four clinics, and when a book is all filled up, you take it back to the office. Then, one of the girls files it with your permanent record, and, of course, gives you a new one. At the end of the rotation, someone adds up all the little initialed boxes, and those sacred signatures coupled with the results of your exams through some magical hocus-pocus formula known but to God determine your final grade."

"I see."

"Always get the book signed, boy, even if the professor is pressed for time. It's no good to try to get it done the next time you're there. The doctors are under strict orders from the school: no backdating, no exceptions. If you have to be a pest, then be a pest. Any questions?"

"No, sir."

We were now at the counter. Roger smiled and winked at the girl before him. "Need a new book, miss," he said, nonchalantly tossing down a dog-eared one. "Make it two, if you would be so kind." He turned to me. "You ready for a new one?"

The girl couldn't have cared less. She scooped up Roger's discard and pitched it into a metal basket already brimming with used, tattered, identical, little red books. She then opened a drawer and slid four new ones across to us. We, in turn, took two apiece and, with a wave of thanks, strolled out of the room. Done. I learned a lesson that day from Roger, one he had no idea he was teaching me. *Act as if you belong.* The proper attitude will make people instinctively believe you are who you purport to be. Sounds rudimentary, and it is. But it's also vital and I should know because the lesson learned that day held me in good stead for the next twenty years.

Once outside the building, Roger handed me his two booklets. "Hold onto these. I won't be needing them. With those four, you should be able to attend clinics for over a year. Now, we need to get you around to meet the various doctors and explain your position. We'll tell them you're going back to school in America shortly and that you've been told to complete their clinic before leaving. They don't know, and could not care less. Remember, boy, these doctors see new faces all the time. Just make sure to get them to sign at the end of each session. So, from now on, carry that little red book with you at all times. Stick it in your wallet: that way you'll never forget it."

I heeded his command. Approaching the parking lot, Roger glanced at his watch. "Almost two," he observed. "Tell you what, let's pop over to my Uncle Edmund's clinic, and I'll introduce you."

Mr. Connolly's surgery clinic was situated in the Cork Infirmary, a private hospital in the heart of the city. Edmund Connolly was a general surgeon and had been in practice for thirty-five years. I had met him several times, mostly at social affairs at the Connollys', and found him to be an easy-going man, totally devoid of any sense of self-importance. He enjoyed a sterling reputation and had patients referred from all over Ireland. Although he did all manner of operations, he specialized in the removal of hemorrhoids. Definitely not a glamorous procedure, but no surgeon could ask for a more grateful patient population. The condition is more often than not excruciating, and the afflicted usually avoid the surgeon's scalpel until the pain becomes unbearable. Embarrassment is the main culprit for this needless delay in seeking out help.

Note, too, I called him Mister Connolly, not Doctor Connolly. Intentional, I assure you. In the British Isles—and one must include Ireland here—not in a political sense but in a geographical one—all surgeons are addressed as "Mister." Should you err and call them, "Doctor," they will reprimand you for the error of your ways. They are proud of the title Mister and guard it judiciously. It's been this way for over three hundred years, and it's a safe bet to say it will remain so for another three hundred.

We were met by a stern nursing sister who immediately recognized Roger. "Good afternoon, Dr. Connolly." What she obviously thought was a smile fleetingly graced her face.

"Sister, meet Dr. Donahue. He is the chief of surgery at Johns Hopkins Hospital in America. The youngest ever, I might add. Anyway, he's heard of Uncle Edmund's fine work and has requested a meeting with the distinguished gentleman."

Her smile now was genuine. This two-hundred pound apparition dressed in white was instantly transformed into a simpering, fawning, fragile, replication of the Lady of the Lamp.

"So pleased to make your acquaintance, Doctor Donahue." She actually me gave a little curtsy. "Let me run and see if Mr. Connolly is free."

"Stop!" Roger wisely saw that his attempt at humor was fast sliding away from him. And I would be the one ultimately to bear the brunt of this woman's wrath. This woman was no one to toy with. I trembled.

"I jest, Sister," Roger continued. "Dr. Donahue is but a humble student. An American, yes, but sad to report, not even a student at Johns Hopkins. However, mark my words, one day he will be famous, I assure you." The prophet had spoken.

Sister lost her smile her in a heartbeat. Her mouth became a tight, lifeless crease with no visible evidence of lips, and her eyes were full of thunder. Sister was not amused. "And until that day comes, Dr. Connolly?" Acid dripped with each word.

"A simple student who merely wishes to study with the master." Roger was now dancing as fast as he could. He turned to me, his eyes saying: it's time to salvage what we can, here. Time to smooth these very ruffled feathers. "Pay close attention to whatever the sister tells you, Dr. Donahue. She knows damn near as much about surgery as my uncle. Fact is she's already forgotten more than you'll ever know!"

"Oh, get away with you, Dr. Connolly."

Roger, the diplomat, was indeed still very much alive and well. Thank God! Did I actually see her blush? The woman was transformed into a prepubescent teenager who had unexpectedly found herself face to face with Elvis. The effect was identical. Roger had sister eating out of his hand. It was time for me to jump in.

"So very nice to meet you, Sister. I apologize for Dr. Connolly's crass attempt at humor."

Real smiles again. "I won't hold it against you, Dr. Donahue. I should have known better, considering the source." Eyes, like daggers, turned to Roger, cutting him to shreds. Only this time, you could tell she didn't really mean it. "Have a seat, gentlemen, and I'll let Mr. Connolly know you're here."

A half hour later, we were once again outside, our mission accomplished. I was to start with Mr. Connolly at eight o'clock the following morning. It was a watershed. Finally, Desmond Donahue was about to start his medical training.

God bless Roger. Over the course of the next seven days, he had me enrolled in two more clinics. One with an American-trained physician, a urologist named Dr. Collins, and the other with a Dr. David Healy, professor of obstetrics and gynecology.

As for Roger himself, he could almost taste the sweet nectar about to be served at the coming feast. He was within spitting distance of garnering his diploma, and he now paced me, hour for hour, in the cavernous university library. It was quite the sight to behold. He would first strip to his shirtsleeves, and then immerse himself in devouring the information from tomes he had not glanced at in a millennium.

* * *

On the last day of April, I received notification that I was scheduled to sit the Part One of the N.B.M.E on June 24, 1970, in Boston, Massachusetts. This did not present a problem because my clinics would be completed by then. My plans called for me to take the exam, then to visit Boston University, Tufts University, and the University of Miami. These colleges were participants in the Cortrans Program, and I had sent applications to each. All I needed was acceptance from one, but I would be ecstatic to be selected by any. My first choice would be Boston, but I quickly reminded myself of what most folks thought of beggars and choosers.

Unfortunately, there was one little fly in the ointment. As I had mentioned earlier, I had ceased attending any of my pre-med classes. Still, final exams were scheduled for the week before I was to leave for America. On the one hand, if I did not sit the exams, I would receive a failing grade for the year's work. But on the other, if I sat my exams and passed, then the year would at least count for something. It was Roger who convinced me to at least make the attempt.

I smugly thought I knew enough in each subject to earn a passing mark. If not, just by sitting for the finals and doing miserably, maybe

I could wangle an incomplete and keep alive the chance to somehow redeem myself later. Nevertheless, I had no intention of studying because my every free moment was spent preparing for the all-important exam in Boston. This meant cramming the texts that the first and second year students used in their courses. Remember, I had a medical background of sorts thanks to my years of work in the various hospitals back in Illinois. I had more than a rudimentary knowledge of anatomy and physiology, thanks to my days working with various pathologists and to my time spent in the hematology labs. But I had so much to learn and so little time! The clinics I was attending certainly gave life to what the books were teaching me, and I was soaking it all up.

As Roger had predicted, no one questioned my presence, or even my right to be at the clinics. My peers were all third, fourth, and fifth-year students, so they had no reason to know whether or not I belonged in the medical school. Our paths wouldn't cross. Moreover, their lives were so hectic that none had time to worry whether or not an impostor was lurking in their midst. *So what? Who cares?* I told them the same story I told the doctors. Simply that I was going to be transferring back to school in America and clinical experience was highly recommended. Sounds good, carry on.

The days dwindled down. April turned to May, which turned to June, and the air on campus turned electric. Finals were now only days away, and for the first time in memory, I could walk into the student union and the place would be all but deserted. Those few souls in residence would have their noses buried in books, absently spooning cold food into their mouths. It was downright eerie.

My only contact with Margaret was by mail and phone. The big summer push was on as she put it, and her days in Paris were as hectic as mine were in Cork. There were times she would fly into Shannon, drive to Dublin for a meeting, turn around three or four hours later, and be back in Paris before nightfall. No opportunity to rut. Such interludes were sorely missed.

Suddenly, it was time for me to sit finals. *A total, bloody disaster!*

My exams were scheduled for three full days, and I arrived early enough that first morning to find a parking space so that I would not be mentally harried before the exam. If a student was not in place by the time the door closed, that was it. No one was allowed entry after the appointed hour. No one.

Eager beaver that I was, I jumped out of my red Ford Escort, gave the door a mighty slam, and stood speechless as I instantly realized I had left the keys in the ignition, and the motor was still running. My car was now locked tighter than a bank vault, and I had no spare key. Sweet God in heaven, what in the hell do I do now? I hopped from one foot to the other, totally beside myself. *You stupid, bloody moron, Desmond!* Of all the bloody, goddamn days to pull a stunt like this, you had to pick today! I could have cried. I actually kicked the car several times and pounded on the roof, much to the amusement of my fellows as they dashed to their appointed rooms. No time to help the twit, today. Tough luck, old boy. One kindly female soul actually made the sign of the cross as she scurried past, but to no avail. The doors did not magically spring open, and neither did the engine have the good grace to die. Oh, no. That little Ford had a full tank of petrol and could be expected to run for a month. I made my decision. Let the goddamn thing run. Just walk away from the son of a bitch. And that's exactly what I did.

An hour later a security guard walked into the exam room and whispered at length to the proctor. The witch pointed me out, and he made his ponderous way down the tightly packed rows of desks with a thousand keys tethered to his belt, all jingling like the music from some demented opera score. His journey ended in front of me.

"I need you to come with me, Mr. Donahue. Seems you left your car running, don't you know?"

As if I bloody well didn't know! "I can't leave the room," I hissed. "If I do, I don't get back in, which means I automatically fail the year." *Can you follow all that, you cretin?*

"I see. Well, what do you want us to do?" He let out a loud snort, earning the enmity of those students around us. "The chief of campus security wants to tow it away, but we can't because it's running, don't you know?"

My patience was wearing thin. "I do know, and I don't care. I don't have a spare key. Order one from the Ford dealer. Do what you have to do."

"I can stuff something up the tailpipe and smother the engine, don't you know?" he said, "but that will in all probability burn up the ignition motor. We don't want to do that now, do we?"

"We don't give a shit! We are in the middle of our goddamn finals, and we aren't leaving. Now, do what you have to do, but leave me the hell alone!"

Without another word, he retraced his steps to the front of the room and disappeared, closing the door with not too gentle a touch. I was seething and had completely lost my ability to concentrate. Dozens of pairs of evil eyes fell upon me. *Goddamn it all to hell!*

It wasn't until well after dark that I had my car back, with me being fifty pounds poorer. Forty went to the Ford dealer, ten in fines to the University. I hadn't done worth a damn on my test, and I still had two more days to go!

After finals, I worked on getting my affairs in order so that I could leave Cork for the entire summer, if needed. I prepaid what bills I knew would be reoccurring, all except my room at the hotel. Mrs. Connolly wouldn't hear of it.

"No, son, we'll rent it out. But, don't you worry, it's yours the moment you return." She was an angel.

And Roger? Well, Roger was Roger right up to the end.

The following week was the week set aside for the senior medical students to take their orals. These were nail-chewing-all–the-way-down-to-the-quick days, and even Roger was spotted with a finger or two in his mouth and on more than one occasion. John O'Banion, on the other hand, was the picture of confidence. At least on the outside. Later, he confessed he had been anything but. John had not eaten a proper meal for a week, and what little he did get down, came back up in short order. But he knew his stuff. John graduated with honors at the top of his class.

On the last day of orals, a frantic Roger called me at the hotel. "Get over here, boy! Christ on a bloody crutch, Desmond, get over here, now!"

"Where are you?"

"In the bloody hallway outside the exam room!"

"What are you doing there?"

"Just shut the hell up and get over here. Bring your books on hepatic function. *Oh, shit!"* he moaned, and hung up.

I was with him less than twenty minutes later, illegally parked in the faculty parking lot, but I was certainly Johnny-on-the-spot.

"Oh, God, Desmond! The board is concentrating on the bloody liver, and that's definitely not my strong point. You've got to help me bone up." The sweat was pouring off him.

It was now eleven-thirty and there were almost a dozen students standing in line, awaiting their moment with the panel of inquisitors. And according to Roger, you had no idea how long you might be in there. Some students were in and out in less than fifteen minutes; others were there for almost an hour. Roger had no doubts as to his chances for getting out in short order.

As each student exited the torture chamber, he would pause to brief their fellows as to their line of questioning. Liver functions and diseases of same. It looked like the trend would hold true for the entire class. Roger and I sat on the floor, slightly apart from the others and began to cram.

At twelve thirty, the three-man panel exited, led by a stone-faced Dean Standiford, and made its way to the faculty dining room for lunch. The troika would be back in one hour.

They returned and continued their torment. Roger was a nervous wreck. Twice he relinquished his place in line, then twice again, until he was the last student. At twenty minutes past four, a tall, angular, woman emerged.

"They want you, Roger. And it's still the liver. Good luck."

He looked at me, and I thought he was going to cry.

"Knock 'em dead, sport!" I gave him a thumbs up sign. "I'll wait for you back in my room. Good luck, boy."

An hour later he called. "I passed, Desmond."

I could barely hear him. "What? Speak up," I commanded.

"I passed. I'm a doctor. Standiford, himself, shook my hand. Oh my God, Desmond, I made it." He broke into huge sobs. His nine-year ordeal was over. Roger was finally a doctor.

Three days later, Roger graduated with the rest of his class. His entire family attended to witness this day which none had expected would ever happen. Roger actually received a round of applause from his classmates, and upon being handed his diploma by Dean Standiford, turned to the crowd and gave a deep bow. The age of miracles had not died. Roger was living proof.

The next morning I drove him to Shannon. He was a sight to behold. The man was still drunk. Not just tipsy, but falling down drunk. His clothes were a mess: shirttail hanging out below his jacket, the knot of his tie down on his chest, and his buttons all in the wrong holes.

"Roger, call me as soon as you get there. I've got to know that you made it, safely. OK?"

"I will, boy. Thanks for everything, Desmond." He patted my face then lurched away, dragging his one overstuffed suitcase along the ground and into the terminal. He had left home, saying good-bye to his mother while avoiding his father, who had no idea where Roger was heading. A coward to the end. I had to laugh to myself as I made my way back to Cork. Roger was a true friend, warts and all. Now he was a doctor, and no one could take that away from him. No one.

And me? I drove to Ballycommon and spent a day with my parents, letting them know that I would be in America, but that I would be returning for the new school year in September.

Back again in Cork, I put my car in a garage I had rented, and after saying my good-byes to the Connollys, set out by train to Shannon and my flight to Boston. I was feeling good. I was on my self-made track to following in Roger's footsteps.

Wait for me, boy, I'll be doctor before you know it.

CHAPTER ELEVEN

After six hours in the air, I was happy to plant my feet on terra firma at Logan Airport. It was late afternoon, Wednesday, and upon exiting the terminal I was slammed by a blast of stale, stifling, humid air. It had to be over ninety degrees, and I felt as though I had somehow landed in Equatorial Africa. And the noise! Utter bedlam. Still, it was great to be on American soil once more.

Back in the spring when I had told my parents of my tentative plans, I had mentioned that I really didn't know how long I would be in Boston. It could be a month, or it could be the entire summer. My mother had insisted that I write my Aunt Mary and ask if I could stay with her. *Who?* Aunt Mary, your Uncle John's widow, your dad's oldest brother. I had no idea that we were in communication with any member of that branch of the family. John had left Ireland with his brothers and sisters in 1922, leaving behind my father. It was my understanding that with the passing of so much time, we had lost touch. Apparently, not completely. Mother gave me Aunt Mary's address; and, being none too proud, I wrote asking if I could rent a room for the summer. She replied in short order stating she would be delighted to have me. I now directed the taxi to her address.

Mary Donahue must have been sitting by the window anticipating my arrival because she appeared on the stoop supported by a stout cane as I was unloading my things. I, of course, had never met the woman, but anyone passing us on the sidewalk that summer's eve would have thought we were the tightest clan in Christendom.

"Bless my soul, Desmond, you're back!" She cried out. "Oh, my, don't you look fine. Come and give your old auntie a huge kiss and a hug."

I'm back? Aunt Mary was in her late seventies, and maybe her mind wasn't what it used to be. Maybe she didn't remember that we had never met. No matter. I did her bidding and gave my old auntie a huge kiss and a hug.

I then handed the taxi driver his fare and a fifty-cent tip. He stared down at his bounty for what seemed like an eternity, then mumbled, "I see Mr. Rockefeller's back in town. Says he'll be spending the entire summer. I must hurry and spread the good news." *Cheeky sod!*

Aunt Mary lived in the upstairs half of a row house in a neighborhood that was solid Irish. I could have been back in Dublin. Every adult who lived on Griffin Street was seated on front porches or on stoops that oppressive summer evening, hoping to catch a breeze. The youngest kids were engaged in raucous games of stickball, tag, or hide-and-go-seek, while the teenagers lounged in segregated groups: boys together, girls together. Only their eyes bridged the divide, their pubescent bodies full of bravado and, dare I say, lust. A thousand lies were whispered to confidantes in the lengthening shadows, all duly sworn to secrecy, as the imagined sexual exploits of the moment's storyteller were made known to an enthralled audience. Tall tales told in 1970 became *so-what* tales a decade later. The sun was fast-setting on the age of innocence. To be honest, it had probably set long before this, only I had been too busy to notice.

My exam was scheduled at Boston University for Saturday. Did I spend my time with face buried in books? I did not. I became a tourist. Here was a city I knew nothing about, and my adventurous explorations for the next forty-eight hours were a time well spent.

Eight o'clock Saturday morning found me and seventy other aspiring physicians tearing open the sealed examination booklets for the Part One of the N.B.M.E. The majority were Americans who had just completed their second year in American schools, and this hurdle was a "must do" before being granted entry into the upper half of the medical curriculum. The balance consisted of students whose status was identical to my own.

So started eight hours of hell. Chemistry, anatomy, physiology and pharmacology. All the basic sciences. Then in the afternoon, problems presented as clinical histories. The student was given a set of facts, and then asked to draw a conclusion or diagnosis based on the information. Formulas had to be completed, correct interpretations made of theoretical laboratory workups, and a follow-on course of treatment recommended, with possible complications anticipated. Mentally exhausting work.

The American students had an advantage in that the style of the examination was familiar to them. By this I mean that they were comfortable with the true, false, select-the-best-answer, select-the-one-wrong answer, multiple-choice type of test. I was used to the essay exam, as were all of the other students attending medical schools abroad, so it was taxing, working in an unfamiliar format. In addition, the Americans had been practicing all year on sample tests; *plus* the majority taking this exam had paid to attend cram courses.

The day flew by and before I knew it, the proctor was rapping smartly on his desk telling us our time was up. I was spent, and from the looks on the faces of my fellows, no one would be boogying in Boston this night.

The next day I accompanied Aunt Mary to mass, then after treating her to breakfast, called Don and Brook in Chicago. I told them that my first year had gone well and that everything appeared to be on track for my being able to transfer back to America the following year. They both offered to pay my plane fare for a visit, but I declined. I had already taken from these two generous men more than I could ever repay, but I did promise to call several times over the summer.

The following week I had interviews at Boston University and with its neighbor, Tufts University. At both schools the staffs were most accommodating. They made sure I had a tour of their respective facilities and readily answered my questions. Their advice was simple. Do well this coming year. Get all the clinical experience you can and study hard for the real test next summer. No commitments were made, and none were expected.

The following week, I flew to Florida to repeat the process at the University of Miami. If only I had had a crystal ball to consult that June day. Who could have known just what an important role this city would come to play in my later life?

Miami was still a small, sleepy town, but growing, thanks to the influx of Cuban refugees. I vividly remember thinking at the time: *I'm in a foreign country where everyone speaks Spanish!*

And boy was it hot! The temperature was 85°, and this at eight o'clock in the morning. *How can anyone work in such conditions?* And from what I had heard, it was like this every month of the year. Not true, of course, but in 1970, what did I know?

My interview at the University of Miami was a repeat of the two in Boston. I was shown the facilities, including Jackson Memorial Hospital which brought back fond memories of Chicago's Cook County Hospital. The Miami city fathers had big plans for this facility, and twenty years later their vision was realized. Today, it's one of the world's leading institutions for medical research. The advice from this faculty was the same. Keep in touch and forward all documents requested as soon as possible. We promise to do the same. I left Miami feeling I had accomplished a lot.

* * *

"Desmond, I want you to call this number and ask for Michael Murphy. He's Edith's son," my Aunt Mary explained, the night of my return from Florida. She was referring to one of her closest friends. "Michael's a painting contractor and does most of the fancy homes in Watertown. He's looking for a reliable assistant, and I recommended you. He said to call him right away."

Bless her heart. Work was something I desperately needed. My savings were diminishing more rapidly than I had budgeted for, so this opportunity was a godsend.

I started with Michael two days later and worked until the middle of September. Twelve-hour days were common, so was working on Sundays. I became a rather proficient house painter by the end of that summer, but more importantly, I was able to save a fair amount of money, which I knew would bring a smile of approval to my banker's face back in Cork.

All too soon, the day came to leave Aunt Mary and Boston. I freely admit I shed a tear as I hugged and kissed my aunt, promising to return and stay with her again the following summer. She had been generous to a fault, opening her home and heart to what in essence had been a stranger.

My mail had been forwarded to me from Ireland by the Connollys, and I learned I had failed my entire pre-med course load.

Not unexpected news, but disappointing, nonetheless. Those tidings definitely contained a warning of bridges irrevocably burned! But, to counter that, I learned the day before leaving Boston that I had gotten a seventy-two on the Part One of the N.B.M.E. Seventy-five was a pass, so I was not the least bit unhappy with my results. To prepare for the following year, I had purchased a couple of hundred dollars' worth of textbooks on physiology—a weak point—as well as study materials crammed full of Part One sample tests.

All in all, not a bad year, considering how poorly it had started.

*   *   *

First things first meant visiting my parents, and then it was on to Paris for a week with Margaret. She was riding high from a very profitable summer's work, accolades and honors being tossed her way from a very appreciative employer. Rumor had it that within several years she could very well be running the entire show!

"We're off to the Palais de Versailles, love," she informed me that first morning. "It's my duty to further your education. I want you to see how the *uber*-rich once lived. It's also for motivation, Desmond." She was concentrating on her driving, looking straight ahead as she spoke, darting in and out of traffic, always searching for some hidden advantage. "Tomorrow, we're going into the wine country for a couple of days. It's the perfect time of year, and I've been able to get a super rate on lodgings. After that, well, let's play it by ear, shall we?"

"Aye, aye, captain." Who was I to argue? I was with Margaret, and that was enough for this country boy.

The days were a blur of exhausting activity, but the nights were heaven-sent. I openly confess I lived that week for the pleasures of its nights. I had so much lost time to make up for, and, oh, how I had missed my Margaret. All too soon this idyllic moment in time came to an end, and I returned to Cork to begin my last year of studies before departing one last time to America and the fulfillment of a dream.

*   *   *

Armed with my official documentation, I once more made the rounds of the various clinics and introduced myself to the professors.

Some new, most not; but all accepted me at face value. I had recounted my story so often that I was beginning to believe it myself. *Act like you belong, Desmond*, the inner voice counseled, advice as valid now as it had been during the last school year.

What a schedule I had laid out for myself. Morning surgery clinics with Mr. Connolly on Tuesdays, Thursdays, and Saturdays. More surgery with Mr. Stephen MacNamara at the same facility on Monday and Wednesday mornings, followed by classroom instruction and labs in the afternoon and evening hours. And during my free time, I camped in the university library. Thank God, Roger was not in town. I would have had the devil's own time avoiding him, and this was to be a year of unbelievably intense effort on my part. Roger would have been a major distraction. Anyway, I was off and running, as fully immersed in my studies as any other medical student at any other college. I belonged. Or so I thought.

Complacency was a state of being I could not afford, and a couple of times that year, I nearly was exposed. Those incidents rudely yanked this Yank back into reality, and although I always acted as though I belonged, I became increasingly more vigilant as the year progressed.

* * *

"G'morning, Matron, g'morning, boy."

"Good morning, Mister Connolly," We parroted in unison. It was the second Saturday in November, eight o'clock in the morning, and as Mr. Connolly struggled out of his raincoat he looked around, irritation written all over his face.

"Where are the other students?" he demanded crossly, addressing neither of us in particular. "And where's my bloody son?"

Silence.

The bloody son was Young Liam, a fourth-year student and a constant source of irritation to his father. Liam was following in his father's footsteps, not out of any love of the healing arts, but because it was expected of him. And he simply did not possess the fortitude to say no. Liam, sad to say, was his mother's boy, happier when hobnobbing at society functions with *mère*, than say, pub crawling with his plebeian cousin Roger, and that other callow fellow, *moi*.

Roger had no use for Young Liam and only tolerated him because he was family. The feeling was mutual. But this morning, Mr. Connolly was none too happy with his progeny. Or the other missing students, for that matter. I thought he would take his ire out on me. Not so.

"Very well, Desmond, it's just you and me, and that's very good for you. Gives you a chance to learn surgery without being bothered by a bunch of idiots hovering around." He turned to the matron. "What's on tap?"

"Two of your patients were discharged this morning so that leaves only Mrs. Beck with us at the moment. However, you have a patient coming in at eight thirty, for a hemmorhoidectomy." She scowled as she rifled through her charts. "Ah, yes, here it is. A Mister Dylan O'Shea."

"All right, boy, let's take a look at Mrs. Beck." The three of us marched single file into the wards.

"Good morning, Mrs. Beck." Connolly smiled down at his patient, and as he introduced me, picked up her hand and gently felt for her pulse. "This is Doctor Donahue, a student of mine from America, and a fine surgeon in the making, too, Mrs. Beck. Pause. Silence. Count. Smile. He laid her arm down. "Please bear with me for just a few moments, and we'll be out of your hair, I promise."

"Oh, you're no bother, sir, really, none at all. I just thank all the saints that I got to you in time."

"Please listen carefully, Dr. Donahue," he began, speaking quietly, but his voice full of authority.

"Mrs. Beck is sixty and the mother of ten. She has suffered from abdominal pain for the past five years, often accompanied with severe diarrhea. You Yank doctors call it IBS, or irritable bowel syndrome. Anyway, about ten days ago, she was incapacitated with sudden onset, excruciating, left-sided pain, along with fever, nausea and vomiting. Now, what do you think the flat plate abdomen revealed, Doctor?"

"Free air in the abdomen?"

"Exactly. We quick-marched into the theater, and performed what procedure?"

"A colostomy?"

He nodded. "What else?"

I shook my head. I had no idea where he was heading now.

"A loop colostomy. And do you know why?" He was fully engrossed in his lecture, and I hung onto his every word. This was what medicine is all about. Oh, you fools for missing this. Especially you, Young Liam.

"Foremost, because of the possible spilling of intestinal material into the abdomen and causing gross contamination," he said. "Secondly, because the procedure allows the bowel to rest and heal." Connolly nodded his head in self-approval. "How long should I wait before closing the colostomy and reattaching the colon? Keep in mind, Doctor, this lady had a very severe diverticular disease. What do you think about three to four months?"

My mind raced. I brought to the forefront of my consciousness all I knew about this disease. No, this was not long enough, and I said so.

"Correct. It will be at least six months, possibly longer. Then we perform a left colectomy. After that, Mrs. Beck will be as right as rain and live for another hundred years."

The patient laughed. "Mercy me, Mr. Connolly, I couldn't stand to be with my Seamus for that long."

"Then dump him and get a new husband. No, you're right, of course. A hundred more years with the same man is too much to ask from any woman." Connolly chuckled at his own humor. "Good-bye, Mrs. Beck. I've got to take this young man back to the clinic and see if there's anything more I can teach him."

Mr. O'Shea arrived at a quarter to ten for his eight-thirty procedure. "You're late, man," Connolly remarked, frustration in his tone.

"Too bloody right!" O'Shea was not in the slightest bit intimidated. He was a wiry little fellow, somewhere in his mid-sixties, and he walked with hesitant, choppy steps. "You'd be bloody late yourself if you had to bicycle twenty miles and walk the last three because your bloody arse hurt so bad."

"Don't look to me for pity, Dylan O'Shea; I've been telling you for years to get those hemorrhoids removed, but, no, you wouldn't listen."

"Well, I'm here now, so let's get on with it. The pain is more'n I can take."

Five minutes later he was on the table with Connolly explaining to me what we were looking at. Not a pretty sight. The pain must have been excruciating. All four quadrants were covered with hemorrhoids, the mass lying externally like so many grapes, most ruptured and oozing blood and fluid. I felt sorry for the old fellow. Mr. Connolly lowered his speculum. "First, I'm going to give you a shot to relax you, Mr. O'Shea; then in about fifteen minutes, you'll get a local anesthetic. After that, we'll take you out of your misery. In went the needle carrying liquid valium, bringing welcome relief to the inverted Mr. O'Shea.

"I want the young doctor to do it." O'Shea was feeling better already. "You're an uncaring brute, Mr. Connolly, that's what you are. I want the young doctor," he repeated.

"Oh, for God's sake, Dylan, shut up or I'll bloody well let him operate on you. Serve you right, it would." He sounded gruff, but he was smiling as he winked at me. "Dr. Donahue's nothing more than a student of mine, you old fool. He's never even lifted a knife before, and you want him to cut on you? I should damn well let him do it."

"Holy Mother in heaven, don't you dare! I was only kidding you, Mr. Connolly. You're the best bloody surgeon in all of Ireland. I wouldn't let another soul touch me."

"That's a whole lot better now, Dylan. You just continue to think nice thoughts about me, and I'll have you fit as a fiddle. Meanwhile, Dr. Donahue and I are going to get some tea, discuss our procedure, and come back in about fifteen minutes."

"Take yer time, gents. I'm feeling fine, so I'll just wait here for you, with my friggin' arse exposed for all the world to see. Take yer sweet time."

We both laughed. Mr. Connolly pulled a drape over the still-muttering O'Shea, and we left for the doctors' lounge in search of hot tea.

Mister Connolly quizzed me for the next several minutes as to the procedure he would follow. "What do you know about the rectal sphincter? What's the name of the nerve we need to block?"

"I don't know, Mr. Connolly."

"Well, you will by next Saturday, boy. You'll know all about the pudendal nerve. Also, the dentate line and a whole lot more, I can assure you. You be ready to talk to me nonstop for fifteen minutes about this a week from now. Understood?"

"Yes, sir."

We operated on Mr. O'Shea, doing half the procedure this day, with the second half of the operation scheduled for six weeks hence. Connolly looked across to me as he was suturing.

"Hope you're paying good attention because you're going to do the next half by yourself. Learn all you can in the next six weeks. For Dylan O'Shea's sake."

More often than not, I was the only student to attend those Saturday morning clinics with Mr. Connolly. One-on-one. Who else could boast of such good fortune? Not many, I assure you.

And my clinics with Mr. Dylan O'Shea were equally rewarding. No, not the same Dylan O'Shea whose hemorrhoids we had removed. This Dylan O'Shea was a fellow surgeon and a friend of Mr. Connolly. They were friendly rivals too, each taking immense pride in the display of nameplates above their respective patients' beds. Rivals, sure, but they always covered for each other whenever sick, on vacation, or just indisposed. And the absent surgeon's patients were treated as if they were the working surgeon's own. They made a good team, and I was fortunate to study under both.

I particularly remember one Tuesday, not long after the incident with the other Mr. O'Shea. I had just had my red book initialed when a man came into the clinic, his left hand encased in a bloody cloth. He was being guided by one of the sisters.

"Thank God, you're still here, sir! This gentleman's had the misfortune to cut off one of his fingers, poor lad."

Sweet Jesus!

O'Shea transformed into a dervish. He seated the ashen patient on the table and unwrapped the makeshift bandage. While he was doing this, the sister was working silently behind him, preparing the instruments and medications she knew he would need.

"What the hell happened?" O'Shea asked, as he studied the remnants of the injured finger.

"I was cutting lamb chops in my bloody shop, when a bloody cat came out of nowhere and jumped up on the cutting block. Scared the living bejesus out of me, it did, and because I was distracted, I cut my bloody finger off. That's what I did. Goddamn all bloody cats to bloody hell."

Still examining and without looking up, O'Shea asked, "How would you handle this? What would you do?"

"How in the hell do I know what to do?" The man screamed at the surgeon. "That's why I'm here! I thought you would bloody well know what to do!"

"Not you, my good fellow," O'Shea replied. "I was asking Dr. Donahue for his opinion."

"Oh, I see. You scared me there for a sec. Scared me right good, you did," and he actually attempted a laugh.

I had my head almost touching O'Shea's as I studied the wound. The index finger on the left hand was severed down to the second phalange, but there was some tissue remaining below the knuckle.

"I recommend removing the remaining portion of the phalange. We should have enough tissue left to create a viable flap."

"Good, Dr. Donahue. That's exactly the course of action we'll take."

The nursing sister handed him a syringe containing a local anesthetic.

"Remember, we must anesthetize both sides of the finger as there are nerves on each lateral side." In went the needle. Then out. Then back into the other side. Relief. The man's color was still rotten, but no longer did I fear that he might pass out.

O'Shea now worked in silence, me hovering, observing his every move, while the sister handed him his instruments as he needed them, never once being told what to do next. I was impressed.

Fifteen minutes later, he stood back and studied his work. "You should do just fine," he told the man, as he bandaged what was left of the digit.

"I'm Jerry Cunningham," the man volunteered, a forlorn look on his face. "My wife is going to bloody well have my hide when she sees this." Apparently, the fear of his wife's expected wrath was too much for him to handle. "Would you be so kind as to call her, and tell her it weren't my fault?"

"Of course, I will. You give me the number and I'll take care of it. But just you remember, it could have been another appendage entirely that you whacked off; then she would have good reason to be mad." Both the nurse and I tittered at the thought. "Meanwhile, I want you to rest here for a while before we send you home." He gave Cunningham a comforting pat on the shoulder and then turned to me. "Let's be off, Doctor Donahue. We have work to do. Thanks for your help, Sister. Absolutely tops, as always!"

My other clinics were with Drs. Buckley and Magee in internal medicine, Dr. Maloney in nutrition and geriatrics, and Dr. Higgins in public health. This was challenging, interesting work, because here they dealt with the everyday ailments of everyday people. I particularly enjoyed the work-ups and treatment of the very young.

"Not much different than our companions in veterinary medicine," Dr. Buckley once observed as we examined a very emaciated and lethargic four-month-old infant. "Like the vet, we must fully depend on our wits to reach the correct diagnosis. We do not have the luxury of being able to communicate with our patients, so we must, by necessity, become Sherlock Holmes, master sleuth. Never rush an examination of an infant, Doctor Donahue. And always keep reminding yourself to be gentle. Never, never, be too proud not to call for assistance if you suspect for even a moment that your opinion could be wrong. Call in the pediatrician. Never tarry when dealing with these most precious little souls." The man was a born doctor and an excellent role model. I learned volumes from him.

Dr. O'Neill was making a name for himself in the field of public health. He, too, was a compassionate man, a crusader who shook the collective conscience of the politicians and forced them into building proper facilities to treat the mentally ill. He had done much research on depression and lectured on the subject every chance he got. He sang the praises of the new medications available to transform those tormented souls back into productive members of society. Dr. Higgins was the best champion the rural poor ever had, and he was one man who over the years truly made a difference. In many ways, he single-handedly brought Ireland into the twentieth century regarding the treatment of diseases of the mind. Lucky me. I was fortunate to study under this man for two separate clinics in the course of the year.

When I wasn't in clinics, I was in lecture halls or in labs. Only twice was my presence questioned.

The first time was during a lecture on physiology. I had arrived late to the amphitheater, and as I clumsily made my way to the nearest empty chair, Dr. Troutman, the lecturer, stopped mid-sentence, face flushed with anger.

"You, *yes, you,*" he said, finger pointing in my direction. "Just what do you think you're doing, coming in here late, and disrupting the entire proceedings?"

"I'm sorry, Doctor…"

"Don't make matters worse by spouting some lame-brained drivel. I'd throw you out, but that'll only cause an even bigger distraction. Just sit down and keep quiet. See me after class."

I have no idea what was covered that day because my mind was in a free fall, full of worry.

There is indeed a God in heaven because as I approached the lectern, Troutman was cramming his notes into his briefcase. He glowered for a moment, then forcefully snapped the case shut. "I'm late, young man, so I don't have time to listen to excuses. You might also pass the same word on to any of the other students you come across while gallivanting in the pubs. Namely, those who might not have gotten the message today." He walked away, leaving me thoroughly chastened, but elated at my good fortune of not having had him pry into my status in the medical school.

I did not attend every session in the labs when the various systems of the cadavers were being examined. These cadavers, bequeathed to the college either by the family of the deceased or by the individuals themselves, are indispensable in the education of young doctors and are handled with care, compassion, and consideration. I had studied innumerable cadavers while employed with the pathologists back in Chicago, so many of the aspects of gross anatomy and physiology were quite familiar to me. Others were not. Such as the nervous system.

It was during such a class that I put in an appearance and joined one of the several small groups working to expose the nerve bundle encased in the spinal column. A female student looked up as I melded into her group. She was plainly irritated.

"Why don't you just go somewhere else and bother another group? I've seen you come in here whenever you please and just take over. Well, not today, so scram!"

"What's the problem over there?" the proctor called out.

"Nothing, Doctor, everything's fine," one of the students answered for the group.

"Everything's not fine!" the offended female sang out, loud enough for all in the lab to hear. My newfound group now held center stage.

"Shut the bloody hell up, Sally!" snapped the one other woman in our friendly little klatch. "Everything's fine," she called out, head now buried in the long-dead spinal column exposed before her.

"Thank you," I said. "I promise only to observe, and I promise not to get in your way."

"Better not," Sally groused under her breath, a woman I'm sure who lived for the final word in any conversation.

I could feel the proctor's eyes boring into the back of my head, so I went to his desk and performed my song and dance. This is who I am. This is why I'm here. Blah, blah, blah. I could've strangled Sally. He accepted my explanation, and I thanked him for his understanding. It could have turned into a nasty situation, but again, the fates smiled upon my countenance.

* * *

The Christmas holidays came and went, but I was not able to get home. Thank God, Margaret had a few days off, and I monopolized her time. People still get sick this time of year, and oftentimes I was the only student present in the various clinics. Mr. Connolly had taken quite a liking to me and was muttering things such as wanting to get me into a fine surgery residency in England after I graduated. I had ingratiated myself with both Mr. Connolly and Mr. MacNamara, so much so that they had both allowed me to assist in operations when their schedules did not conflict with those of the senior students. I made myself available at all sorts of odd hours that year, the result being that I ended up with as much surgical experience as if I had done a legitimate surgical rotation. I had also talked my way into the same agreement with a Mr. Alfred White, a friend of Connolly and a general surgeon at Mercy Hospital, the facility next door to the Cork Infirmary. The experience was invaluable.

"You're coming along nicely, boy," Mr. Connolly said on more than one occasion. "You're a serious, fellow, Yank, and I like that. I suppose it's because you're older than the rest and you know what you want."

"Yes, sir." His praise meant the world to me. I was learning to be a good doctor under his guidance, and I was elated to know that he thought so, too. It was a great Christmas present.

In late March, I wrote to the N.B.M.E to request that I be allowed to sit the exam in Boston this coming June. My plan was to stay in the city for the remainder of the summer, and I desperately wanted to attend a clinic at Boston City Hospital under a Dr. L. Goldstein, one of the finest pediatric neurologists in America. Dr. Buckley wrote a superb letter of recommendation for me, as did Mr. Connolly. Connolly gave me a copy of his.

"As you can see, boy, I told the American that you are overall a good student, but that there are areas you need strengthening. I don't want to give the Yank pediatrician the impression you are some sort of blooming' genius, because you're not. But I told him you're a hard worker, and most important, you have a true desire to learn. OK?"

"Thank you, Mr. Connolly."

"Don't make a liar of me, boy!"

"Don't worry, sir, I won't."

One evening in early April, I was catching forty winks before heading off to the library when some cretin began pounding on my door. I awoke with a start, confused, and more than a little pissed.

"Open the bloody door, boy!"

Roger? Could it be?

Indeed it was. "Well, aren't you going to invite me in, boy?" He was grinning like a hyena and was a picture to behold. Roger was dressed to the nines. He had lost weight, his hair was trimmed, and his shoes were shined. Our Roger was the picture of a prosperous and successful physician. Not a trace of the ragamuffin I had sent off to England almost ten months earlier.

He wore a disdainful look as he surveyed my one-room kingdom. Spying the rumpled bed, he made a loud tut-tutting sound. "Sleeping, eh, Desmond?" He shook his head. "Things were certainly not like this when I was a student. Not on your life. It was study, study, study, day and night, nonstop. My, how times have changed." No longer able to keep a straight face, he started braying like a donkey.

"Blow it out your ear." I had to laugh. Still the same old clown underneath the razor-thin veneer of civilization. Still my crazy friend. "Roger, what the hell are you doing here? Did they fire you in England for incompetence?"

"Watch your tongue, boy."

"Then tell me."

"I'm getting married. I've met a girl in England, and we're going to tie the knot. I'm here to tell my master the good news."

"Me? I'm your master?"

"Not you, boy, you bloody fool! The King. My Pater. The man who's going to have the fit to end all fits, that's who!"

"I think you're bang-on the money on that score, Roger." God only knows what Daniel Connolly would do. *An Englishwoman.* I actually shuddered. "Good luck, old friend, you're sure going to need it."

"You're coming with me when I break the news."

"Oh, no, Roger, no, I'm not."

"Oh, yes you are," he mimicked. "You owe me this, along with many other favors, and I'm calling in one of my markers, boy." Roger, too, was very serious.

What could I say? "OK, I'll go and, hopefully, keep the old man from strangling you. Give me a few minutes to clean up and change clothes. Wait for me downstairs."

The scene played out every bit as badly as I imagined it would. Daniel Connolly was apoplectic, and no one could calm him down. He threw us out of the house. The mother was in tears, and the son wanted nothing more than to get rip-roaring drunk.

Roger was married one month later. I accompanied Mrs. Connolly, Liam, his mother, and Roger's sister to the English Midlands. The other sister, the one married to the Englishman, met up with us in Huddlesfield, and with a forced gaiety, we all witnessed Roger's solemn march into manhood. The father would have no part in seeing his son marry into the enemy camp. Roger was now all but disowned.

On the last day of May, I received confirmation from Dr. Goldstein in Boston that I had been accepted into the pediatrics clinic for the summer program. I was ecstatic.

It was a short-lived euphoria. The next day I received a letter from the Medical Boards offices in Texas, shattering my world into a million pieces. I couldn't believe what I was reading. This just can't be happening! Not now! The words imprinted on that page were my death warrant.

...Upon further review of your documentation in our files, we find that you are now entering your fourth year of medical college in Ireland. It would be totally counterproductive for you to repeat your third year in an American school, especially in light of the fact that you will graduate within the next twelve months with a degree recognized in every state. Our advice is that you sit the Foreign Graduates Exam at that time so that you can gain admittance into the residency program of your choice.

Because of the factors outlined above, we no longer consider you a candidate for the Cortrans Program.

Attached was a copy of the form Dr. Quinn had completed on my behalf over a year earlier. Someone had circled in bold red ink, emphasizing the screw-up of the century. Quinn had written in the blocks marked for years attended:

PRINT THE INCLUSIVE DATES THE STUDENT HAS
ATTENDED YOUR
MEDICAL SCHOOL. FROM: MONTH_*Oct*__YEAR_*1968*___
TO: MONTH_*May*__YEAR_*1969*__

Roger's blind, befuddled, buffoon had written for all the world to see that I had started school in 1968 instead of 1969. Dr. Quinn had just cost me my entrée into legitimacy.

I was beyond tears.

CHAPTER TWELVE

Simply because I felt I had no other choice, I packed and left once more for Boston. This time I sold my car and shipped all my belongings. I had no idea if or when I would ever return.

My life was in an utter shambles. In a few months I would be thirty-three, and I had a sudden vision of John Anderson, the newspaperman, almost in tears because he was a failure at the same age. I could teach John a thing or two about failure, I thought, as I sat in my airline seat heading once more to the New World.

Out of the depths I have cried unto Thee…

However, this time I was sure the Lord would not hear my prayer. *What in the name of all that is holy, am I to do?* No answer. No bolt of lightning epiphany moment. Only emptiness and despair.

My appointment to the pediatric ward at Boston City Hospital was still mine for the taking, so with no other course of action feasible, I started a summer clinic. At least working with those tiny infants and young children forced me to turn my attention outside of myself. It was good therapy.

This ward was a reflection of human nature at its worst. BCH— as the hospital was commonly referred to by its initials—was the city's medical facility which treated the indigent, and its pediatric patients invariably started life in the OB/GYN clinic which was an around-the-clock operation.

So many pitiful infants entered the world too ill to even squall at the moment of birth. They were the progeny of the addicted, and their condition was heart-rending to see. They would lie in their bassinets twitching uncontrollably, suffering the very real pain of heroin withdrawal and, of a new threat on the street, a substance called cocaine. Many others were infected with a host of diseases. The staff struggled in a Herculean effort to try to save these tiny innocents while praying for God to give them a chance at life. Most times they were successful; too many times they were not. It was a most sobering environment in which to work, yet a place where one could make a difference.

My thoughts were never far removed from my own problem. My dilemma was simple. I couldn't just write to the N.B.M.E and say that an error had been made on my application regarding the inclusive dates of my attendance at University College. *Oh, really?* Well get the registrar to send us a corrected, certified copy, along with a letter of explanation. *You mean it's that simple?* Well, blow me away, why didn't I think of that? Of course, had I been a legitimate student, the problem would have been resolved weeks ago, and there would be no need for telling you my life story today.

Summer turned to autumn, and because I had nowhere to go and nothing to do once I got there, I convinced Dr. Goldstein to keep me on stating that I would very much like to remain in America for a full year's training before returning to Ireland to finish my degree. He was impressed. He went so far as to get me an appointment in the OB/GYN clinic. I was now the busiest, non-medical student in America.

Two events transpired that year which landed me in serious trouble with the authorities. Indeed, on the second occasion, my utter stupidity landed me in jail. Were it not for the intervention of several prominent politicians and a similar number of influential physicians, I could have found myself a guest of the state for a long, long time. Thirty years later I still break into a sweat at the thought of what might have been.

The first incident involved my Aunt Mary. She had been suffering from crippling arthritis for years, but in the last few months, her pain had become severe. Noticeable clawing was taking place in her fingers, and the majority of her joints were inflamed. One day, as I was leaving to go to the hospital, I found her sobbing silently at the kitchen table. She was at the end of her rope. The medication her doctor was giving her was of no use whatsoever. I was angry that proper attention wasn't being given this gentlewoman.

"Aunt Mary, I'm going to speak to the experts at Boston City Hospital and see if they have any suggestions for a course of treatment. There are just too many new drugs available, and I'm sure one of them could help you tremendously."

"Oh, Desmond, I can't upset Dr. Murphy. He's been my doctor for years."

"Bullshit!" I hadn't intended to say that. I was exasperated, frustrated, and every other kind of *'ated,'* but I had not meant to be crude to my aunt. "I'm sorry, Aunt Mary, I didn't mean to use that kind of language. I'm sure Dr. Murphy's a fine practitioner, but chances are he's a very busy man and not familiar with the latest treatments. Let me speak to some doctors I know, and I'll tell you tonight what I find out. Hopefully, I'll have some good news." I kissed her forehead and left.

Late that night, I went into my aunt's bedroom to tell her what I had learned. She was asleep, so I gently woke her to share my news. I couldn't wait until morning because I had to be up and gone before dawn. I was going to Chicago to visit Don and Brook.

I handed her a sheet of Boston City Hospital stationery on which I had written the name of a new drug, and the dosage recommended by one of the physicians at the hospital. I had signed the paper as Dr. D. Donahue, not an uncommon practice for a third or fourth year student. I did not add the all-important M.D., however, but I did use the pen I had been given by Don and Brook the night I departed Chicago some three years earlier. Brook's parting words were funny then, but they would be anything but funny in the coming days.

"Take this to Dr. Murphy and have him give you a prescription. It's something brand new, and according to the experts, they're seeing wonderful results. Do it tomorrow. Don't wait until I get back from Chicago. Good night, Aunt Mary."

"Bless you, boy, for taking the time and trouble to think of your old aunt. God will reward you, Desmond, mark my words. He doesn't forget!"

Apparently not. I returned from Chicago to be greeted at the hospital by the local constabulary and an officious someone from an agency in Washington D.C., called Drug Enforcement.

We met in the Hospital Administrator's office. Friendly and cozy it wasn't.

The man from Washington handed me the piece of paper I had given my Aunt Mary.

"Did you write this?"

"Yes. Why?"

"We'll ask the questions, if you don't mind, *Mister Donahue*."

"Why did you write this prescription for Mary Donahue?"

"It's not a prescription."

"Oh? It certainly reads like a prescription. In fact, the patient presented it to the pharmacist as such, and said it was from her nephew, a doctor at Boston City Hospital. It's signed, 'Dr. Donahue.' and it's on official hospital letterhead."

I certainly couldn't argue with that, but I could explain. "I gave that to my aunt to give to her doctor as a recommended course of treatment for arthritis."

"So you admit to holding yourself out as a physician?"

"I do not. This was information I was given by one of the doctors at the hospital, and I wrote down his instructions for my aunt. That's all there was to it. It was never intended to be a prescription. It was information for her to present to her doctor."

For the first time, the local police representative chimed in. "Not quite. The pharmacist saw this as an attempt by someone to prescribe a controlled substance, someone who did not have a medical license, and thus no DEA control number. That's how we caught you, *Mr. Donahue*. No DEA number." Smugness was this Sherlock's middle name.

"I'm quite familiar with DEA numbers, I assure you. As I've just finished saying, this was a recommendation meant for my aunt's personal physician, unfortunately, she misunderstood my instructions and presented it to her pharmacist. This crap I didn't need. It could easily escalate into a full-blown federal offense, and if they found out I was not even a *bona fide* medical student, they could, and probably would, throw me in prison. Not jail. Prison. I was genuinely scared.

The long and the short of it was that I was able to convince the physicians I worked for that this was a stupid error on my part; and with the help of some local politicians, the state dropped the charges against me. But it was an unnerving several weeks until the judge, one Edward D'Agastino, agreed with the state and its decision not to prosecute. He admonished me to go forth and sin no more. He also let me know that if my name came before him again, as he so succinctly put it, no more "Mister Nice Guy."

Aunt Mary thought it was all her fault. She had misunderstood me that night when I had awoken her, and she had thought I was giving her a prescription to take to her pharmacist. She was truly an innocent. On this matter, so was I.

Two months later, I found myself before D'Agastino again and he was out for blood.

I was an unwitting lightning rod for trouble that year.

The second incident was far more serious and actually landed me in jail.

An acquaintance from Cork, John Byrne, now graduated and working in an internship in London, wrote to ask for help in garnering information on a particular residency program in Maine. It was a three-year course in general medicine, and John expressed a keen interest in practicing in America. In fact, he had already sat and passed the Foreign Graduates Exam. Because he could not afford the $150 necessary to physically register and pick up his certificate, it remained unissued.

This was early May, and all such residencies had been spoken for months ago. However, as fate would have it, a physician accepted at the Maine Medical Center had been forced to bow out, and the hospital, desperate for someone to take his place, advertised in the medical journals that the position was again open and welcomed inquiries. John saw this in England and contacted me.

On his behalf, I wrote for and received the application forms. Because time was of the essence, I filled them out, signed John's name, wrote a check on my personal account for the accompanying fee of $120, and sent the package off. I had also paid for and received his Foreign Medical Graduate's diploma, a copy of which was duly enclosed.

Sometime in the middle of June, I was asked to come up to Maine on behalf of John Byrne. I was in for the surprise of my life.

I had been asked to bring my passport, and I complied, thinking nothing of it. I met with a Dr. Kokiel and a Dr. Gibbons, along with state and local law enforcement officials, plus two representatives from the Immigration and Naturalization Service. No one smiled. The first order of business called for me to surrender my passport.

"Mr. Donahue, you have been charged with impersonating a physician, namely, one John Byrne, currently practicing in England," said the representative of the State of Maine. Very serious stuff.

"That's not true!" I replied, full of indignation. "I filled out the forms you're obviously referring to, but only at the request of Dr. Byrne, and I forwarded everything to this hospital on his behalf."

"We've spoken to Dr. Byrne, and that's not what he told us. In fact, he has accepted an appointment in Canada, and told us he had no intention of coming to Maine. Nevertheless, we traced you from the personal check you sent. Same handwriting for both Dr. Byrne and Mr. Desmond Donahue." He looked at me as if he were inspecting a worm. "We then contacted the medical college in Cork, and wonder of wonders, they have no record of you ever being there! Yet here you stand, telling everybody at Boston City Hospital that you are a student from Ireland. On a sabbatical," he added, the words dripping with sarcasm. He paused, reveling in his moment of glory, then continued in a voice aching for the theater. "It's our opinion, Mr. Donahue, that it was your intention to assume this other man's identity for the sole purpose of illegally practicing medicine in this country. That is something we do not take kindly to. Our laws are very specific as to the penalties for such crimes, and you can expect to be prosecuted to the fullest extent of those laws."

"This just isn't true." My mind refused to function. Why in the name of God had Byrne not come forward and told them that I was acting on his behalf? Why did he tell them that he was going to Canada, and why didn't he tell me of his change of plans? Shit! I could very easily be going to prison on this one. And for a long time, if this group were to be believed. I was now very, very scared.

I scrambled in search of an opening. *Anything.* Then, inspiration. "Call Dr. Beckler. He's the president of University College. He'll vouch for me."

Glances all around. This was definitely a new wrinkle. Their faces no longer reflected smug certitude.

Dr. Kokiel spoke. "We will in all likelihood do just that, Mr. Donahue, but in our own good time. Meanwhile, you are to be escorted to the local jail until we can figure out our next step."

I was led away by a uniformed officer and incarcerated for the next twenty-four hours. Then it was back to the hospital. I was kept outside the conference room for almost half an hour.

The same group was assembled, only this time they were huddled around the huge, oak conference table, staring intently at a speakerphone anchored to its center.

"Dr. Beckler, this is Dr. Gibbons. Can you hear me all right?"

"I can indeed. You sound fine, thank you." Dr. Beckler could have been next door. "Tell me, is Desmond Donahue there? Can he hear me?"

"I'm here, Dr. Beckler," I answered, without waiting for permission. This man was my last hope. I prayed: *Dear God, guide him to say the right thing.*

"Desmond, these gentlemen have told me their side of a rather bizarre tale. Now, I want you to briefly tell me yours. Just the facts, boy."

And that's what I did. I gave him the facts.

There was silence on both sides of the Atlantic while Dr. Beckler digested what I told him.

"Gentlemen, can you still hear me?"

"Loud and clear, Dr. Beckler," replied Dr. Gibbons.

"Look, I know Desmond quite well, and if he says he was acting in good faith on behalf of Dr. Byrne, then I believe him. I think somehow communication lines broke down, and Desmond indeed was not apprised of Byrne's change in plans." He paused for a moment, and we all sat stock-still, eyes riveted on that electrical umbilicus connecting two continents.

"Here's my proposal," Beckler finally said. "Clear up this misunderstanding as soon as possible and send Desmond back here to Cork. Desmond, are you listening?"

"Yes, Doctor."

"Good. How does that sound? You come back here, and we will look into your status with the university."

"I'll come as soon as I can, Doctor."

"Well, that should settle it then, gentlemen. Desmond acted naively, but not criminally. I can vouch for him in that regard. That's all I can say. If you need more from me, just call. Good day, gentlemen." Beckler broke the connection.

The prisoner was escorted back out to the hall and remained there for almost an hour while his fate was being decided.

"You are free to return to Boston, Mr. Donahue, but stay away from the hospital and all clinics associated with any medical facility. Do I make myself clear?" This was the State of Maine's representative talking. Unctuous bureaucrat that he was.

"Very clear, sir."

"You will appear in court in Summerville. I suggest you retain counsel and do so with all dispatch. Your passport will be held by Immigration in Boston until after the proceedings."

I heeded his advice and retained counsel. The lawyer was fast, and he was good. He secured letters of commendation for me from Dr. Beckler and from several doctors in Boston. He also solicited references from some influential politicians, character references that definitely saved the day.

Once again I stood before Judge D'Agastino. This was one angry jurist. He listened to all of the testimony, and then gave me a chance to explain my side. He painstakingly read the character references then retired to chambers to make his decision. He was gone a full hour.

"Mr. Donahue, this is my decision. After weighing the evidence, I reluctantly find it in my heart to give you the benefit of the doubt. Do not think for one moment that I did not struggle in coming to this conclusion. The pessimistic, dark side of my nature wanted to give you two years, while the kinder, gentler side reasoned that you just might be the dupe you say you are." He gathered his robes regally about himself. "I will withhold adjudication for one year. If in that time you have not gotten into further trouble, the record will be expunged. I pray I've made the right decision." He paused to glower down at me, barely concealing his contempt. "My advice to you is simply get out of town and don't come back. Ever. Return to Ireland, and see if you can salvage something of your life."

Boom! Down came his gavel as his angry eyes focused on my attorney. "Your client will pay for the court's valuable time, Counselor. See the clerk before leaving the building." His eyes fell on the mound of files before him. "Next case."

I took the judge's advice. Within a week I had retrieved my passport, bade goodbye to a tearful Aunt Mary, and returned to Cork. It was now August 1972, and I paused to take stock of my life. I was a rudderless boat adrift in a gathering tempest and out of sight of land. I had filled my days and nights with endless work these past three years, and for what? I had attended more clinics than most medical school graduates had, yet at the end of the day I had nothing to show for it.

Something had to give, and soon. My savings were all but gone; my past was a littered wasteland, and reality screamed out to me that any kind of a future in medicine was simply nonexistent.

*   *   *

I made my way back to Ireland where Dr. Beckler informed me that Dean Standiford had contacted all the physicians who had admitted me to their clinics and had told them in concrete terms to have nothing more to do with me. No more writing letters on my behalf, no more allowing me into their clinics. Indeed, Standiford informed them all that I was an impostor, and that the authorities should be contacted immediately if I was brazen enough to show my face. Beckler broadly hinted that Standiford had spoken to John Byrne about my true status with the university. Now, it was beginning to make sense. It certainly explained John's sudden abandonment of me.

I piddled away the next couple of weeks visiting family and friends and even managed a reunion with Margaret for a long weekend in Dublin. I said nothing to her about my troubles, and she didn't ask too many questions as to how my studies were progressing. I had written faithfully twice a week while in America, with the added luxury of a phone call on the average of once every three weeks. She had not been as committed to pen and paper as I was, but

I shrugged it off with the excuse that she was a very busy bee, pollinating fertile European minds as to the wonders of Ireland. I was as much in love as ever and hoped the feeling was mutual. Our first weekend together erased any doubts. Actions speak louder than words. So at least that one aspect of my life seemed solid. But for how long? I was beginning to have fears that Margaret would soon find out that all was not well in paradise, and then would abandon me the moment the truth were known.

I had to do something and fast.

* * *

The following Sunday Roger arrived back in Cork. By now he had an infant daughter and all the accompanying responsibilities of fatherhood.

He was aware of my troubles, yet strangely, when I broached the subject later that evening, he brushed the matter aside with a cavalier wave of his hand. "Let's not talk about that for the moment, Desmond." He was a man in motion, even while seated at dinner. Something was on his mind.

"Do you have a problem you'd like to talk about?" I asked, somewhat peeved, yet wondering if there was something amiss at home. His wife and child were still in England, staying with her parents until Roger had a place for them to live.

"A problem?" he repeated, then shook his head. "Quite the opposite. In fact, rather than try to explain what's on my mind, let me show you."

I made a show of preparing to pay the check so we could leave.

"No, not tonight. Tomorrow will be soon enough. In fact, I'll pick you up at eight o'clock, and we'll take a little drive. You'll just have to stay in suspense until then."

Roger, who had never been on time for anything in his life, was uncharacteristically true to his word, and we headed out of the parking lot of The Shamrock Inn bang on the appointed hour.

"Have you eaten, boy?"

"I have," I replied. "Can you tell me where we're going?"

"Athlone, County Westmeath."

"What, pray tell, is there?" Athlone was definitely not the center of the universe.

"You'll see," he replied, enjoying the prospect of having me dangling from his hook. "Meanwhile, tell me about your problems."

And that's exactly what I did. For the next two hours, I recounted the past year in detail and ended with an observation that my future was in grave peril.

"We'll see." By now Roger had a sheet of paper laid out on the steering wheel and was trying to read and drive at the same time. We were in his father's Mercedes, so the trip had been comfortable despite the fact that some of the worst roads in Ireland had passed beneath our wheels. He slowed down at a graveled driveway and swung the big car off the highway. Crawling along now, we drove about a hundred yards up to the porticoed entrance of a beautiful, three-story Georgian mansion. Roger cut the engine and turned to me, all smiles. "Let's take a look inside, shall we, Guv'ner?" He fumbled in his jacket pocket and produced a key big enough to fill the lock of some medieval castle. "Come, boy, follow me."

The place was huge. The first floor held three sitting rooms and two reception parlors, a gargantuan formal dining room, and a kitchen that would put to shame one found in any four-star restaurant. Every room came with its own magnificent marble fireplace. All the ceilings were fifteen feet high, inlaid with the intricate plasterwork of artisans long-dead, while the floors were solid oak parquet. This was a mansion of the first order, and I was speechless as we wandered from room to room.

At the far end of the main hallway, we encountered a locked door.

"Not to worry," Roger said. "We'll go in there from the outside entrance when we finish here." He set a course toward the grand staircase, and we proceeded to the next floor. Here, I discovered six spacious bedrooms, three with adjoining baths. And at the end of the hall, the master's suite, replete with a sumptuous bathroom, all gleaming marble and tile. This wasn't a mansion; it was a full-blown palace. And each room on this floor also came with its own fireplace. Then up we trekked to the third floor. Not as generously proportioned as the lower two, but nothing shabby here, either. These rooms were meant for the household staff, and, again, all had fireplaces.

"Notice the place has steam heating as well," Roger pointed out as we made our way back down to the main hall. Our footsteps echoed throughout the manse, and our voices carried to every room. There were drapes on the windows, but other than that, the house was devoid of furnishings. However, it had been meticulously maintained, and was in move-in condition.

"Don't tell me," I laughed at Roger.

"Then I won't," he replied, the same silly grin still on his face. "Come!" He led us outside and around to a separate, but smaller entrance by the side of the house. He fished out a second key and opened the door.

We entered a well-laid-out, thoroughly modern medical clinic of gleaming stainless and chrome. There were three examining rooms, a small x-ray department, and a bright, airy reception area. I shook my head in wonderment.

"Well, what do you think? Your honest opinion, Desmond."

"What gives, Roger?

"This place belongs to the Eastern Health Board," he replied, referring to one of three governmental medical regions. "The last doctor retired, and I've been offered the job."

"Surely you jest."

He crossed his heart like a little schoolboy "...And hope to die," he said, looking around as if surveying a kingdom. "It's all true, Desmond. The house and ten acres of grounds goes to the doctor, paid for by the government. This is all mine for as long as I stay. There are two other outlying clinics I'd be responsible for, but the really great part is that I can still have a private practice to supplement whatever the clinics generate. Desmond, it's a bloody gold mine!"

"But why you? There must be a hundred doctors who would kill to get this appointment."

"Too bloody true, boy!" He then laughed at the obvious. "I heard about this through some well-placed political contacts."

"I'm impressed, Roger, all the way down to my bloody shoes. So, tell me, is it a done deal?"

"I have to let them know by three o'clock tomorrow. But before I make up my mind, I want to take a run out and see the other two clinics."

Five minutes later we were off to the first clinic situated in Dunwoody, some fifteen miles away. We spent about forty minutes inspecting the facility, then headed in the other direction towards Dublin to take a look at the clinic in Ballyglenn. Then, it was off to the capital to spend the night.

"What about your wife?" I asked, as we drove. Rain had started pouring down in buckets, reducing our progress to a crawl. But Roger didn't seem to mind. Usually, he's the most impatient driver. Dangerous is a more fitting description and, more often than not, he scares the bejesus out of me. It's never fun being with Roger when he's behind the wheel, but today he was a regular gentleman of the roadways.

Roger shrugged, then turned full-face toward me. "Her attitude is if I like it, then she likes it. And I bloody well love it!"

Mr. Practical then piped up to add his two cents worth. "What about furniture?" I asked, remembering those acres of empty rooms.

Roger just laughed. "That cottage is definitely going to take a pound or two to furnish," he admitted, "but Connie will enjoy the process. I'm sure I can get a loan from my parents, but if that doesn't work, well, any bank would fall all over themselves to extend me credit. Hell, it's mine for the bloody asking. Just tell any banker you're a doctor, and he'll throw all the money he can at you." He shook his head. "Money's no problem. I'm going to be rich as the devil in no time, Desmond. As I said before, the entire setup is a bloody gold mine!"

"So you've made up your mind?

"What would you say?"

I laughed. Roger was everything I wanted to be. Correction. Not quite everything. However, he was a physician, married to a fine woman, and now had a little daughter. In spite of himself, he was well on the road to success. And truth to tell, I was jealous. "Roger, I wouldn't think twice. I would tell them long before three o'clock tomorrow that they have their man." I then asked, "When would you have to start?"

"The first of October. Ten days from now."

"Grab it with both hands and both feet. An opportunity like this will never come your way again."

He let out a deep sigh as we entered the driveway of one of Dublin's finest hotels. "You're right, of course. I'm going to tell them yes first thing in the morning." A doorman had materialized and stood expectantly under an open umbrella, waiting for Roger to release his door latch. Roger ignored the man.

"There's just one other thing."

"Yes?" With Roger, it was always one other thing.

"I need to hire another doctor. I'll need someone I can trust."

"You shouldn't have too hard a time there," I assured him.

"The man I have in mind is the man I'm talking to right this moment."

"Roger, I'm bloody well finished! It's over for me, I'm afraid." Hadn't he understood a goddamn thing I had told him during our drive this morning?

"Bullshit, boy! You know more medicine than I ever will. Hell, you know as much as any graduate I've met and, more importantly, you really care about being a doctor." He was now imploring me, oblivious of the doorman's insistent rapping on the window and the line of cars honking their horns behind us.

"Desmond, I'll fix everything. I'll get you all the diplomas and documentation you need. Just say, yes. I need you. You're the only soul I trust."

I could barely breathe. My heart was hammering itself to pieces inside my chest. *Was it possible? Could we pull it off? Was I finally going to become a doctor? Sweet God in heaven, what do I say?* The hotel's driveway was now turning into a camp for an angry, sodden mob. Horns were blaring nonstop, and people were hurling invectives at the two inconsiderate jerks enthroned in their metallic cocoon.

"Yes, yes, a thousand times, yes!"

"Good man, Desmond. I knew I could count on you." Tears welled in his eyes. "We'll be the best damned partners ever, and we'll make a fortune to boot! What more is there, boy? I ask you, what more is there?"

CHAPTER THIRTEEN

"**Doctor Donahue, will** you be covering the clinic tomorrow in Ballyglenn?" Sister Kathleen McGovern, our nurse, asked over the phone, something she did faithfully the day before one of us arrived so that she would not have to face any surprises.

"I'll be there at nine o'clock sharp. How does it look?"

"Not too bad. We have seven scheduled, but who knows how many walk-ins will show up. Doctor Connolly always gets so riled up when they traipse in without an appointment."

"And I'm such a pushover."

"Remember, you said it, not me. See you tomorrow, Doctor."

Three months had passed since that momentous day in the hotel driveway. And true to his word, Roger had become the maker of miracles. He appeared one day while Connie and I were emptying ten thousand moving boxes.

"Desmond, can you come into the clinic for a tick? Got something to show you."

"Don't you keep him long, Roger Connolly," Connie called out, sweeping her hair out of her face. "If it wasn't for Desmond, we wouldn't get a blessed thing done around here!"

"Ta, da!" Roger held up a document for me to see. Could it be? Holy Mother of God, it was! I stood face-to-face with a diploma attesting the fact that one Desmond Donahue had graduated from University College, School of Medicine, Cork, on June 23, 1971. I took it from his hands and just stared.

"How did you do it, Roger?" I whispered. "It's bloody perfect!"

"Let's just say that I have my ways and leave it at that. You're now officially a doctor, and it's time for you to start earning your keep." He was fully savoring the moment as much as I was. "We show you graduated with me, and we can say you spent the last year doing an internship in Boston. It works, boy! It bloody well works!"

"Roger, I need Desmond back this very instant." The lady of the manor sounded peeved. I gave him a thumbs up and raced back to the main hall to do the mistress' bidding. I was floating on air.

Doctor Roger Connolly placed a notice in the newspaper explaining that all three clinics would be open on September 1. It clearly showed the office hours for each location and suggested that patients should make appointments and not just appear on our doorstep. Emergencies excepted. Fat chance. Most people didn't get a newspaper, and the majority of households in the region certainly didn't have telephones. I could not have cared less. I was going to be practicing medicine.

What heady times they were. The days we were in Athlone, Roger ánd I would march from the main house and into the clinic at nine o'clock sharp. After greeting our staff of three, we would commence to divvy up the patient load. We were a good team, and I like to think we gave excellent care to those who sought our help. I confess, I had some serious misgivings about working with Roger, but he surprised me. He gave each patient his undivided attention and never seemed to rush through a consultation. He was not happy to see walk-ins, but he would first treat the patients and then remind them that an appointment would cut down on the waiting time for all concerned. Most had nothing to rush home to, and our waiting room was full of the latest periodicals. Of course, they would tell Roger what he wanted to hear, and then return for follow-up visits at their convenience, not his.

Roger had insisted that I live with them in the mansion.

"What will we do with all this space, Desmond, for just two-and a-half people? It's insanity that you would think about renting an apartment or even a house, somewhere."

However, I wasn't convinced. No matter how big a home, when you have someone other than family in residence, both parties lose their sense of privacy. It can lead to a severe case of frayed nerves and, quite possibly, a loss of friendship.

But it was Connie, who through her genuine sincerity, persuaded me to at least give it a try.

"Desmond, if it proves to be an inconvenience to me, I promise, I'll speak up and tell you. Likewise, I would want you to do the same. Believe me, if you decide you want your own place, I won't be insulted. But give it a try. Please?"

I did. The arrangement continued harmoniously for quite some time. It was only much later that conditions became untenable. By then, Roger was on the skids. His wife and daughter had left him, returning to England, where Connie had reluctantly filed for divorce. But I'm getting ahead of myself.

Connie loved her home and constantly fretted over getting everything just right. In those first few weeks, she must have purchased every interior decorating magazine ever printed, then spent hours cutting, clipping, sketching, and pasting, until one day she announced the decorating was to begin. She had rented a minimal amount of furniture when the family first moved in, but now, a whole houseful of new and very expensive pieces began to arrive.

The Lady of the Manor informed Roger and Desmond that their presence was not wanted during this time, so many an evening we departed right after work and found solace in the area's pubs. Some evenings we would venture as far away as Dublin and return in the wee hours. We would be back on the job after only a few hours of sleep, moving a little slower than normal, but functioning, nonetheless. To repeat. Those were heady days.

I should mention that Connie had hired a live-in nanny to help with Sally. This sweet child was certainly not being abandoned by her mother, but Connie was not well. She had suffered most of her life from diverticulitis, a congenital, deteriorating disease, often excruciatingly painful. The prognosis for most patients is not encouraging, and more often than not, treatment requires the intervention of a surgeon resulting in the installation of a permanent colostomy. Connie was very much aware of this, and I have to say I truly admired her stoic acceptance of what would in all likelihood be inevitable. She had been warned repeatedly that pregnancy should be avoided, but she made her decision to have a child knowing the risks. Begrudgingly, she hired an English nanny, and the two women doted on the happily receptive Sally.

As Roger had prophesied, the money started pouring in. One of the nurses took on the task of processing the mountain of paperwork our success was generating. Remember, we had three clinics, and our labors soon buried us under an avalanche of government and private insurance forms. Many an evening Roger and I would toil long after clinic hours filling out these forms. We realized the importance of doing it right the first time because a form sent back for missing information would mean no money for weeks, maybe months, and that is just not good business. This is one aspect of medicine not covered in school, and it should be. Apparently, the problem is universal.

Roger was a very generous employer. In no time I was doing very well, and I was able to start saving money for the expressed purpose of saving. All my life money had been parked temporarily in a bank only to be spent immediately on the necessities of life. Now, with some of my newfound wealth, I purchased a new car. Another Ford Escort, this time white. Roger tried to talk me into something more substantial, as he put it, but I was not to be swayed. Ireland's roads were designed with the Escort in mind. Or so I told myself. My subconscious cautioned getting an Escort so as not draw undue attention to yours truly.

Our circle of friends rapidly expanded to include a number of professional people from Dublin, and we would spend many a happy, carefree weekend in their company. One was an attorney named Eddy Regan. Eddy had a busy law practice and was highly regarded in legal circles. He was a fun-loving man, blessed with the capacity to work hard and to play harder. And Eddy wrote the book on the play harder part. And a true rival to Roger, and probably more attached to the bottle—if that's possible. But where Roger had a tendency to turn mean and surly under the influence, Eddy was ever the gentleman. Sadly, both met the same untimely end because of the irresistible hold alcohol exercised over their lives.

*   *   *

New Year brought Margaret for ten days, and she oohed and aahed appropriately during the grand tour of the mansion. She and Connie hit it off immediately, and within minutes, were acting like long-lost friends. Margaret surprised me with the interest she took in little Sally. She would spend long stretches with that baby, perfectly content to be alone with her. There were times I would find her in the nursery, seated quietly, staring rapturously at the little sleeping angel.

Feeling my presence, she would turn and smile, then direct her attention back to Sally.

"Could you see one of your own?" I asked, finding her crib-side early one morning changing the baby before the rest of the household had arisen.

"In a heartbeat," she replied, her face positively radiant.

"Maybe we should give it some thought, Margaret." My heart was pounding with the realization of what I was suggesting.

She finished securing the new diaper with two of those monster safety pins, then turned to face me. "Well, maybe we should, Desmond." Clean and comfortable once more, Sally had promptly fallen back to sleep. Margaret took my arm and steered me out of the room, whispering, "I feel domestic this morning, lover boy! Come, I'll whip us up a smashing big breakfast."

Shortly after Margaret left for Paris, Roger's parents came. The days leading up to this historical event had Connie on pins and needles. She had never met Mr. Connolly, but she was well aware of his feelings about the English in general and her in particular. One would have thought that with an English wife Roger would have toned down his vitriolic tirades against the Crown. Not so. However, he had the decency to keep his opinions to himself when around his wife—at least in the beginning. Sadly, as their relationship soured, Roger would lash out and accuse her of being a British spy sent to keep an eye on him because of his outspoken support of the IRA. Stupid as it sounds, Roger was serious. Such was the extent of his alcohol induced paranoia. Rare now was the day Roger drew a sober breath.

Roger's mother must have had a long talk with her husband because the man did keep a civil tongue in his head when introduced to his daughter-in-law and granddaughter. Mrs. Connolly more than made up for his aloofness by letting Connie know she considered Roger the luckiest man alive to have found someone who would put up with his hijinks.

On the morning of the third day, we were all having breakfast when the newsreader on television announced there had been a terrible explosion in the Catholic enclave of Belfast. He said that at least a score were dead, and twice that number severely injured. The deed was blamed on Protestant extremists.

Roger and his father exchanged looks, their faces clouding with anger. Without a word spoken, they got up from the table and went into another room. Mrs. Connolly turned deathly white.

"I fear those two are going to do something sinful. I know that look: I've seen it all my life! Oh, sweet Mother of God, what's going to become of Ireland?"

Roger and his father left an hour later, Roger carrying his medical bag. He paused to speak to me.

"I don't know how long we'll be gone. Take care of the clinics as best you can. I suspect I'll be back in three or four days, but I can't make any promises."

I just nodded.

The father then added his two cents in a voice oozing with sarcasm. "Take care of the women, Desmond." Translation: *You stay safe and warm out of harm's way, boy, while we patriots sally forth to avenge our fallen comrades.*

"Leave Desmond the hell alone!" Roger screamed at his father. We were all speechless. He actually grabbed the old man by his collar and roughly propelled him through the front door causing him to stumble and nearly fall face-first onto the flagstones. Roger's face was purple. "Keep your goddamn trap closed!" we heard him yell as the door slammed shut.

Less than twenty-four hours later, the television gave us the answer we were all expecting. Tit for tat.

A hotel in a Belfast Protestant neighborhood had just been bombed with a large loss of life. Stay tuned for further details.

Daniel and Roger Connolly returned five days later. Both looked exhausted, but could not hide the look of satisfaction on their faces. Roger's parents cut short their visit and returned to Cork the next day.

Roger never said a word as to where they went and what they did. To this day, I could not say, but I know that it involved more than just ministering to the dead and dying. This same behavior was repeated several times over the next couple of years, and if Roger were alive today, it would be an ongoing affair. And Ireland sees itself as the most Christian country in the Western World.

As the year unfolded, we settled into a comfortable routine. The clinics were doing well. The practice allowed us to see private patients, and at the end of any particularly busy day, I would pause to wonder how the lone doctor before us had been able to keep up with the workload. He must have been cast of iron.

In June, the four of us trooped down to Cork to attend Margaret's cousin's wedding. I had been apprehensive about this trip. I would obviously meet up with lots of people I knew from the old days, and they would want to know what I was up to.

I'm a doctor, don't you know? Oh, yes, I had Roger administer the Hippocratic Oath, so everything's on the up-and-up. What? Of course I didn't go to medical school. Total waste of bloody time and, anyway, the patients certainly don't question me on such a little technicality.

I was nervous. My *modus operandi* called for me keeping a very low profile, but unfortunately, Margaret's mother had other ideas. During the reception, the woman dragged Margaret and me from table to table and introduced us to every breathing soul.

"Aren't they just the perfect couple?" she crowed at least a hundred times to her captive audiences. "I pray every day that they're the next ones we hear wedding bells for. It's long past time for this poor old widow to have a grandchild before God calls her home."

Poor old widow? The woman was now in her early fifties, healthy as a horse and still a ravishing beauty in her own right. We were mortified, but Mrs. Kerrigan was on a crusade. These two children have dithered long enough. *Get married! Do you hear me?* I don't care if my shenanigans are upstaging the bride and groom. I will be heard!

Thank God, people were polite and more than slightly amused. They agreed with her wholeheartedly. Another wedding? Great. That translates to mean another party. Heck, yes. Perfect couple. A match made in heaven. Bottoms up! Cheers!

As for me, when anyone asked what I was doing with myself these days, I mumbled that I had been studying in America. No definite plans. Good to see you again. You're looking good, too. And move on. Fast. Luckily, I survived, with no one the wiser, including Doctor Beckler, Dean Standiford, and several physicians with whom I had attended clinics. This was the social event of the year, and everybody who was anybody was here. I couldn't wait to get out of town and back to the obscurity of Athlone.

*   *   *

Roger and I made every effort to attend as many of the monthly County Medical Society meetings as possible. Usually, there would be an interesting and informative guest speaker. New information on any aspect of medicine was something I craved, and often I would be the only person present taking notes. Roger, on the other hand, saw these professional get-togethers as an excuse to party. The meetings were always well-attended, and Roger and I were treated with individual consideration by all of the specialists. None looked down on us as being merely general practitioners.

In Ireland, a GP does not have admitting privileges to the hospitals; thus, those cases requiring admittance we refer to specialists. And because we were the government's doctors for the region, we saw a lot of patients. Patients whose fees were guaranteed. The specialists were all well-aware of this economic fact of life. They also knew we saw a sizable number of private patients as well, their insurance companies paying the freight. We were a source of income, a source to be stroked. Ergo, we were treated as equals in an extremely hierarchical society. These Pooh-Bahs invited us to many posh social gatherings, and we in turn often accepted.

*   *   *

If I had to pinpoint the exact date things began to unravel, it would be September 1, 1973.

Two major events had taken place in Roger's life just prior. In late June, his father was hospitalized following a severe emphysema attack. He quickly turned sour and died within the week. Roger stayed drunk from the moment he got the news until well after the funeral. He was a basket case.

In August, his wife's condition deteriorated due to the terrible strain she found herself under trying to cope with Roger. She had to be rushed to the hospital in the middle of the night, and the next day underwent major surgery to remove a section of bowel, necessitating a permanent colostomy. She sank into a severe state of depression. A cruel blow for any thirty-one-year-old woman to have to endure. And Roger provided her no solace whatsoever. Thank God for the visiting nurses who came daily to aid in her recovery and to teach Connie how to live with and care for the appliance she would have to wear until the day she died.

And because Roger was damn-near non-functional, the load of the practice fell squarely on me. I was covering all three clinics, and there were weeks on end where I would be working sixteen hours a day. I became resentful.

"You and I need to talk, Roger. Things can't go on this way much longer."

It was a Sunday morning, and Roger hadn't shaved or taken a shower in a week. He looked and smelled every inch a derelict.

"Don't bother me, boy! Leave me the hell alone!"

"That's what I'm talking about, you goddamn fool! I'm at my wits end, and I just bloody well will leave you alone. You've all but abandoned your wife and child, you selfish son of a bitch," I yelled back, venting my full fury. "Connie should be getting your undivided attention, not to mention your daughter, but all you can think about is your next goddamn swallow of gin."

That's none of your business," he replied in a petulant voice. "Stay out of family matters, Desmond. Just butt out. It's none of your business," he repeated, the effort of coherent thought taxing his addled brain to the limit.

"I am making it my business, Doctor Connolly," I countered, almost formally. I lowered my voice to a normal pitch and gave him an ultimatum. "If you aren't cleaned up and dressed by the end of the day, I'm leaving. I mean it Roger. I don't know where I'll go, but anything will be better than this. You're a drunken misfit, boy, and you need help." Strong stuff, but I meant every single word.

Roger just stared at me, his face all puffy and misshapen. He looked like a bloated tramp sitting in his overstuffed chair, dressed in soiled pajamas and a ratty Terrycloth robe. A has-been king, lording over a has-been kingdom. He was disgusting. Then, he started to cry.

"You can't leave, Desmond," he sobbed. "I need you. I won't survive without you!"

"Too bloody right, Roger. You'll be on the streets within a month and dead a month after that. Guaranteed. But before that happens, your wife will have left you. Sick as she is, she can't survive here, to say nothing of little Sally. I give you eight weeks, tops. You're a selfish, drunken prick, Roger Connolly." There was nothing left to say. As I turned to leave, I saw Connie, standing in the doorway, pale, clutching the jamb to keep from falling. How long had she been there, and how much had she heard?

She looked at her wreck of a husband, then turned her eyes to me. She nodded, the effort almost beyond her physical capacity. "I concur with everything you've just said, Desmond, and I thank you for having had the courage to say it."

And Roger wailed all the louder. We left him there. I helped Connie back to her bed. I could have throttled Roger for what he was doing to his wife and child.

I left the house and didn't return for hours. I had a full plate of problems to straighten out in my own mind. Such as, what would I do if indeed Roger proved to be beyond salvation? I really didn't want to think about it.

I returned to find Roger seated at the kitchen table nursing a cup of cold tea and staring into the ether. He turned as I entered the room. He was cleaned and dressed, and although haggard beyond words, stone-cold sober. For the first time in weeks. The trembling in his hands was noticeable.

"I'm sorry, Desmond. I truly am. I promise to get myself together. No more drink. I swear on my father's grave, God rest his soul."

"Roger, make the promise to Connie. She's the one who needs to hear those words. I'm glad you're going to get yourself together, but your wife needs to know. Go upstairs and tell her, and at the same time apologize for the grief you've caused. Good night." I left for my room. I was beat. Of course, I didn't sleep a wink that night. The whole situation was a veritable time bomb: the clock now activated, ticking its maniacal, yet inevitable warning of the destruction sure to follow.

True to his word, Roger was fully functional two days later and immersed himself in his work. He kept his promise and didn't touch a drop of alcohol. Within a couple of weeks, he had regained his color, and his brain appeared to be banging away on all eight cylinders. A testament to the healing power of the body. Just maybe this was the turning point. I could only hope and pray.

At the end of November, I took five days off and went home. My mother had written to tell me: "your father seems to be doing poorly, but the stubborn old fool won't go and see a doctor. I need you to talk some sense into his noggin."

My parents now believed I was a doctor, and the pride they felt was thick enough to cut with a knife. And through some sort of divine intervention, this now made me an expert on everything. You want to know about relativity and the space-time-continuum? Hells bells, ask Desmond. How do you send a man to the moon, you ask? Pull up a chair and Desmond will explain. And, of course, I was always being bombarded with medical questions. I checked my father as thoroughly as he would allow and concluded he was simply getting old. After a lifetime of alcohol abuse, his liver was noticeably hardened upon palpation. So, what else was new? The man was sixty-five. He was certainly not going to stop drinking because I commanded it. I suggested he slow down, told him to start taking vitamins, and to eat smaller, but more frequent meals. He was as skinny as a rail, but then again, he had never been a bruiser. Chances were the old curmudgeon would outlast us all. Arthur Donahue was certainly mean enough to do just that. I allayed my mother's fears by telling her so.

I returned to find Roger still on the wagon and treating his wife with a modicum of kindness. Sally was even abandoning the reserve she displayed while around her father, and that in itself was heartwarming to observe. She was a precious child, and could spend hours with her dolls and other toys, seemingly content just to be in her own company. There were a few other children she would play with on occasion, but they would have to be driven over to the castle. Not always an easy thing to do. Her mother and nanny did all they could to make sure she didn't develop into a reclusive child, and, I must say, she certainly seemed normal in every respect.

I had high hopes for the coming year. At the top of my wish list was the hope that Margaret would consent to marriage. She had told me on many occasions that she would not get married in the Church, and I was uncomfortably resigned to this fact. How would I explain this to my parents? That bridge I would have to cross alone.

My future as a physician in Ireland depended entirely on Roger. If he kept up his good behavior, then that future looked secure. However, I had the nagging feeling all was not as tranquil in paradise as it appeared.

The New Year marked the beginning of a long and bitter slide into chaos and despair. How fortunate none of us knows what the future holds. My personal grief, soon to come, I would not wish upon another living soul. The scars from that time are still indelibly etched on my psyche to this day.

CHAPTER FOURTEEN

I **won't indulge** in a blow-by-blow description of Roger's slide into hell. Allow me a paragraph or two, then I'll move on.

By the end of spring, he had taken up full-time residency inside the gin bottle. Rare was the day he attended any of the clinics, and his wife was fast-approaching the limits of her endurance—until he finally pushed her over the edge.

About ten o'clock one night in early May, two men appeared at the house with a curt summons for Roger to accompany them to parts unknown. Connie argued, and then pleaded with him to stay; but he roughly pushed her aside, and without a word to either of us, left in the pouring rain flanked by the messengers from the IRA. When the door slammed shut, Connie turned to me, an almost serene look blanketing her face.

"Goodbye, Desmond. I'm leaving for England first thing in the morning. Please tell Roger to call Eddy Regan. I will have my solicitor in England communicate through Eddy. I'm sorry, Desmond, I truly am." She smiled weakly. "You've been a dear friend, but I'm in a no-win situation. My advice to you is to get out while you still can because he'll destroy you, too. Roger can't be saved; he's out of control." She squeezed my hand, and then gave me a kiss and a hug. With a sad smile, she raised her hand in a last small gesture of farewell and left the room.

Ten days later Roger returned. He contacted Eddy, who told him that Connie was filing for divorce and wanted one thousand pounds a month for support. Through her lawyer, she also demanded a life insurance policy for twenty thousand pounds with Sally as the named beneficiary. All costs of the divorce were to be paid by Roger.

Eddy told Roger that if he did not agree to the terms as presented, then Roger could damn-well find counsel elsewhere. Eddy Regan, too, had had a bellyful of Roger.

"What say you, boy?" Roger asked a couple of days later, not belligerently, but like a man on his last legs and not quite sure what it all means.

"Roger, I'm going to move to Arnprior and run that clinic." He had negotiated with the authorities to manage the medical facility in that small town; and because there were no other takers and because the area had been without a government doctor for months, they had readily agreed.

Surprisingly, Roger did not object. "That's good, Desmond. Maybe you could also handle the shop in Dunwoody, and I'll take care of the practices here and at Ballyglenn."

"Fine, Roger, let's do that." I then told him that I wanted to take three weeks off before starting in my new location. "I'm going to visit friends in America."

"You'll be coming back?" he asked, real panic in his voice.

"I'll be back."

I left two days later, and Margaret went with me. We were not going to visit friends. For months, her mother had been touting the virtues of a small town on the west coast of Florida, a town she had recently visited and fallen in love with. Naples. Smack dab on the shores of the Gulf of Mexico. "It's summer all year round. Go see for yourselves," she had urged. Good advice. I was now planning ahead in earnest.

Margaret and I fell in love with the place. So much so, that I placed a deposit on a condominium close to the water. Naples was indeed a paradise, a town where we could live happily ever after. And the possibility of working in one of the area hospitals looked promising. But I had a problem which would have to be solved before attempting to act on such a plan. The problem? I had no official record on file at University College, Cork, attesting to the fact that I was indeed a graduate. A transcript sent directly from the University would be the first thing asked for by any American employer, and to put it mildly, this would take some doing.

We returned to Ireland full of dreams and serious talk of marriage. "I want to get married in Paris, Desmond. No Church wedding, no priest, which probably means no parents either, but that's the price we'll have to pay. Can you live with those conditions?"

"If that's what you want, then that's what we'll do. Any suggestion as to when?"

"The end of September," Margaret replied without hesitation. "The tourist season will be over, and we can take off for a few days and have fun. How respondeth Desmond Donahue, asketh the bride-to-be?" She was in rare form.

"That's OK by me, the bridegroom-to-be respondeth." We laughed at our foolishness.

I began to count down the days.

We were married on September 24, 1974, in the Hotel Athénée, attended by two dozen of our friends. Most of the guests had also made reservations for an important rugby match for the following day, so everyone was in a festive mood. I flew into Paris the day before, accompanied by Roger, Eddy, and his wife Maureen. Eddy was to officiate, and he had to move smartly in order to secure all the bureaucratic forms from the French Ministry in charge of shuffling such papers. Roger had signed other documents attesting to the fact that both of us had had blood samples tested within the last thirty days and certified we were free of any dread diseases. None of us knew whether this was required by French authorities, but I wasn't about to take any chances.

At four o'clock in the afternoon, we recited our vows, swearing love, honor, and fidelity, each to the other until death do us part. I placed the ring on Margaret's finger and my eyes clouded as I kissed my wife. It was the happiest moment of my life. She returned the kiss, and held me so close and tight that I thought I would burst. "Don't ever, ever let go, Margaret! Hold me like this forever!" I whispered.

Everybody required to sign the marriage license did so; then Eddy placed it in an envelope and handed it to Margaret.

"File this as soon as you get back from your honeymoon. Make sure you pick up a half-dozen sealed copies for yourselves. Don't forget, Margaret, it's that important."

"Yes, Mister Lawyer," she replied, first thing, I promise." She turned to our guests and proclaimed with an exaggerated, sweeping bow, "The bride commands that the festivities begin."

Amidst a thunderous clapping, the toasts commenced, and party we did. Until the next day. The newlyweds excused themselves from attending the rugby match and headed for Monte Carlo with Margaret driving, as I was in no condition to do anything except breathe. Thank God for autonomic reflexes.

Our honeymoon was idyllic. What more can I say? Monte Carlo was grand. The weather was grand. Margaret was grand. I was in heaven. All too soon, the week was up, and I had to return to Ireland.

"I'll see you in Arnprior two weeks from now," Margaret promised, as she bade me goodbye at the airport. "I can't wait to see what our house looks like. I wish I was coming with you."

Within a month, the clinic in Arnprior was operating with the efficiency of a Swiss watch. I had one nurse, Mrs. Delaney, a true godsend. She had been with the Health Region for seven years and knew every household in the county. She had delivered most of the babies born in the past year; the only physician she could turn to for help if a case was beyond her formidable expertise was the town's sole private practitioner, Dr. Terrence Kenny.

She set me straight about Kenny the first day I arrived.

"He's not delighted to have you here, Dr. Donahue," she explained. "He's a greedy one, he is, and he's fuming that you'll be taking money out of his pockets. Be careful of him, that's all I'm saying."

"Thanks for the advice. Once I'm settled in, I think I'll pay him a courtesy call. Certainly can't hurt. That way he can see I don't have any horns."

"Pardon my saying so, but he'll see that in a hurry. There's not much hair up there to hide horns in."

I had to laugh. "Well, I can see that you and I are going to get along just fine, Mrs. Delaney."

The house I had intended to rent burned to the ground the day before I arrived. An omen? I didn't think so then, but I wondered later. Because I was in immediate need of a place to stay, I rented a room at the lone hotel in town, The Lord Arnprior. Definitely not the Four Seasons, and Margaret would not be impressed.

It took two weeks before I could find the time to meet my reluctant colleague. Dr. Kenny was a man about my own age, and while hating to sound like a case of sour grapes, he was devoid of any semblance of personality. Or civility. He kept me waiting for fifteen minutes, and when he finally did come out to the reception area, he wasn't considerate enough to offer an apology.

Our meeting was over in less than two minutes. The prissy little man told me how busy he was, had to get right back to work, but warned me without mincing any words that he would keep his eye peeled to make sure I didn't steal any of his patients.

I readied to leave. "Nice meeting you, too, Dr. Kenny. I can see firsthand what everybody has told me about you is true. You *are* an asshole!"

"See, here, Donahue. You can't talk to me like that!"

"I can and will, any time I damn well please, you little fruitcake." It was all I could do not to punch his lights out.

I relayed to Mrs. Delaney the gist of our meeting. She was delighted. "Oh, my, Dr. Donahue! I would have given anything to have been a wee fly on the wall to have seen and heard that," she said, clapping her hands in glee. Then, in all seriousness, "Do you really think he's a...well...you know?"

I replied with a grin and a suggestive wiggle of my eyebrows. I liked this woman.

"He's trouble, Doctor Donahue," she cautioned, "I'm sure he'll try to make your life miserable."

Just what I needed.

I was too busy to give much thought to Dr. Kenny. Big mistake. I should have swallowed my pride and gone immediately to apologize, even though he was the one in the wrong. Hindsight is twenty-twenty as the Americans say, but I was steaming, and the smart thing to do was not on my agenda.

For the first time in my life, I was practicing medicine on my own. The clinic was soon operating to capacity, so much so that I had to hire a second nurse. All the paperwork had to be sent to Roger for signatures, as it was his name that the clinic was registered under.

Thank God his nurses made sure he signed on the dotted line, and then they mailed the completed forms off for payment.

I also covered the clinic in Dunwoody two mornings a week. Patients who had to see a doctor between times were told to either travel to Arnprior or to Athlone. There really was no other choice. I was spread thin, and the nurse in Dunwoody took care of the small casualties between visits. Overall, it worked pretty well.

On weekends, I would travel to see how Roger was faring. Not good. His nurses often called to say Dr. Connolly hadn't been attending clinics, sometimes for days on end. How much longer could this last until someone complained to the medical authorities? Everyone was covering for Roger, but we all knew that time was running out. Especially for me. One Saturday evening I raised my concerns during dinner in Dublin.

"Roger," I began, "do you have any suggestions as to how I could get a file placed at the University registrar's office attesting to the fact that I graduated? Someday, someone is going to ask for copies of my record, and I'm afraid the day that happens all hell is going to break loose."

Roger put down his knife and fork and began rubbing his face with his napkin. I mean he went at it as if he was drying himself after a shower. That task finished, he proceeded to blow his nose into the napkin. Loud enough for heads to turn. I was mortified, but said nothing. Roger was thinking.

Finally he said, "You've got a point, boy. Let me give it some thought. I'll let you know what I come up with."

"You won't forget, Roger?"

"I won't forget, Desmond. I know it's important." He looked sad as he said this, then changed the subject.

"How's Jane?"

"Jane?" He didn't even remember Margaret's name anymore, and I was hoping for his help? Oh, shit. "You mean, Margaret?"

"You Tarzan, she Jane! A little joke, Desmond. I'm not so far gone that I don't remember her name."

"Oh. Margaret's fine. In fact, I go to Paris next weekend."

"That's nice." He was now a million miles away. He just stared at his plate for an eternity, then asked in a small voice, "What's going to become of me, Desmond? You know I can't stop drinking." He shook his head sorrowfully. "And you know the funny thing? I'm not sure that I even want to. I really have nothing left to live for. I feel my time's running out." Huge tears now rolled down his cheeks.

What could I say? Here was my best friend, a man who had never judged me but had always helped. I was sad beyond words as I tried to comfort him.

"Roger, if you would only seek professional help, I know you could lick this thing. Tens of thousands have felt as you do, but they've beaten it. Why not give it a go?" I pleaded.

He smiled. "We'll see, boy. Anyway, I need to go home. I'm all done in."

The seasons turned, and my life became more removed from Roger's. Whenever Margaret was in Ireland, we would stay in Dublin. We grew closer to Eddy Regan and his circle of acquaintances. They were an interesting group, and we enjoyed their company. However, Eddy was a full-blown alcoholic, and many a night he would quietly collapse into a stupor. Eddy was never a mean or sloppy drunk. Ever polite, he would just suddenly fold his tent and pass out. He would wake up hours later, fully refreshed, and either start drinking again, or go to work, depending on the day of the week. Eddy confided in me that he had never suffered from headaches. Hangovers? Hell, yes. That wretched feeling of being totally washed out, followed by tremors in the hands and arms. But never a headache. Amazing.

Back in Arnprior, Dr. Kenny declared war upon Dr. Donahue. The opening salvo came in the form of a letter published in the Sunday paper. On my birthday. Definitely not a good omen! And it was a masterpiece. Without naming names, he spoke of a certain doctor who had moved into Arnprior and was practicing medicine, quite possibly without a license! Even a congenital idiot would have to know he was talking about me. We were the only two physicians in town, and because he had signed his name to the piece, that left only one man exposed like a pinned butterfly under the microscope of public scrutiny. In closing, he called for an official investigation.

And this from a man who was a poor excuse for a physician at best. Let me cite by example two cases that readily come to mind.

The first involved a thirty-eight-year-old female patient of Kenny's.

Late one afternoon, I was visited at the clinic by a young man who told me his sister was ill and needed attention. He explained that Doctor Kenny had been treating her for several weeks for a stomach disorder. Apparently, the good doctor had been to her home on several occasions yet had never examined the patient. He prescribed antacids and recommended a bland diet. He took his money and ran.

"She's not getting better, Doctor Donahue. Could you come and see her this evening?"

"Fine. Give me directions, and I'll be there after clinic hours."

It took me all of ten seconds to make a definitive diagnosis. The woman was in labor. I immediately called the ambulance service and told them to come to transport the patient to the regional hospital. I advised them to bring along a midwife, fearing she could very possibly deliver en route. Her water had broken and the birth was imminent. To make a long story short, she delivered a healthy boy some three hours later with no complications. Doctor Kenny had been too lazy to examine the woman for weeks. Because she was unmarried, I suppose the thought of pregnancy had never entered his mind when he made his brilliant diagnosis from afar.

The second case was far more serious.

A man in his mid-twenties staggered into the clinic, literally on his last legs, aided by a neighbor.

"Doc, you've got to help Brian!"

One look at Brian, and even a blind man could see he was *in extremis*. "Why isn't this man in a hospital?" I was furious at what I was seeing.

The patient stood before me, gasping for every breath. He was so terribly swollen around the face, neck, and upper chest, that his features were completely hidden by edema. His empurpled, massive tongue stuck obscenely out of his mouth, and the man's eyes, although almost entirely obscured, were full of fright.

"He won't go! We've just come from Doctor Kenny. He said to bring him to the specialist down the street. We stopped at the chemist's shop and told him we were on our way here. He wants you to call him."

That son of a bitch Kenny! He saw that in all probability the man would not survive the night, so to make sure he didn't expire on his turf, he bumped the poor sod off on me.

I sat Kevin down and began to insert a special tongue depressor, hoping to create a better airway. There was no thought of intubating him. His mouth and throat were so swollen it would have been impossible!

"What the hell happened?" I asked the neighbor, as I worked. I was truly alarmed.

"Bee sting on the arm," he explained. "Two, three days ago. Kevin lives alone, you see, so he finally comes to my place this afternoon for help. I took him at once to the doctor, but he would have nothin' to do wit' us. Sent us packing right off to you, he did!"

I scrambled to the phone and called the chemist.

"Martin, it's Desmond Donahue." That's as far as I got.

"Been waitin' fer yer call, Desmond. I've prepared what you need," and he told me what it was. "I'm sendin' it right over."

"Good man. Any suggestion on the starting dosage for the Prednisone?" Chemists--pharmacist as they're called in America-- know more than most doctors when it comes to pharmacology. It's their profession, and only a fool wouldn't consult a chemist, especially when dealing with a new drug, such as Prednisone was at this time. I needed all the help I could get.

"Tricky call, but in his condition, probably a hundred milligrams to start. Then eighty, then sixty, et cetera. Be careful wi' the Benadryl, too. He's so far gone that the slightest bit too much could well put him over the edge. Anyway, you'll have it in a jiffy! I'll also send over some literature for you to look at."

We saved Brian, but it was touch-and-go those first few hours. He was a big, strong man, and that, more than anything, accounted for his survival. The terrible swelling subsided over the next few days, and I made him keep the tongue depressor in until I was satisfied the swelling would not return. I had explained to him how important it was to drink as much fluid as possible and showed him how this could be accomplished by placing a straw all the way to the bottom of a large glass.

"Don't suck up any air," I cautioned. "You can get the straw in your mouth. I've made sure of that." I turned to the neighbor. "Stay with him tonight. I'll be out first thing in the morning." Then back to Brian. "You'll be fine, I promise." I really wasn't so sure, but he needed the reassurance. "Also, you were a bloody fool for not going to the hospital at once. Next time you won't be so lucky. Unless you get immediate help, the next sting will kill you! That's the way these things work."

He nodded that he understood and gurgled his thanks.

Brian survived, no thanks to Doctor Kenny.

* * *

My first visitor that following Monday morning was the chief inspector from the Guard (Police). His name was Morris Moore, and he was the law in Galway.

"G'mornin,' Doctor Donahue. I sincerely hope you're not so upset that ye might be thinkin' of strangling Doctor Kenny. Mind ye, I could name more'n a few souls who might say good riddance, but it would only serve to make my life miserable for a spell. You know what I mean?"

"I do indeed, Inspector. Have no fear, I've got no intention of getting into a feud with Kenny. Frankly, I'm too damn busy." Big talk. I was scared to death what could happen if someone decided to take up Kenny's challenge and really dig into my background.

Morris walked over to the wall, and with his hands clasped behind his back, studied my diploma. He was whistling some obscure tune, tapping time with a foot encased in big, black, official police clodhoppers. Without turning he said, "Doctor, yer the best thing that's happened to this town in quite a spell, and, speaking officially, I can assure you I have no intention of wasting my time trying to uncover muck for Doctor Kenny. Nothin' will come of his scurrilous innuendo. I just came by to tell you this and to ask you not to let this thing stick in yer craw."

Big, silent, sigh of relief. "Thank you for the vote of confidence, Inspector. Rest assured, I'm not going to do anything foolish."

"Good." He held out a huge, callused hand for me to shake. "I'm off. Sorry to have taken your time, but I thought it important."

Of course, I did not just dismiss the incident. Kenny was on the warpath, and he was out to destroy me. I now knew without any doubt that my days in Arnprior were numbered. Maybe in all of Ireland. I needed to light a fire under Roger.

Right after New Year, he came to visit. I knew he had spent the holidays with his mother in Cork, and I had hoped the visit would have buoyed his spirits. Sad to say, this was not the case. He looked worse than terrible and, for the first time, I was truly alarmed that Roger was indeed dying. However, he was the bearer of good tidings.

He laid out the contents of his attaché case on my desk for inspection. The first document was a new diploma, awarded to Desmond Donahue, M.B., B.Ch., B.A.O., and dated 23 June 1976. Today was 7 January 1975. I was thoroughly puzzled. However, the quality was far superior to the one currently in residence on my wall. As far as I could tell, it was the genuine article.

Next followed a "To whom it may concern letter," attesting that I had completed my internship at St. Aloysius Hospital, duly signed by one Doctor O'Devlin and dated 18 June 1977.

He then handed me an official document, direct from the office of the registrar.

7 April 1977
TO WHOM IT MAY CONCERN:
Re: Desmond F. O. Donahue
I hereby certify that the above-mentioned doctor took his medical course in the Medical School of this College. He entered in October 1969, and graduated with the degree M.B., B. Ch., B.A.O. in June 1976. During his pre-medical years in University College Cork, Dr. Desmond Donahue's conduct was found to be somewhat undesirable;

however, Dr. Donahue progressed well academically, and at his final year examination was rated the top honour student of his class. His conduct and performance during his years in our Medical School were entirely satisfactory, and I can recommend him for an internship at your hospital.

Dr. Craig Wilson

Next, was a copy of a transcript, purporting to show all the courses I had completed, along with a grade for each. All superior ratings. I was impressed beyond words. But also puzzled.

And lastly, notification from the Educational Council of Foreign Medical Graduates, an American organization, informing me that I had passed their exam. A crucial document certifying my eligibility to pursue an internship and residency program in the U.S.

Roger commenced to explain. "First, the diploma. Dated for next year. I'll get to that in a tick. Pack it away for safekeeping. You won't be able to order another if you lose it. Make a couple of good photocopies and stash them away, too." He picked up the next item. "The letter of recommendation from Doctor Wilson. Note that it's printed on an IBM Selectric™ typewriter." He then pulled a typing ball from his pocket, still enclosed in its original cardboard and plastic wrapper and handed it to me. "Guard this with your life, boy. It's the same model they're using at the college right now. It should fit into any compatible machine."

My God! I was in absolute awe of Roger.

Reaching into his attaché case once more, he extracted about two dozen sheets of stationery, along with a similar number of envelopes. It was all official University College, Cork letterhead. He thumbed the top half of the sheets for my inspection. All blank paper. Then he exposed the remaining sheets from the bottom half which he proceeded to fan with his hands. Each, too, was blank, except for a signature already in place*: Dr. Craig Wilson, Administrative Officer.*

Roger carefully placed his treasure into neat little piles, and then turned to me. "What does all this mean?" he asked his spellbound audience of one. "Why, for example, 1976 on the diploma? Why stationery with Wilson's name, *et cetera, et cetera*, and so forth."

This was the Roger of old. "It all took some doing, boy, let me tell you. Quite a sum of money had to pass hands to make sure this works. And it will, Desmond. Mark my bloody words, it will work!"

"I believe you, Roger. I damn well believe you, you wonderful, son of a gun." I was now laughing hysterically at my tremendous good fortune.

"There's a copy of your transcript and a copy of this letter signed by Wilson in a special file at the college with your name on it. We don't want to activate it until at least a year from this summer, simply because we know that Wilson will have been long-gone by then. Nineteen seventy-four was his last year, so three years since his departure should be good and safe. His is the perfect signature. I should point out that those papers with his chicken scratches are the real thing. They were pinched from his desk some time ago. Apparently, he kept a stack for form letters, standard replies, and things like that. His secretary had permission to just pop in and take them as she needed. She knew what to write for him. This system saved him time, the lazy bugger! Well, the long and the short of it is that one of my contacts liberated the letterheads before he left and, in turn, sold some to me. They can be used by you to create official letters of recommendation. And to make sure everything looks bloody perfect, all you have to do is be sure they are always mailed from Cork." He pointed to his neat little stack of envelopes.

Roger had thought of everything.

"Now, this next part is very important, so listen carefully. Whenever you find that you have to give a hospital, or whoever, the address of the college, or if you have to write for any reason yourself, always address the envelope to Miss Brigid Ryan. And make sure your name always appears on the envelope. For example, if a hospital writes, have them clearly write on the envelope, Re: Desmond Donahue. Got this so far?"

"I do. But I don't quite understand."

"You will, let me finish." We now sat knee-to-knee. "My contact in the registrar's office has been instructed to be on the lookout for correspondence coming to Brigid Ryan from Desmond Donahue. That tells a certain unnamed person to activate your special file. There is no Brigid Ryan. Correction. There was at one time, but she retired ten years ago and has since died." He studied my face intently. "Remember, Desmond, for this to work flawlessly Brigid Ryan's name and your name must always appear on the envelope. That way, the right person will pick it up and handle it."

My mind was full of questions, but three in particular screamed for attention. "Supposing your person in the office retires? Or leaves? What then?"

"There's always that possibility, but not very likely I suspect. Sure, he or she could get killed in a car wreck, or die of natural causes, but then again, so could you, and all of this would have been for naught. No, this should be good for some time to come. I put all this together after you told me about that little prick Kenny. He could make life impossible for you in Ireland, but I really don't think so. At least I hope not. Anyway, I'm going to write to the authorities and tell them I'm giving up that office, that it's just too much work. I'll give them a month's notice, and then you come back here. OK?"

After all he had done, what was I going to say? No?

"Desmond, hopefully, you will never have to use those documents. Knock on wood, we'll have a long run at the practice here, make gobs of money, and retire to that Naples place you're always telling me about. But, if you find that you must leave Ireland, then I recommend settling in such a place, become established quickly, and use the contact at Cork sparingly. Under ideal conditions, you would only need to get in touch a couple of times right at the beginning, then you should be set for the rest of your life."

I reached over and punched him affectionately on the shoulder. "It bloody well works, boy!"

*   *   *

Two months later I was back in Athlone for good. We closed the clinic in Arnprior, citing difficulty in manning the place effectively. I was not looking forward to working with Roger again, but my options were fast becoming limited. I reluctantly moved into the mansion, a now-sterile dwelling, bereft of any sense of family whatsoever. It was a melancholy time. And I missed Margaret.

Shortly after Easter, and while we were together for a long weekend in Dublin, Margaret dropped a bombshell. She had been subdued and somewhat withdrawn ever since getting off the plane. Not typical. As I prepared for bed, she was seated by the window, silently gazing down on the traffic four stories below. Without turning, she asked, "How would you feel about becoming a father?"

That sounded like an offer I couldn't refuse. "Great! Let's start on it tonight!"

She arose and came to the bed. "We've already started, lover boy. A little rabbit in Paris gave its all to confirm that fact last Tuesday. I'm two months along." She then stared at me, her face soft as a picture in the orange glow of the one bedside lamp. She was the perfect Madonna. "What say you about that?"

I was speechless. I was going to be a father? Oh my God! My mind raced willy-nilly in a futile attempt to keep pace with the pounding of my heart. Finally, in a whisper, "Are you sure?" What a dumb question! However, in defense of my stupidity, statements such as the one I had just heard tend to do that to most men.

"I'm sure, Desmond, and so is the rabbit. Seven months from now we'll have a little bundle of joy."

Did I hear a hint of sarcasm and rejection there? I reached out and drew her close. "Margaret, this is the best news I've ever heard. It's a dream come true!"

"Do you really mean it? You're not just saying that?"

"I mean every word, love, and ten thousand others words I'm incapable of articulating. Margaret. I'm in heaven!"

"I was scared you'd be angry," she replied in a small-girl voice. She gently pulled away, and with a serious tone to match her serious face, remarked, "Here's Margaret Donahue, the great Irish champion of the birth control pill. The same woman who has finally convinced you as to its merits. The woman who has screamed from the mountaintop that every female has the right to use it without fear of interference from either Church or State. And now she finds herself in the same state of unexpected and unwanted pregnancy as all those cutoff from its benefits. Bloody ironic, isn't it?"

"Margaret, no birth control method is a hundred percent. You know that."

By now she had crawled into bed. I leaned over and switched off the light. We cuddled in the dark.

She let out a long sigh, then kissed me primly on the neck. "Thank you, Desmond. I was so afraid you'd be furious. I feel a million times better now."

I returned her kiss. "The mom-to-be needs lots of rest, so the doctor responsible for this condition now orders her to go to sleep. This little family has a lot of planning to do in the morning. Good night, love."

That night, while Mrs. Desmond Donahue slept the sleep of the just, I slept not a wink. I was happy beyond words. But now I knew that my life was once more about to take a turn into the unknown. The time had come to begin thinking very seriously about returning to America and starting life over for a second time. Only now, I would be facing the challenge with my family by my side.

Was I scared? Of course I was. But I was more than ready.

I informed my parents of our news, and they were delighted. Yet guilt was seated squarely on my shoulder. You see, my parents assumed that we had gotten married in the Church, and cowards that we were, we had never told them otherwise. Ditto for Margaret's mother. My hope was that Margaret would at least begrudgingly agree to a belated church wedding, something she was still bitterly opposed to. For me to make her change her mind would take some doing, but for the sake of all involved, I prayed that she would bend to my wishes.

However, this was still the least of my worries. My problems with Dr. Kenny were far from over. As far he was concerned, Desmond Donahue might have been out of sight, but he was definitely not out of mind. This man was proving to be a very formidable nemesis. He had sicced two bulldog reporters on my case, and both men, having tracked me down, were now hounding me for my story. I had avoided them up until now, but they had smelled the blood of reticence and were lining me up for the kill. I was being squeezed by many vises.

Roger, of course, was aware of Margaret's pregnancy, but not much else. He now made no pretense of working any more. The man was drunk all the time, spending his few waking hours at either the horse track or placing wagers on races in other cities. He was beyond all help.

One month later my world exploded. I do not use this metaphor lightly. I mean my world was blown to smithereens, and the fallout of that time is the bane of my existence to this day.

The end came without warning as I was closing the clinic one Saturday afternoon. A guard (police officer) stepped into the waiting room just as I was about to turn off the lights.

"Is this Dr. Connolly's residence?" he inquired, removing his hat as he spoke.

"Aye, it is."

"Is there a Mrs. Connolly, by chance?" He did not appear to be in the least bit happy to be here. Something was up. Something not good.

"There is no Mrs. Connolly, I'm afraid. I'm Dr. Donahue; maybe I can help."

He took a deep breath, then holding himself erect, a soldier at attention, he uttered his tidings in a funereal voice. "It is my sad duty to inform you, sir, that Dr. Connolly was killed in a car crash about two hours ago. Just outside of Dublin."

I staggered backwards and fell into a chair. *This can't be true. Not Roger.* It just bloody well can't be! "What happened?" I forced the words out, my mouth a repository of the ashes of despair.

"He lost control of that little sports car, sir. Apparently, he was traveling at a high rate of speed, missed his turn in the rain, and went sailing off into the woods. I didn't see it myself, sir, but the report says he was killed instantly." He paused and took another deep breath. "Suspicion is that he was drunk, sir. That will of course be verified by the coroner, but it does look that way."

"Has his mother been informed?" I asked, an eternity later.

"No, sir, just you. This is the only address we have for the doctor. I'm very sorry to be the one to bring you such terrible news." He placed his hat back on his head. "I'll see myself out, sir."

I sat in the dark for over an hour before the tears came. And when they did, they wouldn't stop. I pummeled my desk in rage, frustration, and despair. "Why, Roger? Why wouldn't you get help?" I beseeched his ghost. "Why have you done this to your mother?" I implored. "Why have you done this to me? Answer me, boy. Goddamn you, Roger Connolly, answer me!"

We buried him three days later in Cork in a plot next to his father. His mother was inconsolable, as were his two sisters, who had aged a hundred years. The prince was gone. Dead two weeks shy of his thirty-seventh birthday. Dead because of his unquenchable thirst for gin.

Margaret flew in from Paris, and Eddy and Maureen Regan joined us that terrible day. Eddy himself had been in and out of the hospital a couple of times during these last few weeks, and his condition was very serious. Diagnosis? Full blown cirrhosis brought about by alcohol poisoning. Probably terminal.

Margaret, in addition to being pale and haggard, was also markedly puffy in appearance. And stupid me for not being more observant. I shrugged it off as normal weight gain due to her advancing condition.

"I wonder which of us the baby will favor?" I mused.

Her unenthusiastic response was a simple, "We'll just have to wait and see."

I changed the subject. "I think it's time for us to make our break and head for America. We should be in Naples with enough time for you to still be able to travel comfortably and to also get established with a good OB/GYN."

"Make the arrangements, Desmond. Don't bother me with the details. Just let me know when."

"Plan on departing within the next thirty days," I replied, trying not to sound aggrieved by her shortness. "Give notice to Thomas Cook as soon as you get back to Paris, and then come and join me here. OK?"

"Fine, I'll let you know."

Margaret left for Paris two days later, and I returned to Athlone to close Roger's practice. I hired one of Eddy Regan's friends to take care of the legal end of settling the estate, this request coming from Roger's mother who had no desire to take on such a burden. I then devoted my remaining days in Ireland to settling my own affairs and making arrangements for our flight from Shannon to Miami. It was a terribly depressing time, and I found myself anxious to leave. I made a quick trip over to Ballycommon to say good-bye to my parents, but promised to return as soon as the child was old enough to travel so that they could dote on the new generation of Donahues.

I phoned Margaret ten days later to tell her that everything was ready for our departure. No answer. This didn't give me cause for concern, but after I had tried for several hours with no response, I became alarmed. Finally, at close to one o'clock in the morning, she picked up the phone.

"Margaret, where have you been?" Annoyance and relief flooded through me.

An eternity of silence, then, "Desmond?"

"Of course it is! Who the hell else would be calling at this hour?"

"Desmond, this is Eileen. You know, Margaret's roommate."

"Oh! I'm sorry for calling so late, Eileen," I apologized. "Be a love and wake her for me."

Another long pause. Then, "She's not here, Desmond. In fact, she hasn't been here for several days now."

My heart was floating in my mouth. What in God's name was happening? Try not to panic, I commanded myself. "Where is she? Her mother's place, maybe?" I asked, hoping against hope.

"Aagghhhhh. Why did she leave me to this," Eileen moaned into the mouthpiece. "Didn't she say anything to you, Desmond? Anything at all?"

"Say what, Eileen? What the hell are you talking about? Is she all right?" I was now yelling at the top of my lungs, knuckles white from the death grip with which I clutched the receiver.

"Oh, Desmond, she's gone. She's run away with an American she met awhile back. She said she's in love and that she plans to spend the rest of her life with him."

This cannot be happening! This might pass for a normal conversation in some stupid romance novel, but such goings-on did not take place in real life. I was trapped inside a nightmare. *Wake up, Desmond. For God's sake, man, wake up!*

"Eileen, I'll take the first flight out of Shannon in the morning. Please, wait for me at the apartment. I'll be there as soon as I can. Please. Call in sick to work. I'll pay you for your lost wages. Just, please, wait for me. I beg you."

She began to cry. "I'll be here, Desmond. I'm so sorry. I thought she told you."

There was nothing more I could say except, "Goodnight, Eileen."

I raced around the house like a man possessed. Within ten minutes, I was in my car, tearing along the roadway, driving faster than Roger would have ever dared, careening towards Shannon Airport, desperate for answers to this impossible turn of events.

True to her word, Eileen was home to let me into the apartment.

"Tell me everything you know," I pleaded.

Everything turned out to be not much more than she had told me a few hours earlier. All she could add was that the American's name was John, that he was separated from his wife who was still back in the States, and that Margaret and he professed to be madly in love. *Frigging Romeo and bloody Juliet. Bullshit!*

I walked slowly into Margaret's bedroom, hoping to find an answer. A letter, a note, anything. The place had been stripped of all her possessions save for some old clothes she no longer needed. It did not take a genius to see that she had no intention of coming back. I began to open and close drawers. Then, something caught my eye. In the bottom of her bureau lay an envelope, tossed in the back like so much refuse. Picking it up, I felt my stomach involuntarily spasm. It was the envelope Eddy Regan had handed her the day of our wedding. Opening it with shaking hands, I stared at our marriage license, torn into four neat squares and replaced with due care by the cruelest of hoaxers. Margaret had never registered our nuptials! As far as the law was concerned, no wedding had taken place! It had been one monumental fraud. I dropped the envelope and raced into the bathroom where every ounce of bitter bile inside my wretched body went into the porcelain receptacle. I knelt on that cold tile floor, lost in time, wanting only to die.

"Oh, Margaret, what in the name of God could I have done to deserve this?"

"Nothing, Desmond. You did nothing."

I turned to see Eileen standing in the doorway. I had not realized I had spoken out loud in my torment.

"I think she was first going to her mother's," she said, shrugging her shoulders in a gesture of defeat. "After that, who knows?"

"I'm going to Cork," I announced, getting to my feet. "If you hear anything, please call me. You still have my number?"

She nodded. "Good luck, Desmond. I hope it all turns out well for you. I really do."

Mrs. Kerrigan was beside herself when I met her later that evening. Margaret had indeed appeared on her doorstep and announced her intention to take off with her newfound lover.

"Take off where?" the mother had screamed at her daughter.

"Istanbul," the daughter had replied.

"As in Turkey? Tell me I'm hearing things!"

"The very same," came the smug reply.

"Margaret, if you do this, I'll disown you. Mark my words, this is no idle threat. I'll never speak to you again." Then she asked, "What about your husband? What about Desmond's feelings? Doesn't he at least rate an explanation?"

Margaret had laughed in her mother's face. "He's not my husband. We were never legally married! Desmond was always such a fool."

"Is the child you're carrying even his, or are you really a whore?" The mother could have throttled her offspring, such was her anger and disgust.

"Who knows? Who cares?"

That put Mrs. Kerrigan over the edge. "Get the hell out of my house," she screamed, "and never come back! Do you hear me? You're evil, Margaret. God forgive me for having given you life. Out!"

Mrs. Kerrigan was crying as she recounted the visit. Margaret had been gone three days. "She looked terrible, Desmond. I think she's sick, physically and mentally. But she's certainly not insane," the mother quickly added. "I'm mortified having to tell you all this. My advice is to forget her. You owe her nothing. The marriage was a sham. My daughter used you. For what evil purpose, I cannot begin to imagine." She wept as only a mother can weep.

"I'm going to find her, Mrs. Kerrigan. I will not rest until I do and have her tell me to my face that she doesn't love me."

"You'll go to Istanbul?" she asked incredulously, drying her eyes as she spoke. "Where do you start looking once you get there? You don't even know the name of her paramour." She shook her head. "Don't waste your time, Desmond. Don't let her destroy you."

"I've got to try, Mrs. Kerrigan. I'll see you when I get back."

And that's exactly what I did. I flew to that exotic city on the Bosporus, gateway to the east. It may as well have been the backside of the moon. Armed with a two-year old snapshot of Margaret and myself, I walked the streets of that city for three days and nights. I stopped in every travel office I could find, showed the picture, and was witness to a million shaking heads and a million clucking tongues. I trolled the markets, the main streets, the back streets, the hotels, the bars, the restaurants. Nothing. By the end of the third day, I had to admit defeat. I got back on the Pan Am clipper and returned to Ireland.

"Not a trace," I reported to the mother. I hadn't eaten a solid meal in almost a week, and my weight had dropped by at least a dozen pounds.

Mrs. Kerrigan had noticed my condition and expressed her concern. "Desmond, you're going to make yourself sick. God forgive me, son, but she's just not worth it. I'm sad beyond words for your unborn child, but my advice stands. Forget her. Just forget her. That's what I'm going to do. Or at least I'm going to try."

I kissed her good-bye and promised to keep in touch. "I'm going to Dublin for a few days," I explained, as she walked me to my car, holding aloft an umbrella to shield us both from the rain. "Then after that, who knows?"

CHAPTER FIFTEEN

I **left Cork** about ten-thirty and headed towards Dublin in the blinding rain. I was truly at my wits' end and had no idea what my next step was going to be. How in God's name had I thought I could somehow track Margaret down by going to Istanbul is beyond me now, but the decision seemed so rational at the time. What would I have said if indeed I had found her? I have no idea, but that didn't cross my mind as an obstacle either. Mentally and physically I was on my last legs, but on that score, too, I had no conception of just how far gone I was. Trying to forget my own troubles for a while, my thought now was to see Eddy Regan, who had just been released from the hospital and had been told he had very little time left. His liver was now totally non-functional, and even though he was aware of the prognosis and accepted it, I'm sure he hoped his doctors were wrong.

My mind was still on Eddy when I began to experience a shooting pain in my chest, a pain which soon radiated down my arm and across my back. My heart started to beat abnormally. *Arrhythmia.* I knew in an instant what was happening. I broke out into a cold sweat. I was having a heart attack!

Holy Mother of God, this can't be happening! The pain was getting much worse, and my vision was starting to tunnel. I had to get to a hospital was my overriding concern. *I can't die, I'm only thirty-seven years old, and I haven't found Margaret!* I started to cry. By now my driving had become very erratic, and I couldn't see the road through my tears and the incessant rain. Suddenly, out of the corner of my eye I saw a sign for St. James' Hospital. I knew where I was. I careened into the hospital entrance and drove up to the emergency room, barely missing several parked cars on the side of the roadway. I came to a stop on the sidewalk inches from the front door. I was almost unconscious with pain. Two orderlies rushed out, within moments had me on a gurney, and proceeded to wheel me in a mad dash straight into the emergency room.

"Got a heart attack, here!" one of them yelled out. "Get the resident, stat! We're looking at a code blue!"

I was transferred to an examining table, and multiple pairs of hands immediately started working on me. My clothes were removed. Someone started an IV drip while someone else drew blood, and yet another began prepping me for an EKG. Into this scene walked the senior. He lifted my left eyelid, peered in with an ophthalmoscope, studied for a moment, and then repeated the procedure on my right eye.

I remember hearing a voice call out, "This man's a doctor. American, I think." Someone had gone through my wallet for identification.

"That's all we bloody well need!" This from the resident. By now the EKG was printing, and I was being handled as a classic heart case. Mercifully, I lost consciousness.

I awoke to see a nursing sister hovering over me. "Good morning, Doctor." She smiled. "I'll be gone just long enough to get the resident."

They returned a long minute later, the resident studying my chart as they entered.

"Good morning, Dr. Donahue, I'm Dr. FitzPatrick. You gave us all quite a scare and yourself, too, I imagine. So, let me tell you our findings. Your EKG is clean. No evidence of a heart attack. But as you know, we can't rule it out one hundred percent, so to be on the safe side, you need to remain here under observation for the next few days."

I merely nodded. I was utterly exhausted, and although the pain was gone, I was not convinced that he was telling me the truth. "You are telling me everything, right?"

"I'm telling you everything, Dr. Donahue. All indications are of a normal heart. No attack. But, I do want you here for a few days," he repeated forcefully. "I'm prescribing a light sedative. Sleep will do you a world of good". He patted my shoulder, smiled down at me and added, "I'll look in on you before I get off duty."

On the morning of the third day, FitzPatrick came back after rounds, catching me reading the bible. I am somewhat religious; it's hard not to be if you've been raised in Ireland, but I don't wear my religion on my sleeve. Yet, here I was reading the story of Ruth.

Whither thou goes, I go... I put the book down and smiled, almost embarrassed to be caught in the act.

"Good morning, Desmond, I've got some good news. Holiday's over, old boy, I'm discharging you tomorrow." As he spoke, he dragged up the lone metal chair and placed it near the left side of my bed. He sat down backwards, his body facing mine and his arms resting on top of its backrest. "I've asked a Dr. Mulvahill to drop by to speak to you this afternoon, if that's all right with you. Mulvahill is one of the best psychiatrists in Ireland," he added hurriedly, "and I really think you'll enjoy meeting him."

"You think I'm crazy?"

"No, I don't think you're crazy at all, but I do think you are suffering from some form of acute depression. The sisters tell me that when they check on you at night they find you crying in your sleep, and Doctor, you know yourself, that's an indication something very heavy is weighing on your soul." As he spoke he glanced at the bible in my hands. "See Mulvahill, Desmond. He's one hell of a fine physician and about the easiest guy you've ever spoken with. He's not some whacko shrink," he added, unfurling himself from the chair. "Give him a few minutes of your time; you'll be glad you did." He paused at the door. "I'll stop by in the morning to see you off."

At two o'clock a meticulously dressed gentleman appeared in the hallway, paused, and rapped lightly on the slightly ajar door. "Disturbing anything?" he asked.

"No. Come on in."

"Hello, I'm Dr. Mulvahill. You sure I'm not disturbing anything? I can pop back later."

"No, sir, this is fine." I raised myself to a seated position. He came forward and shook my hand, then retraced his steps and shut the door. He then moved to the window, and with his back to me, began to speak.

"You know, there comes a time in all our lives when events conspire to overwhelm us. At some point we all face this challenge, and because we are human, we turn to our fellow man for help and reassurance. It lets us know we are not alone." He then turned and faced me square-on. "No man is an island," he said. "I don't remember whom to quote there, Desmond, but whoever it was spoke volumes. We're an interdependent species," he continued, "and that is why we dominate the food chain. We know when to turn to others for help. It's how we survive. It's the essence of our humanity."

"Yes."

"I've read your chart and agree that you are physically sound. That's very good news. But," he cautioned, "a festering mental anguish, if left untreated, will eventually manifest itself physically; and in your case, you were fortunately given a warning. You're a doctor, so, of course, you are aware of this. You were suffering from an acute anxiety attack the night you came here, and unless you can come to terms with the underlying problem, there will be others. And at some point, it could well induce heart failure. The broken heart syndrome is a very real malady, and the results can often be fatal. We in medicine know this is true, but we really don't know yet how to fully deal with this phenomenon. We traditionally think of it as being induced by unrequited love, but there really are many causes. It makes men give up all hope, and it's truly one of the strangest of phenomena recounted in the annals of medicine. It often manifests itself during war when some men give up the ghost, literally within days of capture by the enemy. And yet, there was nothing physically wrong with them. They just curled up into a fetal position and expired. There exists no rational explanation for the condition, but it's real nonetheless."

I nodded.

"I'm told that you're going back to America soon. True?"

"True."

"Tell me, is there any possibility for you to arrange your schedule so that you could remain in Dublin a short time longer? I would like to help you, Desmond, and I believe I can. You're too young a man to be as burdened as you are. You're obviously bright and have the wherewithal of living a happy and satisfying life."

"How long would you want me to stay?"

"I think I can do a world of good in a matter of weeks. If it's a problem of finding a place to stay, then let me help. I can secure something suitable."

"No, that won't be a problem. I have friends in the area. I can easily arrange that." I was agreeing to his suggestion, yet I didn't understand why I was being so acquiescent. I definitely did not relish the thought of exposing my vulnerabilities to another human being, but something deep within told me I must.

"Give it about eight weeks, Desmond. We can meet for an hour at a time, say, three visits a week?"

Again, I just nodded.

He took a card from his wallet and passed it to me. "Call my nurse on Monday, and she will have you scheduled to start next Wednesday. Let's plan on about four o'clock; that way you will be my last consult for the day. Meanwhile, I want you to get a prescription filled which I'll leave with your doctor here. Start the medication tomorrow as per the instructions. All right?"

"Thank you."

He shook my hand. "We're going to have you as good as new, Desmond, I promise."

* * *

By the following Wednesday, I had made arrangements to sublet an apartment from a friend who was in England for several months, its location a brisk fifteen minute walk to Dr. Mulvahill's office on O'Connell Street.

I was nervous as I entered his suite at a few minutes to four.

"Good afternoon, I'm Desmond Donahue," I said to a middle-aged nurse who was busy writing in an appointments ledger. She looked up and smiled the most dazzling of smiles.

"Good afternoon, Dr. Donahue. Dr. Mulvahill will be with you in just a jiff. Could I interest you in a spot of tea? I'm about to make some for the doctor and myself."

"That would be nice, thanks. Black, very little sugar."

"That's the way I like it, too. Coming right up."

At that moment the door to Mulvahill's office opened, and a young woman in her early twenties came out followed by the physician. "I'll see you next Monday, Bridget. Say hello to your dad for me."

Bridget nodded her reply and slunk out as meekly as a church mouse. When the door closed behind her, Dr. Mulvahill turned to me. "Bridget is a very special girl. I've known her family since before she was born," he explained. "Her mother and brother died in a terrible accident about six months ago, and she's had a very difficult time accepting it. Just she and her father are left, and it's been excruciating for them both. It's helping the Bridgetts of the world that makes my life count for something." He rubbed his hands together. "Ah, I see you have some tea! Good idea." No sooner were the words spoken than his nurse handed him a cup. He took a tentative sip, nodded his thanks, and motioned for me to follow him into his office.

There were several chairs scattered around this spacious, well-appointed room, all comfortable looking and all facing a large leather wingback chair with matching ottoman. That's where he directed me. "Seat of honor," he explained. "So comfortable I often fall asleep in it."

He moved to a chair by my right, and sat. As I mentioned before, Dr. Mulvahill was meticulous in manner and dress. He wore his authority well, not in an intimidating way, but with the aura of a man completely in charge. I would guess he was in his early fifties and was nothing like the textbook image of a psychiatrist. I would learn during later sessions that he made full use of the chairs in his office, moving from one to the other while listening. This sounds distracting, but for some uncanny reason, it wasn't. He smoked a pipe on occasion, always asking permission before lighting up. All in all, a very impressive man. I soon came to learn that he was both brilliant and insightful. Dr. Mulvahill was what every psychiatrist should be. He saved my life.

During those first couple of consultations, as he referred to my visits, we spoke of my early years and my growing up in grinding poverty. I was at ease, and the words tumbled out. I then told him of my later years, of becoming a doctor and practicing medicine. I barely mentioned Margaret.

During my third or fourth visit, he volunteered how he believed in some aspects of the master's work, the master, of course, being

Sigmund Freud. "Freud didn't know everything," he explained, "and neither did such follow-on luminaries as Carl Jung and Alfred Adler, who both helped expand the body of knowledge. They were on the right track a good deal of the time, but this is a field of medicine that's still in its infancy, so we practitioners are not always in agreement with one another as to the course it is taking. But, for the most part, I think we're doing rather well." Then, he abruptly changed the subject. "It's time we talk about Margaret."

I jumped up, heart racing. "That goddamned bitch! If she were here this bloody moment, I'd kill her!" I slammed my fist into the back of the chair, then burst into tears. I dropped back into my seat, crying bitterly, hands covering my face to hide my pain.

Dr. Mulvahill didn't say a word. He allowed me to cry, and a few minutes later I said in a small voice wracked with anguish, "I couldn't kill her. I love her with all my heart. God help me, I love her!"

He handed me a giant tissue which I used to blow my nose loudly, but only after I'd wiped my eyes. I held up the limp square and laughed weakly. "Don't see many of these in Ireland," I said, still sniffling. "I wager you go through a box or two in the course of week."

Mulvahill laughed and handed me another. "Too right. Such an ingenious invention, though, aren't they? So American in function and simplicity," he observed. "Only the Yanks could bring science to bear on filling such a basic need and make millions in the process." He laughed again and had me laughing with him. He gave me a few more minutes to compose myself, while he talked quietly about things I now have no recollection of, whatsoever. Soon, I was back in control of my emotions and glad my real problem was finally out in the open. He had played events to perfection, blindsiding me in such a professional manner that he had exposed me to myself before I knew what was happening. My knowledge of psychiatry is nil, but I do remember thinking: *Is this my Id now fighting with my Ego, or could it be the Id is in a Hiawatha-like death struggle with the Super-Ego? Which is which, and more importantly, which is winning?* I laughed aloud at the convoluted thought and let Mulvahill in on my little secret.

"Well, Desmond, I think it safe to say that we have possibly brought the root problem out into the open. How do you feel about that?

"Good."

"Just good?"

I laughed again. "Just good means a hell of a lot to me right now."

"Then good is good enough for me!" he exclaimed, rising from his chair. "Enough for today. We'll start fresh on Monday, and we'll get to the bottom of this, never fear. Have a good weekend," he said, as we stepped out of his office, his nurse already gone, leaving him to lock up.

I waved goodbye and eagerly began the walk back to my apartment. I hadn't felt this good in months.

Saturday turned out to be a beautiful day, so much so that it was the talk of the city. People traipsed through the streets wearing radiant smiles, and the all the thoroughfares were crowded with happy strollers.

I made my way to Eddy's home. He had called earlier asking me to drop by.

When Maureen ushered me into his bedroom, I was shocked by his appearance. Eddy was dying, and it showed. The whites of his eyes were now an obscene yellow and his skin the color and consistency of aged parchment, evidence of total liver failure. He was propped up by several pillows, a gaunt, haunting figure, unrecognizable as the Eddy of old.

"Eddy, you lazybones, how are you?" I greeted my friend with false bravado.

"Thirsty," he replied, a weak smile on his lips. "My kingdom for a just a wee snort, Desmond, and not the horse Richard the Third called out for!" He laughed weakly at his own attempt at levity. "Tell me, what's been happening? We haven't had a chance to talk in ages."

And that's what we did. We reminisced over the many good times. About twenty minutes later, I noticed Eddy starting to weaken. He must have been aware of it because he turned serious.

"Do you know your blood type, Desmond?"

"B positive. Why?"

"I've received word from friends that Margaret had become pre-eclamptic. Her fetus carried B positive blood, and the pregnancy turned sour. She spontaneously aborted. I'm sorry, Desmond, but I thought you should know."

I sat down hard on the edge of his bed. I was stunned. Eclampsia. Dead. How could I have been so stupid? Of course! Pre-eclampsia. That explained Margaret's puffiness and general rundown condition. Which also suggested her pregnancy was further along than she had told me. I did not know what to say. I couldn't even cry. Finally, "What about Margaret? Where did this take place?"

"Somewhere in France. From what I hear, she has had a very rough go of things, but she definitely survived."

"And still with her American lover?"

"I haven't heard anything to the contrary, so I assume she is."

"You can't tell me where you got this information, Eddy?"

"Not at the moment. I only just heard it myself a few hours ago. Maybe a little later." He let out a long sigh. "I'm truly sorry, Desmond. I debated long and hard whether to tell you or not. I hope I made the right decision."

"You did, old friend, and I thank you." I rose from the bed. "Eddy, you're tired. Time to get some rest. I'll pop by tomorrow." I winked my goodbye, and Eddy winked back.

Shortly after eleven that night, my phone rang just as I was climbing into bed.

"Hello."

"Desmond?"

"Yes."

"It's Maureen Regan."

I could barely hear her.

"Eddy's dead. I went to check on him a half hour ago, and he was gone." No tears, no histrionics, just a monotonic recitation of facts.

"Oh, Maureen, I'm so sorry!" My dear, wonderful, stupid friend was dead at forty because of his obsession with alcohol.

"Desmond, don't come tonight. My mom's here. But do come tomorrow. I know I'll need you then." Without another word, she hung up.

Seven hours later, I was still seated by the window when the sun struggled weakly to gain a toehold on the horizon. First Roger, dead in a car crash because of alcohol, and now Eddy. I had lost my last friend in all the world.

And my only link to ever finding Margaret.

I begged off my Monday's appointment with Dr. Mulvahill because the Regan family needed me to help arrange Eddy's wake and funeral mass. It was a sad time for a number of people, and many of his friends had to pause and think, long and hard...*But for the grace of God...*

Edward Patrick Michael Regan was laid to his final rest on Tuesday morning, accompanied on this last journey from the church to the cemetery by almost four hundred mourners. He had been a popular barrister, praised as being fair and honest in his dealings with rich and poor alike. Many would miss Eddy: he had been that type of a man.

On Wednesday, Mulvahill spoke for a few minutes about my loss. He was concerned as to how I was holding up, and I assured him that I had accepted what had happened.

"Desmond, it's time to tell me about Margaret."

I shrugged my shoulders. "Where do I begin?" I asked, voice subdued.

He smiled. "As they always say in books, 'Let's start at the beginning'."

And that's what I did. I told of my first meeting with this most beautiful of women, recounted how it was love at first sight for me, and explained how I knew that my life would be forever changed. I spoke of our long-distance relationship, of how we were always in constant communication by phone and letter, and how our relationship blossomed. I spoke of how we saw each other every couple of weeks or so and how we had enjoyed so many intimate moments. There was no happier man alive.

The years unfolded, and my love grew exponentially with each passing season. I became a doctor, started to practice, and after a while, decided to return to America. I told of Eddy Regan officiating at our nuptials one weekend in Paris because Margaret had refused a Church wedding. I admitted that I knew now that it wasn't even a legal ceremony and certainly not one recognized by the Catholic Church. I further allowed that if the truth were told, all the participants were inebriated, especially the bride and groom. However, I was adamant in my insistence that I was deliriously happy that fateful day.

I told of how we had decided to go to America and settle in Naples, a city Margaret had grown to love. I recounted that on a weekend together shortly after we had decided on this course of action, she informed me that she was pregnant and that I was filled to overflowing on hearing the news.

My tale continued with the telling of how one day shortly after that, I had phoned to tell her that we would be soon leaving for America, only to learn that Margaret was nowhere to be found! I told how her mother confirmed that Margaret had run off to Istanbul with an American and ended by admitting to Dr. Mulvahill that because I couldn't cope, I simply fell into the abyss of despair.

It probably sounds like this recounting took only a few minutes, but that was not the case. Once I started talking, I couldn't shut up. It took the better part of three sessions for my story to unfold, and through it all Mulvahill just listened and made notes. I suspect now that he also recorded our sessions. He had to have done so in order to have been conversant with the facts as he directed me to move deeper and deeper to explore certain aspects of that relationship during later consults. I suppose those recording disks still exist, gathering dust in some filing cabinet more than forty-five years later, electronic recordings of love lost. Several times I was reduced to tears of anguish and self-pity, only to be counterbalanced with moments of righteous wrath. Through it all Dr. Mulvahill gave me a free rein. He was remarkable.

Now, it was time for him to bring some semblance of order to the chaos that was my life. He spoke in the present tense.

"Desmond, you tell of that first meeting with Margaret and of her reaction when you mentioned you were in Ireland to attend medical school," he began. "You vividly describe the transformation from beautiful woman to venomous harridan when you spoke of your plans. You say her behavior that night both shocked and repulsed, and although the incident lasted only a minute and was never repeated, it left an indelible impression on you."

"All true," I replied defensively. "Remember, her fiancé had just up and left without a word of explanation, off to Australia or some such place with another woman. How in the hell would you feel?" I lashed out.

He ignored the question.

"Well, I understand her reaction," I answered in defense of the accused. I felt he was picking on Margaret, and I was losing my temper again.

"And her fiancé was a practicing physician?"

"That's my understanding."

His next question came at me from left field. "Do you believe Margaret was being faithful to you while you were apart so much of the time?"

My face reddened. I knew where this was leading, and I didn't like it one bit. Events would strongly argue that she had multiple lovers in my absence, but in my blindness to all but perfection when it came to Margaret, the thought never crossed my mind. Desmond loves Margaret. Margaret loves Desmond. There is no room for anyone else. Ours is the perfect relationship.

"Did you feel worthy of Margaret?" he asked, slipping into the past tense.

That question also took me by surprise. "What do you mean?"

"Did you feel worthy of Margaret's affection?" he repeated, then expanded on the question. "Did you ever wonder why a worldly, refined, talented, beautiful young woman who spoke several languages would fall in love with a penniless medical student?"

"Well, sure," I mumbled, "but she loved me all the same." *Why is he doing this to me?* Of course Margaret loved me. My God, we had been intimate on our very first date, just hours after we had met. So, of course, I felt worthy of her affection. Love is like that. *What a stupid question!*

"How many women had you been intimate with before Margaret?"

I had been pacing the floor, getting angrier by the minute at the turn in the conversation, and now this. I unleashed my anger. "That's none of your goddamned business, you bloody mental voyeur! Everything in the minds of you psychiatrists boils down to sex, sex, and sex. That, or peeing in bed as an infant. Those two things are the answer to all a person's problems as far as you quacks are concerned. No wonder people think that everything psychiatrists spout is just so much rubbish." I was on the warpath, looking for scalps, spitting out my words as I ranted, saliva flying in every direction.

"You've answered my question, Desmond, thank you."

"I didn't answer your question, thank you," I cruelly mimicked.

"Yes, Desmond, you did. You used one key word during your response, and that word was a very emphatic none, as in *none* of your goddamn business.

"That is absolute bullshit!" I screamed back. "You're just jealous that I had Margaret. Me, poor Desmond, and not some big, fancy, rich doctor, such as yourself. I've been with lots of women, dozens, actually. How about you?" I mocked.

"Desmond, I think we've covered enough for today," He said with a kind, caring smile as he rose.

I was having none of it! "No, goddamn you to hell, we're not finished for the day. I'll let you know when we're finished!"

"Desmond, I'll see you Friday. Meanwhile, I want you to think long and hard about what we discussed today. Spend the time wisely, you need to start looking at the truth."

He never raised his voice, and by the time I had barreled past his nurse, I was as embarrassed at my crassness and myself as I have ever been in my life—before or since. Dr. Mulvahill was the epitome of kindness and professionalism. However, through that terrible dark cloud of anger I knew he was my only hope, a fragile lifeline tossed my way as I floundered on a turbulent sea.

The follow-on sessions were utter agony. I was peeled open like an onion, layer after layer, until the core of Desmond Donahue was exposed. As I look back, I now see it was I who did the peeling, and that Dr. Mulvahill only guided the process by the use of a single word—or at times—a phrase. Because of his formidable skill, he forced me to see the truth without my rose-colored glasses. Only on one particular issue did he offer his advice.

"Desmond, the question of the child's paternity could lead to an endless debate in your mind, and you would never reach a satisfactory answer. We know the blood type matched. That's a medical fact, and the law of averages would lead any rational individual to conclude the infant was indeed yours. Accept that. It's a valid conclusion, and by accepting it, you allow yourself to go forward. The child's death was a terrible tragedy, but as a doctor you know that these events happen more often than most people think. It's a part of life, and yet it's no easier to bear when it happens to us. Accept the fact this was your child and accept the fact it did not survive. I'm not telling you to forever shut all thought of its existence from your mind, I'm only saying, don't dwell on it."

"I understand, and, yes, I can accept it. I won't deny that it's sad, but I can truthfully say I understand that nothing healthy would ever come from my continued speculation as to whether or not I was the father. Conception coincides with a time when Margaret and I were intimate, so, yes, I will always see it as mine."

"Good. I believe so, too."

After many weeks of therapy, this is what Dr. Mulvahill guided me to conclude about my relationship with Margaret. Let me also say that never did he agree or disagree with my conclusions, but that he seemed satisfied I could now go forward with my life. I will not tell you it was easy. It wasn't. Nevertheless, it gave me the strength to carry on.

Margaret had used me. She had used me to get back at her fiancé, a doctor, for running away with another woman. She was consumed with a hatred that went beyond all reasoning. *Hell has no fury like that of a woman scorned.* No one could deny that Margaret had been scorned. Unfortunately, she chose me as the vessel for her retribution. And she bided her time. She waited until I became a doctor. Or so she thought. She waited until we were married. *Or so I thought.* And she waited until she could announce she was pregnant. She wanted my pain to be excruciating. And for the *coup de grâce*, she vanished with another man. Just as her fiancé doctor had done those several years earlier. She could not get back at him, so she did the next best thing. She created his stand-in. Me. It was my bad luck to be the victim in her demented morality play. He and I had become interchangeable. Too damn bad if you can't handle it, Desmond. *Tough shit!* Now you know how I felt! Exit stage left. End of play.

And the lesson I learned? *First love, last love.* I would never allow another Margaret into my life.

On my last visit, Dr. Mulvahill gave me a prescription he wanted me to take for two months and thoughtfully gave me a letter of introduction to two prominent psychiatrists in America.

"If you ever find yourself needing someone to talk to, please contact either of these men. They are close friends, and either will do anything in his power to help you. They will gladly recommend a colleague in just about any city you might decide to settle in. Remember, Desmond, 'No man is an island.' You know, for the life of me, I still can't remember who said that!" he exclaimed in mock frustration, and we both smiled, remembering how he had used that phrase during our first meeting. "Also, I suggest that if you can see financially not having to work for the first few months once back in the States, then my recommendation is that you don't. Get yourself firmly planted, Desmond; the extra time will do you a world of good."

I stood and grasped his hand. "Thank you for everything, Dr. Mulvahill. You've been wonderful, and I thank God you were there when I needed you. And if I should need help in the future, rest assured I'll seek it out. I've lost my foolish sense of pride." I smiled a cheeky grin. "By the way, John Donne is the name you're looking for. He's the bloke who said we're not islands. It's a line from his 'Meditation Seventeen.' It's the same place Hemingway copped the title for his book For Whom the Bell Tolls. I was full of myself that day.

Mulvahill wished me the best of luck, and as I found myself strolling back to my apartment for the last time, I experienced pangs of true guilt. I had not been completely honest with Doctor Mulvahill. At no time did I divulge that I was a fraud. I simply could not bring myself to tell him that I was not a doctor.

I really felt that had he discovered that fact he would have had me committed.

CHAPTER SIXTEEN

It's **no accident** Florida is called the Sunshine State. The peninsular is blessed with a sub-tropical climate, which means hot and humid in the summer months, balmy and dry the rest of the year. Pretty close to ideal. At least in my view. True, summers can be a challenge, but then again, where in the United States isn't it a scorcher around the time of the midyear solstice? Air conditioning is the great equalizer, and oftentimes when I hear the constant humming of untold numbers of compressors laboring away, I conjure up an image of the entire state being hooked-up to one giant, life-support system.

During my first few days in Naples, I stayed in a hotel, using the time to ready the condominium I had purchased on an earlier trip. Service for electricity, telephone, and water had to be started, and I needed furniture for my new home. Everything came together by the third week, and to celebrate, I just sat on my terrace and reveled in the simple act of lording over my kingdom.

Of course, thoughts of Margaret still flooded my mind, but thanks to Dr. Mulvahill, I understood that it would be a long time before the healing process would be complete.

I took stock of my situation. It was now late fall, and my diploma from medical school would not become "official" until the following June, which meant I had eight months to figure out a direction for my life. My savings were adequate to see me through, as long as I didn't spend money like a drunken sailor. My only major purchase was a new Ford Escort, again red. I turned thirty-eight that October and for the first time in memory was not beholden to the turning hands of a clock.

My condominium was in a gated community, which meant golf, tennis, and three swimming pools, all for the exclusive enjoyment of coddled residents and guests. Many of my neighbors were snowbirds, those fortunate few who could afford to winter in the south and summer in the north. They enjoyed the best of both worlds; all it takes is money.

I tried my hand at golf, but soon found I didn't have the patience to spend the better part of a day chasing that elusive dimpled ball from pillar to post, so I began to channel my energies into becoming passably proficient at tennis. This was the mid-seventies, and tennis had taken America by storm. I spent many a frazzled hour trying to master the finer points on how to get that fuzzy-skinned, white—or the now popular yellow—ball over a one-hundred-foot-high net! I was a first-rate klutz, but perseverance finally paid off and I was soon holding my own. The best therapy to come from all this frenetic activity was that the game proved to be the perfect setting in which to meet my neighbors. The resident tennis pro held lessons three mornings a week, and then offered personalized instruction to those who wanted or needed it. Like me.

People were naturally curious about their new neighbor with an Irish accent. My story was brief. I was a widowed doctor from Ireland, recuperating from an unspecified illness and using this healing time to determine what I eventually wanted to do with my life. I was a miser with words regarding my personal trials, uttering only a sentence or two in response to direct questions. People soon sensed that I didn't wish to say more. A pattern was developing which would become second nature. My fabricated life soon took on a reality all its own, so much so, that in time I came perilously close to believing the story myself. My wife had died in childbirth, and the child she was carrying lived but a few hours. A horrible, tragedy, but something I had to come to terms with in my own way. Folks would cluck their tongues in sympathy, and then ease the conversation onto more neutral ground.

In the spring of 1976, I received terrible news. My sister telephoned from London to tell me father had died. Sixty-seven-years-old. I grieved. Had Arthur Donahue ever known a day of happiness? True, he had been his own worst enemy, and his time on earth had not been easy. Now that he was gone, I was flooded with mixed emotions. I knew I could not bear to see him in his casket or be a witness to my mother's grief. It was the finality I could not accept and knew I would unravel. Reluctantly, I made the decision not to go home. I wired flowers, then sat and wrote a long, somewhat rambling letter to my mother, telling her of my feelings and expressing the hope that my reasons would be received with understanding. I also promised I would come to visit within the next few months. She still did not know the bitter truth about Margaret, although I had mentioned in earlier letters that the child had died during her second trimester. My mother wrote back telling me she fully understood my fears, and how she was so looking forward to a visit from me later in the year.

In June, my diploma became "official," yet I was not mentally prepared to take the necessary steps to become a physician again.

In September I received a letter from Mrs. Kerrigan. She had heard of my father's death and was writing to convey her condolences. She ended by mentioning that she had heard from a reliable source that Margaret was living in Seville, Spain. Alone. Apparently, her lover had decided that a life with Margaret was not what he wanted after all and had returned to America and his wife, who it seemed had forgiven him his trespasses.

The wheels started to turn. Seville? *Why not a trip to Spain, Desmond?* What an excellent suggestion! Maybe you could bump into her. I began to rationalize. On the way home I could stop over in Ireland and visit mother. A perfect plan.

And that's what I did. I found not a trace of my wayward Delilah even though in my heart I knew I had embarked on a quixotic quest. But I had tried.

During my last afternoon in Seville, I was eating lunch at an outdoor cafe in sight of the city's magnificent cathedral when a family of five swooped down on the area and noisily squeezed themselves around a small table next to mine.

"When are we going back to Naples, Daddy?" a little girl whined, then noisily sucked up soda from her glass. "I miss my dog! Let's go to Disney World. Let's go home!" She switched audiences, and pleaded her case in Spanish to her mother.

The father answered her in Spanish, then turned to me and smiled apologetically as if to say: Isn't it a barrelful of laughs traveling with the little darlings?

"Excuse me," I said, "did I hear your daughter say that you're from Naples? You mean in Florida?"

"Yes. Do you know it?" he replied in perfect, yet accented English.

"Know it? I live there!" I exclaimed, delighted to meet neighbors a continent away. "I'm on vacation, but I'm leaving tomorrow. I'll be stopping in Ireland for a week to visit my family; then I'll be back in Florida right after that."

He invited me to join them. He introduced himself as Alberto Alonzo, and then proudly introduced his family. He asked me my name, and then to make conversation asked what I did in Naples.

I recited my canned speech to which he expressed sympathy and then rapidly translated my tale of woe to his wife. She nodded her condolences. The three children just stared.

"A doctor!" he exclaimed. "But so am I. What a small world."

We chatted for about an hour, a restless, squirming eternity for the children. As we paid our bills and prepared to part, we exchanged phone numbers.

"I'll call you at the end of the month, Desmond. You must come to our home for dinner."

Alberto Alonzo and I became fast friends. He was a native of Spain, but his wealthy family had owned homes in both Naples and Miami for many years. He had become a U.S. citizen, but unable to gain admittance into a medical school in the States he had returned to Spain and had completed his education there.

Now he was frustrated. He had twice failed to pass the Foreign Medical Graduates Exam. Badly. The reason for this dismal showing was not so much from his lack of an understanding of English, but rather a paucity of clinical experience. This was the downfall for many doctors trained in offshore schools.

* * *

"I'm now enrolled in a special course in Miami," Alonzo explained that first night after dinner. "It's a nine month program to prepare me for the test and promises good results. But who really knows, Desmond? It may be that I will have to go back to Spain if I ever hope to practice." He wore a long face. "My family wants to stay in America, and so do I. You see my problem, no?"

I did. His was a common tale.

"For the next few months, I must live in Miami during the week and come here on weekends. It will be hard, but it's what I must do." He sipped an after dinner cognac. "I envy you, my friend. You have everything you need to sit the National Boards. All you have to do is pass the exam for your Florida license. You're a very lucky man, *amigo*."

Little did he know.

My life continued its aimless drift. One can only tolerate so much tennis and idleness, and as the New Year unfolded, I began to seriously consider going back to work. My financial situation was such that I needed to at least cover recurring expenses and not eat into my principal, which was disappearing at an alarming rate. But I knew I wasn't ready to jump headlong into the frenetic world of a full-fledged physician again. At least not yet. However, it was time to test the waters, if only the shallows.

Opportunity knocked in the form of an ad for a respiratory therapist at a small private hospital less than a mile from home. Why not? I thought.

I interviewed with the administrator and the head of the department. I showed them my paperwork from the "Roger Connolly Files." They were impressed. I told them of my recently deceased wife and child, and candidly explained that I was not in any rush to get back into the grind of the eighteen-hour days demanded of interns and residents.

"My plan is to spend the next few months studying for the national boards," I explained. "This position gives me the chance to earn a living and will keep me from being forced into something I know I'm just not ready for yet. When the time is right, I'll know it."

"Well, you're a bonanza for us, Dr. Donahue," the administrator gushed. "The position is yours for as long as you like. And any help we on the staff can give you with your studies, why, all you've got to do is ask."

"When would you like me to start?"

* * *

I now had money coming in again. Positive cash flow the Wall Street types like to call it.

Over the months, I had met several area doctors through the country club set, and I told them what I had decided to do. All were outwardly supportive, but I could tell more than a few thought I had become demented. Why would anyone with an M. D. degree waste his time as a respiratory therapist when he could be preparing to feed at the trough of largess reserved exclusively for physicians? Poor Desmond must have lost his mind when he lost his family.

I lived in this state of limbo for almost two years. Alberto Alonzo finally passed the boards and moved his family to Miami at the start of 1978. He had accepted a position in a clinic in Hialeah, one of the many towns sprouting in Dade County. Hialeah is a Spanish-speaking enclave, the perfect spot for a doctor such as Alberto. The two of us would visit back and forth at least once a month, and with each meeting, he would hound me to move to Miami and get on with my life.

"You cannot live the rest of your days in sorrow over the loss of your wife, Desmond. You are now over forty," he reminded me, "and you owe it to yourself to put to good use those many years of hard study. You will never be happy doing what you are doing. I tell you what! I will see what is available in the hospitals in the Miami area and let you know what I find out. At least consider it, Desmond."

"No promises, but, yes, I'll consider it."

Four months later Alberto sent me a clipping from the Sunday edition of *The Miami Herald.* A house physician was needed at Sweetwater Hospital, a private facility in the suburbs.

"This is perfect for you," he exclaimed two days later as we spoke on the phone. "I took the liberty of speaking on your behalf to Mr. Meridian, the administrator. He is a friend of a friend, and looks forward to meeting you. How soon can you come for an interview?"

I laughed. "Just for you, Alberto, so that you don't lose face, I'll call this Meridian chap right now and set it up."

"Excellent. It's time for you to be a doctor again."

I was hired with little fanfare. Donald Meridian breezed through our interview, and then immediately set up an appointment for me to meet the owner, Doctor Murray Whittle. Whittle barely glanced at my credentials.

"When can you start?" No grass grew under his feet. "We're a very busy hospital, Doctor, and I need you just as soon as possible. I don't need to wait for confirmation from Ireland. I know everything is in order! It's just a formality." He flashed a big, toothy, million-dollar smile.

I explained that I had to relocate from Naples, which should take about a month.

"Oh, no, Doctor Donahue," said Meridian. "We needed you yesterday!"

"Donald's right," Whittle chimed in. "We'll get in touch with our real estate agent today and have her find you a place to live. You should be able to move from Naples in the next couple of days and be ready to start with us next Monday. Agreed?"

The gods must have been smiling because two days later I had a sales contract on my condominium. There hadn't even been time to formally list it with the broker when he called to say he already had a buyer, a woman who had agreed without reservation to my asking price.

The following day the agent in Miami called to say that she had the perfect house for me to rent, and with my approval, would take care of making sure the utilities were all working prior to my arrival. No sleepy little backwater town was Sweetwater.

On the third Monday of June 1979, I arrived in Miami to start working as a physician after a hiatus of almost three years. I was ready.

Meridian showered me with reams of paperwork to review and a mountain of forms to be completed. "Got to be done, Doctor Donahue. You know how it is."

After an hour of nonstop reading and signing, he pulled a blank piece of paper from his drawer. "And lastly, we need to get an official transcript and certification from Ireland." He banged out a letter on his electric typewriter as he spoke.

"Here's the address you should use," I volunteered, pushing the information under his nose. "And this is the name of the person you should send it to. I suggest you print *'Reference: Desmond Donahue,'* on the envelope, just as I've written it here. That should speed things up." Such a helpful employee, this new guy.

"Got it. I'll finish up here if you'll just go down the hall to Doctor Whittle's office. Good luck and welcome aboard."

It didn't take long to see why they couldn't wait for me to get started. I later discovered that they had gone through house physicians like most folks go through toilet paper. It was a machine which devoured people. A money-making machine, but only for Doctor Whittle.

The staff was a veritable United Nations. Hardly a soul was fluent in English, and I include in that mix the nurses and doctors. I soon came to see the place was really nothing short of a factory masquerading as a hospital. Let me explain.

Dr. Whittle had contracts to provide medical care to the residents of several area nursing homes. Every day we would send a bus to one or another of these facilities and transport "patients" back to the hospital for routine checkups. They would undergo batteries of tests, usually lasting the better part of the day. We would feed them their noontime meal in the cafeteria, and then continue with procedures well into the afternoon. And all this would be billed to Medicare and private insurance companies. It was assembly line medicine, and ninety-five percent of the testing was unnecessary. But the money poured in. For Doctor Whittle.

My days were long, and oftentimes were my nights. I covered the emergency room twice a week, and it was here I got the chance to practice real medicine. In no time I was up to speed, and on more than one occasion, Dr. Whittle called me into his office to tell me what a good job I was doing. I was none too happy with the fraud I was witnessing in the handling of the geriatric nursing home residents, but craven imposter that I was with secrets of my own to hide, I kept my opinions to myself.

My tenure lasted two months.

"Dr. Donahue, please report to the administrator." I was being paged.

I dialed the number from a house phone. "What's up, Donald?"

"Please drop what you're doing, Desmond, and come to my office, stat."

Meridian, handed me a letter.

Five minutes later, I was on the street.

18 October 1978
Mr. Donald Meridian,
Executive Vice President,
Sweetwater General Hospital,
2500 S.W. 75 Ave,
Miami, Florida, 33155,
U.S.A.

Dear Mr. Meridian:

Your letter has been referred to our office.

We are unable to trace the graduate record of a Dr. Desmond Donahue as you requested. It is possible that the spelling of the name is in error, or alternately, that he may have graduated from one of the other medical schools in the country.

If we can help, please get in touch with us again.

Yours sincerely,

C. R. Hawley

"There's a big bloody mistake, here," I ranted, handing the letter back to him. While I was posturing, my mind was racing. How in the hell could this have happened? The first time I have to use Roger's file, and this is the result. I was both scared and furious. I looked Meridian in the eye. "Did you address the envelope as I suggested?" I asked.

"Oh, hell, Desmond, I don't remember. Is that important?"

I threw up my hands in a show of exasperation. "The college is in the process of transferring all student records to computer tape," I improvised. "I've heard of other screw-ups like this. I'll get on it, stat and make sure you get the correct information. I'm really sorry about this, Donald; it's downright embarrassing."

"I know it is, but, my hands are tied. I have to let you go. If any regulators came in and saw your file, well, we'd all be in a world of trouble here," he explained. "I won't say anything about this to the rest of the staff, but you see my position?"

"Of course I do, Donald."

He shook my hand and gave me a photocopy of the doomsday letter. "When you get all this straightened out, call me. You've been the best house physician we've had in ages. I'll miss you. Good luck."

It didn't take long to figure out what had probably gone wrong. Meridian's letter had been opened by someone else in the registrar's office, probably because my contact was away on vacation. This was one contingency Roger and I had not thought through. Such a small thing. However, the consequences were disastrous for me. I blamed myself. I should have immediately written by the fastest means available, warning my mole of the pending request for information. I would not make that mistake again.

I wrote to my contact in Cork and received a prompt reply assuring me that such a mistake would never be repeated. *Trust me!* I could almost hear the gnashing of teeth a full continent away.

I shrugged off my departure from Sweetwater Hospital to Alberto Alonzo by saying I was not comfortable with the operation. I did not go into details, but by innuendo led him to deduce it was a decision based on moral and ethical grounds. Such a paragon of virtue. Yet sometimes things work out for the best, although it's not always evident at the time.

Shortly after my termination, an investigation of the place was launched by federal and state officials. Apparently, Whittle's Medicare billings were so out of line with other hospitals of like-size that the red flag was raised to the rafters in Washington. The upshot of it all was that the hospital closed, the corporation went into bankruptcy, and the man with the million-dollar smile, Doctor Jerome Whittle, went to jail. I had gotten out just in time. Donald Meridian was exonerated of any wrongdoing, which pleased me. He really was one of the good guys.

And once more, it was Alberto, who came to my rescue, a rescue that took several months. He was looking more and more like a reincarnated Roger.

"I hear St. Anslem's Hospital in Coral Gables is hiring. They're expanding and need residents and surgical assistants. Put in an application, Desmond. What have you got to lose?"

I contacted the administrator and began the process of applying for a position. In due course, I met with a Doctor Pedro Santiago, the Chief of Resident Staff.

"Everything looks to be in order, but of course, no promises until we have what we need from Ireland." He smiled as he spoke in a voice rich in the accent of his native Cuba. No cutting corners here, no talk of needing me yesterday. This was a hospital run with the efficiency of a Swiss watch. Doctor Santiago exuded confidence, a man fully in command of himself, and a doctor in control of his environment. But not riding a high horse. A gentleman in every sense of the word. And I was pulling his chain most convincingly. All these years later, I still regret my hoodwinking this man. He trusted me and I betrayed that trust. I can equivocate, and I can rationalize, but it still washes with the same result. I tell myself that desperate men do desperate things, but my duplicity with this man still causes me acute embarrassment to this day.

As soon as my interview was over, I dashed off a letter to Ireland alerting the mole to the impending inquiry from Doctor Santiago.

Second time was the charm. All documents arrived back in order. I was home free!

"Congratulations, Doctor Donahue. Everything we've received from University College is excellent. You've passed the first hurdles, but before we commit ourselves, I would like you to show us how well you can assist in surgery. If that works out to everybody's satisfaction, then I can formally say that we would like you to join us here at St. Anslem's. This is a probationary period," he cautioned, allowing himself an out. "During that time, we can see if you fit in with us. However, on the obverse side of that coin, it allows you time to assess us, and to reach a decision as to whether or not you want to continue an association. Sound fair?" So much time had passed that I was beginning to despair of being offered a position. He ended with demand: "We need to have you pass a physical exam. Standard procedure for all new employees. A rule mandated by our insurance carrier. We're all beholden to them, Doctor Donahue. No one can escape their clutches. Insurance companies rule the world!" He chortled at his own humor.

"Thank you, Doctor Santiago. I accept your tentative offer, and I'm delighted at the possibility of working at St. Anslem's for many years to come." There was just one thing nagging me from the corner of my mind, and I gave voice to my concern. "I look forward to working with your surgeons during the evaluation phase, but I must remind you it's been a while and I'm probably a little rusty."

"Not to worry. We don't want you to perform an open heart procedure. At least not right away," he laughed. "I know how long it's been, so relax. The important thing is that you can blend in with the flow here. That's really what we are looking for. Compatibility."

We shook hands. "Thank you. Just let me know when you want me back."

I headed home in my Escort, flying on a cloud a hundred miles above the city. I had done it. *I was in!*

*   *   *

I was as nervous as Mark Twain's once-scorched cat that first morning in July 1979 as I drove to the hospital to scrub for surgery. This was the acid test. The buck stops here. My mind was a dervish, full of trite phrases.

You can do it, boy, I distinctly heard Roger whisper in my ear as I maneuvered that last hundred yards into the staff parking lot. His voice was so real, his presence so overwhelming, that I caught myself involuntarily glancing at the passenger seat. And I actually answered him. *You're right, Roger, I can! Stick around and watch me do my stuff.* Roger just laughed beside me.

The first surgeon I scrubbed with was a man named Doctor Lamping. He was all business, and as he prepared for the initial case of the morning, he dryly went over the procedure and explained what he expected to find. Doctor Santiago scrubbed right along with us. He was going to observe.

We all marched into the theater and took our places around the draped, sleeping figure under the lights, my taking up the position of second assistant.

Lamping looked to each of us in turn and asked, "Everybody ready?"

We all nodded.

"How about you, Doctor?" he asked, addressing the anesthesiologist seated at the patient's head.

"All systems up here say go."

So began my very first case at St. Anslem's Hospital. We were here to remove a gall bladder from a markedly overweight Latin male. This is normally a rather routine procedure, a non-event in the hands of someone as skilled as Lamping. But because of the obesity factor, everyone was on their toes in the event the unexpected happened.

The attending surgeon sets the mood in any operating room, and everyone falls in line as if on cue. Some are easygoing, telling mildly off-colored stories or jokes; some sing songs or hum annoyingly out-of-tune to the piped-in music, and some even recite poetry. Those guys are really boring! But each invariably develops his or her own style. And some are bloody tyrants. These are the individuals who yell and scream from the moment they first pick up their scalpel and tend to keep up a vitriolic diatribe until the last closing suture is in place. They will then march out of the theater without so much as a thank you to the exhausted OR team. Many a time I have seen these surgeons hurl instruments at the staff or heap such verbal abuse on them that the unfortunates have fled the theater in tears. Not common, but it does happen more than we like to admit. These are usually the *prima donnas*, brilliant, but mostly in their own minds. To their colleagues they are horses' asses.

None of the above described Doctor Lamping. He rarely ever smiled, but he sure was good at what he did best. Surgery. No antics here. He never engaged in idle chatter and always gave full attention to the task before him.

That morning, Doctor Santiago circulated around the table, standing for a few minutes behind each position before moving on to the next. Within the hour we all trooped out of the theater while the patient was trundled off to recovery. We huddled to brief the next case.

"Breast biopsy," Lamping said, as he placed a host of x-rays onto the light board. "Our patient's a forty-two-year-old mother with a family history of breast cancer." He stood close to the pictures, intently studying them as he spoke. "Let's pray the biopsy is negative, but I'm not encouraged with what I see. All right, let's get started."

Unfortunately, Lamping's words proved prophetic. The biopsied material was sent down to pathology while we waited in silence for the diagnosis. The verdict was not good. The tissue was malignant. A radical mastectomy was indicated.

This is one life-saving procedure most surgeons hate to perform. The necessary physical mutilation leaves indelible scars on both the body and the soul. Some women cope better than others, usually those blessed with a tremendous support system of family and friends. Many of the less fortunate sink into a state of depression, thus hindering the recovery process. Totally understandable. There is never a sense of satisfaction of a procedure well-done after a radical mastectomy. It's one operation in which everyone loses.

Thirty days later Doctor Santiago rendered his verdict.

"I've gotten excellent reports from all the surgeons, Desmond. Even Doctor Lamping had good things to say about you, and he is not the most generous of souls when it comes to handing out compliments. Your clinical knowledge and operating room acumen were praised by all who've worked with you. So, if you would like to stay, well, the job is yours for the taking.

Thus began my thirteen-year association with St. Anslem's Hospital.

CHAPTER SEVENTEEN

Life took on a semblance of normalcy. I was back in the mainstream. As an employee of the hospital, I enrolled in the group medical, dental, life insurance, and pension plans. It was the American way, and I was a part of the system. It felt good. I informed Brook and Don of my good fortune, and we all promised to get together at Thanksgiving or Christmas.

St. Anslem's Hospital enjoyed a reputation for excellence, not only in the local area, but also throughout the state. It was a "Not for Profit," a magnet for the top specialists in a score of disciplines. I was proud to be associated with such talented professionals, and my learning curve expanded exponentially.

I slipped into a comfortable routine, and with the uneventful passing of the first few months, came to worry less and less about the possibility of exposure. As I've said before, this fear was a constant companion, and even subconsciously, I found myself ever on guard. I would always do more listening than talking whenever a group would gather in the doctors' lounge between cases. Some of these men had very lucrative practices, but I came to see that more than a few had truly empty lives. Their whole existence revolved around making more and more money and seeing how fast they could spend it. Bigger houses, better cars, newer boats, more toys. What they couldn't spend, their wives did. They were in constant communication with their stockbrokers, men they would converse with for hours on end, moguls all, living lives held hostage to the vagaries of Wall Street. These healers had ceased caring about their patients as people long ago and made no bones about it amongst themselves. They were in medicine for the *lucre*, period.

Could mine just be a case of sour grapes? I honestly don't think so. I've met untold numbers of fine doctors who haven't become jaded by the money, men and women who have a balance in their lives. They love their chosen work and take a full measure of satisfaction in what they do. They have retained their humanity and demonstrate a genuine concern for their patients. As far as they are concerned, it's the icing on the cake to be compensated so well for what they do. I believe most would still choose to be doctors even if the money were not so good.

I would be a hypocrite to say that money was not—and is not—important to me. It is. In many ways, money was the strongest motivating factor in my making the decision I did. I have known grinding poverty firsthand, and, yes, I have long held a morbid fear of ever finding myself again in like circumstances. However, my drive emanates from my unbridled fascination of all things medical. The money is secondary. I have never wanted to have the most, the best, the newest, the biggest. My satisfaction has always come from having made a difference in someone's life.

Life at St. Anslem's was anything but boring. Of course, there were many routine cases we handled on a daily basis, some classified as simple procedures, others more demanding and challenging, but routine, nonetheless. We call these elective surgical cases, which means they are not emergencies. All are planned procedures, often a month or two in advance, so when the day comes when the patient is wheeled into the OR, there are no surprises. This is life in a perfect world. Alas, the real world is not governed in such an orderly manner, so true emergencies are always lurking in the shadows in any busy urban hospital such as ours. It's during these times everybody earns his keep.

My workday would begin at 7 A.M. I would go directly to the doctors' lounge and change into greens. Next, I would check the chalkboard to see what cases I had been assigned, and then I'd zip downstairs to the cafeteria for breakfast.

I would make my way back up to the surgical unit to scrub with the rest of the team, and we would invariably enter the OR bang on the hour of eight. Time was money, and all seven theatres were veritable beehives of activity, save one, which was kept free to handle emergency obstetrics cases.

My professional services as a surgeon were paid for by the hospital as a salary, and the surgeons whom I assisted were very much the beneficiaries of this arrangement. They did not have to reimburse the hospital for my time. My being present to assist, freed up partners who could work on other cases. Ergo, more procedures were performed, and the operating room turnover increased dramatically. The bean counters saw it as efficiency in the use of resources. This made for a stronger bottom line on the balance sheet, which meant the hospital administrator was a very happy man.

If the operating schedule was light—not a common occurrence—I could be finished around three or four in the afternoon, and the rest of the day belonged to me. However, many a day we would still be cutting and sewing well into the night. On those occasions, I would just grab a spare bed in the hospital, sleep for a few hours, and start my routine all over the following morning. *C'est la vie!* I was doing what I enjoyed.

My personal duty schedule was such that I was on-call one night per week, one Saturday and one Sunday each month, and, of course, available on a moment's notice if a true emergency arose. The same applied for everybody on staff. Such an emergency would be something on the order of a major aircraft accident at Miami International or maybe an industrial explosion anywhere in the county. Very rare, but the hospital continuously practiced for such eventualities. We were always poised to respond to the community's emergency medical needs on short notice. If this sounds unique and self-congratulatory on the part of St. Anslem's, I assure you, that was not the reality. All hospitals have such plans and are evaluated on their ability to respond in times of crisis.

The days that I was on call—but not required to be physically at the hospital—I would remain in touch by phone and beeper. It was a very short electronic leash, but it freed me to be able to do other things. I didn't have to sit around hour after hour waiting for something to happen.

As is so often the case in the life of a doctor, a ringing phone is a harbinger of bad news.

"Desmond, are you awake? Desmond, wake up, dammit!"

"Who is this?"

"It's me! Lance Datsmann. Desmond, I need you in surgery. You haven't been drinking, have you?" A trace of real concern evident in his voice. Friday night, Saturday morning. *Oh, shit!*

Fully awake, I snickered at the suggestion. "Don't I wish. No such luck for me, I'm afraid. I go on call at six in the morning, Lance, and it's now just twenty past two," I added, glancing at my bedside clock. "I need my beauty sleep. Whatever it is, I'm sure it can wait until then. G'night."

"No, dammit, don't hang up! I need you now, Desmond. I'm at the hospital, and I've got a major accident case on my hands. It's a doctor's daughter from Los Angeles," he explained rapidly, then mentioned the name of a world-renowned surgeon.

"How bad?" I asked, hopping out of bed, the phone buried in my ear.

"Very bad. Single car accident, two known dead and two transported to Jackson Memorial, and two, including the California girl, here. Desmond, please shake a leg."

"I'm on my way, Lance."

"We'll already be in surgery. They've just about finished the workup in Emergency, so she'll be upstairs momentarily. Prepare for a long day, pal."

When I arrived in the operating theater, there were two teams huddled over the table. I sidled up next to Lance and observed him and one of his partners engrossed in the task at hand. I needed a moment to get my bearings and to receive a quick briefing. The second team was composed of orthopedic specialists, and they were just starting the tedious process of repairing the young woman's seriously damaged legs.

"No head trauma?" I asked.

Lance glanced in my direction for a microsecond, shook his head, and continued his work. "None, thank God. The other kids in the car all have severe head injuries, but this young lady happened to have been wearing a football helmet. Crazy, huh? Seems they were partying up in Fort Lauderdale after attending a U. of M. game in the Orange Bowl earlier in the evening. That helmet sure as shit saved her life. Okay, Desmond, jump right in here as my assistant, and let's keep the flow moving."

Both teams worked on her for nine hours. Bilateral fractures of both legs were repaired and implanted with rods and traction pins by the orthopedic team. A long, tedious, grueling, delicate procedure, while we, the general surgical team, tended to the balance of her injuries.

Our patient had suffered from mesenteric thrombosis, a condition caused by blunt trauma to the abdomen. This meant that the inferior mesenteric artery had ruptured, filling the abdominal cavity with blood. Our first order of business was to clear the area in order to make a detailed diagnosis and accurate assessment as to the true extent of her injuries.

We were on a roll. Once the site was drained, we set to the task of removing her ruptured spleen, and then followed with the repairing of a small, ragged perforation of the liver. And while Lance and I were busy as bees working in the abdomen, his partner had intubated her with a pneumothorax tube, critical for the job of re-inflating her collapsed left lung, punctured by two fractured ribs. We continued our painstaking, methodical examination of the abdominal cavity. *Bingo!* We uncovered a portion of the small bowel that had been torn and mangled, necessitating the removal of some eighteen inches of the organ, followed by a re-sectioning of the two ends. To repeat, it was a long day for all involved. Yet, nobody was aware of the hours slipping away. Time stood still while our patient used up ten units of blood in her struggle to survive.

Lance finally stood back and gazed down at his sleeping charge. He let out a heaving sigh. "She's young, she's strong, and she'll survive, but it's going to be a long, painful rehab to full recovery." He turned to the team. "Thank you all for a super job." From behind his mask, he smiled a tired, but happy smile. "Now, I've got to see if her parents are outside and give them our encouraging prognosis." He waved a second thanks and shuffled stiffly out of the theater a couple of steps ahead of the rest of us.

We all followed her progress for the next several months via reports from her home in Los Angeles. Her surgeon-father could not say enough good things about the treatment his daughter had received and expressed those thoughts most eloquently in a letter to the editor of *The Miami Herald's* Sunday edition. It was music to our ears from one so famous. One year later, she was back at the university, continuing her studies. That's the kind of happy ending that makes one's heart sing.

Other cases, while serious, are also occasions for laughter. Sounds odd, but let me explain through example.

This particular case also happened to involve Lance.

It was shortly after five o'clock on a mid-week afternoon when we were alerted in the lounge that a multiple gunshot injury was coming up from Emergency. Such cases were becoming more and more common in Miami in the early 1980s, and we steeled ourselves for the worst.

Minutes later, a Latin male was trundled in on a gurney, very conscious and very agitated. He, of course, was trailing an octopus-like assembly of IVs, multiple translucent tentacles, all dripping blood and other fluids into his veins. And he would not lie still for love or money. A deliberate choice of words. All his clothes except his undershorts had been cut-off downstairs, and as he was being transferred by the orderlies to the table, money began to fall out of his boxers. I'm not describing a dollar or two shaking loose, I'm talking serious money! Bundles of it, and all hundreds.

"Take it. Take it all. I pay you now!" he pleaded to his speechless audience in thickly accented English.

"That's very generous of you," I said, the first to recover, and answering for us all, "but we'll wait and get paid later, thank you just the same."

"Let's just see how much more you've got in there, sport," added Lance, slicing the man's underpants off with one run of a sharp pair of scissors. The remaining bundles spilled onto the table and cascaded down onto the floor. "Good lord, man, don't you believe in banks?" Lance's eyes were the size of saucers.

"You keep it all, Doctor," the man implored. "If you don't take it, the police officer downstairs will just steal it from me."

"Well, for your information, this ain't Bogota, pal. However, we do thank you for your generous offer, but I'm afraid it has to go to the police." He turned to an orderly. "Bag it, count it, and take it back down to Emergency. All of it," he added, with mock-severity.

Directing his attention back to the table, he announced, "What do you say, folks? Is it time we put Daddy Warbucks to sleep?"

While we worked on Mr. Rockefeller for the next two and a half hours, repairing the damage caused by three bullets in his legs and two in the groin, we carried on like a bunch of high school kids, each trying to upstage the other with outrageous ideas as to how we should have spent the money.

It turned out there was twenty thousand dollars tucked away in his shorts, and because he was the uncooperative victim of a drive-by shooting, the cops kept the loot as evidence. After six weeks in Recovery, he disappeared one day by simply walking out of the hospital. I mean the man just vamoosed! And in so doing, stiffed the taxpayers of Dade County for almost two hundred thousand dollars in treatment costs in the process.

*   *   *

Mine was not a life of all work and no play...indeed, this Jack was never a dull boy. I did have a personal life, but memories of Margaret were still a crippling force, and I had promised myself I would never again be burned by unrequited love. This is not a good attitude to harbor when entering into a relationship—or while attempting to sustain one. This personality flaw, coupled with my very real need for secrecy, no doubt made me appear to be a cold, uncaring individual, one incapable of returning affection. Therefore, the conclusion reached in the minds of the several women I met over the years was that I was a selfish, self-centered, conceited jerk! Or worse. The reality was that I could sustain a shallow relationship indefinitely, but should intimacy crest to a point where I would be forced to lay bare my soul and expose myself for the shameful fraud that I was, I withdrew. True intimacy was a luxury I could ill afford.

When I embarked upon my journey, little did I know what terrible a price I would have to pay. That it would mean an existence bereft of wife and family or anyone with whom I could share the joys and sorrows of life. Remember, the only other soul who knew my secret was himself dead these past four years. Roger Connolly. My mother certainly didn't know, and my father went to his grave not knowing. And, of course, my many siblings had no idea as to who and what I truly was. Many were the days I would ask myself: *Is it worth it, Desmond?* I was envious beyond words of my friends who had what I so deeply yearned for and oftentimes heard Doctor Mulvahill's voice and the words he spoke during our first encounter in that hospital room in Dublin.

"No man is an island..."

Maybe, just maybe, I was proving to be the exception. Not by choice, but because I had never thought this act of duplicity through to its logical conclusion. Like Faust, I had sold my soul willingly, never imagining there would be such a monstrous price to pay. I was a prisoner of my own making.

Most women gave up on me in short order, cutting their losses by running in search of greener, more emotionally secure pastures. Some were made of sterner stuff. These hearty souls must have reasoned that with time, affection, and patience, they could bring me around. All knew the story of Margaret and the unborn child, so of course, I was a tragic, true-life, romance novel figure in their eyes. But no woman can cleave to a man who will not return love and affection in kind. Thus, my relationships were spiritually empty, affairs only of the flesh and shallow beyond words. How many fine women did I heartlessly spurn, forcing them away? I honestly don't know. However, I was the loser in the majority of those instances.

Of course, there were also women who were after me solely because I was a doctor, and they could have cared less if I had two heads. In their minds, the word *doctor* is interchangeable with the word *money*. The world calls them "gold diggers," so I had no feelings of guilt over any dalliance with the few that I met. These women enter relationships with eyes wide-open, incapable of hiding their true purpose in life. It's a business proposition they seek. I'll trade sex and companionship for money. I'll overlook the fact that you are physically repugnant. You have the gold and that's all that matters. For every gold digger, I suppose there's got to be a gold mine, but I possessed no mother lode, so those prospectors soon abandoned my bed and headed back into the fray.

* * *

Disturbing news came in 1981when the State of Florida sent word to all hospitals that staff physicians had to show evidence of having passed the Educational Council of Foreign Medical Graduates exam and the national FLEX test. The former was not mandatory, but the latter sure was. Pressure was coming from the state legislature in response to complaints that Florida—and South Florida in particular—was home to many exiled Cuban doctors who were not taking the required steps to become licensed. This practice must cease. Three years was the timeframe in which all house physicians had to comply.

I had already passed the first exam—didn't I have a file from Roger to prove it? So, I took a copy to Doctor Santiago. He filled out some mumbo-jumbo paperwork to placate the state and mailed it off. He also sent a copy to the hospital administrator to be placed in my personnel folder.

"When do you propose to sit the FLEX?" Santiago now asked.

This was the mandatory exam required of all foreign graduates. FLEX is an acronym for Foreign Licensing Exam. No longer were the individual states being allowed to posture like so many sovereign duchies and administer their own exams. This one national test replaced all that and was recognized as the ultimate licensing authority by all fifty states.

Ooooh shit.

"I'll have to take tons of time off to study. It's been years since I graduated. I'll need to go over all the fundamentals again, some from scratch. You know how it is." I was verbally waltzing him wildly around the floor!

Doctor Santiago arched his eyebrows and peered at me over the top of his reading glasses. "Be that as it may, that's what you're going to have to do." He rummaged around a pile of papers on the top of his desk and plucked out a brochure. "Take a look at this."

This was an announcement that the University of Miami was sponsoring a class for foreign medical graduates, a preparatory course to ready them for the FLEX. It described a comprehensive, intensive, six-day-a-week, ten hours a day, three month program of instruction. Classes would be held in a conference room in a local hotel.

"I'll set you up with a leave of absence, Desmond. Get this course under your belt, then sit the FLEX. The program has an excellent reputation, and a lot of our people have gone through it. Heck, for someone with your training and background, it should be a cakewalk." His tone let me know that his terms were non-negotiable. I wasn't about to argue with Pedro Santiago, M.D.

The price of admission was fifteen hundred dollars, payable in full upon registration. I signed on the dotted line that afternoon.

For the next twelve weeks, I reported to the Four Ambassadors Hotel at the stroke of eight, six mornings a week, along with forty or so other wannabes. And I worked my tail off. The curriculum was everything Doctor Santiago had promised—times ten. This was the most challenging, informative, several hundred hours of medical instruction available anywhere. I was bombarded with information and saturated with knowledge by some of the best medical specialists in their fields. Three months later I passed the final exam and was granted a certificate of completion from the University of Miami, School of Medicine. I was proud beyond words. Some twenty percent of my classmates did not fare as well, and they were all graduates of real medical schools in Europe, South America, Mexico, and the Caribbean! And, I hasten to add, some were graduates of U.S. schools who had failed the National Boards more than once.

Look at this, Dean Standiford, I taunted my nemesis from the safety of my mind. *Look what Donahue's done, no thanks to you, you shithead*! And to you, Doctor Santiago, thank you from the bottom of my heart for your wisdom in giving me no choice.

"Now, you're ready to take the FLEX at the next sitting," he advised on my first day back on the job. "I need you for bigger and better things. Congratulations on your fine showing."

The rest of the staff welcomed me back, and life continued as before. Except no one knew of my dilemma. If I sat the test and passed, there would be a comprehensive background investigation before any license would be granted, and I would not survive such a query into my past. The problem in Boston would lead to the problem in Maine, which would lead back to Cork, which would lead the investigators to learn that I was not a doctor! Then, all hell would break loose! My no-win position was anything but enviable.

My colleagues were all supportive and encouraging. They wanted to see me get my license. Indeed, more than a couple hinted at wanting me to join their partnerships. Some were more encouraging than others, such as my good friend, Jack Trader, a well-respected internist with a thriving practice in Miami. Jack and I somehow managed to squeeze in a couple of games of tennis every week.

"Dammit, Desmond, get off your duff and take the frigging exam, already!" He couldn't for the life of him understand my dawdling.

All right, Jack. I hear you. I'm sitting it next go-around, OK?"

"About time," he groused as we enjoyed a beer after a long set on the court in his home. Jack was a perfectionist in all things, and to many people he was a royal pain in the ass. "You don't want to spend the rest of your life as a house physician! Or do you?"

If only you knew the truth, Jack.

Therefore, to keep everybody at bay, I sat the FLEX test—and failed! I had made a conscious decision to fail because had I passed, I would have been boxed into a corner and uncovered. This way, I could buy some time.

My friends were sympathetic. "Don't feel badly, Desmond. Tons of doctors fail the first time out. No big deal. Get your head on straight, study hard, and knock them dead next sitting."

"I will."

Eventually, the furor from the state to get everyone to pass the FLEX died a natural death, so I burrowed deeper into the sanctuary of the bowels of the hospital by doing my job and doing it well. What more could I possibly want? Surgery was everything to me. *Screw what people might think, Desmond!* You just do what you know is best I repeatedly told myself, *ad nauseam.*

The pages of the calendar continued to turn faster and faster as I lay safe and snug in the cocoon I had so meticulously crafted about my persona.

*   *   *

Twice in the years between 1981 and 1988, I embarked on a wild-goose chase to track Margaret down. She was with me every day, a demon I could not exorcise. There were times I was driven to bouts of depression over this lost love, but never did I suffer as I had in Dublin when Doctor Mulvahill had rescued me from myself. I knew my continued infatuation with Margaret was not a healthy thing, but I had it under control. Or so I told myself.

Both times, I had heard that she was living in Mexico. My first trip south of the border took me to Acapulco, the second to Mexico City. *Nada!* Did I see myself for the fool that I was? I did not.

In August 1989, I went to England to attend a family reunion, the first time the Donahue clan would be together since who knows when. Thank God I went, for this proved to be the last time I would see my mother. She had flown over from Ireland accompanied by my youngest brother.

She had been in failing health for some time, plagued with Parkinson's disease, hypertension, and coronary insufficiency. Nevertheless, her spirit was as indomitable as ever, and she wore a permanent smile, radiating pure joy. Earlier in the year, she had made a pilgrimage to Lourdes in France, the site where the Blessed Virgin had appeared to a peasant girl named Bernadette some one hundred years earlier. Bernadette, you will remember, was the name of my little sister who had died in infancy, and mother had always wanted to go to Lourdes because of the closeness she felt to Christ's mother. Such was her faith. It was a high point in her life.

"Desmond, it was wonderful! Imagine me, standing on the same spot the Mother of God once stood. It was beautiful, son, beautiful beyond words!"

What a time we had that last summer of my mother's life. We spent untold hours recounting old times, laughing now at events which had reduced us to tears of misery those many years ago. My mother sensed her time remaining was short, and she made it her duty to spend at least an hour alone with each of her thirteen children.

"Oh, Mamma, you'll outlive us all!" we cheered, none believing a word of it.

"Serve you all right if I do!" she rejoined.

We knew her sands were running out, but we were in denial.

At the end of the week, I bade her goodbye with a promise to return to Ireland at Christmas.

She hugged me as tightly as she could. "That would be grand." Drawing me closer, she whispered in my ear, "I've always been so proud that you took the rainbow to America." She became suddenly quiet and patted my back. "You probably don't remember what I'm talking about, but that's all right, son." I could now feel her crying on my shoulder.

I returned her hug as tightly as I dared, tears flowing down my cheeks. "Of course, I remember, Mamma," I whispered. "We were at Clew Bay, standing on the cliffs, and I was so scared. I held your hand as if I would never let go, and you pointed to a rainbow which you said would come back for me one day and take me to America. You said it was a magic staircase. I remember as if it happened yesterday, Mamma."

In the waning days of September, she was admitted to the hospital in cardiac distress. My brother was with her, and he called to inform me she was resting, but not comfortably. She wasn't complaining and she wasn't in pain, he explained, but her breathing was pronounced and labored, a sure sign of stenosis. I immediately contacted a medical supply house in Miami and ordered two special orthopedic pillows to be flown to Ireland for her.

The next day, I called the hospital and spoke to the sister in charge of her ward.

"Your mother's fading fast, Doctor Donahue. She is still lucid and very much at peace. She received the last rites this morning and is now just praying for the end." The sister paused for a long moment, then said, "Doctor, please call me back in a half hour. I'm going to see about rigging up this phone to take it to her bedside so you can talk to her. Can you ring me back?"

Oh, God in heaven, yes!

I returned the call from the doctors' lounge at the hospital. I thought I was in full control of my emotions, but when I heard my mother's voice, weak but recognizable, I burst into uncontrollable sobs of anguish. Several of the doctors knew of my mother's illness, and when I started to cry, they silently left the lounge and closed the door, graciously allowing me privacy for my final goodbye.

"Desmond, child, don't cry for me! It's my time, and I'm ready to meet my Creator. You children have been fourteen diamonds in my crown, and I have been blessed by each of you. Wipe away the tears, son. Remember, Desmond, I love you into eternity, and I'll always be with you." As weak as she was, she did her level best to give me comfort. Her last words will be with me forever. "Goodbye, my son, and remember me to God."

She died on my birthday, October 5, 1989. I was devastated beyond words. My anchor was gone. I was now truly alone.

A few hours later, her doctor called me at home.

"Doctor Donahue, I got your number from your brother, and I just had to call. I want to offer my condolences and to let you know that your mother slipped away in total peace. In all my years, I have never seen such a look of absolute serenity on a patient's face. God truly came for her this day. I've never before said such a thing about another soul, but I assure you, God came and personally took your mother. I was in the presence of a saint this day and can tell you with all the certitude I can muster, your mother is now in heaven."

"The Lord giveth, and the Lord taketh away..."

Within a month of my mother's death, a special person entered my life. For years, I was too stupid to see the goodness of this woman, but thank God, she persevered because maybe she somehow saw something worthwhile in me.

Her name was Elizabeth.

CHAPTER EIGHTEEN

"**Desmond, I'm calling** with a change of plans," Jack Trader said. "Scratch tennis this Wednesday. Susan's asked me to invite you to join us at the Colonnade Hotel for drinks. Seems she has a friend she wants you to meet." This was Sunday afternoon, and Jack was putting me on notice.

"I don't know," I waffled, "maybe some other time." I really wasn't up to meeting anyone new.

Jack was not about to take no for an answer. "Desmond," he commanded in a no-nonsense voice, "Wednesday, six o'clock, no tennis, no argument." Then, he switched the pitch. "Do it for me, please," he wheedled. "I need to keep peace in my valley, if you know what I mean."

Resignation filled my blackguard's heart. "OK, Attila, six o'clock."

And that's how I met Elizabeth. My first impression? Dazzling. Dazzling in the sense that even a blind man could see this woman was special. She was medium in height with ash blonde hair surrounding a face of fine, regular features, and when she smiled, her eyes sparkled like the finest Columbian emeralds. (I suspected at the time, tinted contact lenses. *Wrong!*) She presented a natural and effortless beauty to the world, a woman who was also gracious, witty, and thoroughly charming. I was impressed. No, I was speechless. *And* intimidated. So much so, that I did not follow-up on my promise to call as we shook hands on parting that first meeting.

Disinterested? Hardly! I knew Elizabeth could have her pick of any man at any time, and I was not the competition. *What could you possibly offer the likes of Elizabeth, pray tell?* I asked myself repeatedly in the following days. And my answer was always the same. *Nothing.*

Two Saturdays later, as I was absently studying ten thousand competing brands of breakfast cereal in the supermarket, a voice interrupted my reverie.

"Hi, Desmond. Remember me?"

And there she was. *Oh God!* In a nanosecond I shrank to some two centimeters in height, scurried under the nearest shelf, and disappeared from sight! *Safe! Home free! Is she still there?*

"Hello, Elizabeth. How are you?" My ability to converse with such a casual ease has always made me the envy of every man in America.

"You forgot to call me, Desmond," she chided playfully, but with not a hint of accusation. No trace of a woman scorned in her voice. Totally in control, leaving me to squirm on the barb of a self-fashioned hook, a pitiful, pathetic worm.

I mumbled a halfhearted, lamebrained, ineffectual excuse, and then blurted out an offer of amends by asking her to dinner for the following Saturday. Surprise! She accepted.

Our first date took us to Key Biscayne, an island community east of Miami. This is the last slice of American terra firma separating the continent and the Bahamas. It is a tropical paradise, boasting miles of the finest white-powdered beaches anywhere. This is not just my opinion—even though I purchased a home there shortly after meeting Elizabeth. No, it's the opinion of the world's toughest critics. Tourists. Those folks who vote with their wallets. And the ballot boxes of Key Biscayne are stuffed to overflowing with such votes of confidence twelve months a year.

During dinner and more so over the ensuing weeks, I learned that this lady had suffered many tragedies, yet had somehow managed to stay on an even keel.

To begin, she was a widow with three children. She had lost her husband to pancreatic cancer five years prior at a time when his business was on the brink of exploding into the stratosphere of success. The children were inconsolable. She somehow found the strength to persevere and had managed to raise her two sons and one daughter with an enviable grace under extraordinary pressure. A remarkable woman in every respect. Even Desmond, the eternal cynic, was impressed.

Shortly after the New Year of 1990, my friend Jack Trader died. He had been fighting lymphoma for about four years, and he really believed he would beat the odds. It was a belief held to the end. He had refused to reorganize his life by deferring to the silent killer within, and his daily routine included a full office and hospital schedule, followed by a regimen of strenuous exercise most evenings. He took a holistic approach to his treatment, and no one could ever say that the man did not fight the good fight. His passing was a heavy blow to family and friends. Jack was just sixty.

His death was followed soon after by the death of another friend, Bob Murray, a victim of the same disease. His widow, Kathy, fell apart with the loss of her husband of forty years, and unable to cope, asked me to work with her attorneys on settling Bob's estate. It was not a happy time in my life.

The death of these two men got me to thinking more and more about my own mortality. I was now fifty-two. Not old, but no longer young. I decided it was time to get more life insurance along with a more suitable disability policy. I made application for both and took the required company physical that included blood and urine tests, along with the requisite poking and prodding. All the results came back normal, and the policies were issued without fanfare. I made Elizabeth the primary beneficiary, overruling her strong objections in the process. Our relationship had progressed to the point that I had a special feeling for Elizabeth, a feeling I had not known since the days of Margaret. I must confess though, I had not bared my soul; thus, she knew nothing of my secret.

Several months later, feeling constantly tired and suffering from general fatigue, I underwent a complete physical to assure myself everything was fine. It wasn't. The bloodwork results came back showing a positive indication of hepatitis C. "Could be wrong," the internist said, "so let's do it again." Second time charm. Negative findings for hepatitis. But a third test—just to be sure—showed the same results as test number one. Now, I was thoroughly confused and more than a little alarmed. I consulted one of the leading specialists in Miami, which meant more blood tests and a liver biopsy. *Boom!* Positive for hepatitis C.

"In all probability you picked it up during surgery," the specialist explained.

I could only nod. That had to be it. The biggest fear of anyone working in the operating room is being nicked by a scalpel during a procedure and having infected blood pass from patient to healer. In this day of AIDS and hepatitis C, contamination is every surgeon's worst nightmare.

He started me on a several months long course of treatment. The prophylaxis included shots three times a week of a relatively new drug called Interferon. Given in massive doses of five million units per treatment, Interferon greatly assists the immune system and does wonders in halting the spread of cirrhosis in the liver. However, it also has a downside. The aftereffects are horrendous: nausea, vomiting, chills, fever, and blinding headaches. This was my lot for six months. I continued meeting the surgery schedule every day that I could, but it wasn't easy. Many a day I wanted nothing more than to stay in bed and sleep for a hundred years, if only to get relief from an ever-exploding head.

I knew recovery would take months, so I did my best to aid the process by eating right and resting, instead of fighting the tiredness when it threatened to overcome me. It paid off. By the end of the year, I was cured.

* * *

If there is one day that I would have to say marked the beginning of the end, that day would be March 1, 1991. The morning started out normally. I went to surgery as always, but around eleven, answered a call from Kathy Murray.

"Desmond, I'm sorry to bother you but I need a favor."

"Shoot."

"My car's giving me fits. The steering is stiff, and it makes a sound like an angry mule when I try to turn the wheel. Do you have a clue what could be wrong?"

I did. I had the same model Datsun 280ZX. The power steering fluid was low. I told her this and stated that I would drop by after work.

I arrived at her house close to dusk. The recalcitrant vehicle was parked on the grass in the front yard underneath a giant ficus. This particular tree sported a root system that seemed to cover the entire state of Florida. Of course I exaggerate, but not by much. I popped the hood and studied the car's innards in the fading light. I couldn't see any signs of a leak, so I filled the power steering unit with the necessary fluid.

"Okay, Kathy," I called out, "turn it on and let the engine warm up!"

She remained in the driver's seat with the window open so she could hear me and waited for my next command.

A full minute later, I called out again. "Put it in reverse and back-up slowly." I wanted to see if there were any telltale signs of fluid stains in the grass.

Boom! The car sprang forward, its open hood striking me savagely on the head while the front right wheel slammed into my left leg, tripping me over the tree's roots and throwing me to the ground in a tangled heap. I was out cold.

Kathy jumped out of the car, certain that she had killed me. She was yelling and crying hysterically when I finally came to.

"Help me up. Help me into the house." I struggled to my feet, and leaning heavily against her, staggered inside.

"Oh God, Desmond! I'm so sorry," she wailed, cleaning my bloodied face with a towel. "Let me call fire-rescue. You've got to get to a hospital."

"Let me just lie still for a few minutes, and I'll be OK," I said, trying to reassure her. "What the hell happened?"

"I don't know, Desmond. I thought I put the car in reverse, but maybe it went into fourth gear instead. It just lurched forward." She was crying so hard it was a struggle to understand what she was saying.

"Not your fault, Kathy, I'll be fine." My head was killing me, and my leg felt as though it was being attacked with a red-hot poker.

I should have gone to a hospital that night, but didn't. Somehow, I managed to drive home and stumble into bed. I slept in fitful snatches, a searing pain pounding inside my head, and my leg was now a swollen, throbbing mess.

I struggled up at dawn and made my way to work.

"What happened to you?" asked the surgeon I was scheduled to assist that morning.

"Auto accident," I volunteered weakly.

"Lie down, here," He commanded, pointing to one of the couches.

I explained as best I could what I thought my injuries might be, and while I was struggling to tell him, Doctor Stenopolus, an orthopedic surgeon, joined us. Both men came to the same conclusion.

"You're going down to radiology, stat. We need a complete skull series: a set of pictures of your neck and back and a set of your knee, leg, and foot." Doctor Stenopolus picked up a house phone and told radiology to expect me shortly. "We'll also want to do a myelogram," he said, as I started for the elevator. "You'll be checked in as a patient, Desmond. No arguments, OK?"

I was too weak to argue, and my head hurt so much that I couldn't even nod. I gave a little shrug to let them know I would do their bidding.

The next morning, it was decided an MRI scan was also needed. "Let's be sure there's nothing we might have been missed with the X-rays." Doctor Stenopolus had taken full charge of my case.

Later that day, he stopped by to give me his findings. "Let me start by saying you could have been killed, or at the very least, severely injured. Possibly paralyzed. You must be leading a clean life." He winked as he spoke, while I lay flat on my back on a pillowless bed.

"Here are the results. No fractures evident on any of the views of the skull and cervical areas. The MRI shows herniation at the C five, six, and seven positions. Your left knee joint has a small tear in the anterior cruciate ligament, but it's not too serious." He referred to his notes. "There's a large hematoma on the skin surrounding the upper portion of the posterior Achilles and a hairline fracture of the cuboid. All in all, you're a damn lucky man."

"Amen to that," I replied.

My rehabilitation was slow. The spinal injuries, of course, were my biggest concern. I really wanted to avoid surgery, and at one point, I had to be re-admitted to the hospital for a two-week period I was placed in traction and treated with steroids with the hope this would take care of the numbness and shaking which had developed in my left arm and hand. I underwent physical therapy twice a day, and after discharge, continued this regimen for the next two months. Unfortunately, it proved ineffectual. Doctor Stenopolus now referred me to a neurologist and a neurosurgeon. Their findings indicated that surgical intervention was necessary to repair the damage to the disks at the C6 and C7 position of my spine.

This was the first of three operations I had over the next eighteen months, and throughout, I lived in constant pain.

Because I had been unable to work, I applied for disability coverage under the policy I had purchased two years earlier. After a delay of several of months, the company wrote to tell me they were denying coverage.

What?

The reason given was that I had a pre-existing condition, namely hepatitis C, thus rendering the policy invalid.

I wrote back and reminded them that I did not have the condition when the policy was issued, and stated that their medical staff had examined me, had studied my blood, and had found me to be in good health.

They replied with an Alice in Wonderland explanation that I had had a moral obligation to inform them several months into the policy period that I had contracted the hepatitis C virus.

I wrote back to tell them such a thing was nonsense and to remind them that I never claimed coverage for lost work due to hepatitis, but that my claim was the result of a not-at-fault auto accident.

Their reply was the same. Coverage denied.

As if this were not enough, my medical carrier was dragging its feet on paying my hospital bills, citing that my auto carrier was responsible under the PIP section of the policy to pay first. This was turning into a fiasco, with me caught squarely in the middle. And the hospital administrator was starting to complain about not getting paid.

The insurance companies were wearing me down. I was fast approaching the end of my proverbial rope, trying to navigate through foreign, hostile waters. I needed help, so I turned to my friend, Mike Middleton, an attorney.

After contacting Mike, I committed the one cardinal sin any client can commit when consulting with his attorney. I was neither truthful nor candid as to all aspects of my life, and this stupidity cost me dearly. The blame for my subsequent downfall rests squarely on my own shoulders.

* * *

I met Mike in his offices in Coral Gables two days later. He was aware of my accident and expressed his sympathy that I was not mending as fast as had been hoped. I spent the next hour telling my tale of woe while he scribbled feverishly on a big, thick, yellow legal pad. He would interrupt to ask an occasional rapid-fire question, and then continue to scribble as I answered. He finally laid the pad on the table.

"Quite a mess," he observed. "No wonder you've decided to come to me. I'm surprised you didn't do it sooner." He gave a derisive laugh. "What you're going through is what I deal with every day. There's not an insurance company in the world which doesn't love to cash premium checks all day long, but God help a policyholder who might have a claim. That means they might have to pay out on a loss, not how the game should be played in their eyes. Therefore, they stall, offer to pay a fraction of what the claim is worth, or deny coverage entirely. And that's usually the point when we attorneys are called in. Then, the companies start to piss and moan that we are the villains responsible for driving up the cost of insurance. Hypocritical bastards." Mike was now pacing, a warrior for the downtrodden and full of righteous wrath.

He finally settled back down into his massive leather chair. "OK, first things first. We notify your disability carrier that we're going to sue them for breach of contract, bad faith bargaining, and anything else I decide to throw at them. Then, we'll see what I can do about the hospitalization insurer, your auto carrier, and Mrs. Murray's auto carrier. This is my headache now; you just concentrate on getting better."

I left his office knowing that I had made the right decision. As I mentioned, Mike was a friend of longstanding, but more importantly, he enjoyed a reputation of being a crackerjack attorney. He was the right man to have in my corner.

I underwent the first operation. It was arthroscopic surgery on my knee entailing a partial menisectomy of the medial meniscus. Translation: part of the pad that acts as a shock absorber behind the kneecap was removed. This pad protects the smooth articular surface by cushioning the joints so that they do not come together to abrade.

Simultaneously, I was fitted with prosthesis to wear in my shoe to elevate my heel, critical to help the torn Achilles tendon in the rejuvenation process.

Next, I had the first operation on my back. The procedure called for the surgeon to do a discectomy, or removal of the herniation of the disc material at nerve root C6 and C7.

The procedure is measured in terms of immediate success. If numbness to the arm and hand disappears, then, *voila,* the patient is healed! My fingers and arm felt fine. Great news, indeed.

Alas, my triumph was short-lived. Within a few months the symptoms reappeared, only this time progressively worse.

I returned to work after a few weeks of recuperation, but on my first day back, I was called up short by the surgeon I was assisting, Doctor Harry Arnold.

"Desmond, you aren't going to cut the mustard here," he growled, as he studied my palsied left hand, shaking uncontrollably even while tightly wrapped around a retractor. "We can finish up without you, but I want to speak with you when I get out. Wait for me in the lounge. I have a friend in Chicago I want you to see. He's one of the top neuro men in the country, and you sure need his help."

Dr. Harry Arnold was a leader in the field of sports-injury surgery, and if he thought I needed help, then my condition was far more serious than I had realized.

The man he called was a Doctor Wendell Ewing. Harry cut through miles of red tape and set up an appointment for me to fly out to the Midwest for a consult with his friend. At least I could take comfort in the fact I would be examined by the best.

Back on the insurance front, the disability carrier was not budging. The adjuster was preparing to go to the mat. Mike called for one last attempt at reason before entering the court.

After the requisite niceties on both sides, Mike proposed a settlement, expressing for the umpteenth time it was his hope we would not have to go to trial. I listened on the speakerphone.

"Sorry, counselor, my company is adamant on this one. We feel good about a jury finding in our favor, so I guess we'll meet in court. Nothing personal, right?"

"Nothing personal."

This was followed by a glacial pause. Finally, "By chance are you the same Mike Middleton, who won that two-million dollar verdict last week up in Gainesville?"

"Guilty as charged." Mike winked at me as he spoke.

"Didn't you also win a judgment in Brevard County recently for over a mil?"

"Guilty again."

"Tell you what. Let me speak to my people one last time, and I'll get back to you."

"You're almost out of time, sport. Trial starts in the morning."

"Just hold your horses, Counselor; I'll call you back within three hours."

"I'll be here." Mike hung up and turned to me, a huge grin dissecting his face. "Yes," he shouted, punching the air with his fist. "They're going to settle, Desmond, and I'll bet the goddamn farm on it."

Three hours later that's exactly what they did. They agreed to settle my claim and pay Mike's attorney fees outside the settlement amount. I was on cloud nine. I sure had been one smart rascal the day I decided to hire Mike Middleton. I could have kissed him.

"That's one down, one to go." Mike was happy, but ever the professional, realized the job was not complete. He reached into his drawer and withdrew a letter.

"This is from your auto carrier," he said. "You remember I told you awhile back that I was going to ask them to join us in suing Mrs. Murray's insurance company because her carrier had denied coverage under their policy?"

"Sure. You said that you would have to go against my insurance company to pay for my injuries under the uninsured motorist section of the policy if Kathy's insurance policy was not sufficient to pay the loss." Under his tutelage, I was becoming quite the expert on insurance coverage. A man had to be a Philadelphia lawyer to understand what these contracts said.

"Right," he continued. "Well, the long and the short of it is that they have declined to join forces with us." He shrugged his shoulders. "I can't say that I understand their reasoning because they have to know we will go after them for acting in bad faith. It's going to involve a lot of depositions being taken on both sides, which invariably ends up with a ton of mudslinging."

He must have seen something in my eyes because he ended on a positive note. "Never fear, Desmond! We're going to win, even if they're crazy enough to take this all the way to trial! Anyway, as I told you when I first took on your case, you let me worry about the legal end of things. You concentrate on getting better."

"I leave it in your hands, Mike. I think you're doing a super job, and I appreciate your help no end." I passed him an envelope containing the latest unpaid medical bills. My palsied hand was shaking uncontrollably.

"More dunning notices?" He asked, peeking inside.

"Afraid so." I then briefed him on my upcoming trip to see Doctor Ewing.

"He sounds like just the ticket. If you have to go under the knife again, let's pray this will be the end of it." Mike walked me to the door. "Keep the faith, pal. This whole mess will eventually end well."

I flew to Chicago and met Dr. Ewing. It didn't take long for me to see why this man was praised by his peers.

After the requisite small talk, I handed him a packet of supplemental x-rays which I had hand-carried on the plane. These were in addition to a huge file I had shipped air express the week before. He placed them on the side of his desk, and then asked me to detail my medical history since the date of the accident. Doctor Ewing took notes during my monologue, allowing me to talk uninterrupted. He then beckoned me to join him by the light box mounted on the far wall. He dimmed the room lights and studied the negatives. I stood silently beside him.

He scrutinized the pictures for several minutes, eyes darting back-and-forth through the pre-op series, and then over to those taken postoperatively. His jaw tightened. I could see he was miffed at what he saw.

With a flick of his finger, he snapped off the light and returned to his desk. "Have a seat, Doctor Donahue."

He waited until I was settled.

"Any reason why your surgeon in Miami didn't fuse the C six and C seven, not to mention the C five? All imperative, in my opinion, if one wants to make sure there would be no collapse above the injured area."

I didn't know what to say. I just stared, waiting for him to continue. I could see he was loathe to speak ill of a fellow surgeon, but he clearly was not happy with what he had seen.

He sat back in his chair, twirling his metal pointer between his fingers.

"I recommend more surgery, Doctor..."

"Please, it's Desmond..." I interrupted.

"And I'm Wendell." He regained his train of thought. "I'm talking about a multi-level fusion. What I want to do is take a graft from your leg and use about four inches of bone to strengthen and support you at the C six and seven, and then fuse those disks. Next, I want to fuse the C five. This will take the pressure off the nerves, and you should experience an immediate and permanent cure for the tremors. Not to mention the pain," he added in afterthought. "And best of all, this should rule out the need for future operations. Any questions?"

I had plenty. We spent the next half hour going over the procedure, and at the end of the session, I was fully confident in what he proposed. "When can you do it? I'm ready any time you are."

"The day after tomorrow. I'd like to take some more pictures today, and then do a few tests in the morning." He picked up his phone. "Any objection to admitting you into the hospital this afternoon?"

I shook my head. "Let's get it done."

Without going into a lot of technical ballyhoo, suffice to say the surgery was successful. The recuperative period was long and painful, requiring me to wear a huge cervical neck brace for the next seveal months. The healing process did not take place as fast as I had hoped. I suspect nature was reminding me that I was growing old.

CHAPTER NINETEEN

*N*ow seated before Mike in his conference room on this the next to the last day of 1992, I had just spent the last several hours doing something I had not done in more than half a century. I had laid bare my soul to another human being, and it was the most humbling experience imaginable.

Darkness had descended over the city hours ago. A weary Mike Middleton picked up the bulging envelope from attorney Carl Weston and slid it over to me. It was obvious to us now that this bulldog of a lawyer had been suspicious of me for months, and acting on his suspicions, had hit pay dirt. Carl Weston had single-handedly uncovered the awful truth about the charlatan who called himself Doctor Desmond Donahue.

"Desmond, I want you to go through everything in here, page by page, then we'll talk some more."

"Now?"

"Now."

As I opened the packet, a blizzard of correspondence from Cork tumbled out. I set to my task. It spelled out in graphic detail how I had not graduated from medical school, instead, had soundly flunked the one and only year of pre-med. Several letters from the current dean informed Carl Weston that they had a running file on Desmond Donahue—a file made fat with the passing of time—a file filled with fact and innuendo detailing how I had been holding myself out as a doctor these many years, first in Ireland, and then later in the United States. Other documents were equally emphatic in their denial of my ever having attended any clinics. This information had caused Carl to redirect his sights to Boston, and then Portland, Maine.

How utterly, irrevocably damning was the evidence against me.

A Desmond Donahue from Ireland had been arrested for issuing a false prescription in Boston.

The same Desmond Donahue was tried on the aforementioned count, but the judge had withheld adjudication.

The same Desmond Donahue had later come to the attention of the authorities when he tried to assume the identity of a legitimate doctor—and almost succeeded in gaining admittance into a residency program in Portland, Maine.

Further evidence showed how the same Desmond Donahue had hoodwinked the authorities into letting him sit the Foreign Medical Graduates Exam, using forged documents signed by a Doctor Quinn on the medical school staff in Ireland.

It was all there. The onion had been peeled, exposing the rotten innards for all to see.

I sat back in my chair, surprisingly calm. It was finally over! The charade, which was my life, had been laid bare by Carl Weston, Esquire. No wonder he had refused to give Mike the time of day whenever he would broach the possibility of a settlement.

Mike's words now taunted as they raced through my mind once more. *"Poor old Carl went on a fishing expedition only to find there were no fish in the pond."*

I now sat in that room undisturbed, wondering what would come next.

For weeks, I had asked Mike to approach Carl with a motion for discovery, but not knowing what I was afraid of, he had brushed aside the suggestion as unnecessary. And, of course, stupid Desmond had not told counsel the truth as to who and what he was. I had now presented Mike with one unholy, bloody mess.

When he returned, he just sat and stared at me. I couldn't look him in the eye.

Finally, he spoke. "Why didn't you just tell me the truth from the beginning?"

I slowly shook my head. "I wanted to, Mike. A thousand times I wanted to, but always at the last moment I couldn't bring myself to tell you. I guess I didn't think Carl would dig up my past. I convinced myself it wasn't germane."

"That should have been for me to decide," he replied, not a trace of anger in his words. Had I been in his shoes, I would have wanted to strangle me!

"I've got to know one thing, Desmond. Did Margaret really exist? And what about the child?"

I took a deep breath, and then let it out slowly. "Mike, she still exists. Present tense. She's not dead. And, yes, she did become pregnant, and, yes, the fetus did die before birth. And, no, we were not married, even though we went through that ceremony in Paris."

"Well, at least that's something. I want you to give it to me from the top all over again, going back to the first day you remember."

At times he paced the room as I spoke, a seething tiger in a cramped cage, but other than to interrupt for clarification of a point or two, he gave me full rein. Finally, I was finished. It was well past midnight.

"What now?" I asked.

He scratched his head. "I honestly don't know. I have to figure a way for damage control, and then try to press your case strictly on its merits. Carl sure as hell has done his homework and then some. I suspect he's going to want another round of depositions and soon," Mike added, thinking aloud. "Chances are he'll want to go to Ireland for testimony from some of the principals there, which means I'll have to go, too."

"Is that really necessary?" I asked. "Can't we just concede the facts, and I'll admit that I'm not a doctor?"

Mike shook his head. "No, Carl will want sworn depositions to present to the court. There's no way out of it. I'll have to go to Ireland."

"Does that mean I have to go with you?"

"No, you get to stay here and keep out of trouble. This is one hell of a goddamned mess you've dumped in my lap."

"I'm truly sorry, Mike. Do you want to withdraw? I'll certainly understand if you say yes."

No, I'm in this all the way. Just tell me the truth from here on out, OK?"

"Thanks, Mike."

Carl Weston commanded my presence for a follow-up deposition for the first week in January 1993.

This time Mike was ready and continuously instructed me throughout the proceeding not to answer the majority of questions posed me. I obeyed.

To say Carl was exasperated is putting it mildly.

"I'll get a court order compelling him to respond, Counselor."

"So be it," Mike replied. He was playing for time.

Mike and Carl Weston went to Ireland in March 1993 and deposed Doctor Craig Wilson, Doctor Ian Farris, Doctor C. R. Hawley, and Howard Collier.

Wilson studied the transcripts of my purported medical school training, along with a copy of his letter of recommendation, and declared all were forgeries. "It certainly looks like my signature, but I would never have signed that letter."

Next came Doctor Hawley's testimony. He was handed a slew of documents, all purporting to show that I had attended various hospital clinics and had successfully completed my training. The last attested that I had been granted a diploma in June 1976.

"All forgeries," he assured the court. "Doctor Beckler, now deceased, would never have signed such fraudulent documents."

Then, it was Doctor Farris's turn, the current Dean of the Faculty of Medicine. He corroborated the testimony of the other two. All documents presented to him were forgeries.

Lastly, Mister Howard Collier, the finance officer and medical records keeper at Mercy Hospital, Cork, was deposed. He assured the court that Desmond Donahue had never attended clinics at his institution and smugly added that that he had the medical records dating back to 1882 to prove it!

The pace quickened.

Carl Weston scheduled another round of depositions, so ordered by the Court, and I appeared once more in his offices on April 28, 1993.

He grilled me unmercifully. He picked over every aspect of my life from the time I set foot back in Ireland in 1969 to the present.

It was all but finished.

* * *

The court of the Honorable Oliver Roscoe, Circuit Court of the 11th Judicial Circuit, in and for Dade County, Florida, came to order at 9:30 A.M., August 10, 1993.

Representing the plaintiff: Michael Middleton and Barbara Olds, the latter hired because of the turn of events. She was an expert in the appeals process, and Mike was under no illusions but that Carl Weston was seeking nothing less than a dismissal.

Representing the defendant Kathy Murray: Carl Weston.

Judge Roscoe stated for the record that the Court had asked for a representative of the State Attorney's office to be present. He introduced a Mr. Leon Medvedev. This was not a good sign.

The gallery was crowded with representatives of the media, tipped off, I'm sure, by Carl Weston, who wanted his triumph recorded for posterity. He was wearing a new suit for the occasion, looking spiffy for his fifteen minutes of fame.

Carl was the first to speak. What follows is an excerpt from those proceedings.

Mr. Weston: "Your Honor, Mr. Donahue told at least seventeen lies about being in medical school and receiving a medical degree. He told thirty-four lies just during the first ten pages of his deposition.

The story that Mr. Donahue gave about the death of his wife and child shows a pattern to deceive. He spoke in abstruse medical terms of cross-matching, of things beyond a barrier, of dissecting, and rhizomes, and he did all this for one reason only: to fool me. His entire story is false, yet artfully told, with the intention of convincing me of his worth as a physician and his pathos as a person.

He lied about his whereabouts, alleging that he was in Ireland from nineteen sixty-nine to nineteen seventy-six. He told us under oath that he was at the Irish Medical School during those years. It's just not true. We have the records indicating he went to pre-med for one year but failed miserably, and he never did get into the medical school. He was in Ireland from nineteen sixty-nine until nineteen seventy. It's a part of the record, but there is no record he was there after that.

But we did discover that while in Massachusetts, he was arrested and charged with writing prescriptions for a controlled substance, distributing a controlled substance, fraudulently obtaining a controlled substance, and practicing medicine without a license.

Subsequent to that, he went to Maine and said his name was O'Reilly. He obtained the records of Dr. O'Reilly—and there is a real Dr. O'Reilly, Your Honor—and he attempted to get a job using O'Reilly's credentials. That's when the medical school in Ireland found out what Donahue was up to.

On April 8, 1993, we again took Mr. Donahue's deposition, and yet after he had access to all the documentation from the Irish university, he continued to lie.

He said he commenced his studies in Ireland in nineteen sixty-eight. Then, he said he didn't recall how long he was at the University College in Ireland after he had told us earlier under oath that he was there for several years.

In the first deposition, he said he didn't remember if he was prosecuted in Boston. He could not remember where he lived or worked from nineteen seventy to nineteen seventy-three. He couldn't remember where he worked or lived from 1970 to 1979.

"Yet, he has no memory problem as he has so testified under oath. I submit to the court that a man who has been working at St. Anslem's Hospital since 1979, and says he doesn't remember. That is lying.

He testified that he didn't know if he had held himself out as a doctor in Ireland, yet after prodding from his lawyer, he finally said, 'Well, yes, I did hold myself out as a doctor.' He would continue to tell lies, and his lawyer would have to say, answer this, tell the truth.

In his earlier deposition of January 5, 1993, he denied that he told Dr. Ewing he was a physician. We took Dr. Ewing's deposition. Dr. Ewing read from his notes: *Here is my history. I'm a fifty-two-year-old surgeon.*

Mr. Donahue has made a claim for bodily injuries. His lawyer demands the defendant's insurer pay $300,000 because the plaintiff is a doctor who has been injured.

The plaintiff has made fraudulent representations to support his claim; and as far as the law is concerned, Your Honor, I ask that this case be dismissed. Thank You, Your Honor."

The Court: "Mr. Middleton."

Mr. Middleton: "Your Honor, the memorandum that Mr. Weston has filed is basically what he has just argued. If I may, I would like to go through that.

The first thing we need to point out, Your Honor, this is not a motion to dismiss for sham pleading. There is nothing that has been alleged in the pleading that is false. The pleading states that Mr. Donahue was in an accident and that he was injured. The testimony from all the doctors has been he was injured.

The motion to dismiss the case says that Mr. Donahue has engaged in a fraudulent scheme to collect damages through fraudulent documents. As far as fraudulent documents are concerned, there are no forged documents before the Court. No forged documents have ever been submitted by plaintiff, or plaintiff's counsel, so I don't know what fraudulent documents have to do with this.

In the memorandum the defendant cites thirty-four lies. Your Honor, it's all one lie. It's a situation where someone did not falsify anything in order to gain from a lawsuit, but falsified things to obtain a livelihood.

In Mr. Weston's memorandum, he says Mr. Donahue gives false testimony concerning his medical training. That's true, he did. Mr. Donahue lied about being in college in Ireland. He lied about his clinical training, he lied about medical school, and he lied about being an intern. That's all one lie.

Whether or not he was married is inadmissible. It is not relevant to anything. It's unfortunate, and I'm pleased at the word used by Mr. Weston in his statement. He used the word pathos. That *pathos* has the same root as *pathetic*, and it embarrasses me to say this with my client sitting here, but he *is* pathetic. He's lived in a fantasy world where he would tell people he was a widower, and he would tell people he was a doctor. But that has nothing to do with this lawsuit. Yes, he did lie, and that is of importance to this court, but it wasn't told to the court or to Mr. Weston to gain anything.

The court should be appalled. I'm appalled, but it's not something that was done to commit fraud to the court. It's a lie that he's lived, it's a lie that he is stuck with, and a jury will have to take that into account. But to dismiss the claim? No, Your Honor."

This did not sit well with Carl Weston. He jumped up.

Mr. Weston: "May it please the court. Your Honor, one of the major claims in this case is the loss of earnings and earning capacity.

A claim was made that this man is a doctor who got hurt. If this is not blatant, I don't know what is. Your Honor, the defendant has nothing further. Thank you."

Now, it was Judge Roscoe's turn. I took a deep breath and exhaled slowly. It all came down to this man, and how he would rule.

The Court: "I had intended to call Mr. Donahue to address these issues, to advise him of his rights, and to address each of them. However, I don't think that's either necessary or appropriate at this point in time. I will first say that I appreciate the candor of Mr. Middleton in acknowledging that statements made under oath were lies. It is an affront to this court, it's an affront to this community, and it's an affront to anyone who believes in justice to permit somebody to continue with a lie. Not only would it be inappropriate for this court not to impose sanctions, but it would be an affront to society to let something like this pass without imposition of sanctions. Criminal court will handle any sanctions, if they so choose. If the State Attorney chooses to proceed in this matter, then it will be handled appropriately in the criminal division.

The court cannot countenance this perjury, the court cannot fortify the illusion, and the Court cannot just sit idly by and allow that to happen. Nor is this court going to tax the intelligence of a jury at the expense of the public for the plaintiff to utilize our system of justice in spite of his consistent perjury.

Listening to what has transpired, the Court is full of contempt for the plaintiff, and at the very least, *and I mean at the very least*, the Court will grant the defendant's motion.

The defendant has incurred expenses, substantial expenses, and it will not be inappropriate for this Court to impose those costs against the plaintiff.

Now that the lies have come forth and have been made public, Mr. Donahue, I would hope that you should turn your life around and stop living that lie. Whatever may have occurred in the past, is past, but you will pay a substantial penalty for that. But if you can't turn your life around and forget that past and start your life afresh, then you are going to wind up in a lot more trouble.

At this point I will grant the motion reserving jurisdiction. Court will stand in recess."

Final Judgment was issued that same day. In his opinion, Judge Roscoe cited prior case law to substantiate his finding. It ended with these words:

Accordingly, it is hereby ORDERED and ADJUDGED that:

1. This action is dismissed with prejudice so that Plaintiff will take nothing by this action, and Defendant shall go hence without delay;

2. That Court reserves jurisdiction to tax costs in favor of defendant and against plaintiff, and to impose upon notice and hearing such further monetary and other sanctions as may be appropriate.

DONE AND ORDERED in chambers at Miami, Dade County, Florida, this 10th day of August 1993.

CHAPTER TWENTY

I **recall nothing** of the drive from the courthouse to Key Biscayne and only vaguely remember entering my home and bolting the front door. Strangely, I do recollect going from room to room and shuttering every window until the place was as secure and as dark as a tomb. I unplugged the phones, turned off my pager, stood back and surveyed my kingdom. Had I missed anything? No. I went into my bedroom, flung myself down on the bed, and curled up into a ball.

Only then did I break down and begin to sob. Uncontrollably. Until I could cry no longer. Hours passed. Wracked with a terrible thirst, I struggled to sit up, but too tired to do so, abandoned the effort. Sometime later, chimerical images of people took form in the darkness and once assembled, they all began to speak in an incomprehensible babble. I clamped my hands over my ears in protest.

I recognized my parents as they emerged from the shadows, and with their coming, the rest of the group fell silent. I now identified the others. Closest to me stood a defiant Margaret, and next to her all my brothers and sisters, including the long-departed Bernadette. And behind them, Eddy Regan and Doctor Mulvahill.

I was mortified to be in their presence. Except Margaret's. I managed a quick glance toward my mother and saw tears glistening on her cheeks, the sight of which rent the very fabric of my soul. My breathing became labored, and my heart pounded.

As if heeding some unspoken command, all turned in unison to face a new arrival. It was Roger, and seeing him after all these years, I started to cry again.

Roger stumbled toward me. The others parted ranks and retreated into the shadows, leaving us alone, the only two souls in the universe.

"I'm reading your bloody mind, boy!" Roger began in a voice filled with bitter bile. "Always could, right from the moment I first laid eyes on you. Knew immediately you were an egotistical snot." His words were slurred. Roger was drunk. "And now you're blaming me for your troubles. It's all Roger's fault, don't you

know?" he mimicked wickedly. "Roger made me do it!" He paused long enough to allow his words to find an unwelcome home. "Well, it's too bloody late for that! Fact is, I'm here to tell you it's time for you to come join me. All you've got to do is traipse on into your bathroom and rummage through that medicine cabinet of yours. I've already peeked inside, and it's a regular bloody little pharmacy you've got yourself there. So, pick your favorite poison, boy, just as I did all those years ago."

I was paralyzed at the thought of what Roger was suggesting.

"Desmond," he unexpectedly wheedled in a sudden change in tactics, "I need you to come drink with me." The truth was out.

"Get Eddy," I replied, "he's already there."

Roger shook his head, sadly. "I can't. Eddy will have nothing to do with me now. He's taken the pledge, don't you know. Hasn't touched a drop in ages. So that leaves only you, and anyway, you've got nothing to stay there for."

Truer words were never spoken.

"Desmond!"

I jumped at the sound of my name being called from across time and space. It was my mother.

At that moment, I also became aware of a horrific banging way off in the distance. Roger must have heard it also because in the next instant he was gone.

"Desmond, if you don't open this door, I'm going to call nine-one-one!"

It was Elizabeth!

I made my way to the front door, but didn't open it. "Leave me alone," I called out. "I'm fine, Elizabeth; I just don't want to talk right now." I paused, unsure of what to say next. Then, inspiration. "I'll call you tomorrow."

"Promise you won't do anything stupid?"

"Promise," I replied, then waited in silence until I heard her drive off.

I returned to my room, lay down on the bed, and stared into the inky nothingness above my head, waiting for the group to reassemble.

Only Roger returned and wasted no time picking up where he had left off. "You've really got to get a move on, Desmond," he said, glancing at his watch. "Just go into the bathroom and get it over with. *Now hurry!"*

I started to get off the bed when Doctor Mulvahill appeared. "No, Desmond, that's not the answer," he said in a voice as soothing as I had remembered from those many years ago in Dublin. "I'm sending Roger away so that you can sleep. Then in the morning, you and I will have a talk."

Thank God, I found both the courage and the good sense to obey Doctor Mulvahill and not Roger Connolly that awful night.

I awoke the next morning with a splitting headache and rationalized it had all been a dream.

Or had it?

* * *

The next few weeks were among the worst of my life. I spiraled into the abyss of clinical depression. At some point Elizabeth managed to get through to the real Desmond cowering in the corner of my tortured mind and persuaded me to seek professional help. The psychiatrist I finally agreed to see wasted no time in prescribing a powerful mood elevator. Slowly, over the next two weeks, the medication took hold, but several follow-up visits were needed to convince the doctor that I harbored no thoughts of suicide. However, I must admit there were times during those dark days that the idea of ending it all held a certain appeal.

I now look back on that period of clinical depression as a friend, a friend who had forced me to analyze my tattered past. No longer could I delude myself that I had done nothing really wrong. Indeed, I saw my life for what it truly was: a self-created nothingness, a sham born of unbridled arrogance. And I had no one to blame but myself for the fate that had befallen me. Certainly not Roger. No, I had deliberately preyed on his weakness, used him as ruthlessly as I had used so many countless others in a furtherance of my own corruption. Mine was a life filled with treachery and deceit. And during those days of introspection, I even came to terms with the man who had become my nemesis, Carl Weston.

How could I have allowed my life to take such a course? Sadly, it was a question I had known the answer to from the moment I had made that conscious decision to cross my Rubicon two decades earlier in Cork. Put in the simplest of terms, it was my all-consuming fear of poverty, a fear so powerful that as a child it had caused me to despair of life itself the day little Bernadette had died in my mother's arms. I had thought I would go to my grave never having known any other condition.

I offer this as insight, not as an excuse.

And now that terrible fear had blossomed anew. And for good reason. My debts were staggering. Not only did I owe damages to the Court, but also to the insurance company. And, of course, I was deeply in debt to my lawyers. I would have to sell everything, including my home, in order to make amends. I had come full circle back to the hopelessness and poverty of my youth.

Surprisingly, even though I was understandably morose, I was no longer filled with self-pity. I had looked inward, saw myself as others saw me, and was appalled. I mentally revisited the untold numbers of patients I could have harmed while masquerading as a physician, and thoughts of what could have been but for the grace of God filled me with dread. To think that I had had the temerity to trample all over the Hippocratic Oath, that most solemn vow which begins with the venerable words: *First, I shall do no harm.*

Many was the night I lay in bed and gave up a prayer of thanks that my parents had gone to their graves never knowing what I'd become.

Only through much effort was I able to present to the world an outward appearance of being in control. Inside, I was living every moment with a full complement of demons kept mercifully at bay by medication.

How long could it last before something snapped inside? Thankfully, the answer came a few weeks later.

* * *

One night toward the end of January, I was awakened by the sounds of a raging winter storm. Startled, my first coherent thought was, oh my God, it's another Hurricane Andrew! Then I told myself, no, it's not the right season, and soon calmed down. I lay back and listened to the wind as it howled and tormented the trees. I became a little boy again, and my mind conjured up visions of things evil and alive as the lightning flashes created monsters in the shadows. Demons, having escaped from netherworld dungeons, were now stalking the earth, searching for me.

At first light I arose, had breakfast, and then settled in my living room to stare out the window at a world in turmoil.

Around three o'clock the fury abated, and I found myself inexplicably overcome with an urge to venture outside, drawn by some mystical force pulling me toward the ocean.

I donned a yellow slicker and sallied forth, my head held low against the stinging rain. I was the only living thing afoot. Even the gulls had abandoned their homes on Key Biscayne, having fled inland in search of sanctuary.

Once on the beach, I made my way around mounds of seaweed and other flotsam that had been flung ashore as if by some deranged giant. The roiling surf beckoned me closer. The sea's primitive force and savage beauty ensnared my soul. I stood mesmerized.

At some point the wind died and the rain stopped. Still, I remained transfixed, staring out to sea.

"Look, Desmond, a rainbow!"

Thoroughly startled, I realized it was my mother's voice, as real as if she were standing beside me. And in that instant, I was back on the cliffs of Clew Bay in Western Ireland.

I looked out over the water, and there it was, as majestic a rainbow as ever God had created.

"Isn't it lovely?" she marveled. Then she whispered, *"I give it to you as a gift, my son. I want you to ride its magical staircase to a new beginning. You see, God's giving you a second chance, child, so seize the moment. Seize it with both hands, Desmond, and never look back! God has heard you, lad, and all He asks in return is your promise to do good with whatever time you have left."*

Her hand reached out for mine. I grabbed ahold and squeezed as tightly as only a five-year old can when anchoring to his mother. She smiled down at me as she ran her fingers through my sopping hair.

"May the Lord keep you safe in the palm of His hand until your journey is done. God bless you, my child."

And with that prayer, my mother vanished, gone as mysteriously as she had come. I found myself enveloped by an indescribable sense of peace and wellbeing. I was reborn.

I turned my face skyward toward the new sun and smiled in the direction of heaven. It was time for me to go home.

*   *   *

Mike appealed the judge's decision. He felt that it was wrong to link my past misconduct with my right to relief for a very real injury. The Appeals Court rebuffed that argument in record time.

Meanwhile, the State's Attorney's office conducted its own investigation and concluded that my testimony in deposition was indeed perjured, but only as it related to my claimed medical background. All other aspects of my life's story were found to be true. My child had died, and I did lose Margaret.

The court fined me $3,500. Rather than have me pay this sum to the treasury of the State of Florida, the judge had me write the check to a memorial fund recently established to aid the family of a police officer killed in the line of duty. I was also given a suspended sentence of two years.

Several months later, two investigators from the State Board of Medical Examiners came to my home to inform me that the board had found me guilty of practicing medicine without a license. They did not berate, nor did they exhibit any evidence of disgust, and for that kindness, I am sincerely grateful. As they left, both wished me well and hoped that I could now move on with my life.

The debit column in my ledger was awash in red ink. I owed the insurance companies thousands of dollars in repayment for the money they had spent investigating my past, and I also owed Mike. I did not have time to sit back and feel sorry for myself. I had to get to work.

But where? Doing what?

As fate often has it, my dilemma was solved when a friend invited me to come to work in his antique business. I proved to be a natural. I've always enjoyed working with wood, restoring objects to their former beauty. Within months, I was attending auctions and buying for myself. I was hired by clients to find those special pieces needed to finish a decorating scheme. I branched out on my own.

Four years have now passed. I left the courthouse that August morning, full of dread at having to meet my friends, expecting all to vilify me. As it turned out, those fears were groundless. They proved to be a most charitable group, especially my colleagues from St. Anslem's Hospital. Several have since become closer.

Elizabeth was also there for quite some time afterward, exhibiting grace and style under the most trying of circumstances. However, we slowly drifted apart until one day she was simply no longer in my life. I truly wish her the best. She deserves no less. There are not enough words in the language to thank this woman.

I can honestly say I am now finally at peace with myself. The past is dead and buried, and I have come to appreciate the joy of being a part of a community of friends, of being able to live each day without that constant fear of exposure.

I have also recently made plans to leave South Florida to go somewhere nobody knows me. I want to start anew, to contribute something worthwhile in whatever time I have left.

Finally, I must admit that Dr. Mulvahill was right those many years ago in Dublin when he quoted John Donne: "No man is an island."

It has taken me this long to learn the simple truth found within those words.

AUTHOR'S AFTERWORD

The night before Desmond left Miami, he came to my house to say goodbye. He also brought with him a big, old-fashioned leather satchel. We had been friends—not close—but we had bonded years earlier soon after he learned I had spent a year in Ireland as a child. Desmond knew I understood what those early years of grinding poverty must have been like and felt I could identify with his wanting to escape to a better life in America.

He handed me the satchel. It was heavy.

"You mind telling me what's inside?" I asked, hefting it a couple of times while studying the impressive, obviously new padlock that secured a leather strap girding its outside.

"The story of my life," he said, sounding somewhat sad. "Ian, what came out during the trial and what was printed in the newspapers afterward only scratched the surface. And a lot of what was written was simply not true." He must have seen the skeptical look on my face because he shook his head and held up a hand, silently begging me not to interrupt. "I'm not saying the gist of what was said and written isn't true. It is. I was as bad as, or worse than I've been portrayed. I'm only saying it is not the whole story." He pointed to the satchel. "Inside are a thousand pages of handwritten notes, along with copies of forged diplomas and other documents, plus clippings from Irish newspapers going back more than thirty years, articles from newspapers in Boston and Maine, and bunches of other stuff."

"And what do you want me to do with it?"

"I want you to write my story. I trust you'll do it right."

I looked down at the satchel. "Did you say *handwritten notes*?" I pretended to shudder. "I've seen your writing, chum, and it's worse than bad."

Desmond laughed. "So it might take you awhile to decipher my chicken scratches, but you're up to the task." He turned serious. "I want you to write my story," he repeated, "but ask that you wait fifteen years before seeking a publisher." Noticing my startled expression, he quickly added, "However, it would be OK to market it sooner if you hear that I've died. My only other request would be that you change the names of all of the real people and most of the places you'll find in my notes, especially when it comes to folks in Ireland."

I raised a querying brow. "Wouldn't a biography have a bigger impact?"

"Probably would, but after lots of thought, I've come to the conclusion I must protect the many innocents I duped along the way. They don't need the embarrassment my biography would bring into their lives, not after all these years. Mine has been a wasted life, Ian, but if I can prevent even one person from following in my footsteps, then your fictionalized account of my life will help redeem me." His eyes welled, and he looked away.

"No promises, Desmond, but I will look at everything you've given me, and if I see a doable project, I will produce a manuscript that will do you proud. It might take me a few years, or I could end up abandoning the project. As I said, no promises."

He held out his hand. "I leave it up to you. If you decide not to do it, I understand, and my story dies with me."

We started out shaking hands, but it quickly morphed into a hug.

"I wish you all the best, Desmond. Whatever you decide and wherever you end up, Godspeed and God bless."

He left without a backward glance, and I never saw Desmond Donahue again.

* * *

Thirteen years passed. Desmond became a distant memory, and only occasionally would my wife ask what I thought became of him. Then one day I opened my mailbox, and nestled among several bills, I spotted an envelope with a Thai postmark.

I don't know anyone in Thailand, I thought as I opened it and took out two sheets of paper. The first was a clipping of a death announcement from the *Phuket Gazette, English Language Edition*, dated ten days earlier.

Desmond Donahue (1938 - 2014)

Desmond Donahue, an American expatriate, passed away on Friday, June 13, 2014. He had been diagnosed with inoperable intestinal cancer only one week earlier by the Chief of Oncology at the Phuket Regional Clinic, where he had been employed as an operating room assistant for the past several years. Mr. Donahue leaves behind no wife or family, but had asked a friend at the clinic to have his remains cremated, and his ashes cast over the ocean. That wish was granted two days later, following one of the most violent weather anomalies seen in Phuket in the last fifty years. The rainbow that appeared shortly after the storm passed was described by dozens of witnesses as being the most spectacular they had ever seen.

The second page held a typewritten poem simply titled "A Mother's Gift." A lump formed in my throat as I read Desmond's heartfelt tribute to his mother.

A MOTHER'S GIFT
*   *

I saw my rainbow yesterday,
I saw it in a dream.
I saw my rainbow yesterday,
All seven colors rain-drenched clean.
*   *

Your mother gave me as a gift,
My rainbow seemed to sigh,
A gift you took to travel far
Upon my staircase in the sky.
*   *

But now you know my arc's not all,
The beauty that is me.
For I am more, my rainbow said,
A hidden circle, not to deign, mere men like you, to see.
*   *

There is a message in my words,
My rainbow clearly said to me.
I am ephemeral, as is life,
Fleeting beauty, fading fast, hurtling forth to what must be.

*   *

Your journey's nigh full circle come,
I'm a mother's gift to an eldest son.
Squander not, my rainbow sighed,
What time is left, then quickly died.

*   *

I looked at the envelope again and realized that Desmond must have addressed it for a friend to send to me his death notice and the poem. His penmanship had deteriorated over the ensuing years, so I figured it had reached me only because he had carefully scribed my complete 9-digit zip code in large, bold numerals.

I began working on my friend's story that evening and produced this finished manuscript ten months later. Then, with several strokes of a computer key, I replaced his real name with that of my fictitious Desmond Donahue, as I did with the names of so many others he had met on the wrong road home.

Ian A. O'Connor
Palm Beach Gardens, Florida
June 2015

About the author

Ian A. O'Connor is a retired Air Force colonel, who has held several senior military leadership positions in the field of national security management. His first novel, *The Twilight of the Day*, was a military-themed thriller which received high praise in the *Military Times* for its realism and chilling story line. This was soon followed with the first printing of *The Seventh Seal* by Winterwolf Publishing Company, which introduced readers to retired FBI agent Justin Scott. Both books were re-released in May 2015. His second Justin Scott thriller, *The Barbarossa Covenant,* was released in August 2015.

Ian also co-authored *SCRAPPY: A Memoir of a U.S. Fighter Pilot* published by McFarland & Company. He is a member of Mystery Writers of America and lives in South Florida with his wife, Candice, where he working on the next Justin Scott thriller, *The Masada Option,* with a publication date for the summer of 2016.

Visit Ian at: www.ianaoconnor.com
Contact Ian at: ianaoconnor@ianaoconnor.com